PRAISE FOR *P*

Shortlisted for the 2020 Crim
Debut Dagger Award

"Kim Hays brings a sparkling new voice to police procedurals, giving us engaging and realistically drawn detectives who struggle to balance their personal lives with the demands of a gripping investigation. Set against the fascinating backdrop of modern Switzerland, *Pesticide* will delight crime fiction fans—a standout debut for 2022!"

—Deborah Crombie, *New York Times* bestselling author of the award-winning Duncan Kincaid/Gemma James novels

"Kim Hays hits it out of the park with her debut novel, *Pesticide*, giving this twisty police procedural lots of heart by creating characters that the reader truly cares about. It is a must read for mystery lovers, especially those who prefer their intrigue with an international edge."

—Allen Eskens, bestselling and award-winning author of *The Stolen Hours* and six Max Rupert and Joe Talbot mysteries

"A highly original police procedural, set in Switzerland, with a charming cop heroine who is also a mum, and blending drug deals and organic farming to produce a first-rate yarn."

—Martin Walker, editor-in-chief emeritus of United Press International and author of the Bruno, Chief of Police series

"A convincing and compelling page-turner in a unique and authentic setting, *Pesticide* is a cleverly-plotted mystery that manages to be well-researched, intriguing, and entertaining. Kim Hays writes complex characters and suspense equally well, and her investigating duo, Giuliana and Renzo, are sure to win the hearts of readers everywhere."

—Clare O'Dea, author of *Voting Day*

"Giuliana Linder and Renzo Donatelli make for one of the sharpest, most compelling police duos you'll ever read. Their conflicted attraction bristles with true emotional depth and poignancy as they lead a rich ensemble cast through the surprisingly nefarious world of organic politics. A remarkable procedural set in Bern, Kim Hays's *Pesticide* is Switzerland's answer to Scandinavian noir. Fresh and oh so readable, you won't want to put it down."

—James W. Ziskin,
author of the award-winning Ellie Stone mysteries

"Kim Hays delivers a superbly written mystery set in Switzerland. Two murders, one in the old town of Bern, the other on a nearby organic farm, test the wits of veteran police detective Giuliana Linder and her handsome junior colleague, Renzo Donatelli. The setting is fresh, the characters richly developed, and the plot as intricate as the inside of a Swiss watch. Enjoy!"

—Betsy Draine and Michael Hinden,
co-authors of the Nora Barnes and Toby Sandler mysteries

Pesticide

Pesticide

A LINDER AND DONATELLI MYSTERY

KIM HAYS

Published 2022 by Seventh Street Books®

Inquiries should be addressed to
Start Science Fiction
221 River Street, 9th Floor
Hoboken, New Jersey 07030
PHONE: 212-431-5454
WWW.SEVENTHSTREETBOOKS.COM

10 9 8 7 6 5 4 3 2 1

978-1-64506-046-8 (paperback)
978-1-64506-047-5 (ebook)

Printed in the United States of America

For my sister
Natasha Thomasovna Hays

in love and gratitude for her precious companionship
throughout our lives

Foreword

Bern and Its German

About a million of Switzerland's eight-and-a half million people live in Bern, the second largest Swiss canton and home to the Swiss capital (also Bern) and to generous chunks of two mountain ranges, the Alps and the Jura. French is the mother tongue of ten percent of the Bernese; most of the rest speak a distinctive version of *Schweizerdeutsch* or Swiss-German dialect.

When Swiss-Germans talk to each other, whether they are professors or clerks, TV announcers or truckers, each uses their own local dialect, and, although they may occasionally hear an unfamiliar word, they all understand each other. There are no class distinctions in Swiss speech, just geographical ones. Kids in school learn to read, write, and speak *Hochdeutsch*, the German of books and newspapers, but for most Swiss it remains a foreign language.

The dialect of Bern, *Bärndütsch*, is especially easy for Swiss-Germans to identify. It is sing-song and slow, with long, drawling vowels and some distinctive oddities. Take the word for milk: *Milch* in standard German. Almost all the Swiss dialects pronounce the "ch" as a Scot would, with a hard, guttural sound like the noise you make before you spit. But the Bernese change the word still further, since they pronounce its "l" sound as "u." So *Milch* becomes "Mi-uuuu-ch." Think of a cat about to start a fight.

There are hundreds of words (thousands, actually, but many are old-fashioned and rarely used) that exist only in *Bärndütsch,* like "*Gring*" for head, instead of *Kopf.* The Bernese also use distinctive nicknames ending in "u," like Chrigu for Christian and Pädu for Patrick. In *Pesticide,* lots of characters have traditional Bernese nicknames: Jean-Pierre Niklaus is called Schämpu, for example, and Ueli, Giuliana's husband, is actually named Ulrich, although no one in the book ever calls him that. (For English-speakers, Ueli is hard to pronounce: U as in r**u**le, E as in **e**h, LI as in on**ly.**)

And what about "a" versus *ä*, "o" versus *ö*, and "u" versus *ü*? These vowels with umlauts are sounds that exist in High German as well as *Bärndütsch*—not that that makes them easier for English-speakers to say. Here's a small guide to vowel sounds in Bernese German.

a as in **ah** when you open your mouth for the doctor to look at your throat: **Strasse** (street)

ä as in wa-wa-wa when we want to make the noise of a baby crying, an "a" with your lips spread: **Fränzi** (short for Franziska)

e as in the **eh** that Canadians sometimes say at the end of a sentence (but without the questions mark!): **Reitschule** (riding school—and the name of Bern's alternative culture center, a thorn in the eye of the city's conservative politicians.)

i as in our "**bee**": **bio** (organic)

o as in our "**bowl**": **Polizei** (police)

ö as in our "**bird**" (but no "r" sound) or, if you know French, in "**peu**": **Löffel** (spoon; also a last name) u as in our "rule": **Tschugger** (a dialect term for "policeman")

ü say the sound "ee" and purse your lips almost completely shut: **Zürich**

As in English, there are short and long sounds for each of these vowels. One of the ways to indicate a long "a" is with two "a"s in a row: the **Aare** is Bern's river, which flows into the Rhine. Another example is **Seeland.** It's not "see" as in "I see you," but instead a long "eh."

The first word in this book with an umlaut is *Schützenmatte.* Today this is a large paved space near Bern's train station that's often used as a parking lot. When it first appeared in the city's records in 1477, however, it was a field where men practiced archery with crossbows: a "shooting meadow." It's still a stretch of land to be navigated carefully, especially at night—as you're about to find out.

1

Downtown Bern,
Sunday, June 16, early morning

"Let's get out of here," he said. But when he looked round, he was alone.

They'd just been talking, hadn't they? Now most of the tables behind him were empty, and a man was mopping the floor. He braced his arms, pushed himself to his feet, swayed, and then lurched through the dim bar and onto the sidewalk. Nearby a familiar figure stood hunched against the wall. Good.

Christ, he was blitzed. How had that happened? Some weed, followed by plenty of beer as they'd talked through the plans. But so what? The shots of schnapps—that'd been his mistake. Still, he'd managed; he'd managed everything. Things were set up the way he wanted them. And if he'd messed up somewhere . . . well, it could be fixed. Later.

He heard roars and shrieks: the Dance-In, still going strong. It wasn't often he sold to strangers instead of regulars, but with ten thousand kids dancing through downtown, all working on getting wasted, he'd have been crazy not to unload as much stuff as he could. Selling dope with hundreds of police stomping around—he couldn't believe he'd gotten away with it. The money he'd made, all in one evening! And then getting the whole deal done.

He'd deserved the schnapps.

He tried to see the time on his phone, but his eyes refused to focus. Shit! Was it two? Three? People were moving, but there was no beat. Why had the music stopped?

Clinging grimly to his companion's arm, he squinted at the plaza in front of the train station. When he'd strolled into the bar a couple of hours before, the square had been full of bodies swaying to the music. Now he saw flares of pulsing light and smelled smoke. Through the haze, he made out fires. Heard screams. Felt his eyes sting with tear gas.

Time to walk away. He tugged his friend down the Bollwerk to a crosswalk. When the little man turned green, they wove across the street and came to a stop in the Schützenmatte. During the day it was just a parking lot, but at night . . . Now, the enormous Riding School complex loomed out of the dark in front of him, lit by meager lamps strung across the courtyard. The bursts of graffiti on the building's walls flickered as the hanging lights swayed. He felt—strange. He wasn't alone again, was he? No—he saw a figure leaning against a car. When he beckoned, his friend stumbled closer, scuffing old newspapers and trash like a kid shuffling in dry leaves.

As the two of them shambled toward the Riding School, slapping feet and panting breaths surged out of the darkness behind them, and at least twenty men barreled by. One almost plowed into him. The man's black hood was tight around his head, his nose and mouth were covered, and there was a thick chain wrapped around his arm, one end gripped in his fist. Others brandished metal bars or broken bottles; some carried stuff in their arms. Clothes, shoes, a laptop, a toaster.

A toaster?

They were looting! Guys were actually stealing from shops. He didn't think Bern had ever had a riot like this, where people lit fires and raided stores. It was fucking amazing. But weird, too. The city was out of control.

More boots clattering on pavement. Quick. He stumbled back into the shelter of a pillar, and the next wave of runners swept by. This time it was cops, enormous clear-plastic shields held out like battering rams. Stupid to run with those. The looters would be all over the Riding School before the pigs even reached the front gates. He giggled at how stupid they looked, with their bulbous helmets bobbing in the half-light and their shields banging against their knees.

"Jesus Christ! Let's go," said his companion, grabbing his shoulder.

That's right—they'd been on their way to the Riding School. Which didn't seem like such a good idea anymore. As they swerved back on themselves in a jagged circle, he noticed a single cop running toward them, shield held sideways to keep it clear of his legs, desperate to catch up with the others. *Oh, no. I'm going to miss my chance to bash the boys in black. Wait for me!*

The lone cop hadn't seen them standing in the shadows a few feet away. The impulse to leap out and yell, "Boo!" filled his head like helium. Then he had a better idea.

He stepped out of the darkness as the cop ran by and stuck one leg into his path. The man flew through the air, rocketed to the pavement, and smacked his helmeted head into the bumper of a parked car with a resounding "boing," like a struck gong.

God, he'd never seen anything so funny. He leaned over, hands on his knees, and tried to keep from falling down as he laughed and laughed. Boing!

"Are you out of your fucking mind?" he heard his friend say. But he couldn't stop laughing.

Then the cop was up and on his feet in a heartbeat, howling. God, he was mad. Flinging his shield away, he sped toward them with his visor up and his baton swinging.

This guy was going to hit him. Oh shit! He swayed, trying to stand upright. Tried to say sorry, it was a joke. No use, his voice wouldn't come. He couldn't run, he couldn't even move. He stretched out both hands to hold back the rage rushing toward him. Stop, man. Stop.

The cop was right in front of him. There was nothing he could do.

He closed his eyes.

2

Bern,
Saturday June 15–Sunday, June 16

The old man's body had been removed, and a forensics expert, white-suited from hood to booties, was going over the tiny apartment. Giuliana Linder, also in protective gear, stood out of the way and studied the ancient, peeling wallpaper, yellow with cigarette smoke; the gouged wainscoting; the disintegrating rugs. She'd already taken in the black mold climbing the walls in bathroom and kitchen, and the scramble of clothes, sheets, and blankets heaped in the bedroom. The smell of the place would have been indescribably bad, even without the reek of rotting flesh.

It was the stench that had persuaded a neighbor to call the police earlier that evening; now it was after midnight. As the lead homicide detective on call that weekend, Giuliana had arrived around ten. From the beginning it was a presumed suicide: the victim was a widower of seventy-eight who'd struggled to take care of himself since the death of his wife two years earlier. It appeared that he'd downed most of a bottle of cheap schnapps and hanged himself from a hook in the ceiling that had somehow held his weight. How long ago was a question for the autopsy, but Giuliana thought it had been between forty-eight and seventy-two hours. Self-inflicted or not, the death had to be investigated, so she and her colleagues were still at work.

The figure in white straightened up from a crouch, braced her back with both hands, groaned, and came over to where Giuliana stood. "I hate suicides," she said.

"Yeah," said Giuliana. "Several neighbors tried to help him after the wife died, or so they say, but he was difficult. Mean, depressed, drunk. Still, it shouldn't have come to this."

The other woman sighed. "Someone should have called social services."

Giuliana nodded, even while wondering if it would have done any good. A man couldn't be forced to drink less, get counseling, take antidepressants, and smile at his neighbors.

As the forensics woman turned back to her examination of the floor, one of the men who'd been interviewing residents in the building's other seven apartments—and dealing with their reactions to being awakened after midnight—called out from the corridor, "Are you hearing what's happening downtown?"

From the room's rickety table, a police radio murmured; it had started with bulletins on the police presence at the Dance-In and was now putting out nonstop police-only news about the riots. Giuliana realized she hadn't paid attention for a while.

"Rioters have attacked police with magnesium torches and Molotov cocktails," the dispatcher was saying, "causing fires in the streets. Ambulance drivers, firefighters, and first-aid workers are also being targeted. All available personnel should report to a supervisor immediately for an assignment."

"If you put booties on, you can come in here," Giuliana called to the investigator in the hall. "Right?" she asked her colleague, who nodded wearily.

"Sure. I'm almost done for tonight."

The investigator picked his way through, shuffling in his paper shoe covers across the wooden floor to the frayed edge of the rug. "Jesus. Can you believe this?" he said. "These fuckers are bashing cops' heads in, and we're going to be up shit creek just for using tear gas and rubber bullets."

"Nah," said the forensics woman. "No one's going to blame us for trying to stop *these* guys. Not with all the damage they're doing."

The investigator kept complaining as if she hadn't spoken: "'Police Injure Hundreds in Bern's Deadliest Riot.' That'll be the headline."

"Better than 'Police Helpless as Hooligans Destroy Swiss Capital,'" countered the woman. Her voice grew muffled as she bent to scrape something off the floor.

Giuliana thought of the demonstrations she'd been in when she was young, although the Dance-In was normally more of a giant street party than a demo. There'd been run-ins with the police in her day—but no anarchist block to force things over the top. If this bunch at the Dance-In even were anarchists. Giuliana doubted they had any politics at all; they were just guys who liked upsetting the authorities, fighting, and breaking things.

As if he could read her mind, the investigator said, "American cops would probably shoot these rioting bastards after they threw their first torch. And we get in trouble for dragging some drunk through a pool of his own piss, for Christ's sake."

That recent case had resulted in two cops being disciplined: correctly, in Giuliana's opinion. But now was not the time to say so.

"How about tranquilizing darts?" she said. "As soon as anyone starts trouble, we shoot them to sleep, stack them in paddy wagons, and cart them off to jail. Think how much easier it would be to manage soccer matches."

The other two laughed, and the mood lightened as they waited for the rest of the team to finish so they could wind up for the night.

A quick look at the newsfeed on her phone told Giuliana that the riots were getting worse, and she itched to get back to her apartment. She hoped her brother wasn't out in this mess—and thank God Ueli and the kids were safe at home.

It was after three when she finally walked in her front door. The hall still smelled faintly of dinner, which made her notice her hunger. In the kitchen she cut a slice off the braided Sunday loaf in the breadbasket, buttered it, poured herself a glass of milk, and downed her snack standing up. She was so weary she left the fridge open while she ate and almost forgot to close it. But tired as she was, she went to check on the kids.

As usual, Lukas's bedroom door was open, while Isabelle's was closed. Hand resting on Isabelle's doorknob, Giuliana stopped, remembering her recent promise to her fifteen-year-old not to barge into her room. All right, then, she'd honor her vow at night, too, even if it hurt. No such restrictions applied to Lukas, who was ten, so she tiptoed into his room and sat on the edge of his bed, drinking in his still-childlike smell and the sound of his steady breathing. He was such a heavy sleeper that she risked stroking his hair, dark and curly like her own.

For once she managed to slide under the duvet without waking her husband. God, she was beat. At least it was Sunday and Ueli's turn to get up with Lukas in the morning. They'd planned an outing with the kids, and she needed to write up her notes on the suicide and think about some remaining loose ends, but she could afford to give herself until nine thirty. She stayed awake long enough to set the alarm before losing herself in sleep.

She was dragged back to consciousness by Ueli gently shaking her shoulder and saying her name. Her body trembled with fatigue.

She focused on his face. "What? What?" she mumbled.

Ueli held her ringing cell phone out. "Sorry, love."

"Linder," she croaked. Ueli settled back under the duvet next to her.

"Frau Linder, sorry to wake you. I don't think we've met, but I'm Fabienne Mäder, also with the cantonal police, and I wanted to let you know we've got your daughter. Isabelle Brand, right? That's your daughter? She was arrested at the Dance-In."

Adrenaline surged through Giuliana's body, and she pulled herself upright. "Yes, Isabelle Brand is my daughter." Fighting to control her panic, she turned wide eyes toward Ueli, who catapulted out of bed and rushed down the hall to Isabelle's room. When he returned, he was shaking his head.

"Is she all right? She isn't hurt, is she?" Giuliana heard the squeak of fear in her voice. What could have happened? How on earth could Isabelle have gotten caught up in all that chaos?

"No, she's fine. She's here in central detention along with hundreds of other youngsters brought in during the night. She was reportedly caught vandalizing property and then resisted arrest. I wanted to let you know."

It made no sense that Isabelle had been at the Dance-In; it was even more ludicrous to picture her as a vandal. Talking back to a policeman and pissing him off enough to arrest her? Now that she could imagine. She wanted desperately to drive over to the detention center and pick Isabelle up. But there was no way she was going to ask for special treatment for *her* daughter.

She blew out a long breath. "Thanks so much, Frau Mäder. My husband and I . . ." No, she wasn't going to confess that they hadn't even known their daughter was missing. "Um . . . we're very glad to know she's safe. She's only fifteen, so I'd appreciate it if someone could . . . um . . . keep an eye on her." Even as she said it, she realized she shouldn't have. Asking for *her* daughter to be kept safe. "We'll come get her as soon as minors are released. Is there any chance I could speak with her?"

Isabelle was in a cell, she was told, probably asleep. She'd be free to leave that afternoon, maybe by four. Giuliana thanked the woman again and hung up. She looked at the phone and realized it was only 6:15. She'd had less than three hours' sleep.

Ueli leaned against the bedroom door, arms crossed over his broad chest. His orange hair was flattened to one side of his head, his freckled skin was blotchy from bed, and the waistband of his boxers was twisted. His sleep-tousled appearance would've usually made her smile. But right now he was scowling at her.

"Did you know she—" Giuliana began.

"Where is she? Tell me what that was about," Ueli said, his voice loud. "Where's Isabelle?"

"She's at the main detention center in Neufeld, with the other people arrested at the Dance-In, and they're phoning the parents of all the kids under eighteen—although I think we got one of the earliest calls as a courtesy. Isa must have told them I was a cop. Anyway, she's fine; she's asleep. But I don't understand what she was doing at the Dance-In in the first place." She sat up and perched on the edge of the bed facing Ueli. Because of the heat she'd slept in a tank top and underpants—now she shivered.

"I let her go," Ueli said. "Obviously, it was a mistake. I'm sorry. But she said Quentin had invited her and would look after her."

"You let her go to an illegal street party because she was accompanied by an eighteen-year-old boy we barely know? She's fifteen. What were you thinking?" She pulled the duvet over and draped it around her bare legs as she spoke.

"*I've* met him," he said. "It's not my fault you haven't been around. He seems okay. Plus, she's crazy about him." He scrubbed his face with his hands. "But that's not the point. Aren't they going to let her out? When I think of her locked up with a bunch of people fighting the cops, I . . ."

"Apparently *she* was fighting the cops." Giuliana forced the words out. "And vandalizing things."

"I don't believe that," Ueli said. "Do you?" She heard a hint of uncertainty in his voice. That was the way it was with teenagers—sometimes they did stuff so stupid and risky that you were left reeling. But not this. Not Isabelle.

"No. It's probably a mistake. Don't forget, we can get Paps or Paolo onto it if she needs a lawyer."

"I don't understand why you aren't more upset. It's like you aren't even worried about her."

She felt the prick of tears in her eyes. "Of course I am."

"Okay, maybe that's harsh. Still, I don't . . ." Frowning, he looked away from her and shook his head. "Listen, I'm going to get her. Tell me where the detention center is."

"Please don't go. I'm sure she's safe." She struggled to keep her voice calm. "She got arrested for a reason, and we can't let her think that she doesn't have to face consequences, just because her mother's a cop."

"Forget about teaching her lessons. She *needs* us. She must be terrified. What if she gets hurt?"

"Who's going to hurt her? She's surrounded by police."

"She's still locked up with a bunch of rioters. And . . . well . . . what about the cops?"

Her reply caught in her throat. "What do you mean, what about the cops?" she said quietly.

"Remember that policeman in Luzern who got caught on camera kicking a Rumanian in the head? I know you don't want to deal with it, but cops attack people. Swiss cops attack Swiss people." He said the last sentence slowly, as if she were dim-witted.

Giuliana stood up fast; the duvet fell to the floor. "I know it happens. But she's a lot safer in the detention center than she was at the Dance-In. Even if there hadn't been a riot, the crowd would've been passing out pills like candy and drinking until they puked. God! Suppose someone had given her a roofie?"

"Look, I said it was a mistake."

He looked so miserable that she crossed the room and wrapped her arms around him. His body didn't relax against hers, but at least he put his hands on her waist.

"You did. I'm sorry. Let's not fight," she said.

"I don't want to fight. I want to leave." He shrugged himself out of her embrace. "Maybe it embarrasses you to ask for favors, but not me. I'm going to tell them her mother's a cop and get her out. You can either give me the address, or I'll get it some other way."

She sighed. "I think it's the wrong thing to do. And, besides, it won't work; you'll just embarrass yourself." And me, she admitted to herself. "Honestly, Ueli, I think it's bad for Isabelle to get special treatment. But if you really have to go, then go."

She showed him the location on his phone, waited while he got dressed, and walked him to the door. They didn't speak, but he said a gruff good-bye before jogging down the corridor and out into the bright early-morning sunshine. She knew he was angry that she wouldn't pull strings for Isabelle. But it wasn't right, damn it.

She slumped onto the sofa, head in her hands. She didn't think Ueli had the slightest chance of getting Isabelle released early. He'd throw Giuliana's name around and it would do him no good at all. She cringed. Ueli had a point—she *did* care what her colleagues thought. But was that something to be ashamed of? If it were anyone else's child, Ueli'd be straight onto his laptop, thumping out an article decrying cronyism among cops.

Her head hammered from too little sleep. She took a couple of aspirins and then wandered into Isabelle's room. How had she missed Isabelle's interest in the Dance-In? And going with Quentin? She should have made a point of finding out more about him, if Isabelle liked him so much. Was Ueli right? Had she not been at home enough lately? Was she too obsessed with work?

She shuffled around her daughter's room, touching a lopsided clay pot that Isabelle had made in third grade, moving on to a propped-up strip of photo-booth photos of Isabelle and her best friend, Luna, making faces at each other. She sat down on the bed. Lifting the pillow to her nose, she smelled the scent of her daughter's hair and skin. She hugged the pillow and tried to imagine what Isabelle must be feeling. Was she terrified, as Ueli feared? Somehow she doubted it. Not Isabelle.

Her eyes closed. She slid sideways, and her head sank to the bed, the pillow still clutched to her chest. She'd just lie here a minute or two.

Three hours later, the creaking of the bed woke her. Two large dark-brown eyes, exactly like her own, peered into her face. Lukas was bending over her, breathing chocolate-cereal breath into her nose. "Are you awake?" he whispered.

"No, I'm asleep with my eyes open, you silly-billy." She smiled into her son's serious face. "What time is it?"

"After nine," he said, sitting down on Isabelle's bed. "I woke up at eight and played my wizard game and ate breakfast and watched TV, but I was wondering where everybody went. And why you're in Isabelle's bed. Did Vati and Isabelle go somewhere fun?" She could hear an unspoken "no fair" lurking beneath his words.

"Isabelle spent the night out, and Vati's picking her up. It'll take him a while. Go get *The Thief Lord*, and I'll read to you in the big bed."

Being with Lukas let her set aside her fears. But after half an hour of reading to him, she got out of bed to shower and dress, and the worries returned. When she and Ueli had met at university, he'd already been freelancing, but she'd had no thought of joining the police: in those days, she'd leaned farther left than he had. But her contact with cops during her law internships had made her see things in a new light. She'd believed Ueli had sympathized with her choices. Now, after eighteen years with the police, she found herself wondering how heartfelt Ueli's support of her job really was.

She was zipping her jeans when her cell phone rang. It was her boss, Rolf Straub. Oh God. Surely he couldn't be expecting a full report already?

"Morning, Rolf," she said, clutching the phone between ear and shoulder as she pulled on her socks. "I assume you want to ask me about last night; I haven't . . ."

"Morning." Rolf interrupted. "I'm calling about something else. Another case. I'm very pleased you're the one in line for this."

A not-so-little voice inside Giuliana's head screamed no, no, no. Not because she couldn't handle two cases within twenty-four hours, but because her mind was so filled with Isabelle's arrest and Ueli's departure that she wasn't sure she could process a new crisis.

"Sure," she forced herself to say as she padded into the living room to see what Lukas was doing. "What's up?"

"You know Jonas Pauli, a young uniform who sometimes helps homicide with phone calls and paperwork? He was out on riot detail last night, and he seems to have bashed in a man's head with his billy club."

Giuliana knew Jonas, who couldn't be more than twenty-five—eager, hard-working, and blessedly short on machismo. Jonas, a killer? Her husband's words came back to her: "Swiss cops attack Swiss people."

"He killed a rioter?" she asked, lowering her voice because of Lukas, who was sitting on the floor building something out of Legos.

"A rioter, a bystander? We don't know yet. The body was found in the Schützenmatte parking lot outside the Riding School. A young man about the same age as Jonas. I'd like you to investigate."

"Of course. What's happening with Jonas?" She stooped to stroke Lukas's head. He ignored her. She crossed the hall to the kitchen, where she filled a large mug half-full of milk and put it in the microwave to heat before turning on the Nespresso machine.

"He's handed in his weapons and badge and will be off duty during your investigation."

Giuliana was nodding to herself—it was the usual procedure.

"Who's on the roster as my backup?" She added the equivalent of a triple espresso to her mug of hot milk, sliced a piece off the loaf she'd attacked the night before, and buttered it thickly.

"Sabine," answered Rolf.

"Great," Giuliana said, and meant it. Sabine Jost had been on the homicide squad for over twenty years, a trailblazer for woman detectives. "And my prosecutor?"

"A youngster called Oliver Leuthard. Haven't heard anything against him."

"That's good. How's Jonas coping?" She carried her coffee and bread back into the living room to eat at the table near Lukas.

"He's crying a lot." Somehow Rolf's tone conveyed both sympathy and censure.

"Does the press know about . . . him?"

"They're reveling in the riots, but this death hasn't come out yet. So I need you to get onto this and stay on it until it's solved."

"I'll be there as fast as I can."

"Thanks. Sorry about your Sunday," said Rolf, the workaholic, whose Sundays Giuliana suspected were spent reading investigators' reports. He hung up.

"Hey!" she called to Lukas in his sea of Legos. "I need you to spend the day with Nonna and Grospaps. That wasn't the original plan, but Vati and Isabelle aren't home, and it turns out I have to go to work. Sorry, love. You going to be okay?"

Lukas shrugged without looking up, and guilt pierced her. First, she abandoned Isabelle in jail, and now she was deserting Lukas. She opened her mouth to offer a more elaborate apology, but before she could speak, he turned and gave her a grin. "There. I'm finished. Come see."

She sat on the floor next to him and studied the half-vehicle, half-creature he'd been building as he showed her every method of destruction he'd given the thing. Cross-legged on the floor, she pulled him onto her lap and kissed the top of his head.

It was only after her mother had cheerfully agreed to have Lukas for the day, and Giuliana had changed into thin linen pants and a short-sleeved blouse, run a brush through her shoulder-length hair, twisted it into the knot she always wore at work, and made sure her purse had everything she needed that she remembered: Ueli had the car.

She slammed her hand onto the kitchen counter, which hurt but did nothing to make her feel better, and then she called a taxi. On the way to the station she texted Ueli. No message came back.

3

Bern's Nordring police station,
Sunday morning, June 16

Jonas Pauli sat slumped, red-eyed, elbows on the grey metal of the table in an interrogation room. His lawyer, Werner Rindlisbacher, sat beside him. Giuliana knew Werner, not only because of his work with criminals she'd investigated but also through her defense-lawyer father. Now she faced him across the metal table. Opposite Jonas sat Sabine Jost, the second homicide detective on the investigation, and in a corner of the room, a man in uniform sat at a laptop, writing everything down.

"Jonas will answer your questions," Werner said. "But he shouldn't have to go on all afternoon. He hasn't slept for thirty hours."

Giuliana nodded. It wouldn't do her any good in court to be dependent on evidence Jonas had given while he was in this state.

"Thanks, Werner," she said. "Jonas, I'm going to be in charge of this investigation, so if you tell me your story now, I'll have something to work with today. Then we can go over the details tomorrow once you're rested."

The young man glanced up and met her eyes. He looked so wretched she wanted to comfort him. But this was not the time for reassurance.

"I'm just . . . so sorry," he said. "It's hard to believe I could have . . . This guy, he tripped me, and I fell on my head. Hard. I was so angry I ran back and thumped him with the club. I never thought one blow could kill someone. We trained and trained not to lose our tempers, and then when I go on riot duty . . . Oh God." Jonas bent over until his forehead almost touched the table.

Sabine looked up from the slim stack of papers in front of her and asked Werner, "Is there evidence confirming the fall he described?"

"Yes," Werner answered. "We had a medical exam done. He has lots of scrapes and bruises. Nothing significant on the head, since he was wearing a helmet. But it fits."

That may be, thought Giuliana. *But he could have received those injuries before or after he hit the victim.*

"I want you to describe the whole sequence of events. Why were you running toward the Riding School? Did you get a command?"

Jonas shook his head. "We were facing off with twenty, maybe twenty-five rioters near the train station, and then they ran. I heard one of the cops yell, 'They'll hide in the Riding School. The fuckers will get away—catch them.' I don't know if it was a command from a senior officer, but lots of people broke formation and started running, so I ran, too."

It was understandable: almost everyone around him would have been senior to Jonas. She wrote "Command?" in her small spiral notebook and nodded for him to continue.

"We weren't organized, just running together down Bollwerk. Then I tripped over my shield and almost fell. By the time I started up again, I was way behind the others, so I was going through the Schützenmatte as fast as I could. I noticed a man on my left moving toward me, and suddenly I was flying toward a car. He'd stuck out his leg and tripped me."

"Did he threaten you afterward?" asked Sabine.

"No. I was shaky after the fall, but I jumped up fast, because I thought it was an attack. The guy was standing there, laughing. I mean really laughing. So I ran over to him and . . . well, I was so angry I hit him with my billy club. That wiped the grin off his face," Jonas said savagely. Then he pressed a hand to his mouth.

Giuliana just nodded. "Did he seem badly hurt?"

"No. He put his hands up to his head and sort of swayed in place. He stank of pot and booze."

All this—the tripping and Jonas's retaliation—had probably taken place in under a minute. Thinking had not been part of the program.

"The emergency techs who discovered the body found a police baton lying next to it—was it yours?"

Jonas was staring down at his hands, gripping the edge of the table as if it were a cliff edge. "Yes. It just . . . fell. I didn't pick it up. I don't know why. I was . . ." He broke off, chewing his lip.

"Was it found more or less where you left it, Jonas?"

He shrugged. "I guess so. I just dropped it and ran. I did grab my shield first, but . . . I was alone in the dark. The other guy standing there might have . . ."

"What other guy?" Sabine asked sharply, before Giuliana could say the same thing. Rolf hadn't mentioned a witness to the attack. That changed everything.

"There was another man. He stayed back in the shadows, like he was trying to hide, but when I hit the drunk, this guy ran over, yelling at me. I wanted to get away from him, so I ran off to the Riding School to find the other cops."

"Tell us about the second man. What was he saying? Did he have a weapon?"

If it was possible, the youngster seemed to shrink in on himself even further. His body sagged, shoulders slumped, arms crossed. He raised his eyes to meet hers, and then his head drooped.

She hardened her heart. "What did you notice about the second man?"

"Nothing. I don't know. He came at me out of the dark, shouting, and I just ran, like I said."

"Did you at any point check on the man you hit?" Giuliana asked.

At this, Jonas sat up straighter, and his voice became animated.

"Not then. But three, maybe four hours later, when things were quieter, I was on duty near the train station. I couldn't leave, but I asked one of the ambulance men to go down to the Schützenmatte and see if someone was lying there hurt. I figured the guy I'd hit would be long gone, but I wanted to be sure. About an hour later I was still on duty, and the tech I'd spoken to came back with a couple of other cops, and they talked to me and brought me in."

Giuliana would have to speak to the medical tech. She wrote "EMT" in her notebook and saw Sabine jot down the same letters. Their eyes met, and Sabine smiled at her.

"But the other guy could have called an ambulance after I ran off," Jonas said, reaching across the table and taking hold of Giuliana's wrist. "He was standing right next to that laughing bastard. Why didn't *he* call for help?" He shook her arm before letting her go.

In the short silence that followed, while Giuliana reviewed what else she urgently needed to know, Jonas started to cry.

"I shouldn't call him a bastard. He's dead. But he *tripped* me." For a moment, Giuliana was reminded of ten-year-old Lukas.

"Do you have enough to get started?" Werner asked them. "Jonas needs to get some sleep. His parents and girlfriend are waiting to take him home."

"Just another minute. Look at me, please, Jonas," Giuliana said.

He lowered his hands from his face, and his swollen eyes met hers.

"Are you sure you hit the man only once?"

Jonas drew in a long, shaky breath. "I'm sure. I hit him one time, on the top of his head."

"Okay. That's all for now," Giuliana said. As she and Sabine stood up, Werner and Jonas did the same. Werner put a hand on Jonas's shoulder and steered him away down the corridor. Giuliana and Sabine left the meeting room and turned toward the homicide office, where Rolf was working. "What's your impression?" Giuliana asked her colleague, stopping in the hall to talk softly.

"He comes across as truthful. But a lot depends on the autopsy and the lab report on the baton, doesn't it?"

"Yes," Giuliana said. "Most people wouldn't die from one blow to the head with a billy club, but it depends on so many factors. There's no point in speculating yet; I'll get a request for witnesses into tomorrow's paper. We need to find the friend Jonas described."

Sabine cocked her head, her mouth twisted. "With the press, the public, and half the politicians in the city and canton frantic to track down every rioter, do you think *anyone* who was involved in last night's mess is going to identify themselves to the police?"

"If a friend of yours was beaten before your eyes, wouldn't you react?"

"I would," Sabine answered. "But if I was the kind of border-of-society type that hangs out around the Riding School, would I walk into a police station and accuse a cop of brutality? Maybe I'd be afraid of being clobbered myself."

Giuliana opened her mouth to argue, then heard Ueli's voice in her head and said nothing.

They briefed Rolf, and he went home, leaving the homicide room to them. Giuliana asked Sabine to phone the lab about the baton, while she hurried to the basement café for something to eat. Her morning slice of bread seemed far away.

As she ran down the stairs, she thought again of Ueli, probably at that very moment fighting police bureaucracy for Isabelle's release and being stonewalled at every turn. And she thought of her daughter, her strong, self-confident Isabelle, who tried with teenage bravado to hide all her sweetness. Was it wrong to believe that her child needed to lie in the bed she'd made for herself?

But either way, Ueli was handling it now. He was dealing with this crisis, just like he handled so much of the stress in their family life, so that she could get on with her job. The thought calmed her.

Right. She needed to visit the site of the homicide and check on the autopsy, but first she had to eat.

As she grabbed a tray, she noticed Renzo Donatelli having coffee alone in a corner under a ragged poster about knife crime. He wasn't a homicide detective but a general investigator, a *Fahnder*. On a case the previous fall, he'd been assigned to do her door-to-door work, and she'd been impressed by how much detail people had revealed to him about their dead neighbor—and how cleverly he'd summarized what she needed to know.

She slid a plate of cheese and fruit onto her tray and glanced around the café with its white institutional walls. On this Sunday afternoon, it was almost empty. Which was good, she thought, because it meant she could sit with Renzo without . . . She tried to squash this thought. Renzo was an excellent cop—why should there be any shame in talking to him? The problem was his appearance: he looked like he should be on a billboard, advertising aftershave or underpants. And he seemed to have latched onto her as a mentor. Flattering, but . . . difficult. At least at thirty-four he was twelve years her junior, so no one was going to imagine he had a thing for her. But still . . .

She wasn't sure what perverse bravado had made her agree to his suggestion after Christmas that she join him once or twice a week to work out and have a quick breakfast afterward. God knew she could use the training. And Renzo, who was an early-morning fixture at the gym across from the police station, had come up with a challenging exercise program for her. It should have been a great plan, and it was, really, except for her wondering what her colleagues thought about it. That, and her worrying about how much she enjoyed his company.

Enough overanalyzing. However conflicted she might sometimes feel about Renzo, there was no doubt he'd become a friend. Shifting her tray to one hand, she gave him a wave and headed over.

4

Nordring police station,
Sunday afternoon and evening, June 16

Renzo had noticed Giuliana as soon as she entered the cafeteria. Why was she at work? Maybe that old geezer she'd been assigned to the night before hadn't hanged himself after all.

From across the room he watched her move down the food line. He forced himself to do nothing to attract her attention, but still she waved and started toward his table.

"Hey," he said, as she set her tray down across from him. "Why aren't you out enjoying this weather?"

"I've got Jonas Pauli, with Sabine as second, so here I am. What about you?"

Renzo shrugged. "Fränzi decided to take the kids to her sister's cottage in the mountains for the weekend. My brother-in-law spends the whole time trying to get me to invest in some fund he's peddling, and it's hard to avoid him when I'm a guest in his house. So I decided to stay in Bern and attack my car-theft paperwork. Fränzi won't miss me: she can complain about me better when I'm not there."

As soon as the last sentence was out of his mouth, he wished he could call it back. Over the past months of post-gym breakfasts, he'd been unable to resist confiding in Giuliana about Fränzi's hatred of his job. But to sound so pathetic! He hurried on to ask, "What's the story on Jonas?"

He watched her demolish her food as she gave him a quick summary. "All of which means I won't be at the gym tomorrow morning," she finished. "I'm sorry. Let's see if I can make it on Wednesday."

"That would be great," Renzo said, mentally reviewing his schedule. "Now that I'm almost finished with these car thefts, I should be able to get myself onto your case. That is, if it would be useful," he added, hoping he didn't sound too keen.

"I'd love to have you. Once we get the victim identified, we'll need more investigators. The timing should be just right."

She drained her water glass, stood, and touched his shoulder. "Sabine and I are off to the Schütz. Good luck with your paperwork."

He reached up and squeezed the hand resting on his shoulder. "It's hard to imagine Jonas beating a man to death. He's a good kid."

"Yeah, he's beside himself about it." Walking toward the used-tray stand, she added, "The dead guy's just a kid, too."

Renzo stared after her until she'd vanished down the hall. Time to get back to work. Instead, he twirled his coffee cup in its saucer and thought about Giuliana's husband. Although he'd never met Ueli, he'd looked up his photo and biography online; he'd even read some of his articles. However much Renzo vented to Giuliana about his problems with Fränzi, she never said anything negative about Ueli. Just happy family stuff. She'd told him they'd been together since their early twenties. *Decades of bliss*, he thought bitterly, and then cheered up at the idea of changing assignments.

Walking upstairs to his desk, he began planning his strategy for joining Giuliana on the Pauli case.

"What's with the shit-eating grin, Donatelli?" a cop from Vice called out to him.

He came back with, "My wife's out of town," which earned him a leer. To himself he said, I'm going to work with Giuliana.

But that was something he never talked about, with anyone.

"Our autopsy sure got fast-tracked," said Sabine, perched on Giuliana's desk in the homicide room. With only two of its usual eight busy detectives, it was abnormally quiet.

"Lucky for us that the press has started asking questions, and the boss wants better answers to give them," said Giuliana. She didn't mean Rolf; "the boss" was the commandant in charge of the cantonal police force. "But I think he's making a mistake, waiting until tomorrow afternoon to hold an official press conference. We'll have known about the death for thirty-six hours by then."

"Well, at least it doesn't look like a cover-up," Sabine commented. "The online newsfeeds seem to be reporting more or less what we know at this point."

"Whatever we do or say, it's still a cop beating a bystander to death," said Giuliana. "Thank God *I* didn't have to tell a bunch of journalists that the vic was hit twice. Why did Jonas lie, when he knew what the autopsy would show?"

Sabine shook her head. "Did he, though? I'd have sworn he was telling the truth."

"Me too," Giuliana said. "So, just for the moment, let's assume he really did hit the kid only once. Since we won't have any forensic work on the club until tomorrow, we don't know what will come out of that. But we can speculate."

"No phone or wallet on the body." Sabine summarized what they both knew. "Let's say Jonas hit the guy once and threw his club down, like he said. Someone picked it up, whacked the vic again and robbed him. That would be a realistic scenario in a druggie hangout like the Schützenmatte. Except for the hundred-fifty francs in his pocket. And the thousands in his money belt—which is weird anyway. But I guess if the robber was in a hurry, he could have grabbed the wallet and missed the rest of the cash."

Giuliana was shaking her head before Sabine had finished. "We know from the autopsy how drunk and stoned the guy was. A mugger wouldn't have needed to hit him again to get his wallet and phone—with one-point-eight in his blood and a bang on his head, he'd have been gaga anyway. You're right about the five thousand francs in the money belt. Why did the vic have it on him? Because of the Dance-In?"

Sabine shrugged. "If Jonas *is* telling the truth, then we need to think about the second man. He's the most likely mugger. Or he may have had other reasons for giving his friend a whack on the head."

"That's assuming Jonas didn't make up this 'friend' to give us another suspect besides himself," Giuliana said. "I've made sure the request for witnesses will be in the newspapers and online tomorrow. But before we start looking for a possibly imaginary person, we've got to figure out who the dead man is."

Giuliana had talked to Heinz Neuhaus, a *Fahnder* like Renzo, whose team of investigators had spent the afternoon crisscrossing the neighborhood around the Schützenmatte with a photograph of the victim's dead face. Even at the best of times, the men and women who hung out at the Riding School were not inclined to help cops. Now, less than forty-eight hours after the riots, they were openly hostile.

"If only we could get the vic's photo into tomorrow's papers," said Sabine.

"Yeah," Giuliana said. "But imagine what *that* gruesome sight would do for our image. I just hope Jonas doesn't become a scapegoat. Maybe the boss will decide that all those Dance-In folks who got a face full of tear gas or pepper spray—and their parents—will feel less pissed off if a cop gets thrown to the wolves."

Giuliana got home shortly after ten and went straight to Isabelle's room to find her daughter fast asleep and Ueli sitting by her side in the dark, a strand of her red-blond hair in his hands. He'd texted Giuliana at five to say he'd finally gotten Isabelle out, picked Lukas up, and brought both kids home. Isabelle, he'd reported, was fine, but hungry, filthy, and exhausted.

Ueli stood, and Giuliana took his place on the bed, touching her daughter's arm. Usually a light sleeper, Isabelle didn't stir; her face with its paler version of her father's freckles looked peaceful, despite her ordeal. Giuliana wanted to throw her arms around her child, lift her to her breast, and rock her. Instead, she stroked Isabelle's arm and got up to follow Ueli out.

"I can't believe it took those bastards all day to let her go," Ueli said, once they'd closed Isabelle's door. "She didn't want to talk about what happened, but she says no one hurt her."

"That's good," said Giuliana, moving into their room to get ready for bed. The words "What did I tell you?" banged around inside her mouth, but she clenched her teeth and kept them from escaping. She was sure no one had hurt Isabelle at the detention center, but she wasn't so sure about the Dance-In. Something bad must have happened to her daughter, or she wouldn't have gotten arrested.

If Giuliana had been able to get home earlier, she and Ueli could have talked about that morning's disagreement, and he could have unloaded about what must have been a difficult day. She could have told him how much she, too, had been thinking about Isabelle. Right now, though, she was so exhausted that simply putting one foot in front of the other took effort. Ueli's emotions seemed like one more problem to cope with.

Giuliana had called Rolf before leaving the station to let him know how little progress had been made identifying their victim, and he'd been curt. He probably felt even more hounded than she did.

She heard the click of Ueli's laptop keys from the living room. He always had a deadline, and his wasted Sunday would mess up his meticulous research-and-writing schedule. Most of her felt sympathy, but a tiny, nastier part of her thought, *Serves you right.*

She looked in on him before going to bed. "Can we talk?"

"I'm listening," said Ueli, although he kept typing.

"I'm very glad Isabelle's okay, and I'm sorry you had such a hard time getting her out." He typed on. "This morning I was put in charge of a new homicide, and I'm going to be busy. Tomorrow I have to leave at seven fifteen."

Normally, Ueli would have asked about her assignment. This time, he shrugged. "So what else is new? The kids and I will cope."

Giuliana drew in a sharp breath, but her angry words died before they could emerge. He was right. It was how they made their two-career family function: she worked as much as her job required, and Ueli handled the children and household and shaped his writing assignments around everyone else's schedule. She waited another moment, but he kept typing, so she kissed the top of his head and went to bed.

Tired as she was, she stayed awake, having silent conversations with him. She wasn't even sure if she'd had any sleep when she finally heard the bed creak and felt the mattress sink under his weight. She reached out in the dark, and her hand had to move a long way before it touched his warm back where he lay, facing away from her.

"I'm sorry," she whispered, and hoped he wouldn't think she was apologizing for not getting Isabelle out of detention. She was sorry they'd disagreed and sorry that her police work made his life more difficult. But she didn't regret her decisions.

"I know you are, love," he said. She'd hoped for "I'm sorry, too." But at least he'd answered. "Good night," he added. Eventually she slid her hand off his back and across the cool sheet to rest under her chin.

Shortly before her alarm buzzed the next morning, Giuliana got a text from Renzo. "Assigned to another death. Hope to see you Wed at gym."

5

Haldiz, a village in the lake country of Canton Bern, Sunday afternoon, June 16

François Schwab still hadn't arrived at the Lakers' executive council meeting, and it was five after four. Matthias Ruch was surprised and disappointed. He never saw enough of Frank, and their chats after Laker meetings were something he looked forward to out of all proportion to their length. But another part of him was relieved, because the main item on the day's agenda was the effectiveness of copper sulphate, which many of their members had been using to fight potato blight. Bio Suisse regulations permitted organic farmers to use it, and everyone on the Lakers' executive council and in the larger association agreed with the practice. Only Frank was against it. Frank and his principles! Matthias admired him, but God, the old man could be pigheaded.

The Lakers didn't have an office, so they met at the parish center next door to the church. The room they'd been assigned today was papered with children's drawings of what had to be the parting of the Red Sea. Behind Christian Hirschi's head, there was a particularly dramatic jumble of red waves, blue fish, and drowning Egyptians. As Matthias stared at it, Christian called the meeting to order.

"Anyone know if Frank's coming?" he asked.

"Start without him," urged Jean-Pierre Niklaus, who knew Frank just as well as Matthias did. "And for God's sake begin with the spraying and get that over with before he gets here. I think we'd all like to make it home before suppertime, right?"

There were nods of agreement, but Matthias was glad to see they were accompanied by smiles. He wasn't the only one who respected Frank in spite of his stubbornness. No one at the table had been an organic farmer as long as Frank. Matthias had heard it said that no one in the whole of Switzerland had been *bio* for so many years, but he thought that unlikely. Frank was something of a legend in the organic-food business; stories stuck to him.

It was Frank who'd named their association, seven years before. They were vegetable-producing small landowners, most—but not all—organic farmers, who lived in the Seeland or lake region of the cantons of Bern, Fribourg, and Neuchâtel. How was anyone supposed to make a name out of that mouthful?

Their very first meeting had been deteriorating into a free-for-all when Frank pounded on the table. "This is ridiculous," he'd roared. "We know who we are and why we're here. Who cares what we call ourselves?"

"But we have to have a name for our letterhead," Doris Gerber had said.

"Letterhead!" Frank scoffed. "What does that have to do with the price of leeks? We live in the lake country, so let's call ourselves the Lakers." He said the last word in English, adding with a grin, "The Swiss Lakers, so no one will confuse us with the Los Angeles ones."

They'd eventually come up with something more official-sounding for their letterhead, but the name Lakers had stuck.

"I was with Frank on Wednesday," Matthias said, "and he told me he'd be coming. Let's not wait. If he doesn't get here, I'll fill him in later."

Matthias meant to try Frank's phone again when he got home from the meeting. But another group of pickers had just arrived from

Poland, and while they'd worked for him before and knew what to do, there was still a lot to get through. Suddenly it was evening, and he still hadn't heard from Frank. The goats were bleating to be milked, but he decided to try the phone first. He felt for his cell and then realized he must have left it by the sofa where he'd been sitting with the picker boss.

Inside the house, he kicked off his rubber boots at the door. Edith was fixing supper with the help of one of the apprentices—the other would be in the barn with the goats. He gave his wife a wave that promised more attention later and walked through to the main room. He wanted badly to sink into a flowered armchair as he picked up his phone, but he was still wearing his filthy coveralls.

Frank didn't answer either his mobile or his landline: that probably meant he'd decided to go into Bern, Biel, Neuchâtel, or Fribourg for the evening. The four cities were fifteen to twenty miles from Haldiz in four different directions. The thought didn't particularly comfort Matthias—sure, Frank was fit, but when a man of over seventy couldn't be accounted for, it was impossible to keep the words *heart attack* from flashing before one's eyes.

It wasn't until eight, after milking, supper, and putting his two younger children to bed that Matthias got on his bike and headed for Frank's. The warm June evening glowed with golden light and smelled richly of earth. He rode slowly down the lane, among rolling hills, patches of woods, and fields where hundreds of farms had thrived for centuries. Far in front of him, the Alps gleamed on the skyline, made small and delicate by distance. Behind him, he knew without turning, were the mountains of the Jura range, modest when compared to the Alps but imposing in their proximity. Out of sight but easy to reach were the three lakes that gave the region its name: Bielersee, Murtensee, and Neuenburgersee.

By the time he reached Frank's place, Matthias felt soothed by the land. He left his bike against a low stone wall and banged on the kitchen door. No answer. He tried the handle; the door was unlocked. But that wasn't uncommon.

"Frank, you there?" Matthias listened for the sound of feet somewhere inside. Nothing. He took off his shoes and checked every room in the old two-story house. He even braved the heat of the unfinished attic under the enormous overhanging roof. When he didn't find Frank sprawled somewhere in need of CPR, he allowed himself to relax a little. Still, he knew he wouldn't get to sleep that night unless he did some more scouting, so he headed out the side door into the courtyard.

"What the hell are you doing here?" he asked one of Frank's hens as it wandered out of the nearest cucumber bed. Beyond her, he heard the clucking of other chickens. That was strange: during the day Frank gave his chickens free range, but he never left them out of doors after six. It would be like ringing a dinner bell for foxes and pine martens.

As he walked through the yard, a chemical smell began to tickle at his throat. At first, he couldn't find the source, and he tacked this way and that, a sense of unease mounting. Now some other stench, sickly and rotten, lurked underneath the smell of chemicals. Eventually his nose led him toward one of the outbuildings. It was Frank's potting shed.

The shutters on the windows were closed, as was the door, which was secured by a simple hasp and padlock. But the padlock wasn't fastened. Matthias stood for a moment outside the door, overwhelmed by foreboding. He knew what he was smelling—working on a farm, it was a smell you learned to dread. With resolve, he removed the lock and opened the door.

The swollen corpse looked nothing like the living man, but it was Frank all right. He lay on the floor between two long potting tables, his skin tinged greenish-blue, his long white hair matted with dried blood. Everything in the room, including Frank, seemed to have been sprayed with something chemical that Matthias thought must be a commercial pesticide. He could scarcely draw breath without gagging.

He closed the door and staggered back across the courtyard toward the farmhouse. Under the eaves near the kitchen door was a bench and he sprawled there, drawing in deep gulps of air. He couldn't think—he kept seeing Frank's distorted face; smelling the ghastly smell of dead flesh. With a complete lack of logic, he found himself thinking how upset Frank would have been about the pesticide on his property. In his shed.

After a few minutes, he felt calm enough to dial the emergency number. Then he phoned his wife. "Edith," he said, and couldn't go on.

She knew him too well to waste time. "It's Frank, isn't it? What's happened?"

He'd planned to tell her everything, but he couldn't. Not on the phone. "He was lying dead in the potting shed. Been there a while. I called the police."

"Let me come and wait with you. They'll take forever to arrive." Haldiz was much too small to have its own police; even nearby Erlach had only a part-time force.

"I feel like I want to be alone. Just for a while. Can you . . . ?"

"I understand. Of course I do. Call me if you need me."

Matthias had looked after Frank's livestock and crops many times, but it was hard to think now, hard to move.

The sound of the chickens finally got him off the bench. He drove them into their coop and went to check on the mare, Grace Slick, who was usually out in a fenced paddock behind the house. He found her there, placid as usual, cropping grass next to the old claw-footed bathtub that served as her water trough. Grace would be fine to spend another night outside. Were there any other urgent chores he could do tonight to help Frank?

Tears sprang into his eyes. No one could help Frank now.

He considered waiting for the police indoors, but the setting sun was drenching the farm in warm yellow light, so instead he went to fetch Frank's guitar from its stand by his favorite chair and sat again on the bench under the eaves to tune it. After that, with many false starts and mistakes, he began to play a slow version of "Crossroads," a song that Frank, a diehard Eric Clapton fan, had first played for Matthias when he was a child. He was amazed how the lyrics flowed into his mind as he touched the strings, although he hadn't sung the song for years.

I went down to the crossroads, tried to flag a ride.
Down to the crossroads, tried to flag a ride.
Nobody seemed to know me, everybody passed me by.

He repeated the same verses over and over, trying to banish the other refrain that kept forming in his mind: I wish you hadn't been alone, Frank. I'm so sorry you had to die by yourself, my dear old friend.

Almost an hour after he'd found Frank's body, the first police car arrived, and soon after that the death was declared a probable homicide. Matthias could hardly believe it, and yet he couldn't see how it could be anything else. Only after a forensics team arrived from Bern did he finally take himself home, riding his bike through the dark lanes.

He found Edith asleep on the living room sofa, a single lamp still burning. He knelt beside her and rested his face against her breast. The sound of his name in her sleep-slurred voice and the feeling of her hands stroking his back loosened the fist clutching his heart. She put her arms around him, and he sobbed into her nightgown.

6

Nordring police station,
early Monday morning, June 17

The call for Renzo to join the team investigating the death of François Schwab came at three in the morning. Fränzi groaned something from her side of the bed. Renzo felt his usual jolt of excitement.

Less than half an hour later, he was shaking hands with Noah Dällenbach, whom he'd worked for before. Noah was only thirty, four years younger than Renzo, which sometimes made him wonder why *he* hadn't risen that fast. Since Noah was low-key and likeable, though, it was hard to hold his success against him. He was also an excellent marathon runner, but instead of rubbing his colleagues' faces in that, he bragged about his wife, an Ethiopian whose record was even better than his.

The second detective on the case was Erwin Sägesser: thirty years older, eight inches taller, and a hundred pounds heavier than the slightly built Noah. He was a different breed of cop altogether. Renzo admired Erwin but was still a step away from liking the older detective, whose caustic remarks were legendary.

"Rosmarie Bolliger is our prosecutor on this case," Noah told Renzo. "She's already on her way to the Seeland; I'm heading there with a team in a few minutes to examine the corpse and scene. I'd like you to help Erwin research the victim, his work as an organic farmer, the village of Haldiz—at this point you can check on pretty much anything you think could be useful. I'll let Erwin know as soon as I have more specific background requests."

Erwin was already reading up on Frank Schwab, so Renzo started with organic farming in the Seeland.

"Ever been on a farm?" Erwin asked him, as he scrolled through website pages.

"A visit in fifth grade. I'd never realized cows were so damned huge."

Erwin nodded. "I had a great-uncle who was a farmer, but I grew up a city boy through and through."

Renzo picked out some statistics. "Says here there are more farms in Bern than any other canton—over eleven thousand. So I guess it's about time I visited another. Not sure how this one will be different, being organic."

Erwin asked, "A lot of them organic?"

"Ten percent, apparently."

"I don't get what the fuss is about," Erwin said. "I know this *bio* shit is supposed to be better for you, but does it taste better? It certainly costs more."

"Yeah. We don't buy it." Renzo was scribbling notes as he read, not sure yet what would be important but eager to soak up background on Haldiz while he had time.

"Schwab was arrested at a demo when he was sixteen," said the older man a few minutes later. "There's a ten-year-old *WOZ* article here that tells all about him."

"What the hell was there to demonstrate about in Switzerland way back then?"

"Seems like the movement to separate Jura from Bern was already alive," said Erwin. "Schwab's mother came from a village in the Jura region called Glovelier, and he was arrested 'with a group of family members,' it says here. Last name Chavanne."

Erwin skimmed the article as he talked. "More involvement in the Jura protests. Never in the violent wing of the movement—or so it says here. Later some arrests for squatting in unoccupied buildings. Started a commune on a farm he inherited in Haldiz. Sex 'n' drugs 'n' rock 'n' roll, it sounds like. Founding member of various organizations, including one pro-legalizing weed. Look, here's a photo of him in his twenties. Boy, does he look the part!"

Renzo leaned over Erwin's shoulder. On the screen was a bearded man with long brown hair and a bandana tied around his forehead. He wore a fringed leather vest over a flowered shirt and had a guitar slung on his back, its embroidered strap across his chest.

"Here's a more recent one," Erwin said, pulling up another picture. "Looks like that Rolling Stone who was in the pirate movie."

The older version of Schwab wasn't quite as ravaged as Keith Richards, but he still looked nothing like a typical Swiss farmer. The long hair, now white, was in a ponytail; the beard was gone. Something about the creases around his eyes suggested a sense of humor.

"And how does all this relate to murder?" Erwin mused. "I'd say an old flower-child farmer who supports legalizing marijuana just might have had an interest in the dope market. I predict a big barn full of grow lights somewhere on his land."

"According to the farming association he belongs to, the Lakers, he kept chickens and grew veggies and herbs and a bunch of different salad greens," Renzo said.

"Right," Erwin scoffed. "Herbs! I think that should read 'herb.' Someone's going to have to check every square inch of his place." The older man glanced at Renzo's Italian-made loafers. "This case is just made for you, Renzo. Strolling around the countryside enjoying the fresh air. I'm looking forward to seeing your shoes and those nice clean jeans of yours after you've walked all over a sixty-acre farm!"

Renzo couldn't help grinning at the look of evil glee on Erwin's face. "God, I hope not. What kind of shoes *do* farmers wear, tramping around in mud and shit all day?"

"I think they wear rubber boots," Erwin answered, "or maybe wooden clogs."

"Wooden clogs? It's not the Middle Ages. As for rubber boots, forget it."

"You're going to eat your words, pal."

7

Haldiz,
Monday afternoon, June 17

Luckily for Renzo's shoes, a narcotics cop with a dog joined the investigators, and it was they who got to conduct the muddy search of Schwab's property. Noah, who'd followed the body back to Bern for the autopsy, assigned Renzo to interview Matthias Ruch, and Renzo suggested that he also follow up with Christian Hirschi, president of the Lakers. Noah told him to use his judgment.

The first thing Renzo wanted was a feel for the village, so he parked in the lot by the train station, glad for the lightly overcast sky and cool temperature. Walking up one main street and back down another, he encountered stores selling clothes, groceries, and farming supplies, plus a church, a cemetery, a hairdresser, and three restaurants—quite a lot of infrastructure for a village of fewer than fifteen hundred people. His drive to Haldiz had been past field after field of vegetables but no buildings, and now he saw why. The farmhouses, with their living quarters in front and barns behind, were grouped in the village, while the crops were planted in a vast circle all around it. Men in coveralls kept passing him on foot, bicycle, and tractor: presumably heading back into the fields after a midday meal at home.

His phone rang; it was Noah, whose initial hello was lost in an enormous yawn. "Sorry, up all night," the detective began. Renzo appreciated that—no bullshit about being so tough he didn't need sleep. Anyone who could run twenty-six miles in three hours, as Noah could, didn't have to prove anything, at least not as far as Renzo was concerned. "I wanted to let you know the autopsy results. Schwab was hit on the head, just as we thought, but it only knocked him unconscious. Cause of death was asphyxiation."

"He choked on the pesticide?"

"I think that was the scenario the killer wanted to create, because he was drenched in the stuff—it was in his mouth, nose, ears, hair . . . But in fact, that was all done postmortem. Looks like once he was unconscious his face was pressed into a pile of soil on the ground. His lungs are full of dirt."

"Making it look like an organic farmer was killed by pesticide—surely there's a message there."

"A killer with a sense of irony, huh?" Noah said and yawned again. "Do you have any questions for me? Otherwise, I'm going home to grab a couple of hours in bed."

"I'm all set to do my interviews," said Renzo.

"Okay. Erwin's our iron man—he's still awake and coordinating the search of Schwab's place. He'll call if he has a job for you. And listen, we want to keep the cause of death and all the details secret. Officially, he died from the head wound, okay?"

"Got it."

Since his appointment with Matthias wasn't until three, Renzo decided to stop for a late lunch. He deliberately chose the most central and old-fashioned-looking of Haldiz's restaurants, hoping to find someone who'd give him a shot of gossip. Walking into the Star's wood-paneled dining room, he introduced himself as a cop on the Schwab case to the woman who greeted him, and was rewarded with a sharp look.

"I'm Nadine Löffel," she told him. "What can I do for you?"

"How about some lunch?" he said. "I'll have a plate of whatever's left of the special. And a glass of beer." He took a seat as far away as possible from the few customers hunched over coffee or small glasses of schnapps, and the woman brought him a plate of meat and gravy, mashed potatoes, and steamed fennel, along with a cold beer and a basket of whole-wheat bread.

"You're lucky. That's the last of the pot roast, and the cook's gone home until dinnertime."

She hovered, as he'd hoped she would, so he said, "I never imagined I'd be looking into a violent death in a little place like Haldiz. Did you know Herr Schwab?"

"Of course," she answered, leaning one hip against the edge of the table. Despite the excessively black hair, bright lipstick, and tight clothes, Renzo pegged her at close to sixty. "My ex-husband's from Haldiz, so I've been here since our wedding and I stayed on after he left me. Frank's a regular. During the past year or so he came in a lot with a young man. A good-looking one." She raised her eyebrows at Renzo and gave a smoker's husky chuckle that threatened to slide into a coughing fit.

Here we go. Renzo flashed his most flirtatious smile. "Why don't you have a seat and tell me about that, Frau Löffel. Are you saying François Schwab was gay?"

"Just call me Nadine. And I can personally testify to the fact that Frank wasn't gay." Renzo caught a knowing grin. "Not that he was a boyfriend of mine or anything serious like that. But after my husband walked out, Frank kept me company a time or two. And he certainly didn't have any trouble getting the job done. Still, these days you never know. After all, he and Louise never got married."

Renzo started to ask about Louise, but Nadine wasn't finished yet.

"The cute boy—Simu, he's called—wasn't a nephew or anything. I asked around. So who was he? Maybe the two of them had a lovers' quarrel, and Simu killed him. I heard Frank's head was bashed in," she said, leaning closer. Then, perhaps realizing how bloodthirsty she sounded, she pursed her lips and shook her head. Renzo half-expected her to join her hands in prayer, but the performance stopped short of that. "Poor man," she added.

"That's right," Renzo told her, glad to be able to start spreading Noah's "official" cause of death. "I can't imagine what a farmer could do to annoy anyone." He worked a note of puzzlement into his voice. "He must have been a harmless enough old fellow."

"Frank, harmless?" she snorted. "It's obvious you never met him. He loved riling folks, just *loved* it. I don't mean he got into bar fights. He simply didn't believe in compromise. Oh, he'd listen to advice and even take it sometimes, but once he'd made up his mind, there was no budging him."

Renzo smiled, his interest piqued. "Stubborn, huh?"

Her answer was another snort. "Can you imagine what everyone thought of his decision to turn his farm into a commune? When Frank's great-uncle died, and he inherited that place in the late sixties, this village was the back of beyond. Frank grew up in Biel, but he worked on that farm every summer as a kid. Of course, it wasn't organic then. No one had *heard* of organic then. But when the uncle died, Frank had just come back from traveling around the world. He moved onto the farm with Louise, and they started gathering in friends. Sometimes it seemed like there were twenty people staying—although there was so much coming and going, it was impossible to know who actually lived there."

Renzo had seen *Woodstock* at a high-school film festival; now he tried to transplant those shaggy-haired kids with their flowing clothes to Haldiz.

As if she was picturing the same thing, Nadine said, "Imagine Frank in his bell-bottoms, with braided hair hanging halfway down his back, coming into the Landi to buy his supplies. He'd stand there with the other farmers discussing the weather and the price of chicken feed. My father-in-law said almost everyone accepted Frank's way of life because they'd known him since he was a kid—and because he knew how to farm. Plus, they saw all those long-haired girls in flimsy dresses hanging around his place and figured he was the luckiest guy in town. But, believe me, they didn't take kindly to the men. Nothing wrong with them, I guess—but random hippies were too much for Haldiz."

"Was anyone living with Frank when he died?" asked Renzo. The food was gone—he'd enjoyed every bite, and he wiped up the gravy with a piece of bread.

"As far as I know, he was alone. People would come by to stay with him for a while, but his place got quieter and quieter over the years. No more rock concerts in his fields, no more Volkswagen buses and motorcycles at his door, no more peace-and-love types hanging out here at the Star. Except for Louise—she kept coming for a long time. Then she was gone, too, although eventually they got back together."

"Louise was his girlfriend?"

"Off and on for years, although she was married to someone else for a while. I can't remember the last time she had a drink in the Star. As I said, Frank never married, never had a family. I wonder if Louise will inherit the farm."

Renzo wondered that, too; he would find out soon enough. Right now, he wanted to bring Nadine back to an earlier point.

"You said Frank's stubbornness could irritate people, but now you make it sound like he was popular. Is there anyone in Haldiz who *didn't* like him?"

Nadine gave Renzo a quick glance. "Let me just check on the last table," she said and moved off to the schnapps drinkers. Renzo pushed his empty plate away and felt, all of a sudden, like laying his head down and taking a nap; his early morning was starting to make itself felt. He longed for a coffee, but he didn't want to ask Nadine Löffel for one and destroy the gossipy feeling they'd built up. To his delight, she brought two full cups when she came back, put them on the table, and plonked herself down next to him again. With one last look around to make sure the other customers were busy, she took up his question with enthusiasm.

"Frank didn't really have any enemies but, as everyone in Haldiz can tell you, he and his next-door neighbor, Jean-Pierre Niklaus, had problems. You'd think Jean-Pierre would have been driven crazy decades ago by all those hippies swarming around, but he and Frank were about the same age, and they were friends as kids. The trouble between them started when Frank decided to go organic. He'd talked about *bio* from the get-go, or so I've heard, but he couldn't begin until his soil and groundwater tested free of chemicals. That takes three or four years. Then he started slowly, with only a few fields, to make sure he didn't bankrupt himself. Remember, only fanatics bought organic food in those days. But over time he found good markets for his stuff, so he converted the whole farm."

She made it sound as if he'd gone over to the dark side. Renzo wondered if her ex-husband had also been a farmer: if so, not an organic one, he felt sure.

"More coffee?" she asked him, and he risked a yes. The restaurant was empty now, so she kept talking as she took away his cup to refill.

"I came to Haldiz in the early eighties, and by then Frank's whole farm was organic. He was convinced that just about every farmer in town would switch when they understood how well it worked for him. It crushed him when no one else wanted to, though of course plenty have converted since. He was especially disappointed about Jean-Pierre. And then came the chemical wars. Every time Jean-Pierre sprayed his crops, Frank worried about the stuff blowing onto his fields. Once, about six years ago, it really happened, and Frank lost a few rows of radishes. Lost them as organic, I mean—he could still sell them. To hear him go on about it, you'd think Jean-Pierre had done nuclear testing! Their friendship never recovered. But that's nothing you'd kill a man for. Poor old Frank." This time, her sorrow sounded genuine.

Renzo thought about the pesticide coating Schwab's corpse and the inside of his shed. Niklaus, huh? He'd need to talk to the man. The thought made him glance at his watch: fifteen minutes until his three o'clock appointment with Matthias Ruch.

"This has been great—you've given me a much better picture of Schwab. Thanks. Now I've got to get to work. What do I owe you for lunch?"

"On the house. Come back any time. I'm around practically every day, and most of Haldiz shows up regularly. The Bear down the road is the white-tablecloth place; we're for locals."

She said it proudly. A tough old girl, Renzo decided, with an admiration he hadn't felt at first. He shook her hand warmly and set off to the parking lot, where he'd left his car. Before driving away, he thumbed "J-P Niklaus" and "Louise" into his phone.

8

Haldiz,
Monday afternoon, June 17

Approaching the Ruch farm, Renzo realized he'd have to park down the road. The paved space and some of the lawn around the farmhouse were chock-full of vehicles—three cars and a truck, a tractor, and a couple of small, homey-looking trailers. A skinny girl of about fourteen sat on the steps of one of the trailers, eyes glued to her phone. Two young kids splashed in a plastic pool on the grass nearby. Renzo, who had a three- and a four-year-old, was not impressed with the teenager's dedication to babysitting.

"Ciao," he called to her as he walked toward the farmhouse, which combined living space and barn in one large building. She didn't look up.

Another teenager, an older boy, was sweeping the courtyard outside the farmhouse with a long twig broom, forming straw and little brown pellets into neat piles around his feet. He looked up as Renzo approached and smiled. "Hello," he said, leaning his broom against the wall. "Are you the policeman who's come to see Matthias?"

"That's right. Renzo Donatelli."

Renzo held out his hand to the boy, who gave him his right elbow to shake instead. "I'd better not give you my hand. Goat dung." He gestured at the pellets. "I'm Robi Hofer, one of the apprentices. Mättu told me to get him when you arrived. He's with the goats. One nanny has a blocked teat."

The boy jogged over to the barn, and moments later a lanky man in his forties with thinning brown hair loped toward Renzo, wearing long-sleeved workman's coveralls and wooden clogs. Clogs! So Erwin had been right after all.

"Come into the house," Ruch said. "I'll get you something to drink. I've got about half an hour, and after that, if you have more questions, you can follow me around. I don't mean to be rude, but there's a lot of picking going on, and I have to keep an eye peeled. You probably passed some of the pickers' kids as you came up the drive. They live here while their parents are working."

He left his clogs on the doorstep and continued in his socks, leading the way into a small entry room with a tile floor and sink. Once inside, he washed his hands, unselfconsciously stripped off his dirty coveralls, hung them on a hook, and pulled a pair of jeans over his boxers. Renzo followed him into the kitchen, where he filled a kettle and set it on the gas stove.

"I didn't get to bed last night until around three," Ruch said as he found two mugs on the draining board, "and I was up before six like always to milk the goats, so I have to warn you, I'm not all here. I keep worrying about Frank's farm. We can't let his crops go to waste, and his chickens and mare need tending."

Renzo, leaning against the kitchen table under the window, was struck by Ruch's concern. He—well, Fränzi, usually—sometimes watered plants for their neighbors, but he couldn't imagine taking on responsibility for an entire farm out of neighborliness.

Ruch was still talking. "Christian Hirschi—you're going to talk to him, too, right?—he's already phoned Bio Suisse, and they are going to find a retired farmer or an ag student to run the farm, but a group of us will take turns going over there and doing the minimum to keep things in shape until someone shows up. Sit down and have some coffee," he told Renzo as he brought the kettle to the kitchen table.

Then he turned to fetch a sticky-looking sugar bowl, a jar of instant coffee, and a large pitcher.

"I should warn you: this is goat's milk. Would you prefer the normal stuff? My wife has some coffee cream somewhere." Ruch looked vaguely around, as if he hoped the cream would poke its head out of a cabinet. Renzo couldn't imagine drinking goat's milk outside a refugee camp, but he smiled at his host. "Don't worry. I take it black."

There was silence as Ruch doctored his drink with milk and sugar. He spoke first. "Are you sure Frank was murdered?"

"He was. I'm sorry. I've heard that you knew him well."

"Yes. I started helping him out when I was twelve; his farm was still a commune then. He was a second father to me for years. Once I inherited this farm, I had less time to see him, but I've gone over there once a week for years to take him milk or cheese from our goats, a loaf of Sunday bread from my wife—things like that. We chat about crops or livestock. Or my kids. Actually," he amended, "we generally talked about *my* problems."

"So you visited him weekly at his place?" Renzo prompted.

"I saw him at the Star from time to time, too. We'd drink a beer together. He ate a meal at our house at least every month, and a couple of times a year he'd join us on a family outing. I guess he was like an extra grandfather for our children."

"Did he live alone?"

"Yes. He has a partner, Louise Fehr, but she's based in Bern. They were together off and on for fifty years, but she hasn't lived in Haldiz for a while." He took a gulp of coffee. "Odd thing, isn't it, for a man who housed so many people to end up by himself, but he was okay with it. Besides, when I say he was alone, I mean he didn't have family or friends living with him. But he always took apprentices and interns from the agricultural schools, and some of them lived on the farm for a while. Plus, there were researchers from FiBL coming and going, and scientists from abroad, too, who wanted to talk to him about his methods and observe his work."

"What's 'feeble'?" asked Renzo.

"Sorry, organic-farmer jargon. FiBL is a major research institute for organic farming near Basel. Frank started converting his farm to organic in 1970, before FiBL existed, and he was always one of their favorite guinea pigs—he sometimes let them conduct long-term experiments on his land. Agricultural researchers have come from all over the world to meet Frank." Matthias rubbed a hand across his eyes.

Could these visits have had something to do with Frank's death? Renzo wondered. Research sabotaged? Results stolen? "Were any researchers here recently?" he asked.

"A South African professor, about a month ago."

Renzo nodded and made a note to look into it. "Did Frank do any work abroad?"

"I don't think he's been away for more than a few days at a time in decades. But when he finished his apprenticeship, years and years ago, that was when he took off to see the world: London, Paris, cities in India and Australia. He ended up in San Francisco: that's where he and Louise met. They saw Monterey Pop. Can you imagine that? Janis, The Who, Jimi, Grace Slick—he heard them all live, just as they were getting started. Not Cream, though. He'd have loved to shake Eric Clapton by the hand."

Renzo tried to remember his *Woodstock* film again. Was Grace Slick a group or a person? He smiled vaguely before saying, "Organic farming wasn't Schwab's only cause, though, was it? He pushed for legalizing marijuana. Did he grow it? Sell it?"

The farmer fidgeted with his spoon. "Grow, yes; sell, no." He turned and stared out of the window above the table, sighing. "Frank smoked dope for as long as I knew him, and he grew some, too, but only for himself. The THC content was over one percent, so of course it was illegal, but he found Swiss marijuana laws ridiculous and never seemed to take them seriously. I never knew him to sell a single ounce, though. I asked him, a couple of years ago, if he'd ever sold dope, and he got offended."

Renzo judged Ruch to be completely sincere, but that didn't mean he was right. Still, a drug-related murder didn't explain the pesticide-drenched corpse. He sipped at his coffee before saying, "Tell me about this feud with Jean-Pierre Niklaus."

Ruch's eyes opened wide. "You can't be considering Jean-Pierre as Frank's killer. The two of them grew up together. Sure, there was that business about the pesticide, but that was years ago. Frank didn't hold a serious grudge over it."

"The question isn't so much whether *Frank* held a grudge, since he's the one who's dead." Renzo watched Ruch closely as they talked. His eyes were tired, and there were deep lines in his forehead, but he seemed completely honest. In fact, it had been a while since Renzo had interviewed anyone with such an open face and manner. "Did something come to a head between them during the last few weeks?"

"Definitely not," Ruch said without hesitation. "If Frank and Jean-Pierre had a blowup, all of Haldiz would know. It's not easy to keep a secret around here."

"And then there's a young man named Simu," Renzo continued, leaning back in his chair and crossing his arms.

Ruch stiffened. "Uh-huh. Simu." He said the name as if it tasted bad.

"You don't like him."

"I don't even try to hide it, do I? But God knows that doesn't mean I think he'd kill Frank. It's not exactly that I don't like him—I've never really gotten to know him."

Renzo wondered about this. Nadine had said this Simu was around Frank a lot, yet Ruch claimed not to know him. "Someone suggested the two men might have been lovers," he said, curious about Ruch's response to this idea.

Ruch snorted and shook his head. "Jesus. The things people say! I think I would have noticed during the past thirty-five years if Frank liked men more than women. But I can see why people around here are puzzled by Simu. He's been at Frank's place off and on for at least eighteen months. Not living there, but he did sometimes stay over. Usually, if someone's a regular in the village, we get friendly over a beer or standing in line at the Landi. But not with Simu. He did drink at the Star now and then—that's how I met him. But he didn't talk about himself. I don't even know his full name."

"But you've known Schwab most of your life. Didn't you ask what this Simu guy was doing on his farm?"

Ruch's face twisted. "Of course I asked. Several times. Frank was vague. 'The kid's working on a project, and I'm giving him a bit of a hand.' When I suggested that Frank bring Simu to dinner at our house, he said, 'Simu's not the family type.' Whatever that means."

"Do *you* think Simu killed Frank?"

Ruch stared down at his fingers as they tapped the table, and Renzo became aware of a not-unpleasant animal smell that hung around the farmer, even though he was outwardly clean. Goats, he supposed.

Eventually the farmer raised his head and said, "I'm the wrong person to ask. The truth is, I was jealous of Simu. He hung around Frank's place the way I used to when I was young, before I had a wife and four kids and my own farm to worry about. I'm ashamed to say it, but I resented his friendship with Frank." He barked a humorless laugh. "If Simu were dead, I'd be your biggest suspect. I only wish it *had* been him instead of Frank. God, I'm going to miss him."

It felt like Ruch had more to say, so Renzo waited. The farmer looked profoundly exhausted, a bone-deep tiredness that went beyond the loss of a few hours of rest. Renzo tried to imagine what it must be like to live at the mercy of weather, insects, fungi, blocked teats, and seasonal pickers. Not to mention fragile markets and fickle customers.

Ruch remained silent, and Renzo realized he was crying. "Sorry," the farmer said in a choked voice. He got up and found a box of tissues in a kitchen drawer, wiped his eyes, and blew his nose. "My father was never an easy man to get along with. All these years I've had Frank, instead. I can't picture life without him. My wife and I talked about his coming to live with us if he got too old to work his own farm. But he was only seventy-five and fit as a fish in water. I assumed I'd have years with him, and now he's gone."

"I'm very sorry for your loss," Renzo said. He knew the formal words didn't help, but he meant them. He thought of his own father and felt his heart contract. It had been three years since his dad's death, but the rage and helplessness still took hold of him unexpectedly. "I need to ask you one more question, before I go. Would you like to take a few minutes first, or—?"

Renzo's phone rang: good timing. It was Erwin. Renzo left Ruch in the kitchen and ducked into the far corner of the living room. From there he took in a battered sofa draped with kid-sized soccer kit and a corkboard wall dotted with children's drawings. A pitcher stuffed with cornflowers, poppies, and speckled foxgloves sat on an end table.

"Just what I thought," Erwin said. "There's a field of weed hidden away behind a line of trees, about as far from the village as you can get without leaving Schwab's land. No big barn full of grow lights and irrigation tubing, just an old-fashioned outdoor crop of something the narcs call Northern Lights. Apparently, it's a strain that doesn't produce a strong smell. Estimated street value at least a hundred thousand francs. Enough to murder for, I guess."

Erwin might not be surprised to learn Frank grew a small fortune in dope, but Renzo was. This clashed with everything he'd just heard from Ruch.

"Do you want me to grill the Haldiz folks about this?" Renzo asked. "Or are we keeping it to ourselves?"

"It's no secret—we're going to shape our investigation around it. So go right ahead and get everyone's reaction."

"What about next of kin?" Renzo asked. "Has anyone figured out who needs notifying? Should I ask Ruch for names?"

"Good plan—do that. I'm going through his telephone records now, and I'll have his papers and computer by the end of today. So far, we haven't turned up any living family. He had a sister, but she died in her twenties in a skiing accident. She didn't have kids. But there may be cousins."

Renzo heard a click and the silence of a dead line, as Erwin hung up without saying good-bye. Renzo knew better than to take his abruptness personally—just Erwin being himself. Damn—he'd forgotten to tell the older cop about Frank's girlfriend, Louise Fehr. Well, it would have to wait.

He stood in the sunlit living room and saw that one of the mismatched, comfortable-looking armchairs flanking the sofa had a sleeping cat curled up in it. Ruch had said that Frank grew a few marijuana plants, which surely didn't mean a whole field. Had Ruch lied to him? Or had Frank lied to Ruch? And if Frank was dealing dope, was it a recent development? Did it mean his organic farming business was failing? That would show up when they examined his finances.

Under all these practical questions, Renzo felt another rise to the surface. It was the question of Frank Schwab as a drug dealer. Renzo wasn't particularly bothered about people smoking dope, but the image he'd been forming in his mind of Frank, the wise organic farmer receiving homage from foreign researchers, didn't match this new picture of Frank the dope dealer, lying to his close friend. Because Renzo believed that Ruch truly hadn't known about the field of marijuana. So perhaps the mysterious Simu had something to do with this.

Back in the kitchen, Ruch had stopped crying and was leaning on the worktop by the sink. Patches of his short, grey-brown hair were wet where he'd washed his face, and he had a glass of water in his hand.

"I know you have a lot to do," Renzo said, "but I need just few more minutes. First, are you aware of any family members we should notify about the death?"

"Most of them live around here, so they'll probably get the word informally. But I'll give you the names of a couple of cousins in Haldiz and also in Glovelier, where his mother was from. Just in case."

He walked into the living room, where Renzo heard him rummaging through papers, and returned with an old-fashioned dark-red address book, a small pad of paper, and a pen. He sat at the kitchen table and began copying names and phone numbers out of the book, saying, "Louise lives in Bern. Have you told her yet? This is going to be hard for her—they were very close."

"I just learned of her existence today," Renzo said. "We'd like to break the news to her in person. Can you give me her address and phone number, too?"

A woman in her early seventies didn't usually murder her long-term lover, but Louise Fehr had to be treated as a suspect. Renzo hoped he could be the one to speak with her first. Did she know about the marijuana field? he wondered. He sat back down at the kitchen table, watching Ruch, who was just finishing his list.

"I really need to get back to work," Ruch said, as he handed the paper to Renzo.

Renzo knew he was about to distress the farmer again. It was a useful tactic for getting informants and witnesses to spill their guts; still, he liked Ruch too much now to want to vex him.

He folded his hands loosely on the table in front of him. "One last thing. The phone call I got—it was about a whole field of marijuana the police found on Herr Schwab's land. A hundred thousand francs worth."

Ruch's mouth fell open—he couldn't have looked more surprised if he'd tried. "Are you sure?"

Renzo nodded.

"So I guess you think I lied to you," Ruch said. He pushed his chair out with a screech and turned away. His shoulders were hunched, fists clenched.

"Could someone have used the land without Frank's knowledge? This Simu, for instance?" Renzo asked.

"I'd like to believe that," said Ruch, his back still to Renzo, "but it isn't possible. Frank walked those fields every day."

"Sixty acres is a lot of land."

"I don't mean he covered all of it every day, but by the end of the week he'd have examined every field, and then he'd start over. It was one of his principles, checking his crops and soil, handling his livestock, staying alert for small changes that might be a forewarning of pests or disease." Ruch stared out of the kitchen window, arms hugging his chest. "He would have known what was on his land. It was that field behind the trees, wasn't it?" He didn't wait for Renzo's answer. "He told me a couple of months ago that it was being used for an experiment. I assumed he meant FiBL had planted something there." He sat back down at the table and hid his face in his hands. "Jesus," he said. "I can't believe Frank lied to me."

Renzo stood, meaning to leave Ruch to grieve. But the farmer rose, too, heaving himself up out of his chair like an old man. Renzo followed him as he pulled on his coveralls, shouldered open the door to the courtyard, and slipped into his clogs. He offered Renzo his hand, asking, "Where are you off to now?"

"Christian Hirschi's."

Ruch's chin came up, and he gave a half smile. "That's good. Frank was a great pioneer, but Christian is taking organic farming into the future. Not much over thirty and he's already in charge of our association—he represents us at Bio Suisse. It won't be long before he's speaking for all the organic farmers in the Seeland. Last year one of Migros's TV ads for organic food starred him. You'll like him. *And* his wife." Ruch grinned.

"Good," Renzo answered. "We'll talk again, Herr Ruch. In the meantime, good luck with all this." He waved his arm around the farmyard, and Ruch nodded, turning away.

A sudden question made Renzo call after him.

"Frank's buddy Simu. What's his dialect?"

"Bern, for sure," Ruch called back. "Not the Emmental or the Alps. The city."

Back in his car, before considering where to go next, Renzo phoned Erwin.

"What's up?"

"Schwab had a girlfriend, Louise Fehr. Lives in Bern, is about his age. That's all I found out, except that they've known each other for over fifty years. I'll text you her address and phone number."

"I'll follow up," Erwin said. "Anything else?"

"There's a guy in his twenties named Simu that needs accounting for. Sort of a hanger-on of Schwab's, with a city dialect. No last name so far, no info on what he was doing around the farm. I'll keep asking."

"Guy who found the body seem suspicious?"

"Nope." Renzo twisted and wiggled in the driver's seat, fighting drowsiness, and glanced back at the farmhouse he'd just left. He couldn't imagine Matthias Ruch pulling a goat's tail, let alone killing a close friend, although experience reminded him to keep an open mind. "Says he and Schwab were close, but he had no idea about the marijuana."

"Right." Erwin snorted his doubt and was gone.

9

Haldiz,
Monday afternoon, June 17

It took five minutes to drive from Ruch's farm to Hirschi's, and that included a brief wrong turn. Hirschi's house and the attached barn were only a block from the railway station, with fields stretching off in three directions. The sky was growing bluer, and the temperature was perfect. Renzo felt a breeze out of the north—a *bise*—cool his face and found himself reflecting on how pretty and peaceful the country was. Then the roar of a tractor reached his ears, and he caught a whiff of the liquid manure sprayed on the fields. He imagined having no place to take Fränzi dancing on a Saturday night. Time to stop romanticizing life in the sticks.

He parked on one side of Hirschi's long driveway. He could see why a major grocery chain would use this farm in an ad for healthy food. Wholesome: that was the word for the place. Brightly painted wood trim, checked curtains, and carefully tended flowerbeds and window boxes gave the old-fashioned house a picture-book quality, while the flagstone courtyard appeared freshly hosed, and the rear half of the building that was the barn managed to look both cozy and professional.

Christian Hirschi answered the door wearing new-looking jeans and the style of shirt Renzo had supposed Swiss farmers only wore at festivals—light blue and printed with tiny white edelweiss. Wholesome was a good word for Hirschi, too, with his stocky build, muscular arms, and blond hair. Renzo considered the contrast between Hirschi's ruddy good looks and Ruch's thin, weary face and admired Ruch's generosity. A lesser man would have resented this lively, successful young neighbor, not praised him.

"Come in. I hope I can help you," Hirschi said. Swept into the house by his host, Renzo could smell real coffee brewing. A woman emerged from the kitchen. "This is my wife, Asunción Rivera," said Hirschi, his voice full of pride. Renzo offered the woman his hand. Now he understood Ruch's sudden grin as he'd mentioned Hirschi's wife. The woman was dramatically beautiful, with a mass of sleek black hair and a striking figure that was accentuated by a white blouse, bright belt, and tight jeans. Her perfume was musky.

"Please sit down, Herr Donatelli," she said in strongly accented High German, halting but intelligible. "Let me give you a cup of coffee and some cake."

Renzo was taken aback. Laid out on a low table between a sofa and three armchairs was an arrangement of china cups on saucers, cream in a pitcher, a matching sugar bowl, an uncut cake, and a French-press pot of coffee. Who does this for an interview with a cop? He watched Hirschi's wife cut into the chocolate loaf cake and place a slice on a plate for him.

"This is kind of you," Renzo said, hoping he didn't sound too surprised—or suspicious—as he took the cake and coffee. He sat in one of the green armchairs and drank a swallow from the delicate cup before setting it down and reaching for his phone.

Hirschi smiled. "My wife enjoys entertaining guests. This was her idea. We were already expecting one of our buyers this afternoon. She thought you should profit, too." As he spoke, he sat down in the middle of the sofa, his wife next to him in the corner farthest from Renzo. He stroked her arm, and she turned her head and gave him the ghost of a smile.

"Thanks very much, Frau Rivera," Renzo said, and she gave him the same vague smile. As he took a bite of cake, he glanced around and noticed how neat the room was. The furniture wasn't elegant, but it was all quite new-looking, and none of the tables or shelves were cluttered with envelopes, newspapers, mugs, and all the rest of the stuff that accumulates in a well-lived-in home. The Migros ad featuring the couple and their farm went through his mind again. Something about the room reminded him of a furniture catalogue. He'd rather live in Ruch's cozy, beat-up place.

"He might be a useful person for me to meet, this buyer of yours," he said to the couple. "Do you think Herr Schwab's produce went through him as well?"

"I'm sure it didn't," Hirschi said. "Are you familiar with the Bio Suisse label? The bud?" Renzo felt that his host's courtesy was real but not effortless. It was as if he had to concentrate so as not to become distracted. By his wife? Renzo wondered why she was present. Had she known Schwab?

"It's the sign for Swiss organic food, isn't it?" Renzo answered.

"Not quite," said Hirschi, leaning forward. "It's the Swiss Ministry of Agriculture that decides whether a farm is *bio* or conventional, but most organic farmers also want to be certified by Bio Suisse, because shoppers are familiar with the bud label and look for it. Still, you can grow and sell organic food without Bio Suisse certification. That's what Frank did."

Renzo was astonished. "Frank didn't belong to Bio Suisse? I thought he was dedicated to organic ideals. And he's involved with FiBL."

Hirschi nodded. "Frank was one of the grandfathers of organic farming, which made him a law unto himself. He was much too stubborn to deal with all the Bio Suisse requirements. His farm was recognized as organic by the government and by himself—that was enough for him. Since his produce didn't have Bio Suisse status, the big grocery chains—Migros, Coop, and Fraîche—wouldn't take it, but he wasn't keen on *their* rules either, so he didn't care. Years ago, he started selling his vegetables and eggs to a lot of little health-food stores all over Bern and Fribourg, before the big stores had ever heard of *bio*, and he still supplies a lot of them."

"I see," Renzo said, thinking that he'd need to tell Noah and Erwin to look for a list of health-food-store managers among Schwab's papers. They represented a whole new source of information about the farmer. Perhaps even a source of suspects. "How well did you know Herr Schwab, Frau Rivera?" he asked his hostess. She had the capacity to sit very still, without fidgeting, and the cup of coffee she'd served herself appeared untouched. When she turned to him, he had the feeling she was coming back to him from far away.

"I?" She smoothed her hands over her thighs. It seemed an automatic gesture, free of seductive intent. Still, Renzo was very aware of her. "I didn't know him at all."

Her husband took her hand. "Asunción has a group of Spanish girlfriends in Fribourg. She hasn't had a chance to get to know people in Haldiz yet."

Yet? How long had the couple been married? The wife appeared to understand and speak German, so Renzo assumed she'd been in the village for at least a few years.

"And you, Herr Hirschi? Did you have contact with Schwab, apart from his involvement with the association of farmers you head?"

Hirschi had to swallow a bite of cake before he could answer. "I saw Frank several times a week—in the village, at the Landi or the Star, sometimes on his farm if I drove by, but only to say hello. We didn't have any special business with one another, except on the executive committee."

"From what you've seen and heard during the past six months or so, would you say Herr Schwab had fallen out with anyone? Had he been acting strange? Gotten involved with anything new?" Renzo wished he could focus his questions better. It's only your first day, he reminded himself.

Hirschi took a gulp of coffee and shook his head. "I'd like to help, but I can't think of anything special."

"And Simu? The young man who's been hanging around Schwab's farm? Do you know his full name?"

"No idea. I didn't warm to him, I can tell you that."

"Did you ever talk to him alone?" Renzo could feel his irritation rising at all these useless answers, and he struggled to keep his voice pleasant.

"Not really. I mean, we may have stood around exchanging a few words now and then, but I don't know anything about him."

"Are you aware of any problems Herr Schwab was having on his farm? Money problems? Pests in his crops? There must be a lot of troubles that can knock a farmer sideways." Renzo knew how ignorant he was about the life men like Hirschi and Ruch led; he expected the farmer to roll his eyes or say something dismissive. Instead his face sharpened, and he answered emphatically, "Troubles? You can't imagine." He touched his wife's cheek. "Asunción's father farms, too, in southern Spain, so she knows a lot about the ups and downs of the farming life. That's how we met, nine years ago, when I was working for her father on a sabbatical from this farm. We've been married for four years now."

Renzo glanced at the woman, expecting her to add her reminiscences to her husband's, but when she just threw another smile in his direction, he returned to Hirschi. "And Herr Schwab?" he persisted.

"We all suffer when the weather doesn't cooperate, but if Frank had any particular difficulties, financial or otherwise, I wasn't aware of them."

"Would it surprise you to hear that we found a field of marijuana on his land?"

Hirschi shrugged. "Well, I don't approve, but I can't say I'm surprised. Frank lectures anyone who'll listen on how stupid our drug laws are."

Renzo kept his smile in place with an effort. He'd expected a lot from Hirschi: an overview of Frank's situation from someone who was acquainted with most of the organic farmers in the region and their finances. The head Laker, though, courteous as he was, didn't appear too concerned about helping him figure out why Frank had died.

There was a knock, and Asunción got up. Instead of going to the door, as Renzo expected her to, she disappeared into the house, and he heard her walk upstairs.

Hirschi ushered the buyer from Fraîche into the room, introduced him, and gave him coffee and cake. Adrian Pfeiffer was a tall, thin man in a white shirt, dress slacks, and a sports jacket. Something about the precise way he began to fork up bits of cake reminded Renzo of a classic *Tüpflischisser,* a man who made a living dotting i's and crossing t's. But of course he was a purchasing agent. Almost as bad as an accountant, that was.

"I know you two have business to discuss," Renzo said. "But I'm investigating the death of François Schwab, Herr Pfeiffer, and I wonder if you had any dealings with him."

"Schwab dead? What happened?"

"Head injury," answered Renzo, watching Hirschi as he uttered this lie. But Hirschi's expression, which had turned grave at the mention of the death, didn't waver.

"What?" Pfeiffer exclaimed. His cup clattered as he set it down. "Was he . . . did he have a fall?"

"It's a suspicious death. That's why I'm here. Did you know him?"

"I suppose anyone who has anything to do with organic produce in the Seeland region knew Frank—or knew *of* him. I can't believe he's dead. I just talked to him."

"What about?"

"He phoned to ask me about selling produce to Fraîche. Just general inquiries. We didn't talk long."

Hirschi stood up and held out a hand to Renzo. "I hope you don't mind, Herr Donatelli. That is, if we're through? Adrian and I have a lot to discuss."

We're not through until this murder is solved. Still, Renzo showed himself out. He had enough to be getting on with.

In the courtyard, he stood to consider. It was after four, and he was eager to get home in plenty of time to put the kids to bed, even if he had to show up at the office afterward. But before he plunged into the *Autobahn* traffic, he wanted to think about what he'd learned, so he could summarize it for Noah and Erwin. What exactly had he dug up that they could use?

He got into his Fiat and, turning away from Bern, drove uphill toward the forest that separated Haldiz from the next village. Just below the first trees, an unpaved road ran along the ridge of the hill; halfway along it was a single bench under a tree. Its back to the Jura peaks, it faced the vast stretch of planted fields. Renzo turned onto the track, parked, and sat on the bench. From this height he could just make out the shining surfaces of two of the region's three lakes. Far, far away, half hidden in the summer haze, the grey-and-white Alps hovered like ghosts on the horizon.

Rows of vegetables stretched down the hillside and out in all directions. Food, millions of francs worth, was all around him, field after field of cabbages, eggplants, onions, cucumbers, peppers, tomatoes, and more kinds of lettuce than he'd ever eaten. A profusion of green, broken here and there by an expanse of glass roofing or vast sheets of white plastic. Tiny figures dotted the rows, standing and bending, standing and bending—pickers. Maybe locals, maybe seasonal workers from abroad. He wondered which of these fields belonged to Christian Hirschi. And where were Frank Schwab's sixty acres?

How orderly it all looked. When he thought of "organic," he pictured masses of untamed vegetation. But organic food was big business, and, as Hirschi had told him, carefully regulated. He could understand Frank having trouble with that. Sure, he must have felt triumphant—his private passion had become a world cause. But that change had created so many strict rules defining exactly what *bio* meant, a far cry from the hit-and-miss farming on his original commune. Had he still found his work fun, all these years later?

Renzo shifted on the hard bench and took out his phone to look over his notes. Talking to Louise Fehr was crucial. So was finding Simu.

The fact that all three people he'd talked to didn't know the kid's name was strange. But there were bound to be phone calls between him and Frank. Noah must have ordered Frank's phone records. They'd find Simu.

What else had struck him? That Ruch hadn't had a clue about the field of weed. Could Frank really have sold dope under the nose of a man who was like a son to him without his knowing it? Of course, he only had Ruch's word for their closeness—maybe Frank had felt differently. And the tension between Ruch and Simu: he'd keep that in mind.

Anything else? The picture-perfect quality of the Hirschis' farm hadn't carried through to the interview. Renzo had figured Hirschi would be full of himself, given his youthful successes and the admiration people felt for him. But he wasn't. He'd also expected him to be pantingly eager to help the police, a real suck-up. But both of them, Asunción and Christian, had seemed remote, as if whatever else was going on in their lives consumed so much of their attention that they'd lost interest in what was going on around them. Problems in their marriage? They hadn't seemed hostile to each other. Illness in the family? Hmm. At least he hadn't sensed they were holding back about Frank.

His mobile rang. Expecting Noah with a question or Erwin with news of Louise, he was surprised to recognize Ruch's hoarse voice.

"I've been thinking since you left, and I'm sure it's Simu. He's been growing dope on Frank's land. That explains what he was doing here, in Haldiz."

"But—"

"I'm not saying Frank was fooled. As I said, he knew every inch of his land. But I'm positive he wouldn't have thought of the stuff as his crop—to him, it would have been Simu's. And Simu was the one who sold the weed."

Renzo could hear relief in Ruch's voice. He needed to keep Frank on his pedestal. Renzo didn't blame him. People made excuses for those they loved. But he himself couldn't see much distinction between growing marijuana yourself and letting someone grow it on your land.

Switzerland's whole marijuana policy might be an illogical mess, but profiting from drugs was still illegal.

"Check Frank's bank account. You'll see he wasn't selling drugs. And find that bastard Simu."

"We will," Renzo said.

The call over, he checked his watch and decided to give himself fifteen more minutes to relax and enjoy the countryside. But after first staring at the fields to see if he could figure out what vegetables were growing and then debating whether a white patch on the horizon was snow or cloud, he knew it was hopeless. *Relax, my ass.* He got into the Fiat and gunned the motor, keen to get back to his kids.

10

Downtown Bern,
Monday morning, June 17

Heinz Neuhaus, the investigator whose team was working on identifying Giuliana's victim, was the last to arrive at the staff meeting and the only one without a cup in his hand. His round face was red, and he was slightly out of breath. But he was on time—it was eight thirty exactly. Giuliana took pity on him.

"There's still time for you to grab coffee, Heinz. Go ahead."

Sabine and their public prosecutor, Oliver, smiled in assent; Rolf Straub grunted, which she chose to interpret as agreement. While they waited for Heinz, she crossed the small room and slid both windows on the far wall open wide. Despite the traffic noise that filled the room, the air was a relief in the stuffy space.

The meeting moved quickly. Giuliana had already emailed everyone a summary of what Jonas had told her on Sunday, so they knew about the discrepancy between Jonas's story of one blow and the doctor's identification of two.

"Nothing right now is as important as putting a name to our victim. No revelations from forensics to help us, although they're still processing stuff from the area around the corpse."

"Speaking of revelations," said Sabine, "Jonas did approach the emergency med tech on Sunday morning, and the tech found the dead man and reported it. As Jonas told us."

"Good to know." Giuliana opened the folder with the autopsy report.

"The victim was a healthy man, mid-twenties," she summarized, "with more than enough alcohol and THC in his bloodstream to make him do something dumb like trip a cop. The first blow, delivered to the crown of the head with Jonas's club, wasn't serious. The second blow, to the left temple, was much harder and caused bleeding to begin in the brain, which led to death between one and two hours later. The time of death was after three in the morning and before six. That doesn't help the case for or against Jonas, since he thinks it was around two when he ran through the parking lot."

"From what you're saying," said Oliver, "I assume the doctor wasn't able to determine how much time separated the blows."

"Only to say that they were delivered less than half an hour apart. If someone came along afterward and killed our victim with Jonas's club, he did it soon after Jonas left."

She continued summarizing the report. "The victim's THC levels indicate that he was probably a habitual marijuana user. I know we've already emailed his photo all over the department, but I'm going to double-check with Jürg Thönen in Narcotics that he hasn't been picked up at some point for using, buying, or dealing."

She turned to Heinz.

"Anything to add about ID-ing him?"

"You know from my report that we're getting almost no cooperation from people we approach around the Riding School. But that photo of the corpse we're showing them is pretty unrecognizable in any case."

Giuliana smiled at him. "Sorry, Heinz. What a thankless job. I'll ask Bruno Menotti to do a sketch of the kid looking alive, and your team can start using that." In fact, she thought, maybe if there were an artist's sketch of their victim, Lilo, the press officer, would let it be released to the general public. "I've already set up for Jonas to describe the other man—the one he says was standing with our victim. Sabine, could you ask Bruno to make time for both drawings?" Sabine nodded and took up her phone.

Rolf broke in. "We're gathering information too slowly. If we don't get a move-on, the commandant will have to stand up at the press conference this afternoon and admit that we still don't know who the dead man is. I like your suggestion that he might be a dealer, Giuliana, and we'll use that, but we need more."

She opened her mouth to point out that a bloodstream full of THC made someone a user, not a dealer—and, anyway, it was just one of many leads she planned to pursue. But Rolf was not in the mood for interruptions. "Identify the victim: that's your first priority. Then get us the evidence to indict Jonas. Either that, or find us signs that someone else finished off what Jonas started. Hopefully before the commandant's official press conference."

"I'll do my best," said Giuliana, forcing her voice to stay level. The press conference was in seven hours.

"Good," Rolf said. "I'm off to update the commandant."

Who would clearly be overjoyed at the words *drug dealer*. Giuliana sighed and rested her chin on her clasped hands, looking around the conference table. Oliver was typing notes into his mobile. Sabine, still talking on her phone to the sketch artist, gave a thumbs-up. Giuliana's gaze moved to Heinz, who was trying to hide his impatience to get back to some real work.

"You'll get Bruno's drawing of the victim as soon as I do," she said. "I'm going over to the Riding School."

"My people were all over that place Sunday afternoon and evening," said Heinz, "and they got no help at all. In fact . . . well, you know what it's like being a cop at the Reitschule. If you ordered a beer, ten guys would spit in it before it reached you."

"Yeah. I know. I'll go find Lars Gehrig," Giuliana said.

"How are you going to manage that?" asked Oliver. "I'd say you have about as much chance of talking to him as to the queen of England. And she'd be polite."

Lars Gehrig was the original activist responsible for the conversion of the Riding School from an abandoned building—a former nineteenth-century training arena for horseback riding—to Bern's alternative culture center. He'd been a larger-than-life figure there for close to thirty years. Officially, no one ran the Riding School. It was a communal entity, all decisions were made by committee, and everyone involved was equal. But Lars, Giuliana knew, was far more equal than others. He was quoted in the local papers about once a week, usually criticizing city officials and the police.

"I helped him take over the building," Giuliana said. "Then I stayed around to clean it up and get the center started. I've known him since I was a teenager."

Sabine's eyebrows rose dramatically, Oliver whistled, and Heinz let out a guffaw. Giuliana grinned and raised her eyebrows. "I had a life before I became a cop, you know."

"Good luck with Lars, then," said Oliver, who dashed off to Robbery to discuss another case he was prosecuting. Sabine left to go through photos of the corpse on her computer to choose one for the police artist, and Heinz went back to his team, presumably to cheer them up with news of the sketch. Alone in the meeting room, Giuliana took an absent-minded sip of cold coffee and got out her laptop. She found a main phone number on the Riding School's website, but no one answered. Giuliana wasn't surprised. She ran her eye down a long list of contact emails and numbers. She knew the two performance spaces wouldn't be open on a Monday morning, nor the bar, so she tried the Great Hall, where horses had once practiced their paces. Nothing.

She and Lars had never exchanged mobile numbers. By the time cell phones were commonplace, he'd become the unofficial voice of the enormous, graffiti-covered youth center and she a policewoman. In the late 1980s, when he'd been a driving force behind the occupation and conversion of the building, she hadn't needed a phone to communicate with him, since she'd been one of his acolytes. In the summer after she graduated from *Gymnasium*, the run-down complex of buildings had been her mission. She'd spent days there, mostly cleaning up filth and clearing out junk, but also sitting in on some of the earliest and most chaotic committee meetings. Twenty-eight-year-old Lars had been omnipresent then—a charismatic figure with a shock of tightly curling reddish-brown hair. Even then, his biting wit at the expense of the System was a journalist's dream. The press had loved him. So had she. The memory of her short but desperate crush on Lars made her smile now. He'd neither made fun of her awkward overtures nor taken her to bed. As the mother of a teenage girl, she could now appreciate how tactfully he'd dealt with her, even if she'd suffered from his rejection at the time.

First university and then Ueli had loosened her dedication to the center and Lars. Still, the two of them had stayed in touch for a decade before drifting apart. Now they spoke only when they ran into each other in the city. It had been years since she'd visited him at the center. She didn't know if he still had an office next to the concert hall. Well, she'd find out.

It was a ten-minute walk from the police station to the Riding School, which was next to the main train station on the other side of the Lorraine Bridge. She crossed the Schützenmatte, full of cars and tourist buses. Dodging an abandoned shopping cart and two completely stripped bicycle frames, and ignoring the stink of urine, she passed under the railway bridge leading into the train station. One of the bays under the bridge had been turned into a skateboard run. She stopped a minute to watch three boys of about fifteen skating up and down the sides of a large concrete depression, practicing jumps on every turn. A few more years, and Lukas might be ditching school to hang out here.

Better skateboarding than sniffing glue, she told herself.

She turned back to the Riding School, crossing the courtyard to approach the massive wooden doors that opened onto the wide exterior passageway between the Great Hall and the main building. There wasn't an inch of stone on the building's exterior, even to the top of the neo-Gothic tower, that wasn't covered in layers and layers of graffiti. "The night belongs to us," she read. "Solidarity with Gaza," and "Go vegan." The most common was "Fuck the cops." She laughed softly.

On any given Saturday night, the Riding School forecourt was packed with teenagers and twenty-somethings clutching bottles of beer, but now, on a Monday morning, it was deserted, carefully swept, and surprisingly pleasant. It was watched over by a large, realistic stone sculpture of a horse's head, still mounted above the main doors of the Great Hall. This slope-sided courtyard was partially roofed by a large blue tarp; under its shade rose stadium-like steps that also served as seats. Small garbage cans with plastic bags neatly folded over their rims dotted the area, none overflowing. Set apart from the graffiti by its official look, a message on one wall read: "No deal, no steal, no cops." What a hope! This courtyard and the area around it, including the Schützenmatte and the bridge bays, were full of dealers most evenings. Which meant the police knew where they were; there was a lot to be said for that.

The doors into the passageway between the two main buildings were closed and covered in large black letters with a list of rules banning sexism, racism, homophobia, and any form of exploitation. That should have made her feel cynical, but instead she was pleased to see that the idealism of her days at the Reitschule was still alive. Everything looked deserted, but one of the huge doors swung open when she pushed on it. Inside, the roofed alleyway between the two buildings was lined with bistro tables, benches, and large potted plants; beyond them she could see into the larger flagstone patio, which was crisscrossed with masses of Virginia creeper. The green stuff grew up the walls, too, three stories high. That was new since her time. So were large red graffiti that made her giggle out loud: "Abolish capitalism," was side by side with "Rich Parents for Everybody." She didn't think she and her fellow volunteers had had such an appreciation of absurdity; they'd been a sober and romantic bunch.

As she stood in the patio, admiring the climbing roses—all new since her time—and reading the signs posted on doors opening off the space, she heard voices above her head. There were two women in an office with a tiny balcony on the floor above the courtyard.

"Hello," she called.

A small woman in her fifties in a tunic and baggy pants and a younger, much larger woman in some kind of caftan both came out onto the balcony.

"Hello," she said again. "Do you know if Lars is upstairs?" She wasn't sure how cooperative they'd be, so she took refuge in vagueness.

"He's not seeing anyone from the press right now," said the older woman. "He'll have another statement about the riots this afternoon at five. He'll comment on the murder in the Schützenmatte then, too."

So Lars was talking to the media an hour after the commandant's press conference, which would give him the last word. Clever. But then Lars always had been exceptionally good with the press. He walked a fine line between courting journalists and making fun of them to their faces as tools of the establishment—and got away with it. Behind the scenes, he was also an efficient manager and excellent negotiator who understood when to stand his ground and when to compromise quietly.

She'd gained more understanding of Lars since the age of nineteen. Whatever he stood for in public, his personal politics had become more expedient over the years. No matter what he said about the police and the city government, he could work with them when he had to. It had taken years for the Reitschule to develop into a viable and self-supporting center for entertainment and culture in Bern—a successful business, in other words—and Lars, like any businessman, was not going to look kindly on the mindless, chaotic violence indulged in by Saturday night's rioters. But to please the Riding School's young clientele—to protect its brand, in business terms—the center had to maintain its pro-anarchy, anti-law-and-order stance in public. Especially to the press.

"I'm a friend, not a journalist," she said to the two women.

"He doesn't want to be bothered now," the younger woman said. Although she didn't raise her voice, she sounded fierce. Giuliana wasn't worried; she knew the two women couldn't throw her out. That was one of the Riding School's sacred policies: they were open to everyone. Including drug dealers and rioters fleeing the police.

"Okay," Giuliana said amicably and walked back into the passageway and out of their sight. She made a lot of noise opening and closing one of the double doors to the courtyard, in case the women were listening, and then walked quietly to the nearest staircase, which was through the bar. Without conscious thought, she found herself heading up the stairs to the Dachstock, the upstairs concert hall, where, according to a poster on the wall, "stoner metal and sludge" would be performed that Friday. Did Isabelle like music called sludge? Suddenly she felt she should know.

"Lars," she called as she moved through the auditorium, heading for the offices she knew were behind the backstage area.

"Over here." She heard his voice. Suddenly there he stood, framed in a doorway, a phone pressed to his ear, wearing a red T-shirt with a black anarchy "A." As she got closer, she saw the circle around the "A" was actually the Venus symbol for female. Anarchy and feminism. Typical Lars. Closer still she noticed that the signature halo of curly hair was thinner, the wiry body thicker, and—Lars in reading glasses? But his lopsided grin hadn't changed. Suddenly she wished she'd checked herself in a mirror before dashing over.

"Giuliana," he whispered, his hand over the phone and his eyes dancing. "Come in. I'll be another minute."

The office window was wide open to let a faint breeze into the overly warm room, which was just big enough for a desk and swivel chair, a straight-backed visitor's chair, and one well-worn but comfy-looking armchair by the window.

True to his word, Lars was off the phone quickly. He came over to where she was standing by the window, looking out at the Aare. "Giuliana," he said, kissing her cheeks. "It's great to see you."

"I'm glad to find you up here just like in the old days," she said, taking the chair across from Lars's desk.

"Feeling nostalgic?"

"Absolutely. I can remember dashing around this place like I lived here—and now my daughter's a regular."

"The Giuliana of those days: all wild dark hair and huge, intense eyes. And energy—my God!"

"My energy was short-lived, but yours . . . You've made this place truly successful."

He put a finger to his lips. "Shh. Don't say that. First of all, it's not *my* work; we did it all together, as a community, and, secondly, we're not successful. Only businesses are successful, and businesses make a profit. That's a dirty word around here." He winked at her conspiratorially.

Without warning, his eyes narrowed despite his still-jovial tone. "If you're here to trade on our friendship so I'll let your police run around arresting every second customer for throwing stones at the cops on Saturday night, you can forget it."

"I *am* here to trade on our friendship, but it has nothing to do with the riots. Not exactly. I need your help to identify a dead man. And it's not only so we can figure out who killed him. We need to find his family."

"The boy murdered by the cop? You want me to help you with that? You expect me to betray . . ."

She could hear Lars swinging into his public persona.

"Lars, stop. This is me. I know what you think you need to say, so just take it as read. It's still my job to investigate this death, and, believe me, if a policeman killed this man, he'll be indicted. But in the meantime, we need to identify the victim, and there's a good chance he was a Riding School regular. I had my people showing his photo around yesterday, and all they got was curses."

"Don't sound so indignant," Lars countered. "I remember a time when you would have been cursing cops, too."

"Perhaps, but I've grown up," Giuliana said.

"I'm still not going to help you. You want to find one of my Riding Schoolers guilty of murder to get your own killer off the hook. I'm not going to be a party to that."

Save your performance for the journalists, Lars. But she didn't change her calm expression—just looked into his eyes until he broke her gaze and stood. He paced the room for a moment and then turned to her.

"You just need to identify the guy?"

"Yes. That's what's important now. Depending on who he is, we may need to come back and talk to people who knew him, just as we'd interview the friends and colleagues of any homicide victim. I can give you a photograph of him, and I'll email you an artist's sketch within the hour. If *you* circulate them, people here will make an effort to figure out who he is. And I need to know." *Before our press conference,* she added, but only to herself.

He hesitated, and she knew he still couldn't stomach the idea of helping the police, even when asked by an old friend. He needed to see an advantage to himself.

"Come on, Lars," she said, "think about how you can use this. I heard you have a press conference today at five. Journalists will ask why you let the rioters run in here to hide and why the Reitschule continues to give shelter to violent criminals. You can deflect that if you focus on the murder victim. You can say you are—what's a good word?—spearheading an inquiry into this young man's terrible death." Her voice slid into a chant. "The Riding School will ensure that his killer is brought to justice. Just let the police *try* to deny that one of their own—"

"Etcetera, etcetera," interrupted Lars. "I can see you've got the style down pat. Good God, when did my earnest little Giuliana turn into such a cynic?"

"I don't care what you say to the press," said Giuliana, dodging his question, "as long as you help me get an ID."

She imagined Rolf wincing at her words. But none of them could influence what Lars said anyway; he was bound to be critical of the police. If anything she told Lars generated the victim's name before the press conference, no one would care what had passed between them.

She opened her shoulder bag, took out a copy of the dead man's photograph, and passed it to Lars, who examined it.

"Jesus," he said in disgust. "It's a good thing you're having a sketch done—I can't ask anyone to look at that photo. I'm almost sure I don't know him. But I'll do my best to find out who he is. Is the commandant going to release this at his conference?"

"Last I heard, no. So you really are crucial to the investigation at this point."

"If this guy's a regular at the Reitschule, someone will recognize him. When that happens, I'll call you."

"Anytime, day or night." She handed him one of her business cards, which had all her phone numbers on it. He didn't have a card—too conventional for him, perhaps—but he scribbled his mobile number on a Post-it, and they kissed each other's cheeks again.

"It's good to see you," Lars said, "even if you did end up joining the baddies. Which reminds me, I play tennis with your brother. Paolo's still one of us."

Giuliana laughed.

"Tennis? You? If anyone finds out you are doing anything as bourgeois as playing tennis, you're never going to be able to show your face again. Talk about the stuff of blackmail—you've just put your future into my hands."

"Hey," he said, laughing in turn, "how do you think I still manage to get into my leathers? Wait until you're over fifty—you'll find out."

This time, cutting back across the Schützenmatte, Giuliana saw—and smelled—what she'd missed in her rush to see Lars: two burned-out cars on the sidewalk across the street from the parking lot. Further toward the railway station, several shop fronts had boarded-up windows. Almost thirty-six hours since the riots, and the wrecked cars hadn't all been towed yet. The extent of the mess nearer the station and on the main shopping streets must be worse than she'd imagined.

As she walked across the Lorraine Bridge toward her office, Giuliana's sense of triumph at having persuaded Lars to help her slid into sadness. He'd accused *her* of being a cynic, but she felt like the one who'd retained her idealism, while he'd become an opportunist. Or was she deluding herself that being with the police meant doing some good? She wondered what Ueli would say about that.

Back in the office she found two drawings on her desk. One was of the dead man, brilliantly brought back to life. The same features were there, but now they showed an expression of alert amusement, almost mischief. With his wavy dark-blond hair, blue eyes, and boyish grin, the victim was handsome. But more to the point, he had become a distinct individual. Someone who knew him would surely recognize him now.

The drawing of Jonas's supposed witness also showed a light-haired man, but there the similarities ended. The second face was generic. She couldn't imagine anyone looking at it and saying, "I know him." He resembled instead any one of a hundred men you could pass on the streets of Bern every day.

She sighed over the unremarkable face. Had this man watched Jonas Pauli beat a friend to death and failed to tell anyone? Or had he been the one to pick up the club where Jonas had dropped it and deliver a vicious blow to his companion's temple? Or was he no one, the product of Jonas's defensive imagination?

Her thoughts were broken by Rolf sticking his head around the door. The black circles she'd noticed under his eyes in the morning now looked like bruises.

"You met with Lars Gehrig? He knew the victim?" barked Rolf.

"No, but he agreed to help. I'm about to send him this sketch, which is excellent. He'll show it around the Riding School. But . . . but you know there's nothing going on there during the day. Even the bar and restaurant are closed on Mondays. So his chances of getting an ID before the press conference are . . ."

She stopped. Rolf stood in the doorway, leaning against the doorframe like it was all that was keeping him standing, rubbing his eyes. Then he nodded and tried to smile.

"We've still got a few more hours," he said.

Giuliana smiled back, but Rolf missed it; he was already trudging down the hall.

Giuliana came to a decision.

She phoned Sabine. "Thanks for leaving me the sketches. The one of the vic is outstanding, isn't it? Heinz will be . . ."

"He already is," Sabine broke in. "I had copies made and gave them to him for his team. He's very hopeful. They're over at the shooting gallery right now, talking to the junkies and anyone else they find hanging around near the Schützenmatte."

"Great," Giuliana said, although she imagined the social workers at Contact, the supervised injection site, might be more helpful than the smackheads. Still, it was a good idea. "I'm going to make some copies and go back over to the Reitschule. I want to put this sketch into Lars's hands myself and make sure he does what he promised me."

"You got him on board," said Sabine. "I'm impressed."

"Don't believe it until he comes through," she answered. "While I'm back over there, would you call Jürg Thönen? I tried him earlier and didn't reach him. I'll leave extra copies of the sketch on my desk for you to pass on to him for his people. Maybe this will jog a memory."

"Right."

Shortly afterward, a folder full of letter-sized colored photocopies in her bag, Giuliana ran down the main stairs and out the front door just in time to catch the no. 20 bus at the stop across the street. An angry driver honked at her as she dodged his car, but with the press conference less than five hours away, she didn't wave an apology. She was too busy wondering whether Lars would make good on his word.

11

Downtown Bern,
Monday afternoon, June 17

Giuliana phoned Lars from the bus, but he didn't answer. Five minutes later she walked into his office again and found him gone. Another phone call; still nothing. Shit! She left him a phone message and placed a small pile of the portraits on his desk, with a note reminding him how urgent the identification was.

Lars really would ask about the dead man during the next couple of days, if only so the police would owe him a favor. But the more she'd thought about it since their meeting, the surer she was that he'd make no effort to ID the youngster before the police press conference. That would ruin the fun of having the city's top cops look incompetent in front of a crowd of reporters. Not only had one of their men apparently killed a bystander, but also thirty-six hours later they still had an anonymous corpse on their hands. Giuliana imagined Lars's speech to the press an hour after the commandant's. "Criminal incompetence" would be the mildest accusation he'd throw out.

Surely someone must be hanging around on a Monday afternoon in this damned labyrinth. She stepped out of Lars's office and yelled, "Hello! Anyone here?" When no one answered, she began searching, floor by floor, trying closed doors and poking her head into random spaces—offices, meeting rooms, small auditoriums, storage closets. She unearthed nine people, including the older of the two women she'd seen earlier in the day, who was working alone at a press in a room full of printing equipment. None of them could give a name to the young man in her sketch, although two admitted he looked familiar.

She came upon a locked door labeled "Workshop." Someone behind the door was hammering, so she knocked hard and called out, "Hey, sorry to bother you, but would you mind opening up? My name is Linder. I'm trying to identify the youngster killed in the Schützenmatte. We need to be able to tell his . . ."

A deadbolt turned, and the door was thrown open by a man of about sixty wearing carpenter's overalls. He grinned at her.

"Well, we've both gotten a bit older, haven't we?" he said. "But you still look pretty hot after twenty-five years. Come in."

The man seemed so pleased to see her that she hadn't the heart for a sharp retort, so she walked into the room, and he closed the door. He was skinny and bald with thick glasses. There was something about the way his ears stuck out . . .

"I know you," she said. But no name came to mind.

"It's okay," he said comfortably. "You were twenty and chasing after Lars in those days. I was a rusty old geezer of thirty-five. A lot rustier now, I'm afraid. Kari," he added, thrusting out his hand. "Kari Spirig."

"Of course," Giuliana cried, shaking his hand with vigor. "I remember now." She eyed the vast room, which had a sawdust-covered floor and a beamed ceiling. Carpentry tools were mounted in rows on the walls, and there were workbenches under the large, barred windows. "You're the guy who fixed up the building after the takeover."

He ducked his head, still grinning. "Well, one of them. I used to sneak over here with my tools when the boss could spare me, and sometimes when he couldn't. After a while I got too busy to do much Reitschule work, with my own business and all, but now I'm retired. So I decided to do some volunteering. Monday's a great time for me to get work done. No one drops in with their problems."

"Broken chair problems or life problems?"

"Both, I guess." He shrugged.

"And now I'm here with a problem, too. Do you know this man?" Giuliana asked, holding out the sketch of her victim.

He took the piece of paper in both work-stained hands and studied it.

"This is Simon Etter. He's a regular. He's also a friendly guy, so I've chatted with him, at the Rössli"—that was the Reitschule bar—"and here, in the workroom. Did you say he was dead? Don't tell me he's the one who was killed Saturday night by the cop?"

We don't know yet who killed him, she wanted to protest. Instead she nodded. "Thank God you've given him a name. Now we've got to find his family. Etters are pretty common—is there anything you can tell me about him? Was he from Bern?" She paused as she realized she had to explain, even if it smashed the man's pleasure at seeing her again. "I'm a cop myself now, Kari. Homicide. This boy is my case."

Kari's smile was mischievous. "I was wondering when you were going to tell me." He turned away and, moving to a tall cabinet against one wall of the room, brought out IKEA folding chairs, just about the only plastic objects in the workshop. He opened both so that they faced each other, dusted one with a rag from his back pocket, gestured her into it, and sat down in the other. "Of course I know you're a *Tschugger*. Seven-day wonder when a couple of us from the old days found out way back when. But, hey, we need more good folks to become cops, don't we? Now, stay still and let me think a minute."

Giuliana sat and did nothing, which was a relief. It was pleasantly cool in the thick-walled workshop. She knew she should be worrying about getting the name "Simon Etter" to Rolf before the press conference. Instead, she enjoyed the smell of fresh wood and watched motes of sawdust float through the air in the light of the afternoon sunshine. Her eyes closed.

The carpenter shifted in his seat and touched her knee to get her attention. "Etter sold weed. He came to the Reitschule to have fun and go to concerts, but most evenings he was here to do business. The stuff he sold was relatively inexpensive, the way outdoor grows have to be these days, and he talked up the fact that it was organic, which appealed to lots of his customers. It was good-enough weed—I bought some now and then." He cocked his head at her, and she nodded, so he went on. "As for how you can find his family, I know he worked for the post office."

She started, and he caught her thought before she voiced it. "No, he didn't drop doobies into mailboxes. He enjoyed making that joke when he mentioned his job, but actually he sorted letters, which gave him convenient shifts. I also know his mother is a widow, even though he was only in his early or mid-twenties. She and at least one of Etter's sisters live in the Bern area. Maybe he told me more about his family, but that's all I remember." Kari crossed his arms adding, "Oh yeah, he had an apartment nearby. University area, maybe? Can you find his folks with that?"

Giuliana wanted to jump up and hug Kari, but instead she just grinned. She felt light with relief. "That's more than enough—that's terrific. I still have one more favor to ask. I'm going outside and call all this in to my boss. Then I'd like to ask you what Etter was like."

"You go make your call, and I'll think about it," Kari answered, walking back over to the drawer he'd been working on before she walked in. He was sanding wood as she left.

To make sure she had privacy, she slipped out of the building and sat on the stadium steps in the corner of the courtyard under the tarp. As she waited for Rolf to answer, she noticed two posters on the wall next to her, side by side. One was for a seminar on Marxism, the other for a craft beer festival. She swallowed a snort as Rolf answered.

"A dealer?" He sounded elated by the information—at least by the standards of his normal deadpan delivery.

"Just marijuana," she cautioned.

"Killed in the Schützenmatte, right next to the Riding School. Giuliana, this is exactly what we need. The boy wasn't just drunk and stoned; he was a dealer. And Jonas says he only hit him once and left his club right there. If whoever was standing next to Etter picked up the club . . ." Rolf trailed off. Giuliana knew the relief she'd felt at hearing Etter's name must be nothing compared to Rolf's. But what he'd said worried her. It sounded like he was wrapping up her case before it had begun. She'd been afraid Jonas Pauli might get sacrificed during the commandant's press conference, but now it looked like there was going to be a whole new scenario shoved down reporters' throats.

Damn it, why don't you let me investigate my case before you hand it over to PR like a shrink-wrapped package, she wanted to say. But this was Rolf. He always had her back. She'd wait until after the press conference and then see where things stood before she confronted him. Looking at her watch, she saw that the conference was in less than two hours and felt a jolt of panic.

"You don't expect me to see the press, do you?" she asked.

"No, no. Same as always. You carry on with the case, and if any journalist tracks you down and asks you anything, you refer them to Lilo."

Sending the media to the press officer had always been her strategy before, but she'd never been assigned such a high-profile homicide.

"Well done for getting the information to us in time," he added.

"Thanks. Sabine and I will find Etter's family as fast as we can, but I doubt we'll get to them before the press conference."

"No problem. We have enough for now."

To Sabine, whom she called next, she passed on everything she'd learned about their victim. "I'll get some of Heinz's team off the streets and onto the computers to help me find the mother," Sabine said. "Then I'll go tell her. You coming?"

"Go without me, and I'll finish up here at the Riding School and call Narcotics for more info, now that we have Etter's name. Break the news today—no questioning—and tell her you'll be back in the morning with me so we can talk about her son. Line up as many family members as you can for tomorrow morning; I doubt anyone's going to talk straight about Etter in front of the mother, but we'll figure out a way around that. Sound okay?"

"All good," said Sabine, although she sighed heavily before hanging up. Giuliana felt guilty leaving the worst of all possible tasks to her colleague, but reminded herself that she, too, would be confronted with the bereaved family's grief during the next day's interviews.

"There was something about Etter that put me off," Kari told her, once she was back on her plastic chair in the workshop. "That's what I've been trying to figure out." Although he'd just sat down himself, he stood up again and began to walk around the room. Giuliana knew why he was restless. Speaking ill of the dead—it was hard to do face-to-face.

"He was excellent company over a beer." Kari spoke as he stood at one of the worktables fingering something. "Friendly, funny, a good storyteller. And you could count on him to show up when he said he would."

Ah. Swiss punctuality expected even of drug dealers. Giuliana suppressed a smile.

"In spite of all that positive stuff, I often felt he was sizing everyone up, trying to decide what benefit each person and each situation could bring him. Not a monstrous ego, not that. More of a 'What's in it for me?' that lurked behind even the most casual chat."

"Not exactly the ethos of the Riding School," said Giuliana.

"Exactly," Kari agreed, turning from the window he had drifted over to and coming back at last to his chair. "Of course, a lot of the Reitschule blah-blah about community and democracy is bullshit, but in Simu's mouth it felt particularly fake. If you'd met him at the Davos Economic Forum wearing a suit and talking about hedge funds, nothing would have jarred, but at the Riding School . . . I'm making him sound too serious, though. He was a light-hearted guy. Spontaneous. Or so he seemed. But when I really start to think about him, that's what I come up with."

It was rare that someone Giuliana interviewed communicated so much about what was under an acquaintance's everyday façade, and she told Kari as much.

He acknowledged the praise with a nod and, taking a deep breath, said, "I have a son in the Waldau. Well, in and out, in and out. For years. I've learned to think . . . differently about people."

Without thinking she leaned forward and reached out, grabbing both of Kari's hands where they rested in his lap. She squeezed them as she met his eyes. Just for a moment. Then she let go and sank hurriedly back into her seat. God! Could anything be more terrible than having a child in a mental institution? Suddenly afraid that he'd take her sympathy for pity, she saw to her relief that he wasn't offended.

"Yeah. It's bad. But I also have a terrific daughter and son-in-law and three grandchildren, so . . ." He trailed off and then asked, "What about you?"

"A journalist husband and two kids. Our boy's ten; our girl's fifteen. Things are good."

Or they were until recently, she amended after parting from Spirig. Isabelle arrested at an illegal street party; Ueli critical and distant. Not good. At least Lukas was fine—he'd better be.

Walking back across the bridge to the police station for the second time that day, she noticed how hungry she was. She'd missed lunch again. Which made her think of seeing Renzo in the cafeteria the day before and getting his text. She wondered what case he was on. Normally she'd know—homicides in Bern were uncommon enough that the whole police department kept up with them—but she was so focused on her own case that she'd forgotten to ask Rolf.

At the bakery a block from work she treated herself to a wedge of apricot-and-custard pie to eat at her desk. Conscious of wanting to avoid encounters with TV cameras or reporters, she snuck through the parking lot door and up the back stairs to the homicide office, where five detectives were at their desks.

Erwin Sägesser glanced up from his computer. "Your case-room is set up now," he said, before she could set her things on her desk. "Sabine's in there. I think they've found your Etter."

"Great. What are you working on?"

"A farmer killed in a Seeland village. We'll have our own case-room by tomorrow morning. Right now the techies are too busy with the press conference to get to us."

"Is Renzo working with you?"

"Yep."

She heard a hint of reservation in his tone. Erwin belonged to a generation that sometimes used slurs when they referred to Italians. But she didn't think it was Renzo's ethnicity so much as his appearance that made Erwin roll his eyes at her now. He confirmed her suspicion by adding, "Sending Renzo to talk to farmers in Haldiz is like putting . . ." An orchid among turnips? A bottle of Glenmorangie with a six-pack of Miller Lites? Giuliana waited, but Erwin had no metaphor for what he wanted to say.

"He'll surprise you, Erwin," she told him. "People talk to him—men, too, not just women. Even farmers."

Erwin glowered. Then he shrugged. "We'll see."

Two doors down she found Sabine in a smaller room that had now been set up with two desks, one desktop computer, and a meeting table. Sabine jumped up from one of the desk chairs to meet Giuliana at the door. "We've got Etter. He worked a morning shift at the postal center, seven to one. To leave time for his drug business, I guess. Twenty-four years old, apartment on Brückfeldstrasse. His only police record consisted of two citations for riding his bike through red lights, which didn't get his fingerprints into our database, or we'd have found him right away. That's all we've got so far, but Heinz's people are still on it. As for his family, his father died a few years back, and his mother lives in Deisswil. He has three older married sisters, one also in Deisswil, two in other villages near Bern. I've broken the news to the Deisswil sister on the phone, and she's going to come with me to tell the mother. Thank God for that. I'm meeting someone from the care team in the parking lot in"—she checked her watch—"less than ten minutes; he's joining me. Anything I need to know before I go? I remember we're not asking any questions until tomorrow, especially not about the dope business, but should I be on the lookout for something special?"

Giuliana summarized what Kari Spirig had said about Simon Etter.

"Ambitious, huh?" Sabine said. "I'll keep that in mind. Oh right.

I've asked the sister I spoke with to make sure the other family members are there tomorrow for questioning."

She turned to leave, but Giuliana stopped her with a hand on her arm. "Thanks, Sabine. I'm sorry you have to go through this."

Sabine smiled at her with unexpected warmth. "I promise—next time we're on a case together, you'll get to tell the family. But there's no point in both of us suffering."

With Sabine gone, Giuliana called Jürg in Narcotics. Maybe he'd have a theory about why anyone would want to get rid of a young man who sold a relatively insignificant amount of marijuana. An ambitious young man, she corrected.

"You, too, huh?" he said, at the sound of Etter's name, which meant someone from the commandant's office had already been squeezing him for data. "All I have on him is from informants and the undercover folks, and it isn't all that new. As far as I know, Etter worked alone selling pot and only pot and had no known contacts with any organizations. Strictly small time, usually dealing on the Grosse Schanze or at the Reitschule."

Nothing new, but it was good to have Kari's statements confirmed. Jürg brushed off her thanks. "I understand that what you really want to know is what's going on in the Bern drug scene that could lead to the man's death. The commandant was onto us asking the same question. No one has an answer—yet. But it's become a priority, believe me."

"It's my case, Jürg. I get the impression the commandant's hot on the drug trail, but I don't just want to hear what you find that points to a drug killing. I also want to know if you think that theory's bullshit. *I* don't have any agenda, except to solve the case."

"Got it," Jürg said. "Right now we can't imagine how a minnow like Etter could have gotten into the path of even the smallest shark. But I've had him on my mind for less than two hours, so give me a little time. I'll check in with you by tomorrow evening at the latest. Okay?"

"Great. And thanks," she said. She called Oliver, her prosecutor, to fill him in; then she began a brief written report for Rolf. This reminded her that she still hadn't written up Saturday's suicide. Shit!

She'd have to do it soon, before her notes from that night no longer made any sense to her.

A few minutes later her phone rang. She fumed at the interruption before she saw it was Renzo. She'd just take a minute to ask him about his new case. Leaning back from the computer screen, she took the call.

12

Nordring police station,
Monday late afternoon, June 17

"Hi," she said, "Erwin told me . . ."

Renzo interrupted her. "I talked to Erwin, too. He said you've got a name for your dead body. Simon. A youngster who sold marijuana. Do you know if it was organic?"

"What?" She paused to process the question. "How could you . . . ? He told his customers it was organic. Whether it really was . . ."

"It was. He grew it on the land of a famous organic farmer. It's too much of a coincidence otherwise." He gave a manic chuckle.

"Renzo! What are you talking about?"

"I'm working on the killing of a farmer in Haldiz, François Schwab, who was a *bio* hotshot and a big supporter of legalizing dope. The locals say that for the past year a guy named Simu, last name unknown, has been hanging around his farm. We found a field of marijuana on Frank's property, and his best friend is convinced it must be Simu's. But where is this Simu? I just heard that your dead guy was a Bernese dope dealer named Simon. Anyone from Bern named Simon gets called Simu, so . . ."

"When was your farmer killed?"

"Sometime Friday afternoon or early evening. And your boy died early Sunday morning, right? Two people involved with local organic marijuana killed less than forty-eight hours apart?"

"You're right," said Giuliana. "It can't be a coincidence. Are you still in Haldiz? Because the easiest thing would be for me to email you the portrait of Etter that Bruno Menotti drew. Anyone who's seen him a few times would recognize him from this sketch."

"I'm halfway back to Bern to put my kids to bed," Renzo said. "I called Erwin a few minutes ago, and my brain didn't click on the name Simon Etter until now. I don't want to turn around, but I can go back with the drawing later tonight. I don't mind."

Giuliana knew better than to suggest that Renzo miss bathing and reading to Angelo and Antonietta for anything short of an emergency. She hated to make him go back to Haldiz at all. It wouldn't be necessary if the place had its own policeman. The larger village of Erlach was ten minutes away by car, though; surely someone there was on duty—or on call.

"Thanks for the offer, but we'll get a local person onto it. I'll ask Monika to compare Etter's fingerprints and DNA with whatever they've picked up at the farmer's place, too."

"Good luck with that," said Renzo. Giuliana heard the smile in his voice. Monika Utiger, the head of the lab, hated being rushed—it made her grumpy as hell.

"Look," he added, "with our two cases coming together like this, you're going to need me to fill you in on what I've been doing. I mean, of course you'll talk to Noah and Erwin, but . . . don't you think we should get together for a chat? Maybe later tonight?"

No wonder he and Fränzi were having trouble. Giuliana tried to keep all censure out of her voice as she said, "No, I need to stay home tonight. We'll catch up Wednesday morning after gym. Okay?"

There was a long pause before he answered. "Okay, then. Bye."

She slipped her phone into her pocket and walked to the nearest window. A pack of boys, a couple too small to throw as high as the basket, were running around the neighborhood basketball court below her with a ball. It was almost five; the police press conference must surely be over. Which meant Lars's was about to begin. Oh, God. She'd never let Lars know that Etter was identified. In truth, he hadn't done a thing for her but act cooperative and then disappear, but she couldn't let him crow to the media about his own crusade to ID the police's corpse when it already had a name. Assuming Lars had an informant among the police or press, which she imagined he did, he'd have learned that Etter was identified, but she couldn't risk it. She took the phone out of her pocket and, her eyes still on the basketball court, where a boy of about eight was trying to dribble, she pressed redial for Lars. No answer. All she could do was leave a message. She gave him the facts about Etter, no apologies, nothing about Kari Spirig being her source. She didn't owe Lars anything, she reminded herself.

Much more important was telling Rolf about the two Simus being one. Which she did. Twenty minutes later, having only had time to brush her hair and twist it back up into a neater knot, she was sitting at a round table with not only Rolf but also the commandant, along with Lilo the press officer and Noah Dällenbach, whom Rolf had informed about a possible change in the status of his case. In this meeting room the chairs were padded and had arms, and the overhead lights shone gently on the attractive grain of the thick wooden tabletop. Giuliana sat as straight as a board; she had to force her hands not to clench the armrests. Even the large fuchsia hanging in the window did nothing to improve her mood.

The *Kommandant der Kantonspolizei Bern* was probably a pleasant husband and friend and a loving grandfather. Middle-aged and middle-sized, he kept himself fit, was never known to yell, and believed in rules; Giuliana had never heard a whisper to suggest he was corrupt or had favorites. For that, she respected him. But she never felt comfortable with him. He was too stiff and self-righteous.

". . . only serves to confirm," the commandant was saying. He turned from the press officer to Giuliana and Noah, sitting side by side. "Frau Linder, Herr Dällenbach, thank you for joining us. You don't need my advice when you are in Rolf's capable hands." Out of the corner of her eye Giuliana watched Rolf give a stiff nod. "But I would like to emphasize to you how important it is to follow up on the relationship between these two men, Etter and"—he glanced at his notes—"Schwab, and find out exactly what links their deaths to the narcotics trade in Bern. The sooner we can come back to the press and public with a solution to both homicides, the better." He didn't say, "And I trust it won't involve murder-by-cop," but he didn't need to. His next words confirmed what was on all their minds.

"Jonas Pauli is in serious trouble in any case, as you all know."

Yes, thought Giuliana, *but for excessive use of violence, not for voluntary manslaughter—or worse. And I'd like it to stay that way*, she had to admit to herself. Any killer but Jonas Pauli.

She remembered Lars's words: "You want to find one of my Riding Schoolers guilty of murder to get your own killer off the hook." She'd been angry when he'd said it. Now she saw exactly what he'd meant, how convenient it would be for the cops.

But she had no plan to run her case by pursuing what was convenient.

"Do you have any questions?" the commandant asked. "Or comments?"

Stop telling me how to solve my case. She wasn't going to say that, so she and Noah responded with polite negatives. The press officer, a woman so well-groomed she seemed to gleam, added her piece. "It's vital that you refer any questions from the media to me; in fact, I'd appreciate it if you'd text me if you are even approached." She seemed to be staring at Giuliana as she spoke. Aha, she knows about Ueli being a journalist. Giuliana made her expression pleasant as she nodded.

The commandant rose and shook their hands. "I'm always available to you," he said as he walked them to the door. When it had closed behind them, Noah and Giuliana grinned at each other and slapped palms.

"It must be two years since he took that human relations course, and he's still talking the 'open-door' talk," Noah said as they made their way back to Homicide.

"The funny thing is, I believe he means it," Giuliana said. "I think he'd be delighted if one of us popped in with a respectful question about how he runs things."

"Speaking of running things, how are we going to run these two cases? I suggest that for the present I stick to what happened in Haldiz, and you stick to Etter's death here in Bern. From now on, though, we'll be looking for connections."

"I agree. Let's hold tomorrow's eight o'clock meeting together, with both our staffs, before we go our separate ways. I'll start cc-ing you on all my reports, and you can do the same. Shall I run this plan by Rolf? I'll phone him before I go home in any case."

"Good. I'll make sure Rosmarie, my prosecutor, knows, too. And, by the way," Noah said, as Giuliana was turning into her case-room. "I know you like working with Renzo, so start asking him to follow up on your stuff. You don't have to check with me. He and I need to touch base anyway, so I'll let him know that he'll hear from you. It'll be a big advantage to have him working both cases, and if he has a problem taking assignments from two people, he can let me know."

"As long as he's fine with it, I think it's a good idea," she answered, staying carefully low-key. "Thanks for sharing his time. See you at the meeting tomorrow." As she turned away from Noah, she replayed his first words: "I know you like working with Renzo." No, no implications there.

In the case-room she went back to phone calls, leaving messages about the following day's joint meeting for Rolf, Sabine, Heinz, Oliver, and Jürg. As she was about to set her mobile down at last, she saw that a call from Lars had come in. Steeling herself, she got back to him.

"Hello, Lars. Did your press conference go well?"

He was silent a little too long.

"I was pleased with it. But I would have appreciated more notice about the identification of your victim. Odd, the way you came over here, reminisced about old times, begged for my help, and then turned around and IDed the guy yourself. I've been trying to figure out what you were up to, old friend." His tone was light, but she wasn't fooled.

"No ulterior motives in sight, Lars." Her tone matched his. "Things moved fast, and we didn't connect. You've been busy, too." That was as far as she was willing to go toward reminding him that he hadn't answered her phone calls and had been gone when she'd stopped at his office a second time. "You'll be glad to hear that we've already found the boy's family, and we've made some progress toward finding his killer, too. Turns out Etter was a small-time dealer of weed who used the Reitschule as one of his bases." Which by now he surely knew from the news online, but she didn't want to appear to be hiding anything from him. "We'll send a couple of people over tomorrow night to talk to anyone who knew him."

Lars's snort came clearly over the phone. "Don't forget all of us are convinced your cop killed him."

"No matter who killed him, we still need to know more about him. The commandant met with me less than an hour ago to tell me how eager he is to have this case solved. He'd be very pleased if you . . ."

"Of course he'd like me to smooth the path for your investigations. But that isn't my problem. I need a pat on the back from the cantonal police like I need a hole in the head. Jesus, imagine how that would look on the evening news."

"You know perfectly well I'm not talking about public praise. I'm talking about fewer cops hanging around your forecourt, less hassle for your customers."

"Are you offering me a written contract with guarantees? I make nice, and the commandant calls off the dogs?"

She channeled good humor into her voice. "A contract—that'll be the day. It's just that the more we can find out about his connections at the Riding School, the sooner we'll leave you alone. Think about it."

"I'm done thinking about Etter," he said, but this time there was something perfunctory about his anger. He *was* thinking about it, trying to figure out what advantage to the Reitschule he could extract out of the situation. Okay, that was part of his job.

And part of her job was to deceive him. Because although it was true that no cops would be around that night, that was only because the Reitschule's bar and restaurant were closed. The police would be contacting their usual informants, and the undercover cops would drift to the places where drugs were sold and start conversations about the murder. With or without Lars Gehrig's cooperation, information would be gathered about Simon Etter and the Riding School.

"Got to go," he said. "I'm sure the police taped my press conference. Have a look at it." There was something in his voice that worried her, but she had better things to do than spar with Lars anymore.

Still, she'd try to anticipate his moves. Giuliana speed-dialed her brother, Paolo, and started explaining all about Etter and his association with the Riding School as soon as she heard his hello. He wouldn't care if she skipped the sisterly chat for once.

"Lars is in a position of power," she finished up. "He can put out word that everyone should be obstructive, or he can suggest cooperation. Of course, a core of Riding Schoolers considers it their lives' work to block the System and will do that no matter what Lars says: even he's part of the establishment for them. But some people will be inclined to tell us more on Lars's say-so."

"What do you want me to do?" Paolo asked.

Good old Paolo. Another person might have asked that question in a tone that meant, "And just what do you expect me to do about all this, for Christ's sake?" But Paolo asked it cheerfully, as if helping her was one of his life's small pleasures. Giuliana smiled at him, even though he couldn't see it.

"Nothing. But I know you're his lawyer; he told me so. This way, if he calls you for advice about how to proceed, you've heard my side of the story."

"I take it you aren't in the position to promise him less police harassment."

"I said something to him about that already—but the truth is I doubt I could get him any concessions, no matter how hard I tried."

Paolo laughed. "Well, that's an honest answer. Now that I know what's going on, we'll wait and see what happens."

"Thanks, Lo."

After that, Giuliana couldn't bear to contemplate another phone call. She packed her oversized pocketbook with files, poked her head into the door of the homicide office to say good-bye to the two colleagues still sitting there, and left for home.

Tonight, she and Ueli were going to talk to Isabelle about what had happened at the Dance-In. It was past time for that conversation. But all the way home, instead of thinking about her daughter, she wondered why Lars had told her to watch a tape of his press conference. The more she thought about it, the queasier she felt.

13

Bern's Kirchenfeld neighborhood,
Monday evening, June 17

Ueli's hands toyed with an empty coffee cup and Isabelle picked at her cuticles, while Giuliana ran her fingers through her hair again and again. They'd managed to pretend everything was normal until Lukas went to bed. Now there were no more excuses for avoiding the Dance-In.

At last Ueli leaned back, crossed his arms, and looked at his daughter. "What happened Saturday night?"

"You'll both get mad," she answered. Her voice was firm, but her eyes were scared.

Giuliana couldn't understand why parents ranted at their kids for doing the same idiotic, reckless shit that they'd done as teenagers. But surely she hadn't been as young as Isabelle when she'd started defying her own parents. Isabelle was small-boned; her fair, faintly freckled skin bruised easily; her red-blond hair was as fine as a baby's; her amber eyes dominated her delicate face. Her mother knew she wasn't fragile, but . . .

"We promise not to get angry while you're telling us," Giuliana said, hoping her daughter wouldn't notice what she'd left unsaid.

Isabelle leaned back and crossed her arms over her chest, exactly as her father had just done. How could a slim girl look so much like a burly man with a red beard? Even their wary expressions were similar. Giuliana repressed a smile.

"You know Quentin asked me to go to the Dance-In. With him and some of his friends. I don't know them well—they're all two years ahead of me."

Now that she was speaking, Isabelle's body relaxed a little. She tucked a strand of hair behind one ear and went on.

"I promised Vati that Quentin would look after me, and he did try to keep hold of me in the crowd. But thousands of people were dancing and shoving, and it was loud. Not just the music—people were yelling. I couldn't hear Quentin talking to me. Lots of times guys kind of"—Isabelle looked at Giuliana and took a deep breath—"grabbed me, but . . . nothing bad happened. Everyone was laughing, having fun. It was very hot. People kept passing me beers." This time she eyed Ueli.

"I said no open drinks, Isa," he burst out. "I told you about . . ."

Her exasperated tone echoed her father's. "I know about roofies, Vati, but there was nothing I could do. I don't even like beer, but that was all there was to drink. I was thirsty."

Noticing they were glaring at each other, Giuliana decided to change the subject. "Were you having fun?" she asked.

"I was until Marlies started sucking on Quentin's neck," Isabelle answered promptly and then ducked her head, her pale skin reddening.

"Marlies is a girl in Quentin's class?" Giuliana probed gently.

Isabelle slumped and started worrying at her cuticles again. At last she went back to her story.

"Quentin and his friends were also drinking beer. He was still trying to keep me next to him, but most of the others started drifting off into the crowd. Not Marlies. She just . . . pasted herself onto Quentin, kissing him and . . . and . . ."

Isabelle's voice rose in indignation, and then she broke off. She stared at her hands, growing redder. Ueli caught Giuliana's eye, looking as rueful as she felt herself. Poor Isabelle, coping with the Dance-In *and* a bunch of horny eighteen-year-old companions. Whatever Marlies had been doing with Quentin at the Dance-In, it was a relief that Isabelle was still inexperienced enough to blush about it. Or was she only embarrassed to find herself talking to her parents about it?

"So the two of them disappeared and left you by yourself?" Ueli asked.

"No," Isabelle said, her voice suddenly stronger. She looked up, not meeting their eyes, but with a face full of determination. "That's not what happened. I saw them like that, and then a boy came up and put his arm around me. He looked my age, and he had a nice face, so I went off with him." She was glaring now, defying her parents to reprimand her.

Giuliana hadn't the heart to do it. She could easily imagine how hurt Isabelle had been, how confused and scared she'd felt in the buffeting crowd of drunk and stoned people, how hard she'd tried to save her pride. She was too young to handle such a difficult situation—Ueli should never have let her go. But he knew that now. His stricken expression showed it.

"What did you and the boy do then?" she asked, and was rewarded by Isabelle's look of relief that her mother had not started yelling.

"We were shoving our way forward, toward the DJs. All of a sudden we heard screaming. People started running at us. It turned out they were trying to get away from the fight between the cops and the rioters. We were pushing right toward it." She took a deep breath. "I could see men in black throwing torches and stones at the police, and the police hitting them with clubs. It was awful. Anyone would have been scared." She gave Giuliana another defiant look before saying, "The boy kept hold of me and we made it to a place near Loeb, next to the little bakery."

"So you didn't get mixed up in all the window-breaking and vandalism," Ueli said, clearly relieved. "I knew that had to be a mistake."

"Um." The look Isabelle gave her father was sympathetic. Giuliana noticed that sign of maturity with surprise. Isa was sorry she was about to disappoint Ueli, not sorry for herself. "Not exactly a mistake. You see, this boy, it turned out he was as drunk as everyone else. He saw all those cobblestones stacked under tarps in the center of Kramgasse, where they're digging up the road, and he ran over and picked some up. He wanted to break the bakery windows to get something to eat. I was trying to stop him when a huge cop ran up and sprayed something in his face that made him fall down screaming. I thought the policeman was going to kick him, so I kind of . . . well, I attacked him. That's why we got arrested."

"You attacked a cop in the middle of a riot?" Ueli asked, putting one elbow onto the table and covering his eyes with a spread hand while he shook his head. Giuliana thought he was being a touch melodramatic.

"I didn't hurt him," Isabelle said—as if that was Ueli's concern. "I ran at him and pounded on his chest with my fists, but it was like beating a board. I'm sure he barely felt it. He must have been wearing some kind of body armor. He grabbed my hands and pushed me away, but not so I fell down. Then he handcuffed the boy and me, brought us to a paddy wagon, and ran off into the crowd again."

"Jesus," Ueli said, still shaking his head.

"You know," Isabelle added, smiling at last, "I almost talked him into leaving us there. I promised I'd call Vati and go right home—and take the drunk boy with me. I almost had him convinced. But in the end he arrested us instead."

"You and your grandfather—trying to persuade people to make exceptions. He doesn't always succeed, either—in court or out of it," said Giuliana. She couldn't help feeling proud of Isabelle. She may not have made all the right choices, but she'd thought on her feet and tried to cope. "How was it in detention?"

"It felt like forever," Isabelle said, looking at her mother. "They questioned me and moved me all around. Took my fingerprints. Were you nervous the first time you got arrested at a demo, Mam?"

Ueli interrupted. "Did they shove you? Scare you?"

"No, Vati. I already told you. Everyone treated me okay," she said in a reassuring voice, still waiting for Giuliana to answer her question.

"What about the other men and women being detained? Did any of them bother you?" Ueli asked.

"You asked me that Sunday night," Isabelle said, turning into her usual, exasperated teenage self. "Honestly, Vati, I didn't pay attention to them. Lots of people were yelling at the police and cursing and complaining about stuff, but when no one was asking me questions or making me stand in line to pee or get food and water, I just wanted to sleep. That's what I did most of the time I was there—I lay in a corner on a mat and slept. It was all really, really boring."

Ueli was fidgeting with his cup again. "Minors don't get police records for things like this, do they?" he asked Giuliana.

She shook her head. "No, there won't be a record. She'll have to do around forty hours of community service, I imagine, and maybe meet with a youth counselor if someone thinks she's a child at risk. Although I could probably get her out of that if . . ."

Isabelle interrupted. "No, you don't have to 'get me out of' anything, Mam. I think it would be interesting to talk to a counselor." She raised her eyebrows. "I can tell them how terrible it is to have a cop for a mother." They smiled at each other again.

"Look, Vati," Isabelle said, turning back to Ueli and growing serious. "I wanted Quentin to take care of me at the Dance-In, so I told you he would. But why should he? It's not like he's my boyfriend. I should have phoned you to come get me. It was stupid not to."

Her father pulled his chair around the table until he was beside her and leaned over to give her cap of red hair a gentle stroke. Then he pulled her close to kiss her cheek.

"That's true; you should have. But *I'm* the one who was stupid, sweetheart. I was once an eighteen-year-old boy who got drunk at street parties. I should have known what would happen with Quentin. In fact"—he glanced across the table at Giuliana—"he behaved pretty well. He never abandoned you in the crowd, at least."

"No, I abandoned him." Isabelle's body straightened as she described this tit for tat. She met Giuliana's eyes. "You'd never have let me go if you'd known, Mam. But I wanted to be with Quentin. I would have gone no matter what you or Vati said."

"Let's pretend you didn't say that, all right? I just want you to understand why I wouldn't have let you go," her mother said. "First of all, the city didn't give permission for the Dance-In this year, so it was illegal. I don't allow you to do illegal things. Secondly—and this is the important reason—I thought it would be dangerous. You're fifteen, sweetie. A fifteen-year-old doesn't know how to handle a lot of situations yet. And, honestly, it did turn out to be dangerous, didn't it?"

"It was kind of psycho," Isabelle admitted. "Not just because of the street fighting. Even before that started, I found some stuff weird. But," she said with defiance in her voice, "those things would have been creepy if I'd been older, too."

Giuliana nodded. "I'd find being groped by strange men creepy as well, and I'm forty-six. I still don't think you should have gone, but it sounds like you did your best to make good decisions and stay safe."

"Even though I went off with a boy I didn't know?"

"Well, you said he looked nice, and you couldn't have known he would try to smash shop windows. Running at the policeman was foolish, but you assumed he was about to hurt the boy. I approve of your trying to defend people."

"You would," muttered Ueli.

"What does that mean?" Giuliana asked.

He just shook his head, so Giuliana turned back to Isabelle.

"Unless there is something else you want to tell us, I think you should go to bed. And go to sleep. Don't phone Luna first."

Isabelle didn't argue. She got up from the table and gave first Ueli and then Giuliana a kiss on the cheek. Leaving an arm around her mother's shoulders, she said softly, "Thanks, Mam," before padding barefoot to her room. Giuliana gazed after her smiling. Still filled with love for her daughter, she turned to Ueli, whose face was oddly blank.

"I'm sorry I allowed her to go to the Dance-In," he said.

"We can't always agree on everything to do with the kids," Giuliana said and reached across the table to take his hand.

"And we still don't." He let her hand rest on his without returning her clasp.

She pulled the hand back and leaned her cheek against it. "I'm tired. Can't we just call it a night? We could talk about this tomorrow, couldn't we?"

"We could," Ueli said. "But I don't want you to get up from the table thinking you were speaking for me when you said Isabelle made safe decisions on Saturday night."

Giuliana sighed. "Why not?"

"Our daughter hit a policeman, and you praised her for it."

Her eyes widened; Ueli sounded serious. "Praised her? I don't think she took what I said that way. That's certainly not what I meant. But in this particular case . . ."

He interrupted. "As a cop, you underestimate how dangerous the police are. It makes me sick to think of Isabelle getting pawed in a crowd, but it scares me even more that she was alone in a dark passageway with a policeman and ran at him. Don't you realize he could have hit her, killed her even? Look what happened to the boy at the Schützenmatte, the one all over the news whose head was smashed in."

"You're comparing Isabelle's story to *that*? Now you're being . . ." She stopped herself.

Ueli shook his head and spoke gently. "Come on, Giuliana, you have to see it. Think for a moment, without getting defensive. Isabelle is a young, light-skinned girl. What if it had been Marco's Somali daughter in that passage? Or if we were Tamils or Turks? What if she'd yelled at that cop with a Balkan accent? Do I need to go on?"

"Our cops are trained not to overreact." As soon as the words were out of her mouth, she thought of Jonas Pauli saying, "We trained and trained to not lose our tempers, and then my first time on riot duty, I blew up."

Ueli came around the table to where she was sitting, stood behind her, and put his hands on her shoulders. "The riot must have been terrifying for the cops. And that's exactly when they make mistakes—when they're scared and angry."

"You're talking almost as if the police were responsible for the problems on Saturday night."

"Well, there may be ways in which they were," said Ueli. "I think it's going to take a while before anyone can figure out what caused things to escalate so badly. But I don't want to talk about the whole riot, just what happened to Isa. And what you said to her about it."

"All I said was that I approve of her trying to defend people."

Ueli let go of her shoulders and moved to perch on the table where he could meet her eyes. She could see he was upset—but so was she. And so tired. Why couldn't he just let it go, for God's sake? Just until another evening.

"I don't want Isa believing that you approve of what she did," he said, his voice rising. "I want her to be more cautious than that. In our different ways, you and I both believe in fighting for vulnerable people, but I'd prefer to have a daughter who knows how to stay safe. The truth is—you need to hear this—the truth is that I don't trust the police's judgment. I'm sorry, but that's how it is."

She looked away from him and shook her head.

"Can't you accept some of what I'm saying? Meet me halfway?"

She continued to shake her head, not so much refusing to accept some of his points as rejecting their whole argument.

"Okay, then. If you aren't going to make a single concession, there's nothing more to discuss." He dropped his gesticulating hands to his sides and strode toward his desk in the living room without looking back. "I need to work. Don't wait up for me."

"Look. I didn't mean . . ." Giuliana broke off and watched him walk away. Should she go after him? She hadn't meant to respond so negatively. She too wanted Isabelle to move through the city safely. But not fearfully. Of course she didn't trust the judgment of every cop in Bern. But Ueli had been talking about "the police," and that included her. Which hurt. She decided to let him work in peace for a while. They could both use some time to think about something else.

Not that she could let herself think about something besides police business. And her responsibilities had just increased by one murder. When she'd told Rolf about her and Noah's plan to combine their morning staff meetings the following day, he'd agreed, with a proviso. "I think it would be wrong to take the Schwab case away from

Noah," he'd said, "so I approve of your making it a joint operation. But at the meeting tomorrow I'll make it clear that you have the final say."

Rolf's decision showed his confidence in her, and a clear line of authority would make it easier for her and Noah to work together. But she knew Rolf was also maneuvering her drugs-related investigation to the fore. She wondered how the press had reacted to the commandant's blatant attempt to distract them from Jonas-as-killer. She hadn't taken a moment all day to look at the papers or the evening news.

The TV was across the room from Ueli's desk, but it was a big room. She turned it on, keeping the sound low, and skipped back so she could watch Sunday night's news first. The images of the raucous but cheerful crowd waving hands and beers in the air as they gyrated to the beat of the music blasting out of massive amps contrasted with scenes of panicky youngsters screaming and running in all directions. *With Isabelle in the middle of it,* she thought. *Thank God she's fine.* Footage of the scattered battles—she couldn't really think of them as anything else—between the riot police and the black bloc were all the more frightening for being badly lit, and several times it appeared from the film's sudden cut that the camera person had been threatened. The reporters talked of looting, injuries among the police, damage to property worth millions of francs, and attacks with tear gas, water hoses, pepper spray, and billy clubs on revelers as well as rioters. But there was less criticism of police action than she'd expected. The riot coverage ended with a Sunday morning, day-lit shot of the square near the main station: mountains of trash (which would have been there anyway, thanks to the Dance-In) coupled with wrecked floats, burned cars, charred lumps of debris scattered on the ground, a dangerous amount of glass all over the pavement, and looted display windows in the surrounding stores. She started fast-forwarding before the program quite finished and realized it was because she was so angry with the pointlessness of all the destruction. The rioters hadn't even had a political agenda.

Monday's news denounced the Riding School for hiding members of the black bloc. It also reported indiscriminate police violence and criticized the cops' failure to arrest more of the rioters. A sociologist pontificated on why young men are attracted to destruction, and then came a statement about Jonas's attack on "a young man who has been identified by the police as a drug dealer," followed by coverage of the police press conference. While it was true that the victim had been "knocked down" in the course of the police's pursuit of the rioters, the commandant explained, detectives were investigating the strong possibility that this man's death was tied to another recent killing. Both homicides were apparently linked to the production and sale of marijuana and "possibly harder drugs."

Lars's press conference wasn't shown, but there were scenes from a one-on-one interview with him in the vine-covered Reitschule courtyard. From his mournful face, Giuliana could tell before he opened his mouth that he was going for a "more in sorrow than in anger" approach.

"Today I had a visit from a member of the police force who, years ago, was a personal friend. A close friend," he added, after a slight pause. "She"—another tiny pause, to emphasize the female pronoun—"was asking me about the man who was beaten to death, trying to enlist me in the police's campaign to blame the Reitschule for his murder and distract the public from the cops' own culpability. It's sad to think of them being so twisted—using a youngster's brutal killing to promote their own agenda against the culture center."

The bastard. Giuliana gnawed on a knuckle. He's trying to make me sound like an ex-lover who was out to exploit him. Even corrupt him away from his principles somehow. Oh, God. The press will be after me now with a vengeance, and what will the commandant think?

"Why do you think this policewoman was so eager to involve you?" the man with the microphone asked.

"Because I thought Etter might have hung out at the Reitschule, and Lars runs it, you ass," Giuliana answered the reporter out loud. "And, lo and behold, he *did* hang out there."

"The way the *Bullen* are promoting the drug angle—well, I smell a cover-up," Lars said. And that was the end of the news about Etter's death.

Giuliana turned off the TV. Her heart was tight in her chest. She'd felt clever going to Lars, and now he was twisting her request for help into another sound bite. Still, going herself to the Riding School to get information had not proved to be a mistake, since she'd found Kari Spirig and he'd recognized Etter. That was a comfort.

Calming down, she listened to Lars's last words again: *I smell a cover-up*. If she put her disgust at his betrayal aside, she was inclined to agree with him. If this whole drug-dealer business wasn't a cover-up yet, it was certainly a mass of half-truths woven into a very distorted whole. The implication that Etter might have been involved in selling "hard drugs" was totally unfair—there wasn't a shred of evidence to back it. She just hoped this crap being fed to the press wasn't going to become *her* daily bread. Surely Rolf wouldn't do that to her.

The next morning after the joint staff meeting, she and Sabine would drive to Deisswil to question Simon Etter's mother and sisters. She forced herself to stop dwelling on the TV images and instead think about how she should handle the bereaved women. She went to bed planning the interviews and fell asleep at last, sensing just before she dropped off that Ueli's side of the bed was still empty.

14

Nordring police station and the Old City, Tuesday morning, June 18

Just about everyone working on the Schwab and Etter homicides was crowded around the rectangular metal table in Noah's meeting room. Renzo had worked with all of them before, although he couldn't remember if the narc was called Jürg or Jörg. Noah and Giuliana sat side by side, talking with quiet intensity. Giuliana had her usual notebook out and was writing a word now and then. *She loves this*, he thought, watching her covertly until he noticed Rolf's eyes on him and turned away. Monika Utiger hurried into the room. There was a chair at the table for her, but she didn't bother with it. Too frustrated by her lab's lack of progress on the Schwab scene to sit down, he deduced, although no one showed any sign of wanting to reproach her. In fact, they quieted down immediately to let her speak.

"We can identify the potting shed as the scene of the murder," she told them. "That's the only real news I have for you."

"The autopsy backs that up," Noah said. "The soil in the lungs matches what's under the victim's head."

Monika ignored this. "We found an unbelievable amount of stuff on the body and in the shed. Several kinds of animal dung, peat moss, bone meal, wood particles, terra-cotta fragments. Give us clothing from a suspect, and we can run comparisons. But according to a Bio Suisse consultant, there's nothing out of the ordinary in any of it. Except the pesticide. By tomorrow we should be able to tell you which brand was sprayed around the place. But I don't have a single thing that could move your case along."

Giuliana said, "I know you heard from Rolf only yesterday evening about the two victims being friends, so you can't have had time to do forensic comparisons. But—"

"Fingerprints," Monika interrupted. "I did those last night. Etter's fingerprints are in Schwab's kitchen, which confirms their connection. But you need us to link the crimes, not just the people. Your crime scene in the parking lot was a garbage dump, Giuliana, but it was all city trash, not farm trash, so no connections there. So far. We still have a long way to go with examining everything we've picked up at both scenes."

Renzo saw Giuliana look around the room, meeting eyes, before focusing on Monika and saying, "If these crimes are drug-related, there are two main possibilities. Either both men were killed by the same person, which is the most likely scenario, or else Etter killed Schwab and was killed afterward by someone both men knew through their dealing."

"So you're hoping for traces of the same unknown person at both crime scenes or traces of Etter at Schwab's place of death. Hair, clothing fibers, blood, DNA: all the usual stuff," said Monika, shifting from foot to foot. "We're on it. But nothing so far." As she said this, she looked defiant, as though daring them to complain. No one did.

"Right," she continued. "If there are no more questions, I'll go back to the lab. Reports to Noah, Giuliana, and Rolf on everything, right?"

She was out the door with the thank-yous still on the detectives' lips.

There was a moment while everyone gave a collective sigh of relief. It wasn't that anyone disliked Monika, Renzo knew; it was just that she brought so much tension into a room that her departure had a calming effect.

"Okay," said Noah, dragging out the word. "Now that we have the fingerprint confirmation of the two Simus being the same, the identification of the portrait isn't so important. Still, an Erlacher cop took the drawing of Simon Etter into a Haldiz restaurant last night, and four witnesses assured us that the man in the sketch is the Simu they knew. So there's no doubt about it. Now, let's get back to the marijuana. Jürg, why don't you give us your take on Schwab?"

Listening to Jürg brought home to Renzo just how insignificant Frank Schwab's one field of dope was in the universe of Bernese and Swiss drug crime. The narcotics cop didn't bullshit them: he admitted right off that he couldn't imagine how a small operation like Schwab's and Etter's could generate two murders. Maybe in Caracas or Central LA, but not Bern. So why would someone . . . ?

"Don't worry about the 'why,'" Noah broke in. "That's a Homicide problem. We're used to killings that don't make sense."

"I respect that," Jürg persisted, "but, seriously, guys at Etter's level don't get killed, not even if they've started selling to another dealer's customers. If Schwab and Etter were wiped out on command by someone higher up the food chain, they'd have to have been dealing cocaine or heroin as well as weed. Maybe amphetamines or yaba, but there's not much of a market for those in Bern."

"What's yaba?" asked Giuliana. Renzo had no idea either, but he'd never have asked in front of the group.

"You've probably heard it called 'Thai pills'—it's methamphetamines, usually mixed with caffeine. Little brown tablets. Dangerous stuff." Jürg Thönen talked with his body—Renzo could see that from the way he leaned forward as he spoke, his thumb and forefinger demonstrating how tiny the pills were, his body shrinking in on itself as he described their destructiveness. Still trying to explain the killings' inexplicableness, he added, "Your two vics—they must have cheated a boss. That's all I can think of that could justify this level of violence, and even then . . ." He broke off.

"Good to know," said Noah. "Your people ran the search of Schwab's farm yesterday, Jürg. Are you sure he wasn't drying dope somewhere on his property?"

"We can't find any place that would fit, and 'we' includes the dogs."

"So, it's looking more and more like Etter was the one doing the work, and Schwab was providing the land and some agricultural advice. Right, Renzo?" Giuliana turned to him.

"Schwab's best friend, who's known him for over thirty years, is convinced that's the case," he said, flicking Giuliana a smile. She'd obviously read the report he'd stayed up writing the night before. "There could be a barn somewhere in the Seeland that Etter's renting for processing his weed, but it probably doesn't belong to Schwab."

"Sabine and I are going straight from this meeting to talk to Etter's family and after that to his apartment," added Giuliana. "By the end of the day, we should have found his stash and, hopefully, where he dried and cured it. Based on what you've told us, Jürg, we'll also look for a connection to Class-A drugs."

"He'll have last year's crop already cured," Jürg reminded them, "and this year's is still in the field. So you shouldn't find any stuff drying right now. But the smell lingers. If you haven't found his workspace by this evening, let me know, and we'll send dogs into his neighborhood. Unless that's a problem, Rosmarie?"

The prosecutor on the Schwab case shook her head. "Nope. Should be kosher. If you turn up anyone else's grow boxes, though, talk to me before you bust 'em!"

Renzo broke into the amused pause that followed Rosmarie's comment. "Don't forget Louise Fehr, Frank's partner for over fifty years. She may have answers to all our questions about him—and about Etter."

"The girlfriend," echoed Erwin. "She hasn't answered landline, cell phone, or doorbell. Yesterday we snagged all Schwab's business and personal papers and his laptop," he went on, "and we're sorting everything. Information about Fehr, Etter, marijuana sales: it should all turn up."

Turning to Giuliana, Erwin added, "The situation strikes me as ripe for a falling-out between the two men, with one making money off the other's land. Frank asked for a bigger share of the take and Simu got rid of him. That's my guess."

The big man looked around the table with a confidence that came, Renzo knew, from a long career dealing with greed. He respected Erwin's experience with criminals—but now he disagreed. The Frank that Erwin was imagining wasn't Matthias Ruch's Frank, nor was it Renzo's. He was the only one in the room who knew anything about Frank the person, and *that* Frank had not had a fight with Simon Etter over drug money. But for now, he'd keep that belief to himself.

"I'm going to ask Pauline"—Noah turned to one of Renzo's fellow investigators, a quiet middle-aged woman—"to focus on Etter's presence in Haldiz over the past few weeks, with an emphasis on the Friday of Schwab's death. Renzo, I'd like to put you onto Fehr. She's clearly going to need tracking down. When you find her, please bring her in."

"What's our estimate for the time of death that Friday?" asked Pauline.

"Afternoon between two and six," Erwin said, and poked around in the stack of papers in front of him until he found the right pages. "Knocked unconscious with an unknown weapon. Marks on the back of the head, neck, and shoulders where he was held down in the dirt. No defense wounds on the body. Looks like the killer kneeled on his shoulder blades to make sure he stayed down. Which gave us some clothing fibers. The lab will need all the clothes from Etter's apartment, Giule, to see if anything matches." She made a note.

People were draining coffee cups and starting to shuffle in their seats. But Renzo still had a question.

"What about Jean-Pierre Niklaus?" he asked Noah. Catching blank looks from both prosecutors, he added, "He and Frank feuded over his pesticide getting on Frank's plants."

"I'm interrogating Niklaus at two," said Erwin. "If you aren't busy with Fehr then, join me." Renzo was flattered; he'd never sat in on one of Erwin's interrogations before.

"I have something else that needs following up," said Oliver, Giuliana's prosecutor, to the table at large. "The photographic material from the riots. We have the usual CCTV footage from shops and bars, plus stills and film from police photographers, journalists, and the public.

Despite all this criticism of the police, a lot of people who were at the Dance-In want the black bloc caught, and they're sending us their photos. This investigation has legal access to it all—I've made sure of that. We need to sift through it for images of Simon Etter."

"Back to the hunt, then," said Giuliana, turning to Heinz, who nodded.

"Saturday night is the priority," she went on, "but see if you can find earlier CCTV footage, too—around the Riding School, the Grosse Schanze, and other places Etter might have sold his dope. If anyone gives me a tip about his favorite bar, I'll pass it on."

Renzo felt sorry for Heinz and his team. Trying to recognize faces in amateur photos and grainy film was a pain, even with the help of facial recognition software; he'd done a lot of it over the years. He was glad he got to look for Louise in the flesh.

"Anything you want to add, Noah? Rolf? Any more questions?" Giuliana looked around the table and let the head shakes come at their own pace. The meeting grew silent, and Giuliana didn't break in. Renzo admired that—the way Giuliana's quiet confidence gathered everyone's attention.

"Every homicide creates its own sphere of action," she said, "and we get possessive about our domains, even after a day or two. I'm impressed with the way all of you have joined forces and shared information, and I hope you'll all keep thinking outside the boundaries of 'your' homicide and search for the threads that bind these two deaths together. Right now, we are focusing on a very obvious connection—the marijuana. I suppose you saw the TV news last night and the newspapers this morning. Most of the press is running with the drugs angle suggested to them yesterday by the commandant." She glanced at Rolf before continuing. "But our job isn't to come up with a good story—it's to come up with the true story. There's no doubt that Jonas Pauli, whom many of us know and like, hit Simon Etter once. His baton was found less than three feet from Etter's body. Anyone could have hit Etter a second time, *anyone*, including a total stranger passing by. Remember what Noah said about killings that don't make sense. They don't have to make sense to us, only to the killer. So look at the evidence and think about the different possibilities the facts could point to."

Renzo found himself nodding—he wasn't the only one.

"All right, then. Noah and I will see you tomorrow morning at eight. I've reserved the big meeting room at the end of the hall for us from now on. Have a good day."

Renzo didn't try to catch Giuliana's attention after the meeting. Too many people. Back at his desk, he called all Fehr's numbers, as Erwin had, and heard the same dry, professional-sounding message on each. He left his own number, with an urgent request for her to call back, and drove to the Old City.

It had been sunny but cool when he'd left for the gym that morning; now it was growing hot. Fehr's cobblestoned street, Junkerngasse, was two blocks long. Along that small stretch of city were centuries-old row houses, where beautifully restored, elegant apartments coexisted side by side with unrenovated studios sharing a bath and toilet down the corridor. Which kind of place did Louise Fehr live in? he wondered. There were only four apartments in her building. When no one answered his ring from the street, he tried first the place above hers—also empty—and then the one below: Frau Katerina von Oberburg. The surname was familiar to him—and to many Bernese, he supposed—because it belonged to one of the patrician families that had ruled the city-state for five hundred years. The *Bernburger*. Although Bern had a mayor now, elected in the normal way, the original *Bernburger* still had vast influence in the city and canton.

His buzz was answered. Hmm, this should be interesting.

Ten minutes later, he was sitting across from a small, very wrinkled old woman enthroned in a high-backed chair. It was covered with countless tiny beads forming birds and animals. "It's Yoruba," she'd told him as she saw him admiring it, but whether Yoruba was the artist or the style, he didn't know. The room, whose large windows overlooked the Aare River and the woods on its far side, was a small museum of African sculpture, wall hangings, furniture, and artistic-looking objects, all exploding with color. Frau von Oberburg was as colorful as her living room—impossibly red hair, improbably tanned skin, bright pink lipstick, a necklace and bracelet of enormous green beads, and a dress that swirled all the way to the floor in pale green and what he thought might be called magenta. The skinny old lady seemed to suck energy from the colors around her like a bee drawing nectar from a flower.

"I've never talked to a policeman before," she said, "except to ask for directions. Are all cops as pretty as you?" Her deep voice was surprisingly clear, but the laugh she gave was a cackle.

Renzo grinned. "Well, I've never talked to a *Bernburgerin* before. Are all patricians as colorful as you?"

She threw her head back on its thin stalk of a neck and chortled until she wheezed. Renzo's amusement turned to concern. Should he get her something to drink? Before he could decide, the plump woman who'd answered the door rushed in with a glass of water. Frau von Oberburg took a deep breath, drank, and set the glass aside. The woman slipped out.

"Not only pretty, but cheeky, too. So, what can I do for you, Herr Donatelli?" she asked. "What do you want to know about my neighbor? Is she in trouble? Did she embezzle someone's funds?" She winked at him.

"Not as far as I know." He considered winking back but decided that would be going too far. "I need information about a man who has died, a good friend of hers, and she isn't answering either of her phones. I thought you might be able to help me track her down."

All the mischievous light left the old woman's face. "Is it François?" Her voice faltered. Renzo crossed to where Frau von Oberburg sat shrunken in her chair. He crouched beside her and took her hand in his.

"Forgive me. I had no idea you knew Herr Schwab. I'm very sorry."

After a moment she spoke. "The curse of being old is that everyone starts dying. Before you know it, all the people you care about are gone. But he was at least fifteen years younger than I am. What happened?"

"He was killed. On his farm."

He watched her as he broke this news and read in her face only sorrow and shock.

"Killed? What do you mean?"

"We're trying to understand what happened. That's why we need to talk to Frau Fehr."

"Louise will be stricken."

"Where is she?" asked Renzo.

"In Zürich, with her daughter and son-in-law." Renzo interrupted to ask for the couple's names and address. The old woman yelled for her servant. Renzo suppressed a giggle; he'd expected a tinkly handbell. They waited until the slip of paper was produced and the woman gone, when Frau von Oberburg continued.

"They had twins a month ago, Louise's first grandchildren, and she went to spend a few days with them. She'll be back late tonight. She's so happy playing with the babies; she called me on Saturday bubbling with joy. Don't spoil her visit. Tell her about Frank after she gets home."

Renzo was tempted to do that, but there were so many questions Louise needed to answer that Noah and Giuliana might not accept the wait. It would be their decision. In the meantime, he'd find out what he could.

"What can you tell me about her and Frank? If you don't mind."

"I've known Louise since she was born. She was always a girl after my own heart—determined to have her own way, no matter what her parents wanted."

"Were they also *Bernburger*?"

"They were well-bred and had money, and her father may have bought himself into one of the guilds, but they weren't . . . well, it doesn't matter. What matters is that they had plans for their daughter." The word *plans* seemed to stretch on, heavy with expectations. "She spent the year after *Gymnasium* at a finishing school on the Lake of Geneva. Her parents gave her permission to travel to California to spend a few weeks with an American boarding-school friend and her respectable, conservative family. Those weeks turned into two years. Louise grew her hair to her waist and settled down in San Francisco. She met François at a Vietnam War protest, and the first thing they did was have an argument. Then they fell in love. When he came back to Switzerland, she did, too. But she didn't move back here to Junkerngasse and start looking for a suitable husband. Instead, she moved in with François on the farm he'd inherited in that village whose name I can never remember."

"Haldiz. So you're saying she became an organic farmer."

"Oh, no," answered Frau von Oberburg. "*That* was their problem. They loved each other, but their lifestyles were totally incompatible. François wanted to live on that godforsaken farm and change the world with his organic vegetables. Louise wanted to change the world, too, but not by living in the middle of nowhere pickling cucumbers—or whatever farmers' wives do."

She cackled again, and Renzo was relieved to see her liveliness returning. He tried to relax into his own oddly carved chair, but the back dug into his spine.

"So what did Frau Fehr want to do?" he asked.

"She wanted to invest money."

"A hippie banker?"

The old lady nodded. "Louise was smart, and her family had money. She already had access to trust funds when she was in her twenties, and she realized she didn't understand anything about her investments. She didn't want her money to support businesses she didn't approve of, like the Swiss weapons industry. So she studied finance at university."

Frank had had a girlfriend with lots of money. Did that explain how he could afford to sell to small health-food shops instead of major grocery chains? Was it the reason Ruch was convinced that only Simu Etter had profited from the marijuana? Renzo kept these questions in the back of his mind as he listened to the old lady.

"Did she and Schwab stay together?" he asked. "While she was at university?"

"She spent time in Haldiz, and he came to Bern, though not as often as she'd have liked. It's not easy to get away from a farm. But it was a commune for years, so there were usually other people around to fill in for François if he wanted to visit Louise."

"According to our records, Schwab had no children, but maybe we missed something. Are the twins his grandchildren?"

"No, he and Louise never had children. That's what broke them up. They both craved kids, but he insisted he'd raise them in Haldiz. She'd suffered with parents who wanted to shape their children's lives around their principles, and she was afraid François would do the same to their kids: try to mold them into little *bio* farmers. So they separated when Louise was forty. She married a man she'd known for years, and they had a daughter. About a decade later, they divorced, amicably enough, and Louise went back to François. I've known him ever since they came back from San Francisco together, by the way. A stubborn man, but a good one. See that framed photo on the little desk over there? Have a look at it. Louise is just under thirty in that picture."

Renzo walked over to the desk under the window and held the photograph to the light. He already knew what Frank looked like; here the man's face blazed with happiness. The woman next to him was an earth goddess in a blue tank top and jeans. Tall and strong-looking, with her head flung back in laughter, she had big breasts, full hips, and extravagant corn-colored hair that flowed to her waist.

"They look so . . . balanced," Renzo said, not sure he'd found the right word for what the two figures expressed.

"They were in those days," von Oberburg agreed.

"You said Frau Fehr studied finance." Renzo continued as he returned to his seat. "Did she get a job?"

"She certainly did. She joined one of Bern's small private banks and started a fund. Alternative investments. Wind power, fair-trade coffee, even some of the developments in Silicon Valley. *That* was a brilliant move, as you can imagine."

Renzo wondered if Louise had also put money into marijuana, which certainly counted as an alternative investment. He noticed von

Oberburg's eyes had closed. He waited a moment. Was she searching her memory for more details about Louise?

"Frau von Oberburg," he said softly, and her eyes fluttered open.

She cleared her throat. "Falling asleep—another curse of old age. Do you have more questions?"

"No. This has been extremely helpful. I'm grateful to you but sorry to have brought you bad news."

"It's cowardly of me, but . . . will you break the news to Louise?"

"Yes." *If she doesn't already know*, he thought. It would explain her unwillingness to answer the phone.

"Well, I'll be here to comfort her afterward."

"One more question," Renzo said. "When did Frau Fehr leave for Zürich last Friday?"

"She planned to take the noon train."

Frank had died sometime between two and six that afternoon. But how accurate was the medical examiner's estimate? And had Louise really left then? They needed to know that and much more—but even the police couldn't drag her out of an apartment in Zürich.

That was Noah's decision, too, when Renzo called him from the sidewalk outside Louise's apartment house. He asked for the daughter's number, though.

"I'll ask her to break the news of Schwab's death to her mother, at least," Noah said, "and check that Fehr will definitely be back in Bern tonight. You can pick her up first thing tomorrow morning."

Renzo assumed that "first thing" wouldn't interfere with his and Giuliana's Wednesday workout and breakfast. He was eager to tell Giuliana about Louise. Not just for the sake of the case, but because he knew Giuliana would find her life as interesting as he did.

He jogged to his car in its illegal parking place on Gerechtigkeitsgasse, passing the blindfolded statue of Justice that crowned the medieval fountain at the head of the street. He'd seen it countless times, but this time Justice's strong features, full figure, and cornflower-blue robe reminded him of the young Louise in her blue T-shirt.

15

Nordring police station,
Tuesday afternoon, June 18

Shortly before Niklaus was due to arrive, Renzo found Erwin in the case-room. With the detective's bulk squeezed in behind his desk, the room seemed even more cramped than usual. Renzo perched himself on a low filing cabinet across from his superior.

Erwin leaned forward. "Here's my plan. I'm going to turn this old farmer inside out. You're going to listen, although you can ask a question now and then if something hits you. That won't mess me up. When we're done, unless we've got a confession and are locking the guy up, you're going to take him to the cafeteria, buy him a coffee, agree that I'm a mean bastard, and try to get more out of him. Right?"

"Right," Renzo said. "Want me to meet him at reception and make nice on the way to the interview room?"

"Good idea."

When the call from the front desk came in, Renzo hustled down to the foyer, thinking about Erwin. He recalled a colleague's words: "Just being locked up with the Old Man would make anyone babble." It was hard to put a finger on how Erwin managed to generate so much menace—Renzo wished he could do it.

Seventy-six-year-old Niklaus had been through the metal detector and was waiting in one of the faded blue chairs at the bottom of the stairs. Here was someone who really did look like an old man; years of sun, wind, and work had left him stooped and gnarled. The dome of his head was covered with sunspots above a ring of white hair, and his fingers were lumpy with arthritis. But his handshake was strong and brisk, and his gaze, as he took Renzo in, was penetrating. He was quiet on the way to the interview room, but there was something calm and poised about his silence. Even once he was seated, facing the two of them across a scarred metal table in the basement den, he came across to Renzo as a man with nothing to worry about.

Before Erwin could begin, Niklaus spoke up in his thick Seeland accent. "I haven't been to Bern since last Christmas. I might go on a tour of the Federal Palace while I'm here—always wanted to do that. So, let's get this over with, because you're wasting my time, and I'm wasting yours."

Renzo had to suppress a smile at this, but Erwin frowned. "Why don't you let me be the judge of that?" he said. "How long did you know François Schwab?"

"Since he was born—I'm eight months older. We grew up on the same street."

"How did you get along?"

"Always together when we were small. Then Frank's family moved to Biel, but Frank spent the holidays on his great-uncle's farm. I was jumpy as a cricket waiting for him to arrive. We worked like mules in the fields every summer, but we had fun. When we got older, we chased girls together. And mostly got 'em, too. But that's not what you want to hear about, is it?" He gave a wry grin.

Erwin didn't smile back. "Tell us about your friendship going sour."

"You mean over his hare-brained *bio* farming?" Niklaus sat back in his chair with an exasperated shrug. "All that organic horseshit! I thought when he inherited the farm that the hard work and good times would start up again. But the silly chump came back from America on a crusade. Chemicals in the dirt! In the water! In the air!

The more he preached, the more he pissed me off. As if what we'd all done for generations wasn't good enough for him. Ask my wife, she'll tell you—sometimes it just about broke my heart. He turned that farm into a goddamned commune full of useless jerk-offs." Niklaus glared at Erwin as if he were to blame for Frank's going off the rails.

"What took you over to his place last Friday afternoon?" Erwin asked.

"What?" Niklaus frowned and shook his head. "I wasn't there last Friday. God forbid my boots with their evil chemicals should pollute his precious soil."

Erwin pushed on as if he hadn't heard. "What did he say that made you hit him? He was the neighbor from hell. Always complaining, always knowing best. What was the final drop that made the bucket overflow?"

The old farmer stared at Erwin. To Renzo he looked tired—sad, even. But he did not look frightened. "Listen, you. Frank could be a bossy son-of-a-bitch, and I've wanted to whack him upside the head a hundred times. But I'd no more kill him than I'd kill Grace, that grumpy old mare of his."

Renzo realized he bought this, even as he wanted not to.

But Erwin pressed harder. "I don't believe you." He leaned forward, his hands planted on the table between them, until his face was right in the old man's. "Tell me. What happened on Friday?"

Niklaus leaned away from Erwin's loud voice and his glare, his thrusting shoulders and bunched biceps. But he still appeared more surprised than scared. He gave a slight smile and a shrug. "I spent all of last Friday afternoon out on my land, except when I came inside around four fifteen. I drank some coffee, ate a bit of leftover pie, had a chat with my old woman, and phoned the idiot who's supposed to be fixing my potato harvester."

"Did anyone besides your wife see you during the afternoon?" Renzo asked.

"I saw some people, and they saw me. What you mean is, could I have walked over to Frank's place, beat him to death, sprayed him with pesticide, and been home in time for coffee without anyone noticing? Yep, I could have done that. But I didn't, and I never would. What would be the point? Things between us were never going to be like they used to be. I've had to live with that for the last fifty years. Why would I let it get to me now?"

They sat in silence for a moment, Erwin no doubt hoping Niklaus would keep talking. But the trick didn't work. Niklaus sat impassively, looking from one of them to the other.

Erwin spent another half an hour trying to startle, browbeat, and cajole the old farmer, but there was no shaking his story. Finally, Erwin scraped his chair back and beckoned Renzo out into the hall. "I'm done," he said. "At least for now. We'll nail him if anything relevant turns up in the pesticide canisters on his farm. Buy him a pastry. Maybe he'll forget you're a cop."

Renzo privately thought Niklaus was much too canny for that. But he nodded, headed back into the interrogation room, and offered to escort Niklaus out. "Sorry for that grilling," he said, as they got to the staircase. "Why don't you let me get you a coffee before you go? Our cafeteria's just down the hall."

Niklaus pursed his lips, looking toward the way out. Then he shrugged. "I never turn down free coffee. Lead the way."

The basement café was quiet at that hour, with only a few groups talking shop as they lingered over late lunches. Niklaus put a large, milky coffee and a jelly donut onto his tray, and, having unloaded them at a table, held out his hand to Renzo. "No more Herr Niklaus, you hear. I'm Jean-Pierre."

Renzo smiled at him as they sat down. "I've been out to a few of the Seeland farms now. It seems like backbreaking work. Do you think you'll retire soon?"

"Of course. My wife'll kill me if I don't."

"My father was a fireman," Renzo told Jean-Pierre, "which meant his retirement age was fixed. He had to stop, but he didn't want to. After he left the job, he felt . . . smaller, maybe?"

Niklaus smiled. "Well, not me—I plan to enjoy my retirement.

I'm just waiting for my younger daughter, Jeanne, to get through her studies. She's in Zürich at the ETH."

That was interesting—the best institute of technology in Switzerland. Renzo tried not to look surprised. "Did you go there too?" he asked.

Jean-Pierre threw back his head and crowed. "Are you joking? I shot out of school like a wasp was after me when I turned fifteen. But my baby girl's different. She's studying to be an agronomist," Niklaus said.

"That's great. So many kids don't want to follow in their parents' footsteps. Still, it'll be hard to give up the reins, don't you think?"

"Maybe," the farmer answered. "But I don't plan to turn into one of those dads who can't stop telling his kids how to do everything. Jeanne will manage fine." He downed the last of his coffee and gave Renzo a sly look. "That other *Tschugger* kept trying to talk me into confessing that I went to Frank's on Friday. Well, I didn't."

"So you said."

"But he never asked me if I was there any *other* day last week."

Renzo stared back at Niklaus, who was clearly waiting for him to respond. "So . . . were you?"

"I sure was. And I think what Frank and I talked about was important. But your buddy seemed more interested in hassling me than finding out what I know, so . . ."

Renzo couldn't help but laugh. "You old fox," he said. "Were you going to walk out of here without telling us your piece of news?"

"You never asked me, did you?" Jean-Pierre answered smugly. "But now that you've bought me coffee and a *Berliner*, well . . ."

"Please, Herr Niklaus," Renzo intoned, "the *Kantonspolizei* would be very grateful if you'd give us information about the death of your neighbor François Schwab. Come on, Jean-Pierre," he added, in a normal voice, "don't you want to help us catch this bastard?"

"I do," said the farmer, "and that means you need to take a good look at that little shit Simu. Do you know what that lazy turd was doing? He was soaking his dope field in fungicide. Commercial fungicide, on Frank's land!"

"You mean you knew about the marijuana?"

"Jesus, man, do you think I'm pea-brained? I know what crops my neighbors grow. The kid's stuff isn't as smelly as some hemp, but it still reeks. I watched the boy trotting back and forth to that field, and I kept an eye on him, although I figured Frank wouldn't let anything happen that he didn't approve of. Then, a couple of weeks ago, I was out at night with my dog, who ended up leading me to Simu. The kid was spraying. Plants probably developed mildew or botrytis after the last heavy rains." He sighed. "You'd think I would have felt nothing but glee, wouldn't you, to see Frank get his comeuppance—and from his little pal, too. But it made me mad as hell. I mean, Frank was a pain in the ass, but he was a sincere pain in the ass. And here was this snot-nosed brat, fucking him over."

"Maybe Frank didn't care about the fungicide as long as he made money on the dope."

Jean-Pierre stared at him. "Haven't you listened to a word I've said?" He rocked back in his chair. "Sorry, Renzo. No offense. But Frank would never contaminate his land on purpose, not even one field. And he didn't give a shit about money."

"Everyone cares about money."

"Frank wanted to live a decent life, treat his friends to a round of beers now and then, and grow his vegetables. He always had enough to do that: he had no incentive to make any more. I'd swear it on a stack of Bibles."

Not to mention Frank's rich lover. Louise Fehr's wealth would have given Frank the courage to take risks without worrying about the financial consequences. Renzo decided Jean-Pierre was probably right about the money. "So, you caught Simu spraying fungicide on the marijuana plants. What did you do?"

The old man shrugged. "Nothing. Afterward, though, I thought about it, and I decided I couldn't let it go. So last Wednesday evening, when the kid's car wasn't there, I did put my evil boots on Frank's land"—he cocked one eyebrow at Renzo—"but only on the path leading to his back door. I walked right in there and told him. Believe it or not, I felt bad. I don't know what Frank saw in that boy, but he cared about him."

"So Wednesday night you told Frank that Simu was secretly using fungicide, and by Friday evening Frank was dead."

"That's it."

"Fungicide. Not pesticide."

Jean-Pierre gave Renzo a withering eye-roll. "A fungicide is a kind of pesticide. So is herbicide. Whatever gets ride of bugs, slugs, fungi, bacteria, diseases, even weeds—all the stuff we hate—it's all pesticide."

Jesus! Why the hell hadn't Niklaus given the police this information about Simu spraying the moment he heard Frank was dead? Renzo liked the stubborn old bastard, but he wanted to shake him. Instead, he turned to the formalities. "You told us you were out on your land most of Friday afternoon. But you went inside for coffee and pie. Who can confirm that?"

Jean-Pierre opened his mouth to answer, relaxed as ever. Then he paused and cleared his throat, a wary look coming into his eyes. In fact, his whole body had stiffened. Had something happened on Friday afternoon that he didn't want Renzo to know about? Renzo had no idea what it might be, so he waited until the old man answered his question.

"I . . . I already told that other copper—I was with my wife. Some of my pickers would've seen me going in and out, too. I'll have to think about it, but I'm sure I can give you names. Shall I phone back later this afternoon? Just tell me when." Ha! The old fox had suddenly become a rabbit.

Renzo decided to play dumb. "No need for that," he said. "Now, before you go, are there any more secrets up your sleeve?"

"Nope. That's it," chirped Jean-Pierre, already on his feet. "Thanks for the coffee, son. I'm off to see about that tour of the Federal Palace."

Renzo escorted Jean-Pierre to the street door and stood staring after his stooped figure as he walked away. Then he went back to his desk and checked online. Lots of Niklauses in and around Haldiz, but only one J-P. The name listed next to his was Margret—and she answered the phone.

"Your husband was here for a routine interview," he explained after introducing himself. "We talked about the Friday afternoon that your neighbor, Herr Schwab, was killed."

"Of course. Checking his alibi," she said cheerfully. Renzo blessed TV cop shows. "You must need me to confirm it."

"Exactly," he said.

She sounded delighted to tell him all about Jean-Pierre's rest after lunch, his meeting with one of the veg-picker bosses, and his late-afternoon snack. So far, nothing that contradicted Jean-Pierre's own statement.

"Our Jeanne and her boyfriend had supper with us that evening," she added, "but they were out when Jean-Pierre came in at four."

"Visiting friends?"

"No, no, they were busy. They're both studying farming, see, and they're working on a project that involves questioning some of the other farmers in town and touring their fields. They got home *filthy*. I wouldn't let them sit down at the table until they'd both had showers and changed clothes."

After the phone call, Renzo sat back in his chair. Was this what had spooked Jean-Pierre? Had he remembered that his daughter had been around Haldiz the afternoon Frank was killed, and decided to keep her out of the inquiry? It was understandable that he'd want to protect her from unpleasantness. But Renzo thought the old man had seemed frightened. Worried the police would suspect Jeanne? Why, for God's sake?

Her mother had made her shower when she got home. Had she reeked of pesticide?

His phone, lying on the desk in front of him, told him it was after four. He decided to think about Niklaus and his daughter later. First thing to do was pass all this on to Erwin. Particularly the revelation about Etter using fungicide on his crop. They'd look for traces of fungicide on the marijuana from Frank's field and in Etter's apartment, assuming they found some there.

Hurrying down the corridor to the detectives' case-room, Renzo crashed into Giuliana as she left the bathroom. Automatically, he grabbed her upper arm to steady both of them. He felt the curve of her breast; for a moment they were face-to-face, inches apart. His eyes took in her expressive face framed by waves of almost-black hair. Then he stepped back.

"Whoops! Sorry about that," she said, and he let himself meet her dark eyes. Her smile was affectionate but casual, as ever. Weeks of meeting at the gym and having breakfast together; countless encounters in the building like this; hours of working together on cases; and there was still nothing but friendship in her expression.

He dived into speech to fill the silence. "Hey! Your boy Etter—have you been in his apartment yet? Find any weed?"

"Yep."

"Tell the lab to look for traces of fungicide in his apartment; in his car, too. Frank's neighbor told me Etter sprayed the stuff on his supposedly organic marijuana—which means he sprayed it on Frank's land—and Frank found out just before he died. I'm on my way to tell Erwin."

She gave a whistle. "Whoa! Talk about a reason for the two of them to have a falling-out."

"Exactly."

"Look, I can't stop now, but I'll be at the gym tomorrow no matter what. We'll talk at breakfast, okay?"

He watched her walk down the corridor toward the stairs and called after her, "See you then."

She lifted a hand without looking back, and he remembered what she'd been doing that morning—talking to Simu Etter's family about his death.

16

Deisswil and Bern's Länggasse neighborhood,
Tuesday morning, June 18

"Tell me about Etter's mother and sister," Giuliana said to Sabine.

They'd taken Giuliana's Volvo—Sabine never drove when she could avoid it—and were on the *Autobahn* traveling north toward the village of Deisswil. Giuliana hadn't noticed at the staff meeting that Sabine was as somberly dressed as she was. That morning she'd reached for a brightly patterned shirt to go with her black trousers and blazer, and passed it up for grey-and-white stripes. Sabine had gone for shades of brown. The Etter family would probably be too upset to register what the policewomen were wearing, but colors had still seemed wrong.

"Simon was the baby of the family," said Sabine, turning as far toward her colleague as her seatbelt allowed. "His oldest sister is forty-three and the other two are in their thirties; he was twenty-four. All three women are married with kids, working part-time. No one divorced, no husbands out of work, no one with any record beyond the occasional parking and speeding tickets. On the surface, a conventional, well-behaved Swiss family."

"The mother is in her sixties, then."

"Sixty-eight. The husband was ten years older and died three years ago of complications from diabetes. I found her old-fashioned and fragile even for a woman of that generation." Sabine raised her eyebrows at Giuliana, and they both grinned. Sabine was a very non-fragile sixty-two.

"Traditional, huh? So what do you think? Was she against women finally getting the vote in 1971?" Giuliana asked, only partially as a joke.

Sabine waggled a flat hand back and forth in the air. "Could be. If Papa thought it was a bad idea. But my guess is she didn't know what women's suffrage *was* then."

Giuliana grimaced and then grew sober as the face of Frau Etter's dead son, full of the liveliness that Bruno's sketch had given it, floated into her mind. "What about the sister?" she asked. "Melanie, is it?"

Sabine nodded. "Thank God I had her there when I saw the mother last night. It was—well, you've done it. You know what it's like, telling a parent about a child's death." Sabine turned away to gaze at a field of sugar beets flashing by outside. After a few deep breaths, she turned back and resumed her summary. "Melanie—she's the middle one—seemed sensible and kind. I couldn't get much more than an impression; she was too upset. The other two sisters and two of the brothers-in-law arrived while I was still there and, since I knew we'd be back this morning, I got out of the way and left everyone to mourn."

"Which brother-in-law asked for the private interview this morning?"

"Melanie's husband." She'd checked some notes on her phone, and added, "He's an electrician."

Etter's childhood home was a two-story stucco house on the side of a hill, one of a row of similar structures with small front and back gardens that had been stamped with personality by the hedges, trees, and flower beds that surrounded them. The path Sabine and Giuliana followed to the front door was flanked by orange and yellow marigolds that seemed, under the circumstances, painfully cheerful. The woman who opened the door to them turned out to be the oldest sister. She did not smile, and it was not just grief that kept her face stony. Her expression of barely suppressed anger was echoed on the faces of the two younger women who waited for them at the mahogany dining-room table on either side of their mother. *Uh-oh*, thought Giuliana, *I bet they watched the news last night and read the papers this morning. It may comfort the public to find out that the man who died during the riots was "only" a dealer. But for his family . . .*

Simu's sisters seemed to have protected his mother from the press. Her red eyes, swollen face, and shaking hands spoke of nothing but unbearable sadness. She could scarcely sit upright, let alone answer questions about her son, and after ten minutes of trying, she was supported by her oldest daughter to an upstairs bedroom.

Before her mother was halfway up the stairs, the youngest daughter, who was pregnant, leaned across the table toward the policewomen and spat, "Why should we answer your questions? From what I've read in the papers, it sounds like everyone's glad our brother's dead. Are the police even going to bother to investigate his death? After all, either a cop killed him or one of his fellow druggies did—that's what everyone seems to think. No one thinks about the fact that he was our brother and we . . . loved him." During this last sentence, her voice broke, but, even as she gave a harsh sob, she kept glaring at them.

Giuliana opened her mouth to answer, but before she could speak, Melanie, the middle sister, said, "We knew Simu sold marijuana. Our mother thinks when he died he was still at university working on a business degree, but he dropped out two years ago. We were more concerned with protecting Mam from disappointment than doing something about Simu. I tried to persuade myself it was just a hobby, something to supplement his income—after all, he was working at the post office. Now I can't tell you"—she drew a shaky breath—"I can't tell you how much I wish we'd confronted him months ago. We kept him in line when he was little. But I guess we also spoiled him. He was the baby—such a lovely boy. Oh God. Please tell us: what happened to him that night?"

"We know what happened. A policeman beat him on the head

until he died, and now you're here to cover it up," said the oldest sister from the doorway.

Giuliana and Sabine hadn't been able to utter a word since Frau Etter's departure. Now they exchanged a glance. Giuliana took a deep breath and said, "As far as we know, your brother was not involved in the riot. But we believe that because he was drunk, he attacked a policeman, who responded by hitting him on the head with his baton. Someone hit him a second time, and we don't know who that was. It isn't true that we don't care. We are very eager to find his killer. So please tell us anything that you think could be relevant to his death."

"Sure you want to find his killer—any killer that isn't the guy who actually hit him. Your police colleague, I mean." That was the oldest sister again, who sat back down at the table and put her arm around the youngest, who was sobbing. *She* must have heard the TV interview with Lars. While Giuliana was formulating more soothing words, Sabine spoke.

"*Everything* that happened the night Herr Etter died is under investigation. I'm sorry we can't tell you all about it right now, but I can assure you that we won't let anybody get away with killing him, including a policeman. If you know anything about your brother's activities—not just his marijuana sales but anything at all—that might have gotten him killed, you should tell us."

No one spoke. The pregnant sister was still crying.

"He changed girlfriends pretty often," Melanie said at last. Giuliana heard both censure and affection in her comment. "Remember Annina?" she asked the other two. The youngest sister straightened up and blew her nose, and both women nodded. Some of the worst of their anger seemed to drain out of the room. "What an airhead!"

They'd loved their little brother, Giuliana could see that, and liked the adult he'd become. Their feelings of affection were hard to reconcile with the behavior of a man who, if Jürg Thönen was right, must have fought his way into the A-League of drug dealing and joined the world of serious narcotics. In her mind, it was only illegal to grow and sell marijuana, but it was not only illegal but also evil to sell heroin and other opiates, not to mention methamphetamines. For her, the crimes were worlds apart.

But had Etter really been a part of that second world? So far, nothing she'd learned about him indicated that a drug baron or his hired thug had had any reason to pick up Jonas's baton and give Etter the second blow that had killed him. Even Jonas himself as a murderer seemed to make more sense than that—so far. But the investigation had barely begun.

As Giuliana wondered about Etter, Sabine was encouraging Melanie. "You're saying we should look into the possibility that your brother's death had something to do with jealousy. A boyfriend, a husband, an ex-lover. Good. We'll do that. Anything else?"

Sabine was able to wring the names of several other girlfriends besides Annina out of the sisters, and they produced some anecdotes about his boss and work colleagues, but it was clear they couldn't imagine a reason why anyone would want to hurt their Simu.

When Sabine appeared to have drained them of every relevant idea, Giuliana risked another outburst of anger by asking, "You say you were aware of your brother selling marijuana, and we have evidence for that. Do you have any reason to think he had recently started to handle harder drugs?"

"Absolutely not," said the oldest, frowning. Melanie stirred but said nothing. Deciding to wait with follow-up until she had more evidence, Giuliana asked them for recent photos of Etter, and the youngest started searching her phone, apparently glad of a distraction. Melanie beckoned Giuliana unobtrusively into the kitchen and began putting together a large salad.

"Simu was talking about expanding his business," she told Giuliana as she sliced radishes and added them to a bowl of romaine lettuce, "but only by growing more pot. I'd swear he had no other plans. He talked to Roman, my husband, about what he was up to, and to me again last week. You've got our address, right? Our apartment's close by. Roman's expecting you. It's best if you talk to him alone. One of these days I'll tell the girls, but not right now."

She placed a cucumber on the large wooden cutting board, and then her head drooped. "Simu and I were close, and he really got along with Roman. We should have tried to stop him. Why didn't we?" First one tear, then another, fell onto the cucumber.

Giuliana put a hand on the younger woman's shoulder. "At twenty-four, he was a grown man, at least in his own mind. I doubt he would have listened to you; you might have achieved nothing more than ruining your relationship with him. He was apparently quite good at what he did," she added. "In places where weed is legal, he'd have been a successful farmer and salesman, not a criminal. So don't reproach yourself."

Melanie nodded and gave a twitch of a smile, but she didn't look up. Giuliana left the kitchen and stood for a moment in the hall, galvanized. There *had* been something new going on just before Etter died. Finally, she might find a change in the pattern, a reason for Simu to die. Until now she'd been dutifully investigating Etter's life. Now she was excited.

She went back into the dining room, made sure Sabine had plenty of photos of Etter, and took leave of the sisters. As soon as they were outside, she briefed Sabine. Five minutes later, they drove up to a former farmhouse-and-barn complex that had been converted into apartments. They rang the bell that read R. & M. Aebi-Etter. A wiry man of about thirty-five came to the door. He wore a once-white T-shirt and cut-off jeans and carried a toddler in his arms. Both he and his child—the sex was indeterminate—had shocks of unruly black hair.

"Roman Aebi," he said, holding out his hand. He led them into an open kitchen area, plonked the kid on the floor in front of television cartoons, and pointed at a sofa before sitting down himself on the edge of an armchair. No offers of coffee, no small talk. An efficient man: Giuliana breathed a tiny sigh of relief. No angry outbursts about evil cops, either—so far.

"Please tell us what's on your mind, Herr Aebi," she said.

"Simu was closer to Melanie than to the other two girls," Aebi began, "so we saw him about once a month. I know you know he sold weed. I don't know when he started dealing, but it was before university. When he dropped out of the business program there, it was because he got a chance to grow the stuff himself as well as sell it. Being his own supplier, he could make much more money. He was a good businessman, with or without a university degree."

It wasn't hard to imagine how Etter's sister and brother-in-law had learned he sold weed; he'd probably offered to sell them some.

"Did something change recently that you think could have led to his death?" Giuliana asked. She felt like crossing her fingers—surely her excitement wouldn't be for nothing.

"Yes, that's why I wanted to see you. Simu told me he needed money to expand."

Giuliana and Sabine couldn't help exchanging a grin, which Aebi missed, since he was looking away from them toward his child, frowning. He went on.

"About two months ago, in late April, right after he got his crop planted for the second year, he wanted me to lend him two hundred thousand Swiss francs. Actually, he was asking me to invest in his business. He planned to set up a big indoor growing facility, hire a gardener, create a salesforce—the works. He seemed to have a good business plan, but I said no. We have a mortgage and two small kids. I don't have twenty thousand francs to invest in a new and risky business, let along ten times that much. So Simu asked me to co-sign a bank loan, if he could somehow finagle one. I talked to Melanie, and we decided not to do anything to help him. For lots of reasons. Including that it was illegal." He stopped suddenly and sighed. Then silence.

"Was he angry?" asked Sabine at last.

"I figured he'd storm out, but he took it calmly. Disappointed, yes, but he said he understood. He could find someone in the drug business who'd help him, he said. He'd just wanted to give us a chance to buy into a good thing, to get in on the ground floor. He loved business jargon like that."

"Someone in the drug business," Giuliana repeated. The elation she'd felt in Frau Etter's kitchen bubbled up. Maybe the frame the commandant had built around her investigation, constraining as she found it, held a true picture. If Etter had done a deal with someone way over his head in the hierarchy and then reneged . . .

"Do you know what happened next?" she asked.

"All I know is that this past Saturday Simu called to wish Leon"—he pointed at the toddler in front of the TV—"a happy birthday, and he told Melanie that everything was working out perfectly. That he'd be able to have his cake and eat it, too. That's what he said. She said he sounded proud of himself, like he'd done something clever. She asked him if he was getting in over his head and told him to be careful. He just laughed. Afterward, we talked about it. I told her not to worry. But—" He paused, and Giuliana realized he was struggling with his emotions. "I was wrong, wasn't I?" He got up and began an aimless walk around the room, fists clenched and face scrunched, fighting tears. "Stupid bastard," he yelled and banged his fist on a window frame, causing Leon to take his thumb out of his mouth, stare at his father, and let out a wail. Roman strode over to the boy, scooped him up, and held him tight. "He was Leon's godfather," he said. "Leon won't remember Simu at all when he grows up. That's . . . It's so unfair."

"I'm sorry," said Giuliana.

"You're sure that cop didn't kill him, right? You'd better be." He glared at them, and the little boy cried even louder. "Sorry," he said, and Giuliana wasn't sure if he was talking to them or his son. It was definitely time to leave. He and his wife would need to provide and sign official statements at the police station about Simu's plans, but that could wait a day or two. By now, the crime scene specialists would have finished going over Etter's apartment, and she wanted to have a look at it. Meanwhile, Sabine would interview bosses and coworkers at the letter-sorting center where Etter had worked.

"This talk about Etter looking for an investor in his dope plantation is great, but I don't want to reject the sisters' jealousy idea," Giuliana said, as she drove Sabine to her meetings at Etter's workplace. "I can imagine it, can't you? Two drunk men meeting accidentally on the night of the Dance-In, one angry with the other for stealing his girl; Jonas confronting them; and afterward the police baton lying conveniently there for the jealous boyfriend to grab up."

Sabine was nodding. "I don't know if you heard, but two of the ex-girlfriends the sisters named are women who worked with him, so I'll ask about them today. And follow up on some of the other names as soon as possible."

"Sounds good. You focus on his love life for the time being, and I'll keep after the drugs. Hopefully his laptop is in the apartment; that'll give us a list of his customers. Maybe we'll find his phone. Even if we don't, the phone company should have a call list for us by the end of the day. That'll give us everyone—friends, girlfriends, and buyers. Should keep us both busy for quite a while. And we'll ask Heinz and his team to help."

"Okay." Sabine leaned back in her seat and closed her eyes, and Giuliana was content with silence for a while. She was thinking about what Roman Aebi had said: *You're sure that cop didn't kill him, right?* She felt sure, but that wasn't the same thing as knowing it.

Giuliana dropped Sabine at the postal center and drove on to Etter's one-bedroom apartment. The official searchers weren't finished, it seemed, since their van was still in front of the house, so she put on paper shoe covers, a cap, and latex gloves, just to be careful.

Jan, the man in charge of the three-person search team, was a familiar figure from many crime scenes. With his white overall making him look even plumper than he already was, he stood in the apartment's small, neat kitchen gazing at a row of keys, and when he heard her steps, his eyes above his mask crinkled into a smile.

"Giuliana!" he said. She was reminded of how collegial Jan was, eager to share useful information with investigators rather than jealously guarding his territory against invaders. "You've come just in time to investigate the cellar lockup with me. The most interesting thing about the apartment so far is what isn't here—there's a cord in the bedroom for plugging in a laptop, but it's missing. No cell phone, either, but I'd assumed anyway that was taken off the body."

She sighed. Not having Etter's laptop was a blow. "Any other interesting keys?" she asked, even as she walked over to inspect them herself. They hung on nails just inside the kitchen doorway, keys on simple rings with red plastic labels: Cellar, Storage, Car. What luck to have found a car key! She had the car's make and license plate number from the Department of Motor Vehicles, but she'd assumed it would have to be broken into it once it turned up. Now all they had to do was find the right Hyundai Kona on a nearby street.

"Storage," she commented to Jan. "Does the building have attic storage cupboards for the tenants?"

Jan shook his head. "Just in the cellar. I'm guessing he's rented storage somewhere." She nodded, and together they walked down into the basement shared by all eight apartments, which had a laundry room and eight locked doors on either side of a hall. These weren't labeled, but it didn't take long to find the right lock for Etter's "Cellar" key. Letting Jan flip on the light switch just inside the heavy door, she walked into a small windowless room. The smell of marijuana rolled over her like a truck. From the open doorway she could see that all four walls contained floor-to-ceiling metal shelving units filled with plastic storage bins, clearly not as airtight as they looked. Jan started opening these methodically. At least two-thirds of them were empty, and the rest contained dated Mason jars full of cannabis. There was also a box of Minigrip Redline resealable plastic bags in different sizes, and another box with rolling papers and some premade joints, also in Mason jars. The jars gave everything a homey touch, but otherwise the setup looked very professional.

"Nice to deal with such an orderly victim, for a change," Jan said. "Okay if I get my crew to start fingerprinting in here? And we'll take a couple of samples from different jars."

"Do whatever you need to, and then lock it back up," she told him. "I'll ask Jürg Thönen from Narcotics to get one of his people to check this over when you're done, just in case it reveals something special about his marijuana sales."

She went upstairs to find Jan's two helpers standing in the apartment kitchen and, after checking that she could move freely around the apartment, she sent them down to him and began to prowl around Etter's place. As Jan had said, the one-bedroom flat was neat and relatively clean. It had bright IKEA furniture, healthy houseplants, and a framed poster over the sofa of snow-covered mountains. She took her time, opening kitchen cabinets and drawers and searching through Etter's clothes, wanting to get a better sense of what he'd been like.

There was a large dining-room table that was also used as a desk. The stacks arranged on it (plus one drawer in the bedroom) revealed a normal life's paperwork. Bills, receipts, scribbled lists, take-out pizza flyers, and ads for upcoming music festivals: she gathered all of it up and put it in a large grocery bag she found in the kitchen. But no computer and no phone! All that data somewhere, all that information about his contacts, and she couldn't get her hands on it.

So what did the "Storage" key unlock? Probably his drying room, along with a further collection of filled Mason jars. Although perhaps not all filled—Etter's first marijuana field had been harvested the previous October, and now it was late June. He'd have been starting to run low on supplies, she imagined.

She photographed the key and emailed the image to Heinz, then phoned to ask him to start checking with professional storage facilities about Etter's unit, emailing each business a photo of Etter—and of the key. With that done, she left the apartment, taking the grocery bag full of paperwork with her. She and Sabine would go through it for signs of a bill for storage rental. Or Etter's bank account might tell them that. She was still waiting for his financial records to come in. In any case, all the paper would need to be sorted back at the station.

It was almost two. Etter's apartment was near the university, and the neighborhood was full of small restaurants. She found a parking place in front of one café, sat at an outdoor table, and ordered the fastest thing they could serve her, which was a bowl of cold potato soup with a thick slice of brown bread. As she ate, she tried Ueli, hoping to make up for their impasse of the night before, but only his voice mail answered. "Just thinking of you," she said.

After she'd paid, she leaned back in her chair and idly watched three sparrows fight over a bread crust in the gravel of the restaurant's sunny courtyard. She'd allow herself a few moments to sit in the shade of the awning and do nothing. But even as she felt some of the tension draining out of her, her phone rang.

"Hello, Rolf. I'm . . ."

"The commandant wants to see you." Rolf's voice, always gravelly, sounded ominous. "He watched a tape of the Reitschule press conference. I saw it, too. Lars Gehrig says . . . uncomfortable things. Some of them appear to be about you."

Oh, shit! She should have prepared herself for this. But she'd thought the insinuations she'd heard on the TV the night before were more embarrassing than career threatening.

"I assume he wants to talk about my asking Lars to help us identify Etter. I don't know what Lars said"—only a small white lie—"but we know the man distorts the facts to please the press. Particularly on the subject of the police. I'm surprised the commandant is taking him seriously." Good. Puzzled but not defensive; that was the right approach. She hadn't, in fact, done anything wrong. Maybe it hadn't been smart to say to someone like Lars, "I don't care what you say to the press." But the truth was she didn't. At least, not much.

"I okayed your going over to the Riding School in the first place, and I know it was a friend of yours there who identified the dead boy in time for the police press conference." Rolf's voice sounded lighter already. "But that friend wasn't Gehrig, right?"

"No. *He* promised to help and then disappeared until time for his own press conference." She paused and decided to take a risk. "Listen, Rolf. Would it be all right if I kept my appointment at three with Jürg? He's bringing in one of his young informants to talk to me about Etter. I don't have time to talk to the commandant before that. Could you ask him if I can stop by his office around five?"

"I'll do that. If he still insists on seeing you now, he can call you back himself." Rolf was growling again but not at her. Good old Rolf. He always tried to protect his people from higher echelon craziness. In the meantime, she'd mull over what to say to the commandant. If only she knew what else Lars had said, besides the few words she'd heard on the news. Ha! His press conference was probably on YouTube; she could have a quick look.

So much for taking a break. She got into her car and headed to her meeting with Jürg.

17

Guisanplatz and Nordring police station,
Tuesday afternoon, June 18

Jürg Thönen undermined every narc stereotype perpetuated by TV. Giuliana couldn't imagine him exchanging gunshots with a meth manufacturer or terrifying teenagers until they ratted on their suppliers. He reminded her of her favorite eighth-grade teacher, the one who had roughhoused with the boys but still kept discipline and listened to the girls' problems without crossing any lines. The one who'd made almost anything he explained interesting—as Jürg was now doing for her on a subject her teacher had never touched upon: illegal drugs.

"Swiss-grown marijuana keeps itself separate from any other drug dealing," he told her. "It's all small groups of relatives or friends, three or four people at most, who operate as growers and dealers with no need to mix with anyone else. They don't get involved in any other crime. Lots of their sales are through friends or over the internet; customers order online, and their dope is delivered by mail."

"And it gets through the postal system? I guess they beat the smell by vacuum packing the stuff," Giuliana broke in. She and Jürg were sitting in bright red plastic chairs at a round red table in what he jokingly called his "other" office—an achingly cheery café in a midprice chain hotel. The hotel was near an *Autobahn* entrance on the outskirts of town, and its little restaurant only existed to provide light meals and drinks to its out-of-town guests. Giuliana had never been there and couldn't imagine that many other locals would ever set foot in it, although it had its own tram stop. All of this made it a perfect place for Jürg to talk in person to his informants or undercover colleagues.

"Exactly. Or they do home deliveries. Dramas over invading each other's turf just don't exist for these guys—each operation has its own customer base. The most dangerous time is harvest, when outsiders may try to rip off a grower's whole crop just before it's picked. That can lead to shoot-outs."

"Gunfight at the Happy Hillside Farm," Giuliana said. "Bern's version of the O.K. Corral."

"Hard to believe, huh? But it used to happen fairly often. Now that most weed is grown indoors, it's rarer. The indoor plantations are harder to find, easier to guard."

"What does an indoor place cost to set up?" she asked him.

"A hundred thousand francs at the very least, and that's for something the size of a garage. First, you pay to rent or even buy the space. Then you need to set up LED lighting and automatic watering. You need a filter system to get rid of the smell and provide extra carbon dioxide. A dehumidifier is crucial, too: the plants get diseases if the air's too moist. You can achieve three harvests a year if you work at it, as opposed to one out of doors, but you have to nurse the seedlings along, prune the plants as they grow, check for blight, and keep all the equipment working well. So, tending marijuana indoors is pretty much a full-time job for at least one person, depending on the size of the growing space."

"Sounds like it requires a good farmer," Giuliana said. "Which must be why Etter was doing a sort of apprenticeship with Frank Schwab in Haldiz. From what I've seen of his stash, he was learning fast. Even his one little outdoor field must have made him a lot of money for a kid in his mid-twenties. Tell me. Suppose he decided to use all the money he'd saved from his outdoor dope business to get an indoor plantation going. With three harvests a year, he might assume he'd earn his investment back in no time. Would that be realistic?"

Jürg shook his head. "I doubt it. Don't forget Etter was a guy who, except for the old farmer's help, did everything himself. He had maybe a hundred outdoor plants in a space the size of half a basketball court. He managed to handle growing, picking, drying, storing, and selling the stuff all alone, and still hold down a part-time job. And he had no overhead: almost everything he earned, he kept. Growing indoors, he'd have had a very expensive initial investment, followed by regular rent and electricity costs. Lots of electricity! Plus, he couldn't have managed by himself; he'd have had to pay wages or have partners. So I don't think money would have come pouring in from day one. He'd have struggled at first, maybe for a year or two. As most businesses do when they expand."

"What do you think he earned this past year, selling the weed from his first field?" Giuliana asked. She hadn't seen Etter's bank statements yet, but she doubted he'd been swimming in money. She remembered his attractive but still student-sized apartment, his small Hyundai. "A hundred grand?"

"Yeah, or a hundred twenty-five, I'd guess, if his customers paid fifty francs for ten grams of weed, which would be reasonable."

"Yeah—that's a lot but still not enough," she said. "Whatever he managed to save, he could never have bankrolled his indoor spread by himself. The two hundred thousand he tried to get from his brother-in-law would have been a minimum. He'd have needed lots of cash as a cushion, in case his first year indoors was more experimental than successful. So he'd turn to a backer." Her mind switched from funding to murder. "And maybe he chose the kind of backer who takes a violent dislike to being double-crossed."

Jürg leaned back in his chair, looked up at the ceiling, and smiled as if they were dinner guests speculating on the antics of a local politician rather than cops investigating the cause of a man's death. "If so, I wonder who he chose," he murmured. "The Nigerians and Ghanaians control the cocaine trade in Bern, mainly just the street dealing—when you go higher up the ladder you come to Dominicans. The Albanians tend to have the heroin, but they also have most of the marijuana that isn't home grown—maybe twenty percent of what's on the street. Would Etter have . . ."

"I know I'm interrupting—sorry—but tell me: what about Ecstasy and methamphetamines? And the artificial opiates, like fentanyl? I know meth is made in Eastern Europe and fentanyl mainly in China, but who controls them here in Bern?"

Jürg knocked loudly on the red plastic tabletop. "So far, knock on wood, Bern doesn't have a fentanyl problem, and meth isn't a big deal—yet. Ecstasy is sold in all the clubs, but there's no large organization behind it. So, if Etter were looking for someone in the drug business to help him expand, he might have turned to the Albanians, since they already have an interest in marijuana." Jürg looked at his watch. "Sorry Ivo's late, but I think you'll find it worth the wait."

Ivo was one of Jürg's most helpful informants. He was a genuine fan of the music and company at the Riding School and several other alternative hangouts and of the marijuana he smoked there. But he'd lost a fifteen-year-old brother to an overdose of pills bought in the Riding School forecourt, and this had made him an enthusiastic spy. For the price of a meal, he was glad to tell the police anything he'd been able to pick up about the heavy drug business in Bern.

She'd never seen him, but it wasn't hard to recognize him a minute or two later when he walked into the café. A thin, sullen-faced young man standing at the bottom of the stairs, he wore a grey hoodie, frayed jeans, and dirty high-top sneakers, and his light-brown hair hung in clumps around his head. A piercing through the nasal septum reminded her of snot dangling from each nostril, and tattoos of thorny vines covered what she could see of his arms. Steel plugs had stretched his earlobes into gaping tunnels.

She stood up to greet him. "Hello, Ivo, I'm Giuliana Linder," she said, as they shook hands. "Jürg's getting us coffees." She gestured to her colleague, who was on the other side of the room, talking to a waitress behind a counter.

The smile Ivo gave her was shy, which reminded her what a strange breed informants were, driven to help the police catch criminals by everything from a desire to be important to the need for revenge on a rival. Ivo's own reasons were probably more complex than just sorrow over his brother's death.

"I hear you knew the victim, Simon Etter," she said after he sat down. "What can you tell me about him?"

"He was an okay guy. Could be kind of full of himself but had a lot of charm. Girls liked him. I never heard any talk about his ripping off customers. But I did hear a client of his complain that he was bragging about expanding."

Jürg came back just then from ordering. With his half-bald head and black-framed glasses, the older cop looked even more conventional beside Ivo, although the two greeted each other with fist bumps and chat. Giuliana waited impatiently. Expansion, Ivo had said. Here was confirmation of what Etter's brother-in-law had told her.

Their coffees came with a plateful of pastries. The young man loaded his coffee with sugar, stirred, sipped, sighed happily, grabbed a tart, ate half in one bite, and turned back to Giuliana. "Right. Etter's business. I overheard one of his clients a few weeks back saying something about mom-and-pop shops disappearing even in the world of dope. He was worried that Etter's prices would go up if he got bigger—and that his quality would go down. That got my attention. I'm not interested in little operations, but if Etter was moving into bigger circles, I wanted info. The folks who were talking didn't seem to know more. Do you?"

She summarized what she and Sabine had learned so far about Etter and his business plans; Ivo and Jürg listened. By the end Jürg was rolling his eyes.

"I can see him offering his brother-in-law a chance to invest in his expansion," Jürg said. "With a relative, Etter could pay out a portion of the profits, if there were any, knowing that if everything went to hell, the investor would have to accept his losses. But would he be naïve enough to think that taking a couple of hundred thousand francs from one of the local bosses would be safe? Did he think he could just negotiate a standard venture-capitalist deal with one of them?"

"From what everyone has told us," Giuliana said, "he was smart and hard-working but also a bit spoiled. Perhaps, with Frank's help, small-time crime had worked out so well for him that he figured he could slip into the big time without getting his hands dirty."

"That sounds like Simu," Ivo said. "There was always something happy-go-lucky about him. Part of his charm. He was exactly the kind of guy who'd think he could stick his di . . . foot into a lake full of crocodiles and never fail to yank it out in time."

"Okay," said Jürg. "I think we all have a sense of what we're looking for. Giuliana, why don't you and Ivo stay in touch directly from now on and pass on anything I need to know?"

Ivo exchanged mobile numbers with Giuliana and grabbed the last pastry. He and Jürg had more to discuss, so Giuliana said good-bye and headed for the elevator to the hotel's underground garage and her Volvo. In the lobby, a clock shaped like a cow told her it was twenty to five. Ueli. They needed to talk about dinner: who was making it and if she'd be home for it. Since leaving him a message at lunch, she hadn't checked her mobile, but now she saw he hadn't responded. This time when she phoned, he answered.

"Hi. I'm going to . . ." But she didn't have time to say that she'd be home by seven.

"Sorry I can't talk. I'm doing an interview in Thun, and I'll stay here for dinner. I've texted Isabelle that if you aren't home by six thirty, she should go around the corner and get pizzas or kebabs or whatever she and Lukas want. Okay?"

"Okay. I hope we can talk soon, though."

"We will," he said and was gone.

Lukas would be home from soccer practice at six thirty, starving. She'd try to be there by then, if she could. She could at least cut up some carrots to make the takeout a bit healthier. But first, the meeting about Lars. She found an eight-minute excerpt of his press conference on her phone and watched it.

At five on the dot, she was shaking hands with the commandant. The elegant Lilo was there once again. Giuliana didn't know if that was good or bad, but she knew the press officer was no one's friend. Her goal was to keep the police in the public eye as a force for goodness and justice. Nothing and no one else mattered.

Giuliana began speaking before she was settled in her chair. "I saw a piece of Lars Gehrig's press conference where he insinuated that I was trying to get him to help the police because I've known him since I was a teenager. That's absolutely true. Despite the tensions between the police and the Reitschule, I assumed an old acquaintance would have the decency to want to identify a dead man, so that his family could be notified. If that was a mistake, then I apologize. It was someone else I know from my days at the Reitschule who identified Etter. His assistance was not thanks to Gehrig."

"Contact with Gehrig should be approved by my office," said Lilo hotly, "or by the commandant." Giuliana noticed how reluctantly she added those last words.

"Yes, yes," the commandant said. "But our need to identify the Schützenmatte victim before our press conference was the kind of emergency that supersedes rules. Reluctant as I am to admit that." His tone was deadpan, but she thought she caught a ghost of a smile. Wow, was the commandant making fun of himself?

"Rolf also reminded me of your special background, which explains . . ." He trailed off, noticing her confusion. "Your father, your brother, your husband . . ." He waved his hands as if to imply a crowd of Greens, Reds, and lefties of all colors in her past, present, and future. Maybe someday he'd be adding, "Your daughter." But not too soon, please.

"From now on, however, don't approach the Riding School in your capacity as a policewoman without consulting Lilo or someone on her staff. Unless you are chasing a criminal." Again, a flash of humor. She was going to have to reevaluate the old stick.

"Of course," she said. What a lot of noise about nothing! But she'd gotten off lightly.

Lilo wasn't through yet. "Our office has been deflecting journalists' requests to speak to you since yesterday evening. Have you been phoned or approached?"

"No. Although I haven't checked my landline yet."

"It goes without saying—no press contact at all. That's imperative."

"I can promise you that," Giuliana said grimly, thinking of her conflict with Ueli. Lilo looked slightly reassured.

Giuliana left the office with a lighter heart. So Rolf had reminded the commandant that the infamous Max Linder was her father. Did either of them remember that she'd had a job in her father's defense practice during her first year out of law school, before growing so disillusioned that she'd spent another half-year working for the city as a prosecutor?

That had been a dark time in her life, when she'd despaired of the law as a profession. Only with Ueli had she discussed her changing ideals. Policing could be a form of social service, she'd told her initially horrified husband. Being a prosecutor, she'd explained, had showed her that most crime victims—drunks, prostitutes, frail old women, immigrants with bad German, abused wives, and so many others—were also underdogs who needed protecting. She thought he'd agreed with her. Why had their ideas of policing grown so far apart since then?

A glance at her phone showed her that the dreaded meeting with the commandant had sailed by so quickly that it was only five thirty. She still had time for a chat with Sabine about her interviews with Etter's post office colleagues before driving home. Pizza or kebabs? She'd let the kids decide.

18

Bern's Lorraine neighborhood, Wednesday morning, June 19

Dressed in sweats, Giuliana wheeled her bike out of the garage and shivered in the chill of early morning. Five minutes later, she rode over the Kirchenfeld Bridge, glancing up as she always did at the lacy spire of the *Münster* against the sky. In the quiet of a still-sleeping city, she heard the roar of the Aare flooding over the weir more than a hundred feet below her. She swooped past the *Zytglogge*, glad that gym mornings gave her a chance to see the city center so empty. When she rode her bike home that evening, the streets under the medieval clock tower would be an obstacle course of trams, buses, bikes, taxis, and darting pedestrians, made even more chaotic by the construction ditch down the middle of the main street.

Riding past the art museum toward the Lorraine Bridge, which took her over another loop of the Aare, the aftermath of the riots was still visible. The burned-out cars she'd seen on Monday morning had been removed, but the scorch marks were there, and some storefronts were still boarded up. She tried to cling to her early-morning tranquility, but she felt it slipping away in the face of so many reminders of Saturday night's violence. On the bridge she slowed deliberately and gazed to her right, where behind the skyline of Bern the Alps were displayed across the entire horizon, a panorama of jagged peaks and gleaming snow that never failed to put things into perspective, at least for the space of a few indrawn breaths.

Gritting her teeth, Giuliana left the Alps behind and sprinted from the far end of the Lorraine Bridge to the police station, pedaling like mad. Out of breath, she locked her bike onto a rack behind the station and jogged across the street to the gym, bag slung over her shoulder. She felt wide awake at last, despite a late night reading reports from investigators, examining deposits to and withdrawals from Etter's bank account, and writing her own report. When she'd fallen asleep, Ueli had still not been home from Thun.

She found Renzo rowing. He always got to the gym at least half an hour before she did, to work with weights. Then, while she did her exercises, he usually rowed.

"Morning!" he called, without breaking rhythm. His breathing wasn't even ragged. "I know you just can't wait to get started."

She grinned, stuck her tongue out at him, and adjusted the weights on the first machine. She despised working out. But after she realized she was starting to lose her physical edge, she'd let Renzo set her up with a forty-five-minute routine of floor exercises and weight lifting. For almost six months now she'd kept at it, once or twice a week, and it had made her stronger, faster, and fitter in every way. But there was no enjoyment in it, just satisfaction at having done it. The only pleasure she got during the whole sweaty, painful endeavor was Renzo's rowing. As she rested during sets she watched his body move smoothly back and forth on the machine, his arm and leg muscles tensing and relaxing, his shoulders bunching, the cords in his neck standing out, the sweat plastering his light-brown hair to his skull. Every once in a while, he'd turn his head, catch her eyes, and smile at her, but he never lost his rhythm. At these moments, she let herself enjoy how beautiful he was—and how sexy. The rest of the time she tried very hard to classify him in her mind with her younger brother, Paolo. They were two charming men who knew how to get almost anyone to talk to them. They charmed her, too, but she at least saw through them and laughed at them.

By seven forty-five, she and Renzo were sitting at the next-door bakery café over hot-milk coffee and pastries, both of them dressed for work. Giuliana sipped her *Schale* as she quickly brought Renzo up to date on Etter and his quest for someone with at least CHF 200,000 to invest in his plantation. "Do you think he asked Frank?"

Renzo, munching his way through his first croissant, washed a bite down with coffee and said, "I don't know. But Frank could have afforded it. Even if he didn't have the money, his lover did." He explained what he'd learned about Louise Fehr and then, for good measure, told Giuliana about Jean-Pierre Niklaus and his daughter Jeanne and her boyfriend, who'd probably been on or near Frank's farm when he'd been killed.

Giuliana frowned and tried to fit the different sets of players into patterns that could justify a murder.

"It's hard to imagine Etter turning to Niklaus or his daughter for money, or their being interested," she said. "The old man's eager to retire, and the girl doesn't have a job."

"Yep," said Renzo. "I don't know about Jeanne, but I can't see Jean-Pierre growing dope. That truly doesn't compute. I agree that Etter might have asked Frank for money. But would he kill him for it?"

"No one who's talked about Etter has made him sound violent or even suggested he had a temper," Giuliana said, breaking her own whole-wheat croissant in half and biting off a crunchy end. "But if Frank had promised to lend him money and then pulled out at the last minute . . . It still doesn't work for me, though. A blow on the head might fit that scenario, but not grinding Frank's face in the dirt till he choked and spraying him with pesticide. That all seems too drawn out and ugly for Etter. Although if Frank had just confronted him about spraying the marijuana crop . . ." She trailed off, frowning in thought.

"It's also too elaborate for a thug killing, don't you think?" Renzo was piling plum jam on his second croissant. "Jürg suggested Etter might have approached someone in the drug business, right? And then somehow pissed the guy off so much that he wanted to get rid of him *and* Frank. Unlikely enough, but if it happened, is some Balkan avenger going to take the time to stage this pesticide gig? Especially when he'd have to bring the pesticide with him? I don't think so."

They ate and drank in silence for a moment. "What are your plans for today?" Giuliana asked.

"This morning I'm bringing Louise Fehr into the station for an interview with Noah, if I can find her. I think you should be there, too. She's the one who knew Frank best, but we couldn't get hold of her until now. After that, I figure you'll want to get me hooked into the druggy side of things. You don't want to leave me tramping through mud in Haldiz for the rest of the week, do you?" He gave her a pleading look through his dark lashes that was both heart-stopping and funny. And he knew it. She laughed, and he grinned back.

"You know," she told him, turning serious, "these drug killings . . . the whole setup doesn't click for either of us yet. Soon I'll get some new information, and hopefully it'll all fall into place, but right now a lot of pieces are missing. I've got Heinz Neuhaus and his people, plus Jürg Thönen and one of his boys, not to mention me, all chasing after Etter's drug connections in the city. So I'd like you to stick with Haldiz and the farmers. There may be something going on with this Jean-Pierre and his daughter that has nothing to do with marijuana. Or a bout of tension between Frank and Etter that got out of hand. Or . . ."

Renzo interrupted. "Like the fungicide Etter was using on Frank's land. Everyone I've talked to says Frank's organic principles were even stricter than Bio Suisse's. He must have been beside himself when Jean-Pierre told him what he'd seen—he didn't want to believe it at first. If Etter'd been killed, we'd assume Frank did it in a rage over the spraying."

"So you see why I'd like you to keep tabs on everything that doesn't have to do with drug dealing. You okay with that?"

"Sure. What about Louise Fehr?"

"I've got so much to do that I can't really justify being there, but you sit in with Noah. And speaking of Noah, we'd better go. We've got two minutes to get to what's supposed to be *my* staff meeting, even if Noah's running it."

19

Nordring police station,
Wednesday morning, June 19

Giuliana made it on time to the meeting, but Renzo was late. As they were running upstairs, his phone rang.

"Donatelli," he answered, still moving.

"Good morning, Herr Donatelli," the husky voice said. "Louise Fehr. I know the police need to talk to me about my . . . about François Schwab's death. What time would you like me to come to the station this morning?"

He stopped on the staircase. At last—Louise! In his mind's eye he saw the photo of her in Frau von Oberburg's living room: the golden goddess. "May I pick you up at your apartment at nine?" he asked, although as he checked his watch he saw this would leave him only about fifteen minutes in the meeting. But he knew Noah was as desperate to talk to Louise as he was, and he didn't want to risk her not showing up.

"Please don't pick me up," she said, and something in her tone told him she wasn't just being polite. "I'd prefer to come alone. Shall I be at the station at nine thirty?"

"Let's make it nine forty-five." He felt protective of her, imagining her grief. "Give the guard at the front desk my name."

"Fine," she said, and he heard her release a long, shaky breath as she hung up.

At the meeting table he found two sheets of paper in front of him: Frank's will.

"I've emailed everyone a copy," Noah was saying, "but in case you haven't seen it yet, here it is. I'll wait while you read it, because I'd like feedback."

Renzo hadn't checked his mail before the gym. Now he read:

My dear friends,

You know me so well that you won't be surprised at my wanting the last word, even after I'm dead. I've left a letter for each of you, which you'll get after this document is read, but I can't forgo a chance to boss everyone around one last time. This is, after all, my will!

Even without having met Frank, Renzo could imagine him chuckling over his own pun. And admitting to his bossiness—Jean-Pierre would love that, assuming he ever got to hear about it. He went back to the will.

First comes my beloved Louise. The truth is that I have never been able to boss you around—you are now and always have been your own boss. We have already discussed why I am not leaving you any money or land; it would only be coals to Newcastle. Instead, I'm leaving you a job, that of my executor. As you go through my possessions, please take whatever you like, with the exception of anything mentioned below. And thank you, dear heart, for everything.

Matthias, you are also beloved. I've been labeled "alternative" for most of my life, but I've still had trouble being the kind of man who tells another man he loves him. Easier to write it now than to say it—but I wish I had said it, over and over. You are my friend, my son in all but DNA, and, more and more often during the last few years, my great support. Your wife and children have become my family, too. Thank you for making yourself and them a part of my life.

Remembering Matthias's grief on Monday afternoon, Renzo considered the pain and pleasure these words would give him. He felt his eyes start to fill and determinedly read on.

I thought long and hard about leaving you my land, Mättu, but I decided it would be a burden for you. You work as hard as a man can on the land you have, land that has been in your family for generations. So instead I've left you my money (minus CHF 10,000). "Nice of the old man," I'm sure you are thinking—"perhaps it'll be enough to buy a new truck." Ha! Won't you *be surprised! Did you think I wouldn't take advantage of loving a woman who invests money for a living? I'd also like you to have my guitar, my farming equipment, and my house, complete with contents, except for any mementos Louise chooses. You no more need a second house than you need more land, so feel free to sell it, knock it down, or do whatever you like with it. Unlike my land, my house has no special meaning for me. Nor do my possessions—except for the guitar, which is why I've left it to you.*

I don't have any sentimental attachment to my chickens, either. Keep, sell, or eat them. It's up to you. But I hope you won't mind giving a home to my old girl Grace Slick. She's a bit of a burden, but I know you'll take good care of her.

So how much money did he have, Renzo wondered, as he continued reading.

Simu, it has been fun watching your progress in my Number 17 field. Since no one these days—including me—wants to imagine dying before eighty-five, I hope by the time this will is read you will be long gone from Haldiz and happy in your chosen life. My gift of CHF 10,000 is in memory of your time with me learning to be an organic farmer.

Renzo realized he'd failed to check the date of the will. Obviously, it had been written before the fungicide blowup.

Jean-Pierre, my oldest friend, perhaps you were surprised to be invited to listen to the reading of this will. Before I tell you why you are here, I want to apologize for being such a lousy neighbor. I got off to a bad start, and then—in my stubbornness and pride—I did nothing to improve matters. You're as stubborn as I am, which made everything worse. Now, since I'm dead, it's too late to make amends. So, I'm going to piss you off one more time, probably worse than ever before. I have decided to leave you all my land on the condition that you either farm it organically yourself or sell it to someone who will. My lawyer has instructions to draw up all the documents. I know you will see this as me still trying from my grave to convert you to my way of farming—and that's exactly what it is. But I hope you'll also see it as an act of friendship and reconciliation. I have no children to take over my land, but you have children and grandchildren. If the land I love can't stay in my family, why shouldn't it go into yours? After all, you often worked it along with me when we were kids, just as I sometimes helped you and your father on your place. It would make me very happy to think of your Jeanne farming my land. But it has to stay bio*—that's a given. Think about it. My lawyer will give you some time to consider. If you don't want my place, even to sell, then it will be offered to FiBL for organic research projects. And if FiBL doesn't want it, let the Earth take it back.*

What did Frank mean by that? That it should go back to being forest? Somehow, he couldn't imagine the other Haldiz farmers being pleased to learn that sixty acres of trees would grow up slowly where Frank's crops had been, someday towering over all the agricultural land around them.

That's it. I've left separate instructions for my funeral. No, I haven't lined up Eric Clapton to play for it, but it should be a fun party anyway. Enjoy yourselves, and remember that I love you.

By the time he finished the document, Renzo was hearing Frank's voice as if he were giving a speech at a family wedding. He was surprised how moved he felt, and a surreptitious glance around the table at the faces of the other listeners showed he wasn't the only one. The first thing that struck him was how hard it was, after reading that will, to think of Frank as a criminal. And the bequests—what did they mean to the case?

Noah broke into his reflections. "To answer what I'm sure is everyone's first question, Matthias Ruch inherits just under two million francs, all invested by Fehr in alternative funds. We'll dig to see if Schwab earned any of that money selling drugs. What we've seen of his bank statements so far points to intelligent investment of his farming profits. But we've got over forty years of records to comb through."

Renzo remembered Ruch's worn face and smiled. Life was about to get a lot easier for the farmer and his family. But as much as he liked the man, inheritance and homicide were inseparable. Now they'd have to go over Ruch's alibi for every minute of Friday afternoon. As for Jean-Pierre . . .

Erwin and Renzo were on the same page.

"Niklaus talked to Renzo yesterday afternoon about his daughter taking over his farm without saying anything about this other land she'd get. But suppose he knew what was in the will," said Erwin.

"Hang on a sec," Noah said. "I want to add one more thing. I spoke with Schwab's lawyer this morning, after I found the will on Frank's laptop last night. Most of it was written by him and made official by her just after Christmas a year and a half ago. But without the bequest for Simon Etter—that was added two months ago, in April. Then she got a call from him last Thursday. He wanted to cancel Etter's lease on his field and take the new paragraph out of his will. No more ten thousand francs for Etter. The lawyer told him she'd cancel the lease right away but that Frank would have to come into her office to sign the changed will. He was due there this coming Friday afternoon."

Rosmarie laughed. "Are you saying he was murdered a few days before he was going to disinherit Etter? Just like in an Agatha Christie?"

"That's right," said Noah. "Schwab was killed before he could sign the new will, so Etter would still inherit the money, if he were alive. Now it will be divided between his heirs: his mother and sisters. Not that ten thousand francs is worth killing anyone over—Etter wasn't poor enough for that."

"But what about Frank canceling the lease?" Giuliana asked. "Did that mean Etter'd lose his current marijuana crop? I've seen his stash from last year's harvest—at least the part he keeps in his basement—and he was running low. He needed the plants in that field."

The room buzzed with talk of Etter and his marijuana. The timeline they were developing looked damning. Wednesday night, Jean-Pierre told Frank about Etter using fungicide on his plants; Thursday, Frank canceled Etter's lease and tried to change his will. Friday, he was murdered. Even the spraying of poison all over the crime scene fit the idea of Etter as Frank's killer—although they still hadn't heard from the lab if the stuff all over the crime scene had been used on the dope. But what did it matter? Simu Etter killed Frank in a rage over losing his lease and perhaps his plants, and then got himself killed, maybe because he fell out with his new business partners.

Louise would have more to tell them about the relationship between Frank and Simu. Maybe she'd help him understand Frank and Jean-Pierre's odd friendship, too. Giuliana had asked him to concentrate on everything but the drug trail, which meant thinking about the possibility that Jean-Pierre had known that Frank was leaving him all his land. Was that why he'd lied—well, omitted to mention—the presence of Jeanne and her boyfriend in Haldiz the Friday afternoon Frank was killed? Had Frank been one of the farmers they'd visited that day for their university project?

Within ten minutes of the meeting breaking up, Louise Fehr had arrived at the station and been settled at the end of a long table with a glass of sparkling water at her elbow and Noah and Renzo on either side of her. A clerk sat at the other end of the table copying everything down. Renzo was glad Noah had chosen one of the less grim interview rooms; this one actually had a striped carpet under the table. Called by the guard to meet Louise at reception, Renzo had found a woman weighed down by all of her seventy-three years. He compared her to the photo he'd seen; at this moment, all that was left of that laughing young earth mother was strength. Even in grief and exhaustion, Louise held herself erect, her expression resolute.

"Tell us about your relationship with François Schwab," Noah began. Renzo was surprised he didn't start with the events of the past Friday.

Fehr sat even straighter in her chair, as if holding herself together at all costs. "Frank and I loved each other," she said simply. "But it wasn't enough. I've been thinking a lot about that since I heard he was dead. Frank believed passionately in his work; I believed in mine.

We thought for years that we could make our separate-but-equal lives function, but we hadn't considered children. I wanted a child, one I would raise in Bern. Frank wanted a farming family or no family at all. I tried to come up with a compromise—something to make us both happy—but he wouldn't budge. So I left him. But after ten years, I missed him so much I had to go back. My poor husband. He's a kind, intelligent, hard-working man. Attractive, too. Everything a woman could ask for. But he wasn't Frank."

Renzo acknowledged to himself that Erwin wasn't the only one with something to teach him about interrogations. He gave Noah full points for beginning the interview in a way that would win Louise's trust. The terrible strain he'd seen in her face had disappeared as she'd talked about Frank.

"How did Simon Etter come into Herr Schwab's life?" asked Noah.

Louise slumped a little, and her lips tightened. "Frank was lonely. He had apprentices and researchers working with him off and on, and of course he had me coming and going. But he missed Matthias Ruch. Mättu was twelve when Frank befriended him, and they developed a closer relationship than many flesh-and-blood fathers and sons—much to the distress of Matthias's real parents. Now he's forty-three and has a wife and four kids and a farm to run. He saw Frank whenever he could, but it must not have been enough, because when Frank met Simu at a 'Legalize Marijuana' rally three years ago, they clicked. Simu was a new audience for Frank's tales of the sixties and seventies. He started dropping by the farm sometimes, once he'd finished his shift at the post office. Frank knew Simu sold pot in a small way, but he didn't care one way or the other about that. He was hoping he could get Simu interested in organic farming. Typical Frank," she added, with a small smile. "He could never imagine the land failing to fascinate anyone."

She had been talking calmly, but now she stopped, took a shuddering breath, and sipped her water. Then she clasped her hands tightly in front of her, as if she were centering herself. Renzo gave her an encouraging smile and said, "Simu did get interested."

"That's right," she said. "Frank always grew a few marijuana plants for himself, and that was what did the trick. Or maybe that had been Simu's plan all along. Frank leased him a small field for a token amount, and suddenly Simu was a part-time farmer, asking Frank about measuring soil pH, fertilizing with dung, and all the things Frank cared about. He never took a franc from Simu for the marijuana. It was growing that always mattered to him, not selling. Plus a chance to subvert the System, of course. Frank could never resist that."

Louise looked at them, and behind her dignified self-control Renzo saw a touch of discomfort, a dread of the men's disapproval. But she needn't have worried, at least not about him. He'd stopped judging Frank for now, while he focused on understanding him.

"Then the relationship with Etter changed," Noah prompted.

"Yes," Louise agreed, "things changed." She paused again, and tears appeared on her cheeks. This time Renzo expected her to be overcome by emotion. But she took a white handkerchief out of her handbag, wiped her eyes, and continued. "Before I tell you about that, I want to be fair. Simon Etter is not evil, but he is a deeply self-centered young man. All that matters are *his* plans. As long as you go along with them, you're his friend. I've never been especially fond of him, the way Frank was, but I used to enjoy his company. That was before I realized that someone else's plan is as unimportant to Simu as a fly buzzing against a windowpane. Until it annoys him—then he squashes it. He'll feel sorry. Because he likes to be a nice guy and have other people's affection. In fact, he can't see why someone would turn away from him, no matter how much he's hurt them. He . . ." She stopped and bowed her head. "He hurt Frank."

She'd used the present tense to speak of Simu. If she was pretending not to know he was dead, she was doing a good job of it. It had been Noah's idea not to tell her anything about the death, and Renzo found it a good test. He regretted manipulating her, though.

"How did Etter hurt him?" Noah asked. "We'd like to hear the whole story."

Louise said nothing for a minute or two, apparently collecting her thoughts. "After his first marijuana harvest last fall," she said at last, "Simu kept crowing about how good his sales were. Frank was happy for him, but over time the talk turned to expanding, hiring help, getting into the business 'big time.' Frank dismissed this as hot air. Then, in April, shortly before this year's planting, Simu asked for more land. Frank said no. Then Simu decided he wanted a large indoor plantation instead of the field. He asked Frank to help him build a bigger version of the potting shed or let him use part of the barn. He offered to pay rent and cut Frank into his profits. Frank treated it as a joke, but the project had become deadly serious for Simu. He even began to talk about going into business with people who sold hard drugs, if he couldn't get other investors."

That fit what Simu's brother-in-law and the undercover cop had told Giuliana. Renzo flicked his eyes at Noah and got an okay sign.

"Why didn't Herr Schwab want to stake Herr Etter?" he asked.

Louise's eyes widened in astonishment, as if the question were ridiculous. "I told you. Frank wasn't interested in money."

An echo of Jean-Pierre Niklaus. "We never got to meet your friend," Renzo said, gently. "You have to explain him to us."

Louise nodded. More tears gathered, but again she wiped her eyes and regained control. "One of the reasons Frank lobbied to legalize marijuana," Louise said, "was because keeping it illegal encouraged crime. Serious crime. So he was upset about the idea of Simu working with dealers of heavy drugs. But he saw right away that he couldn't dissuade Simu from expanding. Simu *was* interested in money. So in early May Frank told Simu he'd have to move on if he wanted more growing space, indoors or out. It wasn't just Simu's talk about criminals. Raising marijuana indoors uses a huge amount of energy. Frank would never have gone along with that. No environmentalist would."

"Still, he didn't immediately throw Etter off his land," Noah said.

"I wish he had," she said hotly. "I only wish he had. But that wasn't Frank. He'd watched Simu slave over his field. He didn't want to deny the boy his last crop. They agreed that Simu would be in and out of

Frank's place until after the harvest, and then he'd go. Frank was more sad than angry about the whole thing. I was at Frank's the weekend before last—"

"June eighth and ninth?" Renzo asked. Louise paused a minute before nodding.

"On Sunday afternoon Simu showed up and spent some time in his field. Things between him and Frank seemed harmonious. Then, the following Thursday evening, I drove up to the farmhouse to find Simu and Frank yelling at each other in the courtyard. Frank was as angry as I've ever seen him. He said, 'I'm going to burn every plant, every single one.' Simu shoved him, and Frank fell onto the flagstones. I don't know if things might have escalated, but I ran up. Simu stood over Frank and yelled, 'Burn 'em. Now that I've hooked myself another organic asshole, I don't even care.' And he drove off."

So Etter had found another place to grow his weed. Renzo didn't have time to think through the implications of this; Louise was still talking.

"I helped Frank up. I was leaving for Zürich the next day to visit my daughter and the twins, but if Frank had been hurt, I would have stayed. I wish he had been hurt. Then maybe he would have gone into the hospital for a couple of days, and he'd still be alive."

She paused and pressed her hand against her mouth. A sob escaped. Shakily, she continued. "But there were only scrapes and bruises. He didn't want a doctor. He told me that Schämpu—Jean-Pierre Niklaus; you know who he is, right?—had come over the evening before to say he'd caught Simu spraying fungicide on his crop of weed. When Frank confronted Simu, the boy confessed right away and was surprised Frank got so upset. Frank explained that Simu had contaminated a piece of his land; he couldn't grow anything organic on it now for years. Simu did say he was sorry. Apparently, his plants had developed fungal blight, which he hadn't told Frank about. He said he'd tried the usual organic treatments, which hadn't worked. So he'd gone for the commercial product. 'What else could I do?' he said, as though Frank would agree. 'Anyway, you've got lots more land.' The more Frank realized how little Simu cared about the farm and what it stood for, the angrier he got. He finally told Simu that he couldn't risk the fungus spreading to his own crops; he'd have to burn the plants and start decontaminating the land. Simu was furious about that; he wouldn't listen to any explanations. That's when things escalated, and I arrived."

"Did Frank name the new organic farmer Simu had found to work with?" asked Noah. Renzo noticed that the formality of Herr Schwab and Herr Etter had vanished—Noah was too caught up in the story to hear his slip.

"I asked Frank that. He shook his head and said the whole thing was a mess, but I got the feeling he knew more than he was saying. We didn't talk about it anymore. The next morning we had breakfast together and discussed going to the Ligurian coast for a few days in July. Then I left."

Her hands were clasped even more tightly in front of her. Her eyes stared at nothing.

"What time was that?" Renzo asked.

"It must have been about nine thirty in the morning. That afternoon I took a train from Bern to Zürich. And Monday morning Frank's cousin Léa called my daughter to say that Frank had been bashed on the head and was dead. And my daughter told me." She sounded wooden, like a bad actress droning out her lines.

"Which train did you take on Friday?"

Louise paused. Renzo, waiting for her answer, caught her eyes and realized she wasn't just remembering, she was thinking furiously. When she did speak, it was as though her thoughts were far away.

"Um . . . let's see. Four. I got the four o'clock."

"Frau von Oberburg said you were planning to take the noon train." Renzo kept his voice light. "Why did you change your mind?"

"I remembered some work, some financial forms I had to deal with, so I decided to stay home and get them out of the way."

"You drove from Haldiz to your apartment in Bern directly—is that right?" She nodded. "Maybe you were there by ten thirty. You'd planned to walk out the door about an hour later with your suitcase, take a bus to the train station, and catch the noon train. But you changed your mind and worked at home from then until three thirty in the afternoon." Renzo watched her growing discomfort as he reviewed this schedule. "Is there anyone who can confirm any of that?"

"No. No, there isn't."

She stopped, pressed her fists to her cheeks, and blurted, "Have you talked to Simu?"

"He's dead," Noah told her. Thwarted, Renzo sat back, unable to press Louise further. Didn't Noah realize that her alibi for Frank's death had just gone up in smoke?

"Simon Etter died?" Louise whispered. Her upright figure hunched in on itself.

"He was killed in Bern thirty-six hours after Herr Schwab was killed in Haldiz."

She stared at Noah, saying nothing. Renzo watched as she tried to cling to her self-control in the face of this shock. "But why?" she whispered. "I don't understand. What could have happened?"

"We don't know," said Noah. "We need your help to figure it out."

Louise was crying quietly into her handkerchief. Renzo stood up and poured her a fresh glass of water, trying to remember the last woman he'd seen with a real handkerchief. His grandmother in Orvieto, maybe. He touched Louise's shoulder gently, thinking about the new figure who had now entered the picture, the organic farmer who had taken Etter up on his investment offer after both Frank and Simu's brother-in-law had turned him down. Where the hell did he fit in? And could it be that Louise Fehr was lying about how she'd spent Friday afternoon, the period of time when Frank was killed? It didn't seem reasonable. Yet that was the clear message her hesitancy about train times conveyed.

The silver-haired woman was willing herself into calm; Renzo was impressed with her determination. She blew her nose into one corner of her hanky, drank some water, and then dipped another corner of the cloth into the glass and wiped her eyes with it. She cleared her throat, straightened her already-straight collar and focused on Noah.

"I want to help," she said. "I felt so sure that Simu killed Frank to save his plants, and I still think that's what happened, but Simu being dead, too—it makes no sense to me."

"What friends or contacts did the two of them have in common?"

"I don't know. Simu came and went, working in his field, and when he consulted Frank, he didn't do it while I was there. I assume he'd casually met most of the local farmers during his eighteen months of growing dope in Haldiz. Buying supplies, drinking beer, hanging around—it's a small village, so I imagine a lot of people knew his name. But I don't think he and Frank had any friends in common."

With patience, alternating their questioning, Renzo and Noah asked Louise for details about Etter, but it was obvious she knew less about him than they did, thanks to Giuliana's and Sabine's interviews of the day before. Renzo's hopes of learning something else significant spluttered and died. Her desire to help seemed sincere, but she gave them next to nothing relevant. He fell back to wondering why her schedule for the afternoon of Frank's death had been delivered so hesitantly. Time to try again.

"I'd like to ask you again about last Friday, Frau Fehr," he said. "Can you tell me what you were working on that made you decide to delay your train?"

"I need to go home," she said. "I was awake most of last night, and I'd like to try to get some sleep now. Believe me—I want to know what happened to Frank even more than you do. I'll talk to you as much as you like. But not now."

"We'll need you to review and sign a written version of what you said here," Noah told her, his face clearly sympathetic. "But we can postpone that until tomorrow, if you prefer."

Louise had already stood up and was nodding. "Thank you," she said. "Let me know tomorrow when you want me back."

Renzo stood to escort her out, hiding his frustration under a bland expression. He could believe that she was exhausted and wanted to go home. But the convenience of her announcement annoyed him. She was deliberately avoiding questions about that Friday afternoon, and he wasn't going to let it go. Sometime soon, before the week was up, he was going to have another, less sympathetic talk with Louise Fehr.

20

Münsingen,
late Wednesday afternoon, June 19

With Louise gone, Noah and Renzo returned to the case-room, fetching themselves coffee on the way. Noah sank into the chair behind his desk; Renzo leaned his bottom against another desk and took a swallow from his cup.

"Any idea who Etter's new 'organic asshole' could be?" Noah asked.

"Nope."

"I'd like you to try to find out," Noah said. Renzo smiled—both Giuliana and Noah seemed determined to keep him wandering around the Seeland.

"I'll start with the Lakers," he told Noah. "That's the organization of local farmers Frank belonged to, and most of them are organic. Maybe Simu didn't stray too far from his base at Frank's. If he wasn't planning to partner with one of the Lakers, one of them may still be able to give us an idea of who's in the running. I'll call their chairman, Christian Hirschi, and ask how I can meet with them."

"Is anyone in their right mind going to tell you they made a deal with Etter to grow dope?" Noah asked, cocking his eyebrows. His cell phone rang and he glanced at the screen, then turned it off and looked back up at Renzo.

"I don't think anything will happen at the meeting," Renzo admitted. "It's the anonymous calls and emails afterward that'll pay off. All those good citizens reporting on their so-called friends. 'Why don't you check out the guy at the end of our road?'" Renzo said in a poor imitation of a Seeland accent. "'He just bought a Mercedes and sent his wife and kids to the Maldives for a month. I ask you, where'd he get the money for that?' We'd never get any tips without spiteful neighbors."

Noah's grin twisted. "You're right. I didn't think of that."

"I have another plan, too," said Renzo. "All these farms are inspected once a year—that's how they get certified as organic. Maybe the inspectors would have an idea which farmers could be tempted to give Etter some growing space. They'd know if someone has an empty barn or an unused field. Or if he's short of cash. Or she," he added, even though Giuliana wasn't there to notice.

"Now that's really smart." Noah gave a thumbs-up before hoisting himself out of his chair. "I'll let you get started. I'm off to see how Erwin and his people are getting on with the rest of Frank's files and papers. I'll get a team onto alibis, too: Frank's heirs, for a start, and his neighbors. Giuliana's already busy with the Etter family's alibis. Friends and work colleagues, too. Between us, she and I'll track every step Etter took after he left the postal center at one on Friday afternoon. If he drove to Haldiz and killed Frank, someone has to have seen him. At the very least, a camera must have snapped him."

Bio Test Agro was a farm inspection agency in the small town of Münsingen, twenty minutes from Bern. The firm was accredited to certify farms as organic, with the authority to grant the coveted Bio Suisse bud, too. Renzo had forwarded the Lakers' membership list to the employee he was about to meet and learned that over half its names were on the company's inspection roster, including Matthias Ruch's.

Münsingen was just off the *Autobahn* between Bern and Thun. As Renzo drove toward it, he watched the Bernese Alps loom steadily larger. From the hilltop bench above Haldiz on Monday night, the mountains had had a faraway grandeur. Now he felt he could reach out and touch them. Gazing up through the windshield at the closest peaks, he wondered how they could be intimidating and reassuring at the same time and suddenly realized he was about to miss his exit.

He swerved across two mercifully empty *Autobahn* lanes and onto the exit ramp, followed the GPS map though the small town, and parked next to a field of . . . some tall grass. Could it be wheat? He had no idea. Signs with arrows promised that Bio Test Agro was nearby, housed somewhere among a complex of beautifully kept old buildings. A few minutes' walk brought him into a small, open-plan office with five desks. The sole person in the room, a woman of about thirty in jeans and a red shirt, held out a hand to him.

"I'm Pia Tanner. My colleagues are out on inspections. Let's go into the conference room."

Laptop under her arm, Pia pointed to a drip-filter pot on a burner. "Our budget doesn't run to fancy espresso machines," she said as she held out a mug to Renzo, which he filled. He was already impressed with her. Even faced with an unknown cop, she gave off an air of quiet confidence.

"Thank you for seeing me so quickly," he said, after they'd taken their seats. "Could you first go over the purpose of the inspections your company does? I saw from your website that you inspect farms for the government *and* for Bio Suisse, and there seem to be lots of other certifications that organic farmers can acquire as well. What's the point of having so many?"

"The point," answered Pia, "is money. But before I talk about certification, I need to know if you understand about *Direktzahlungen*, the direct payments the federal government makes to farmers."

"I'm aware they come out of my taxes, but that's about it," said Renzo.

"So let's start there. During World War I, many Swiss starved even though the country was neutral, so after the war, the government tried to eliminate dependence on imported food. Throughout the Second World War, Swiss farmers were able to keep us all fed. Afterward, self-sufficiency stayed central to farm policy. Farmers were encouraged to produce as much as possible of everything, and what they couldn't sell on the open market, the government bought from them at fixed prices. It was a terrible policy. All that frantic production damaged the land, and our taxes were spent on mountains of potatoes and lakes of milk that were wasted."

The small room they sat in was utilitarian but neat, its walls full of closely written posters with photos of different fruits and vegetables. Through an open window behind Pia, he heard the buzz of machinery and saw green and yellow fields fanning out in all directions.

"As fears of the Swiss starving in another major war faded," Pia was saying, "the policy of bribing farmers to grow as much food as possible started to look as dumb as it was. From a money-saving point of view, Switzerland could have given up agriculture altogether and bought all its food from the bigger countries of Europe. But imagine a Switzerland with no cattle grazing in alpine meadows! The Swiss wanted their country to be a land of farms, even if it wasn't economical."

Renzo knew this to be true, since even he, a city-dweller all his life, carried a mental picture of Switzerland as a country filled not only with mountains, lakes, and forests but also with fields of sunflowers, hillsides covered with grapevines, and pastures stocked with cows.

"So in 1992 the National Council decided to pay farmers to farm, instead of guaranteeing payment for their crops. It was like hiring foresters to keep the Swiss woods healthy. Farmers got an annual salary for looking after their land and animals. But not just any way they liked; they had to follow a lot of rules, like limiting the nitrates they added to the soil and increasing the living space they provided for animals. They could also receive additional payments for special services: using the steepest pastures, for example; or increasing biodiversity in their choice of crops, giving hens free range, preserving hedges and marshes on their land as a habitat for wild animals and birds. I could go on, but you get the idea. Those are the *Direktzahlungen* the farmers get."

"But surely they still have to sell their carrots or veal or whatever," Renzo said.

"Of course they do." Pia thumped her forehead with her fist. "Sorry. I seem to be telling this backward. No farmer can live off the government's payments. That money supplements the income generated by the sale of crops. So, yes, farmers sell what they produce to private buyers, and they make money from those sales. Take the Lakers, for example. They band together to share food-processing and marketing costs and streamline their other expenses. Today's farmers are more entrepreneurial than they've ever been. But even with the money they earn through clever business models *and* government payments, they still belong to one of the lowest-paid professions in Switzerland."

"You're talking about all farmers, right? Not just the organic ones?" he asked.

"Essentially, everything I've been saying is the same for both conventional and organic farmers, only the rules about fertilizing, watering, and caring for livestock are stricter for *bio* production—even more so if they want to be acknowledged by Bio Suisse. And that brings us to inspections."

"Are you an inspector?"

"Part-time inspector, part-time farmer, like most of us. There are thirty-five of us, and each year we inspect around fifteen hundred organic farms. We're small. The inspection arm of Bio Suisse, Bio Inspecta, is a lot bigger. It covers five thousand farms a year, plus lots of food production plants."

Renzo imagined all these inspectors sneaking up on farmers to catch them breaking rules. "Everyone must dread being inspected. Does that make your job unpleasant?"

"Not at all. Most farmers like our visits, because we're farmers, too. We appreciate how hard they work. All year long they protect the soil and the water and keep their crops and animals healthy. But no one really knows or cares what a challenge that is and how many setbacks they suffer. We do, and we make that clear to them. At least, I do."

"Are your inspections a surprise?" Renzo pursued.

"No, no," Pia laughed. "You seem to think of us as a kind of police force, but it's not like that. I call and make an appointment weeks in advance, which gives them time to catch up on their paperwork. Once I'm there, we look at the fields together and talk about the crops, then go into stalls and barns, henhouses and pigsties, and I hear all about the animals. Finally, we sit down and go over bookkeeping and receipts, plus the daily animal care records."

"What are you looking for in the paperwork?" asked Renzo.

"Hundreds of things. I'm checking to be sure all the seeds or seedlings were bought from an approved organic supplier, that only appropriate fertilizers are being used, that the animal feed is organic, and that the farmer isn't spending or earning too much money. Vet bills—are antibiotics being used appropriately? It all boils down to balance. Organic farming is about symmetry. Ideally, an organic farm should produce most of its own animal feed—hay and grain and so on—and use the animals' waste as fertilizer. A farm of a certain size that employs good methods and applies the correct quantity and type of fertilizer should only be able to harvest a certain number of pounds of wheat or potatoes or apples. The animals, if they are being fed and treated appropriately, should produce a certain quantity of milk, eggs, wool, meat, and manure. All this should generate a certain amount of money. An experienced inspector can examine the paperwork and notice discrepancies."

"Do you catch a lot of cheaters?" Renzo asked, thinking of Etter's secret spraying.

"Almost none," Pia said. She smiled at his astonished expression. "We're not forcing anyone to farm organically, you know. There are seventy-five hundred organic farms in Switzerland, but that's only fifteen percent of the total number in the country. Organic farmers are a special group of people. Sure, organic food sells better every year, but it's still a small percentage of the food on the grocery shelves, and it takes much more work to produce. If the *Biobuure* don't want to obey the rules, they can become conventional farmers—although, as I said, even *they* have to comply with pretty strict regulations, if they want state subsidies."

Renzo's recent experience with organic farmers—especially, by reputation, with Frank—had convinced him they were special. But he couldn't imagine anyone in any profession following every rule all the time. "If someone does one bad thing, is that the end?"

"Absolutely not. We fill out forms on everything we observe, taking away points for infractions, but someone has to lose a lot of points to get disqualified. Often a farmer is doing some minor things wrong without even realizing it. Particularly in the paperwork—God, do farmers hate keeping records! As I see it, the most important part of being an inspector isn't punishing people; it's helping them farm better and keep clearer records. When we see errors, we usually give farmers until the following year to shape up. Unless they're mistreating their animals—but that's another story."

"I assume the Bio Suisse label is important to the farmers financially."

"Crucial." Pia nodded to Renzo kindly, like a teacher acknowledging a bright pupil. "When you walked in, you asked me why there are all these different certifications. Well, some bring in extra payments from the government and others help farmers market their products to the grocery chains. But it all boils down to money. And even a farmer with a wall full of gold seals and certificates is probably still earning an hourly wage that few other Swiss would consider. But that's life; I'm not complaining. Not much anyway."

She laughed, finished her coffee, rested her elbows on the table, put her chin in her hands, and focused on Renzo. "So tell me, what does this have to do with the murder of Frank Schwab?"

Pia had been straightforward with him, so he'd do her the same courtesy. "We have evidence that one of the organic farmers in the area around Haldiz is planning to go into the marijuana business. It's probably someone who has a large indoor space or is in the process of acquiring one. We'd like you and your fellow inspectors to reflect on your clients in the area and give us some insight into who it might be, with a special emphasis on the Lakers."

Pia Tanner's open, interested face closed like a slammed door. By the time Renzo had finished speaking, she was scowling.

"I see." She stood up, walked to one of the room's windows, and stared out as if she was too disgusted to look at him. "That's worse than asking me to rat on a client who already grows marijuana. You want me to point the finger at someone who isn't producing weed now but might, at some point, decide to try it. What is this—some kind of new, preventive police work?" She glared at Renzo. "Well, I won't be a part of it, and I don't understand what it has to do with Frank's death. He wasn't a drug dealer."

So much for honesty. Giuliana had complimented him the last time they'd worked a case together for his sensitive handling of witnesses. Thank God she hadn't heard him this time.

"Please," he said, "sit down. I may not be allowed to talk about the details of the murder investigation, but I can do a better job of explaining things than that. Forgive me. You took a lot of time answering my questions, and I'm trying to get out of answering yours. Will you come back to the table?"

Slowly, unsmilingly, Pia moved away from the window and took her seat at the head of the table again. Perched on her chair, she folded her arms across her chest, pressed her lips together, and waited.

"Okay," said Renzo. "I'm not interested in arresting someone growing marijuana, much less someone thinking about doing it. I'm looking for the person who might have killed two men this past weekend. There's a lot we don't know, but we do know that before Frank died, a young friend of his mentioned going into the dope-growing business with an organic farmer. Shortly after that, Frank and the young man were murdered. It seems possible that their deaths had something to do with this new marijuana-growing venture. If so, how do we find the new partner, even if it's only to eliminate him—or her—from our investigation? We have no name and no idea who it could be. And the whole business could be irrelevant. This is only one of the ideas we are following up on, trying to figure out why the two men were killed."

He paused. Pia said nothing, but her glare wasn't so dire.

"So you see, I was hoping you might give me your opinion on your

Seeland clients, especially the Lakers. Perhaps, if you look over their names, you'll get an idea that might help us. I'd be very grateful if you'd try."

"I liked Frank," Pia said. "I respected him, too. Lots of us did. His death is terrible."

"The other victim was only twenty-four years old," Renzo said.

Pia gazed down at the laptop in front of her for a long minute and began to type. "We have nineteen client farmers in the Seeland region around Haldiz; I know eight of them: three as acquaintances, and five because I've inspected their farms."

Pia stared at her laptop and chewed on a thumbnail; Renzo said nothing. Finally, she looked up.

"I need to look over my files and contact a couple of the other inspectors. Give me thirty minutes, okay? Why don't you go for a walk?"

"Thank you," said Renzo, standing up. "I'll be back in half an hour."

The inspection agency took up part of the ground floor of a large stone building with the look of a comfortable manor house. Smaller buildings perched nearby around a neat stretch of grass crisscrossed by paths. Outside one structure a few youngsters were gathered. Renzo looked around at what appeared to be a former farming estate converted into a school. Beyond the buildings, he saw planted fields filled with grain and vegetables. A tractor whirred, cowbells clanged, and the hum of crickets surrounded him. The sun shone out of a cloud-scattered blue sky. It was like being inside one of Antonietta's picture books. All that was needed was for a hen in a little headscarf to bustle by, followed by six naughty chicks.

He turned away from the buildings and took a few steps toward a stand of trees in the distance, passing a sign that he'd missed while following the arrows to Bio Test Agro. "*Bio-Schule Schwand*," it said. A school for organic farming. That made sense. He looked at his watch. Fifteen minutes in the direction of the trees, fifteen minutes back, and it would be time to see Pia again. He set off briskly, surprised by how much he was enjoying himself. It was possible that tracking down this weed-growing partner of Simu's would be a dead end. But that was true of most detective work. Understanding all the links between Simu and Frank, however, was no waste of time—he was convinced of that. Louise Fehr hadn't been able to tell him what he needed to know, but he'd find out, and Haldiz, not Bern, was the place to do that. He was grateful to Giuliana for assigning him the farming side of the case—and letting him work independently.

The thought of Haldiz reminded him that he had to talk to Christian Hirschi about meeting with the Lakers. Still walking fast, Renzo phoned Hirschi and explained about the need to uncover Etter's new business partner. After some resistance, Hirschi agreed to call an impromptu get-together of the full Lakers association for seven thirty the following morning. "I can't guarantee how many will be there on such short notice," he told Renzo, "but I've got a presentation I can set up to follow your talk. Hmm. I think I can make this meeting useful for me as well as you."

The phone call brought Renzo past the stand of trees and to the fifteen-minute point, so he turned and strolled back the way he'd come. At the Bio Test Agro office, Pia was waiting in the conference room. "Get some more coffee, if you like. I've got one idea for you."

Renzo refilled his mug and sat down next to her, relieved that she wasn't angry with him anymore, even if her attitude had shifted from friendly to business-like. He could deal with that easily if it got him a name.

"Okay. I reviewed the records of the farmers near Haldiz that I inspect, and I got two of my colleagues to do a quick mental review of their clients, which is all they have time for now. They didn't come up with anything. But I did. And I hope I'm not going to regret it."

She gave him a long, somber look. Since he wasn't sure which outcome of his investigation would cause her regret, he simply nodded.

"The farmer I have in mind is going to pieces, financially and personally. He and his wife broke up two or three years ago, and she took the kids. Now he's having trouble getting any help on his farm, employees *or* apprentices, because he can barely pay them anything and snarls at anyone who comes near him. I suspect he's also hitting the bottle. I had to withdraw his certification. He could be desperate enough to try a get-rich-quick scheme. Plus, he recently got rid of the few cows he still owned, which means his barn is available."

She leaned back in her chair and crossed her arms before meeting Renzo's eyes fiercely. "So, if I give you this man's name, you have to promise you'll approach him quietly. I would never forgive myself if I got him into trouble for nothing."

It sounded like he'd gotten himself into plenty of trouble already, with more guaranteed. But all Renzo said was, "I'll handle this as sensitively as I can."

Pia handed him a folded piece of paper. "Name, addresses, and phone number. I don't suppose I can ask you to keep me posted."

"Sorry," Renzo said, shaking his head. "But if your tip leads to the arrest of a murderer, you'll read about it online in *20 Minutes*. Or in your local paper—if you buy one."

"I'm a country farmer—of course I take my local paper. Don't want to miss any news about prize-winning cucumbers, do I?" She lifted an eyebrow in his direction and, finally, gave him a small smile.

Renzo smiled back at her and rose to leave; she stood, too, and held out her hand. As he shook it, he said, "I don't want you to think I only came to pump you for names. I wanted to understand how the inspection system works, and now I do." One thing he'd grasped was how hard it would be for an organic farmer—or any Swiss farmer who wanted government subsidies—to get away with growing a lot of marijuana unless an inspector looked the other way. That was food for thought, but he didn't tell Pia. Instead he said, "So I'm grateful for the excellent introduction you gave me, as well as for this farmer's name."

Pia was smiling as broadly as she had when he'd walked in almost two hours earlier. "Well, I'm not sorry if it helps to catch the person who killed Frank."

Driving back to Bern in an unexpected drizzle of rain, Renzo pulled out the slip of paper with the name. Yves Lüthi. He lived in the municipality of Gals. After talking to the Lakers in Haldiz the next morning, he'd find Lüthi's farm. Right now, what he most wanted was to meet with Giuliana. He wanted to tell her about the interview with Louise, even if Noah had already summed it up for her, and find out what she'd learned about Etter. He wanted to describe his success with Pia Tanner and discuss his plans for the next day. He wanted . . . well, he wanted to see her.

He picked up speed and passed the car in front of him. Back in the driving lane, he groped in his pocket for his phone and pressed "1." Giuliana's code.

21

Nordring police station, Wednesday afternoon, June 19

Since the end of the morning staff meeting, Giuliana had been sorting papers, checking records, reading reports, and phoning and rephoning investigators with instructions. At the case-room's other desk, Sabine was absorbed in similar tasks. A few doors down, in their own room, Noah and Erwin were at it, too, focused on François Schwab's life and death instead of Simon Etter's. Teams of investigators throughout the building were on the phone, requesting alibis and checking them against other people's statements. Some cops were examining traffic footage for signs of Simu's car traveling to Haldiz. The Hyundai had been found two blocks from his apartment, been searched, and was now being tested. Others were going over Frank's and Simu's finances. Lab techs were still comparing the two murder sites, and IT specialists were checking Frank's computer for hidden files. Meanwhile, face-recognition software was running through thousands of photos, riot films, and CCTV film footage, looking for Frank or Simu during a period of sixty hours before Simu's body had been found. Whenever the computer found a possible match, the image was flagged and transferred to another file, where human eyes took over. For one full day, at least, the Bern cantonal police was investing as many of its resources as it could spare into solving the two homicides.

Now it was late afternoon, and neither Giuliana nor Noah had heard a word from any of their staff about a breakthrough.

Giuliana stood up, stretched her arms over her head a few times to ease her neck and back, walked over to the window, and stared out at the street. It was raining hard. She'd stopped walking back and forth to the coffeemaker at about two, when she realized she'd lost count of the number of cups she'd drunk. Now she was drinking tap water out of a plastic Coke bottle, guaranteeing frequent trips to the toilet down the hall. The afternoon's exercise.

Sabine glanced up over the screen of her laptop and sighed. She too stood and joined Giuliana by the window.

"Got a text just now from one of Heinz's people, who interviewed the last girl on our list," she said. "Simu wasn't out with any of them Thursday or Friday night. And none of them can give him an alibi for Friday afternoon."

"So our last sighting of Simu is still the neighbor who watched him walk into his apartment building early Friday afternoon," said Giuliana.

"Yep."

"We've got the traces of fungicide in his trunk," Giuliana said. Sabine already knew this; Giuliana was only comforting herself by repeating it. "Which confirms what Niklaus and Fehr told us."

"If only we had Simu's laptop," Sabine lamented. They'd both taken to calling Etter Simu now, as Erwin and Noah referred to Frank. These were men the detectives were getting to know better than they knew some of their own relatives. "Or his phones."

"Still," said Giuliana, "at least you figured out there were two phones."

Sabine shrugged. Sorting through papers from Simu's bedroom drawer, she'd uncovered a guarantee slip proving that Simu hadn't just owned the iPhone whose calls went through his monthly Swisscom account, but also a cheap second phone that he must have topped up with cash at an electronics store. He used the iPhone to reach all the usual people, but not one of his texts had anything to do with drugs. That business, they assumed, had been carried out on the other phone, to which they had no access. Access to Simu's bank accounts they did have—but it hadn't gotten them further. And no sign of his other storage facility, either.

Sabine turned back to her desk, and Giuliana followed, wondering who else could be contacted about Simu's recent whereabouts. She reminded herself that negative information was also a form of progress; it helped to be able to eliminate every acquaintance Simu and Frank *hadn't* been with just before their deaths. She knew Frank hadn't called Simu on the Friday afternoon before he died—they had all of *Frank's* phone records: mobile and landline. And Frank's bank accounts revealed no inexplicable sums. His income was, and always had been, generated by his health-food-store clients, a market stand in Bern, and some loyal private customers. As for the heirs, Matthias Ruch was in the clear, not just for Frank's death but also for Simu's. Between his apprentices, employees, wife, and four kids, the man was lucky if he got to be alone in the bathroom. She still wanted to review Louise Fehr's and Jean-Pierre Niklaus's alibis with Renzo. And what about Niklaus's daughter?

Her phone rang: Jürg Thönen.

"I've found something," he said. "Can you come to my upstairs office?"

Hope sparked. "On my way," Giuliana said. Calling out "Jürg" to Sabine as she left their workroom, she sprinted upstairs.

Jürg had his own space—it was tiny but private. He closed the door behind her and pulled the chair across from his desk around until it was next to his own. "I want you to watch some film," he explained. The footage showed a young man parking and getting out of his car before moving out of the camera's range. In another clip, he walked into a shop. Finally, he could be seen strolling along the sidewalk toward the shop door, this time with his face fully revealed. Jürg froze the frame and zoomed in. It was Simu.

"That's the clearest CCTV footage I've ever seen. Usually people's own mothers wouldn't recognize them in this street-quality stuff," she said to Jürg.

"That's because this isn't a typical CCTV film. These are top-quality surveillance cameras that we've installed to watch whoever goes in and out of this store. The owner of the place—it's a little hardware store in Holenacker—is in charge of Bern's heroin trade. More or less. The top man's in Albania. But the hardware man runs Bern for him. Has done for years, we think."

"But you don't have enough evidence to arrest him," Giuliana said, giving Jürg a sympathetic look as she stated the obvious.

"Exactly. Your weed-boy must have absorbed a lot of gossip. I don't think many local marijuana dealers have a clue who's in charge of the city's heroin, nor would they be brave enough—or stupid enough—to approach him. They may recognize the lowlifes who sell half-gram shots to the most desperate addicts, but the man in this store brokers home deliveries. Large quantities of smack, huge quantities of money."

"So we're into a new category of crime here, and Etter's stuck his foot right into it."

"Stuck his foot in it is exactly right. Because I have a problem. Now that you've seen these photos, you'll want to talk to this man about your homicides. Of course you do. But if you approach him, he'll know about our surveillance cameras."

Giuliana nodded but didn't say anything. Jürg had already thought this through before he showed her the photos.

"We managed to get enough on him a year ago for a search warrant to check his shop. Didn't find a thing. And his luggage is searched whenever he flies to Tirana and back. Also useless. Since we alerted him to our interest—and all for nothing—he'd be a fool if he didn't suppose we were watching everyone who comes in and out of his shop. But I hate to confirm his suspicions."

Jürg sighed and drummed his fingers on the table, while Giuliana waited as patiently as she could, keeping her questions to herself. Eventually Jürg went on. "His name's Edon Asllani. He's lived in

Switzerland for twenty years; got his citizenship easily after he married a Swiss. His kids probably don't even speak Albanian. Anyway, I've been considering who Etter might have approached for money and decided to check the shop's traffic over the past couple of weeks. It's not exactly Zürich main station at rush hour, so I spotted Etter pretty quickly. One reason we suspect Asllani knows about the cameras is that quite a few of the men and women who go in and out of his shop have their hoods up and their chins down. Etter didn't hide his face."

Giuliana felt restless, but there was no room in Jürg's office for pacing. It didn't even have a window. So instead she tried to run her fingers through her hair without displacing her bun—which was impossible. Realizing what a bird's nest she was creating, she clasped her hands in her lap. "So what about Friday afternoon and Saturday night, when our vics died? I don't suppose you have a nice clear photo of Asllani walking out of his store last Friday after lunch carrying a baseball bat? Or, better yet, a police baton?"

Jürg smiled to acknowledge the joke but still shook his head. "He'd never do anything like that himself. His work is administrative; a request to get rid of someone would be passed up to the boss, who'd farm it out. All that heroin changing hands, and I'm not sure Asllani ever sees any of it. Just the money. But I've looked at the right times," he added, "since I knew you'd ask. No sign of him going anywhere on Friday or Saturday, except home to his apartment at the normal closing time."

"I want to talk to him." Giuliana liked and respected Jürg and didn't want to wreck one of his investigations. But her case came first.

"Yeah, I figured you would. I've already run it by a couple of folks. We agree that if Asllani hasn't slipped up during the past two years we've been watching him, we're probably not going to grab him this way. We'll have to wait to get something on one of his drug runners or drivers whom we can scare into giving us Asllani in exchange for a milder sentence in a safer prison. So we've decided to let you have a chat with him. I'm not sure you'll get much out of him, though."

No point lying to Jürg. "I agree with you. What's he going to say to me? 'Yes, I lent your boy Simu a couple of hundred thousand francs, found out he and his farmer friend were planning to make off with my money, and ordered a hit on them'?" She held her hands in front of her with wrists together, as if waiting for handcuffs. "He'll probably deny having seen Etter, even if I show him the photo taken in front of his shop. But maybe I'll get some useful information. One person after another has told us that Etter was searching for outside investors, but this is the first concrete evidence we have that he tried to climb into the big boys' playpen. I'd hate to let it go. I need Rolf on board, of course."

"When would you see Asllani?"

"Tomorrow morning, as soon as the store opens."

"I'll keep someone on the cameras to alert you to anything before, during, or after your visit that you need to know about. But I'd rather you didn't take anyone with you, even to wait outside. We'd like to keep what we know about Asllani quiet. And you'll be less of a threat to him alone."

"I can do this without backup," Giuliana agreed.

"Someone will text you if anything looks suspicious, and you can walk right out. Keep your mobile next to you."

"I always do." Patting the mobile in the right pocket of her lightweight blazer, she got up and said, "Thanks for this—I owe you."

Jürg gave a friendly wave; his eyes had already gone back to his laptop.

On her way downstairs, she got a call from Renzo. She could hear the sound of *Autobahn* traffic behind his voice.

"Listen, Giule, we need to talk. I've got some new info on top of old info, and before I write up any kind of report, I'd love to sort it out. I thought you could help me do that over a glass of wine. What do you think? I could really use your input."

Suddenly Giuliana could imagine nothing that would make her happier than deserting her desk in the case-room and joining Renzo. The idea of being with a man who sought her advice, trusted her judgment, and sounded eager to spend time with her felt like cool water on sunburn.

"Sure. Let's get a drink. It'll be fine if I'm home by seven. But I've got my bike."

"And it's raining," he said. "Why don't we meet in the parking lot in ten minutes, load your bike into the car, and go for our drink. Afterward, I'll drop you off at home."

"Sounds good."

Which meant she couldn't update Sabine on Simu and the Albanian, nor talk to Rolf about her plan to confront Asllani in his shop. That was what emails and mobiles were for, wasn't it? Still, she couldn't leave Sabine completely in the dark. She swept into the office, where Sabine was on the phone, and packed her laptop and some papers into her bag. Then she got her SIG Sauer P228 and her hip holster out of the locker for her visit to the hardware shop the next morning. Sabine's heated discussion about Simu's bank accounts with someone in the police financial department didn't sound like it was about to be over soon, so Giuliana scribbled a note and laid it on her partner's keyboard: *Evidence that Simu talked to Albanian heroin dealer. I'm going to follow up tomorrow. Call/text me tonight if there's anything I should know. Bye!*

She was waiting with her bicycle when Renzo pulled up, and she helped him move a child's car-seat so they could maneuver her bike into his Fiat. By the time they drove off, they were both damp. As she combed her hair with her fingers, she caught Renzo watching her, before he turned away and started the car.

"Don't worry. It looks nice," he said, before adding, "Now, where are we going?"

Less than ten minutes later they were inside a small wine bar on the steep hill leading down to one of Bern's oldest bridges. The place had more outdoor than indoor tables and was very popular on sunny days. In the rain, the terrace was deserted, and they were the only couple inside, which suited them fine. They took a dark corner table and ordered small glasses of Chardonnay from the Canton of Neuchâtel.

"Frank's will surprised me," Giuliana said after they'd clinked glasses and taken their first sips. "I read your reports on Monday's

Haldiz interviews and on your talks with Niklaus and von Oberburg yesterday, so I thought I knew something about the man, but his writing gave me a picture of a gentler person than I'd imagined. Able to make fun of himself, too. Tell me what you learned today from Louise Fehr."

There were now two women sitting on the other side of the room. Renzo leaned forward so that he could speak softly and summarized Louise's past with Frank; her short-lived marriage to someone else, which had produced a daughter; and her return to the old back-and-forth life between Bern and Haldiz. He went on to give details about Frank and Simu, as perceived by Louise, beginning with their first meeting over two years earlier and ending with their furious encounter the previous Thursday.

"In the relationship between these two, the important thing to Frank was sharing organic farming; that Simu chose marijuana as his crop was irrelevant. But the important thing to Simu was a place to grow marijuana; that it was organic was just icing on the cake. Once Simu tasted success and got excited about growing more weed, taking it all indoors, and so on, the friendship was doomed. They'd already agreed that Simu should move on after this harvest. Nothing blew up until Frank found out that Simu had used the fungicide. That's when he said he'd burn the marijuana plants."

"Do you think it was an idle threat?"

Renzo swirled the wine in his glass while he reflected. "No, I don't. We know about the feud between Frank and Niklaus when some of his pesticide got on Frank's plants. Frank took his principles seriously. If he needed to burn the plants as a step toward decontaminating his land, he'd do it. Plus, he was afraid of the fungus spreading."

"What about Niklaus and the will?"

"I'd be astonished if Niklaus killed Frank," said Renzo. "The text of the will indicates that Frank never told his friend he was an heir. But even if Frank couldn't resist revealing the secret, why should Niklaus kill him? To inherit the land sooner? Jeanne was going to get it anyway in the course of time, and she's still a student. But something's worrying Niklaus, or he'd have told me that his daughter was right there, near Frank's property, just before he died."

"Talk to the daughter about it."

"I plan to," Renzo said, adding, "Louise has something on her conscience, too." He explained the oddly delayed train time.

"Based on what we know so far, can you think of any circumstances that would cause Louise to kill Frank?" Giuliana asked. "To kneel on his back and press his face into dirt until he choked to death and then cover his body with poisonous pesticide?"

"God, no," said Renzo. "But I don't like witnesses lying to me."

"Why don't you leave Louise to me?" Giuliana said. "I have questions for her about Simu, and that will give me an excuse to go by and see her. And, speaking of Simu, he has suddenly gone from having no business partners to having two—the organic farmer he mentioned to Frank as he walked away Thursday night and an Albanian heroin dealer."

She told Renzo about Simu going into a store where Jürg knew a dealer did business.

"I haven't run it by Rolf yet, but I've got Jürg's permission to talk to him tomorrow morning, and I'm going."

"I've set up a seven thirty meeting tomorrow morning with Hirschi and his Lakers," said Renzo. "So morning doesn't work for me. We'll put it off until afternoon."

What did he mean, "we'll" put it off? It was her call. Surprised at his high-handedness, Giuliana touched Renzo's wrist where it lay on the table between them. He turned his hand over to squeeze hers and then let it go. "I'm not going to tell you where the store is," Giuliana told him, "let alone invite you to come along. Narcotics has had this man staked out for a long time; he's their prize. I'm amazed they're letting me approach him at all."

In a flash, Renzo went from smiling to glaring. "How can you even consider doing something like this alone? *Porca miseria*! What a stupid idea! It's too dangerous."

Renzo calling her plan stupid? How dare he? Forget about her being his boss—not even Rolf would use a word like that in light of all her experience, all her years of good calls. She put her fists on the table and leaned forward, spitting out, "What the hell gives you the right to . . ." In the midst of her fury, she felt tears coming. Grabbing her bag, she stood up. "I'll be back," she told Renzo. "Stay here." Then she hurried out of the café.

22

Bern's Altenberg neighborhood,
Wednesday afternoon, June 19

The rain had stopped. Giuliana scurried behind the building where she knew there was a quiet path and a tangle of rosebushes. Facing the flowerbed, she looked down at the river boiling around the piers of the medieval bridge. She hadn't lost it like that for years, not since she was still in uniform. She heard Renzo running up behind her, light and fast, but didn't turn around, even when he said, "I'm sorry." She didn't want him to see her face. But he spun her by her shoulders, took a look at her, and wrapped his left arm around her waist. With his right hand he cupped the back of her head, pushed her face gently into the hollow of his shoulder and stroked her hair.

"Dai, dai. Calmati. Va bene, tutto bene." They were almost the same words her Italian *nonna*, her mother's mother, had comforted her with when she'd cried as a child. Undone by Renzo's tenderness, a sob shook her, and she clasped him back. He tightened both arms around her, pressed her hard against him, and kissed the side of her head.

"Oh, Renzo," she said. She heard the regret in her voice as she spoke, more regret than she'd meant to reveal. She loosened her arms and drew back from him; as soon as he felt her body pushing itself out of his grip, he let her go. They still stood very close to each other.

"I have to . . ." he began.

She pressed her fingers gently to his lips. "Don't say anything we'll both wish you hadn't said."

He kissed her fingers, then took the hand in his and held it against his chest. "But I . . ."

She turned so they were standing side by side and eased her hand away. "Let's go pay for our wine. Then we'll talk. Okay?"

"As I ran after you, I flashed my badge at them," he said.

She laughed shakily. "That must have intrigued them, but I suppose they'd still like their money."

A few minutes later they'd settled their bill and were walking along the Aare. The sky was overcast, and the air cool. The rush of the river just a few feet away filled Giuliana's ears. Except for a single dog-walker, the path was empty.

"I was rude—as a colleague and certainly as someone who works for you," Renzo said, after they'd walked in awkward silence for a few minutes. "I apologize."

"And I overreacted," said Giuliana and then found herself adding, "You couldn't know it, but you were echoing something Ueli has been saying to me lately."

"Oh." The gentle monosyllable drew her out more than any words would have done.

"We're in the middle of a disagreement about my being a police-woman—or at least that's what I think it's about. It's also about my lack of good judgment—as a cop and a mother. It started this past Sunday morning, when I learned he'd let Isabelle go to the Dance-In. She got arrested." It was such a relief to tell someone.

"What? She was in the middle of that hell? And you two are having an argument about *your* poor judgment?" Renzo stopped on the narrow path and turned toward her. "Isn't she fourteen?"

Giuliana couldn't help smiling. "Fifteen. And she was supposedly with a group of other youngsters. But I agree with you—she shouldn't have been there."

They walked on, past a playing field behind a chain-link fence.

Vines grew up the fence, but they could still see three youngsters kicking a ball around.

"So what happened?" Renzo asked.

Giuliana started to describe Isabelle's ordeal but soon found herself talking about Ueli. Over the past two years she'd listened to Renzo's caustic comments about his wife, Fränzi, but she'd never done more than mention Ueli. Now words came pouring out—her fear that he'd only been putting up with her job all these years and her anger at the way he'd talked about "the police" as if every cop thought and acted the same way.

"When we met, we were both idealists, each on our own little crusade to improve the world—or at least the city of Bern. In his articles, I can still see the old crusader, and that makes me happy. I assumed he felt the same about me. But now I'm afraid I've become just a knee-jerk *Bulle* to him," she said. "The kind he despises." She ran out of words.

Renzo wrapped an arm around her shoulders and squeezed her to him. He held her a long moment before letting her go, and they walked on along the Aare. They crossed the river on a footbridge and turned to walk back on a broader route toward the wine bar and Renzo's car. Far above them, seventeenth-century buildings lined the crest of a grassy hill that plunged steeply down to the bank of the river. Only a few joggers and a man with a pram shared the path with them.

"I'm not the best person to talk to about this," Renzo said at last. "Fränzi chews me out all the time for being a cop. Says what a bad husband and father it has made me. As I've told you." He moved to the edge of the wide path and glanced away from her to look out at the Aare. "From the perspective of my marriage, Ueli copes pretty well. I don't want to discuss Ueli anymore," he added, raising his voice and coming toward her. "I want to talk about us."

He started to put his arms around her, but she took both his hands in hers and held them at waist height between their bodies. Instead of letting her hands go, he stepped closer to her. She knew if she moved her chin even slightly upward, he'd kiss her, and the temptation to lift her face was overwhelming. Almost. She talked instead.

"I've felt this . . . intensity from you for a while and hoped I was wrong," she began slowly. "It makes me feel great, Renzo—it's such a . . ."

"If you say 'such a compliment,' I'll throw up," he growled.

She started again. "I love working with you. I love being with you. You are smart and funny and good company. Also very . . . attractive." At that, she risked glancing up at his face; he looked hurt and confused. And he was right to be upset with her. She was a liar and a coward. For the past half hour, since he'd pulled her to him behind the wine bar, she hadn't been able to get enough air into her lungs. Now all she could think about was his body.

She started yet again, trying to be truly honest this time. "Okay. I *do* love working with you—but I also want . . . what you want. But I also want my marriage. So I'm—"

"You've just finished telling me that your marriage is making you unhappy," Renzo said, freeing his hands from hers at last and placing one on either side of her waist. He spoke into her ear, quietly, and his breath on her neck was delicious.

"But Ueli . . ." she began and heard her trembling, breathless voice betray her.

"Fuck Ueli," he said, locked his arms around her, and kissed her. She'd imagined kissing Renzo for months, but this was better than anything her imagination could have come up with. She put all she had ever felt into it until she felt his fingers on the bare skin of her belly. Then she stepped back.

He nodded with apparent understanding. "Where should we go?" he asked hoarsely.

"Home," she said, and saw him frown in confusion.

"Your apartment?" he asked.

She took a moment to calm her breathing as she buttoned her blouse. Then she glanced around. There were no benches on this path—she knew that—so she moved back to lean against the side of a boat shed on the bank, and Renzo followed her, tucking in his own shirt, his face a careful, self-protective blank that made her want to cry again.

"If I weren't married, we'd be headed for the nearest hotel, I swear it to you," she told him softly. "I wouldn't give a damn about the fallout at work, whatever it might be. I wouldn't even care about Fränzi—not until afterward, at least. But I care about my marriage. I care about over twenty years of building a life together, about my children's happiness—and I love Ueli. Yes, he's making me unhappy at the moment, but that's something to be fixed, not the end of a relationship."

Renzo and she were side by side in the shadow of the building. He'd turned his face so she could only see part of his profile, but she could tell that his teeth were clenched: the muscles in his jaw were tight. As she paused, he crossed his arms. She was hurting him. God, she was hurting herself, too, with every word. But what else could she do?

"That's why I've tried before to pretend I didn't know what was going on with you, that I didn't want an affair. Now I can't say no, because I do want you, and I can't say yes because . . . because I'm afraid of destroying my family. It's not duty or guilt or anything like that stopping me—it's love for my husband and children. I'm terrified of . . . of going any further with you. It's hard enough already to call a stop to everything. We can't make it even worse."

"We can see each other so no one will ever know," Renzo said. But he didn't sound like he believed his own words.

"Sneaking around behind Ueli's and Fränzi's backs—we would both hate that. And then we'd end up hating each other."

Renzo turned to look at her at last, and she saw that his eyes were nakedly sad. He took her left hand in his right one and just held it. "What are we going to do?"

"We're going to go on exactly as we do now. I can't imagine what else we can do. What else *I* can do. So I'm going to do nothing. At least, for now. Unless something changes, I'm going to pretend this never happened. Can you . . . forgive me?

Stricken, she watched the emotion leach out of his face as his expression froze.

"You're going to pretend the last ten minutes never happened?" he said, and she could tell he was trying very hard not to yell. Or maybe not to cry. Shaking his head, he turned away from her and took off down the riverside path, walking fast. She drew in a deep, shuddering breath, tucked her blouse under her waistband, and hurried after him.

Once she caught up, they paced along in silence, side by side but three feet apart. The whoosh of tumbling water and the cawing of crows seemed very loud. She'd told him the truth, as best she could. Now she didn't know what else to do. There was no way to mend this situation.

"So you're going to see the Albanian tomorrow morning," Renzo commented at last, and she was so grateful to him she almost cried tears of relief. Thank God. He was going to pretend, too.

"Yes," she said. "And you'll be in the Seeland, first at the meeting with the Lakers and then checking out the farmer whose name the inspector gave you."

They had crossed back over the Aare on the Untertor Bridge and were walking to Renzo's car.

"Renzo," she said suddenly.

He turned to her, and she saw from the way his face lit up that he expected her to tell him she'd changed her mind in some way. That was bad. She looked away and spoke over her shoulder as she made for the passenger door.

"Remember what Simu said to his sister? That with this new arrangement he'd be able to have his cake and eat it, too?"

Renzo didn't answer, and Giuliana didn't look around at him. "Yes," he said at last, unlocking the car. He'd stripped his voice of all emotion again.

She hopped in and fastened her seatbelt, still not meeting his eyes. "Well, it's an odd thing to say. What did he mean by that? It wasn't just a way of pointing out success. It's what you say when you're getting two things, and one of them is free. Or when some bonus is falling unexpectedly into your lap, maybe because you've done something sneaky. Don't you think so?"

"I guess."

"Well, suppose it meant that he was going to keep his plants at Frank's *and* build something indoors."

"After what we've heard about how angry Frank was, that seems pretty unlikely. Unless Simu thought he was inheriting the farm. After all, Frank didn't have any kids. Maybe he'd said something earlier to make Simu believe he was his heir."

Giuliana forgot about looking away. "Renzo, that's a really interesting idea," she said.

Renzo sounded animated at last. "Simu could have said those words to his sister because he knew he'd be getting money from the Albanian, and he knew—or thought he knew—he'd be inheriting Frank's farm, where he could use the barn for growing dope."

"We need more information," Giuliana said, and Renzo nodded.

By five after seven, they were in front of Giuliana's house. Giuliana undid her seatbelt and turned to look at Renzo.

"Are you all right?"

"I'll survive," Renzo said, his voice as dry as tinder. "Just make sure to tell me . . . if you change your mind."

Oh, God, Giuliana thought. What had she done? But all she said was, "I will, I promise," and, before he could say anything else, she'd grabbed her bag and was out of the car and starting down the sidewalk.

"You're forgetting your bike," said Renzo as he opened the driver's door. She waited while Renzo lifted her bicycle out of the back of the car and set it on the road.

"Thanks," she said. "For so many things. See you tomorrow afternoon."

23

Kirchenfeld,
Wednesday evening, June 19

Giuliana stood outside her apartment door. The last time she and Ueli had talked was on the phone, twenty-four hours earlier, with his brusque announcement that he'd be out for dinner. His text today at five had been, "I'm cooking. You home at seven?" She'd answered back, "Yes—see you!" That was all.

Through the door she could hear happy voices, so she took a deep breath and walked into her home. In the kitchen she found Ueli, Isabelle, and Lukas cutting up what looked like the ingredients for a Greek salad. Ueli was chopping tomatoes into chunks, with yellow and red peppers lying ready by his cutting board, Isabelle was peeling cucumbers, and Lukas was painstakingly reducing a big block of feta cheese to smaller and smaller rectangles. A small pile of black olives lay on a plate near Lukas's board. She hugged her son, stroked Isabelle's hair, and gave Ueli a quick kiss on the lips.

"Looks delicious," she said.

"We managed to get Lukas to eat half of a black olive," Ueli said, "but he's resisting the second half." His eyes were saying more. She held them for a long time, smiling. Then she caught Isabelle giving the two of them an inquisitive look.

"I'll go change and be back in a minute," she said, still smiling.

The dinner conversation was dominated by Lukas, whose class had been on a field trip that day to the nearby Nocturama, a small zoo for creatures active at night. In the darkened enclosures he'd seen ocelots, armadillos, sloths, and other nocturnal animals from Central and South America, but all he could talk about were bats. During the flow of information about the migration, echolocation, and even defecation of bats, Ueli caught Giuliana's eye and grinned at her, waggling his eyebrows and shaking his head in fond exasperation. Lukas didn't notice these silent parental exchanges, but Isabelle did. She rolled her eyes in agreement.

"Batshit is great," Lukas said. "Farmers dig it out of caves and use it as fertilizer."

"Batshit is what you're driving me," moaned Isabelle. But her smile belied her words. After dinner, Lukas scampered outside to play soccer with a group of neighborhood kids, but Isabelle remained seated with her parents. Surprised, Giuliana asked her if she, too, wanted some mint tea.

"No," she answered. "I've finished my homework, and I'm going over to Luna's, but first I want to tell you something. You were both mad at Quentin because of Saturday night and so was I. Really, really mad. But he came up to me in the hall today and asked if I wanted to eat lunch with him, so I did. He'd heard about my arrest and told me he felt bad about everything, especially what happened with Marlies. He got worried when I disappeared." She sounded pleased about that. "He wants us to get together Friday night. And I," Isabelle straightened in her chair, "I asked if I'd be tagging along with a bunch of his friends, because, if that was it, I didn't want to go. He said it would be just us. So, we're going to a concert at the Dachstock." In this last sentence Giuliana heard defiance. Isabelle was daring one or the other of them to object to her plan.

Silence followed. Ueli, like she, was probably afraid to respond for fear the other would object, which could plunge them into conflict again.

"What time does the concert start?" she asked.

"Ten," said Isabelle.

She heard Ueli catch his breath and knew he was thinking what she was—why did these gigs have to start so late? Isabelle was supposed to turn out her lights at ten, at least on school nights.

"Your father and I will talk about it, and we'll let you know. Soon. By the time you're back from Luna's."

Isabelle stood there for a moment, looking like she wanted to plead her case, but apparently thought better of it, because all she said was, "Okay." As she got to her room, she called back, "I know, I know. Back by nine thirty. You don't have to tell me."

Giuliana got up to make tea; two minutes later they heard the apartment door close.

"I'm okay with this if you are," Ueli said immediately. "I mean, I'm not happy about it, but I'm not going to forbid her to go."

"She has to be home by one, though, don't you think? That's later than I like, but if the music doesn't start until ten . . ." Giuliana put the mugs on the table and slid one to Ueli. Then she fetched the sugar bowl.

"Quentin probably won't want to leave that early," said Ueli, "so we give her money and tell her she *has* to take a taxi home."

They gazed at each other and nodded in agreement. Then Ueli said, "I want to talk about what happened last weekend."

Oh, God. This was what she'd thought she wanted, too. But now she didn't want to risk opening the wounds again when things were good between them. After what had happened with Renzo, feeling this close to Ueli felt almost perverse, but . . . well, when did love make sense?

"Okay." She poured out a mug of tea from the pot, realized it was too weak, and poured it back. She looked up to find Ueli watching her, frowning. Thank goodness he didn't know she was going by herself to meet Asllani the following morning. She didn't think she could stand to have her professional decisions criticized yet again.

"Everything I said on Sunday morning and Monday night was

because I was worried about Isabelle's safety. It didn't have to do with you."

She drew in a deep breath and let it out slowly. "It didn't come across that way. It sounded to me as if you were questioning my judgment—on the job and at home."

It was Ueli who now reached for the teapot, filled his mug, and added a spoonful of sugar. He stared at his spoon as he stirred.

"I'm sorry if you felt criticized, but . . . don't you think you're overreacting?"

I'm not going to lose my temper. She chanted it like a mantra as she reached again for the teapot and then made a decision.

"Maybe I did overreact. But whether I did or not, I was hurt. I still am. You seemed to be suggesting that we've grown apart, that our values aren't the same anymore. And I can't talk about that right now. It's still too painful. So you know what? Let's wait for this discussion until the weekend. Let's just have a plain old conversation instead. Like—tell me what you're writing."

Ueli gazed at her with an expression she couldn't read. "I didn't mean to hurt you. Can I just say that?"

She nodded and sipped her tea.

"Okay," he went on. "My writing. Hmm. I'm working on an obituary. A pioneer of organic farming died this past weekend, and I want to honor him."

"François Schwab." It wasn't a question.

The initial surprise on Ueli's face passed quickly into understanding. "Of course. It's a Bern homicide, even though it happened in the Seeland. Is it your case? I thought you were working on the youngster who was killed by the policeman during the riots. Allegedly," he added hastily.

"It turns out the two homicides are connected, although we're still working out how."

"Does that mean your colleague didn't beat the man to death?"

"He probably didn't, I'd say at this point. I believe he hit the man once, but even that single, not-very-hard blow with a billy club has to be thoroughly investigated. It could have killed him if a major blood vessel had broken. Or he could have died from a fall caused by the blow. Jonas is suspended and . . ."

She stopped herself, wanting to avoid talk that could lead them back into anger.

"Can you tell me anything about Frank's death?" Ueli asked. "Not for the article—just for me."

"We're stuck at the moment. I'm not saying that to put you off; we have a pile of information that we're still sorting. But we're getting there."

"Funny to think we've been researching the same man this week without realizing it," said Ueli. "What's your impression of him?"

"Sounds like he was a true activist. One of those people who decides very young what he wants to accomplish, for himself and the world, and then follows his plan. But not a nut, and not an egotist, like those kinds of people sometimes are. Stubborn, like activists have to be. Driven, too. But also kind and full of warmth. I wish I'd known him."

"I did know him," Ueli said.

Giuliana reached out and grabbed Ueli's hand where it lay on the table, delight replacing her lingering anger. Ueli had known Frank. And why not? Ueli'd grown up on a farm in Bern, he considered himself an environmentalist, he wrote about agricultural politics often. It made perfect sense that he'd know Frank, and yet, because of their quarrel, she'd never thought of asking him.

"What was he like, Ueli? I'm only getting glimpses of him through interviews."

"He was great company. Being with him felt like a privilege. I once spent a whole day on his farm, following him around, asking questions. He told funny stories about the months when he was first trying to create a farming commune, in the seventies. Later, he talked about what it means to be a good farmer—organic or conventional. He was extraordinarily convincing. In fact, he almost made me regret not working with my parents on the farm." Ueli caught her eye and grinned. "Notice I said 'almost.'"

"Whoa! In all the years I've known you, you've only ever talked about what a frustrating life farming is."

"Well, it is. Frank never made it sound simple. He just reminded me how important it is. How you have to weigh your responsibility to take care of your own land and the land around it; streams and ponds and groundwater; trees, meadows, wetlands, thickets, and hedges, and all the wildlife living in them; even the air: that you have to weigh all the diversity of nature that is under your care with your need to produce food to sell. Frank was an activist, as you said, but he wasn't a fanatic. He didn't recommend that farmers subsist off the land like hermits, give up animal products, or reject normal life in any way. They have to make a comfortable living for their families, and he didn't pretend it was easy. He talked about it as a constant struggle to achieve a balance."

"That's true of most things in life," Giuliana said. "Struggling to find the right balance but never quite managing it. Think of parenting."

"Yeah. It's a struggle—but I think you're a great mother; I don't want you to doubt that, ever. Listen, love, I . . ." He scooted his chair closer to hers, put his arm around her shoulders, pulled her toward him, and kissed her. It was a tentative kiss, but Giuliana happily turned it into a real one. Sitting awkwardly at Ueli's side in a straight-backed chair, Giuliana strained to burrow into his arms before she untangled herself, stood up, and sat down again, this time on Ueli's lap, straddling him. The kitchen chair creaked, and Ueli gave a groan as she squirmed and applied herself again to their kissing.

The neighborhood's many church bells rang a staggered eight o'clock, and Lukas's signature buzz on the door—short, long, short, short, which was Morse code for "L"—sounded from the street. They broke apart; kissed once more, hard; and stood up. "For once I wish Lukas wasn't so good about his bedtime," said Ueli, as they both straightened their clothes.

"I'll tell you another thing about Frank," he continued, as Giuliana trudged to the door to let Lukas in. "He enjoyed a good strong discussion. But I'm sure he didn't deal well with disagreement. Powerful men like Frank prefer disciples to dissenters."

Giuliana, pushing the button to let Lukas in, thought of how Frank and Louise had managed their disagreements over the years. Or sometimes failed to manage them.

"I don't think I'm revealing any police secrets if I tell you that the two people he was closest to are Louise Fehr and Matthias Ruch. Do you know about them?"

Ueli nodded. "I got their names from a farmer friend of mine. I'll call them tonight and try to set up phone interviews for tomorrow. Hmm—I assume neither one is going to be unavailable because of a police interrogation?"

"No," Giuliana assured him, "I can tell you that much. Tomorrow Ruch will be at an early-morning meeting we're calling, but after that, if he or Louise can't speak to you, it won't be because of the cops." She started herding Lukas toward the bathroom to get clean. She made appropriate motherly sounds as she listened to him describe his spectacular kick that *almost* sent the ball into the goal, but her mind was on Ueli. She'd always believed he regarded her detective work as a set of puzzles she was trying to solve. Not a brutal business she should be ashamed of. Now she realized that during the last few days she'd been afraid his contempt for her job would make it impossible for them to talk like this. Leaning against the closed bathroom door and listening to Lukas run his bath, she felt a surge of relief. Things were going to be all right.

Somewhere in the back of her mind, Renzo appeared. She pushed the image away and focused instead on Ueli's kisses. She'd make sure he didn't stay late at his computer before coming to bed.

24

Bern's Holenacker neighborhood,
Thursday morning, June 20

At nine fifteen the next morning, Giuliana walked into Edon Asllani's hardware shop. Since it was a front for crime, she wasn't expecting a genuine-looking store. But she was wrong. Although the place was small and narrow, it was well stocked. The walls to her left were covered floor to ceiling with shelves holding baskets of nails, screws, hooks, hinges, locks, and small tools. To her right there was nothing but pegboard hung with saws, hammers, wrenches, pliers, wire clippers, and rolls of wire. She saw paints, brushes, and rollers against the back wall. Everywhere were neatly printed labels in bright colors identifying the sizes and brands of the wares. There was a clean parquet floor under her feet, and a small counter with a cash register running along part of the wall. Directly across from the front entrance, a door opened onto a back office.

"Good morning. How can I help you?"

The man who walked out of the office spoke Bernese-German dialect with only a slight accent. She guessed him to be in his early forties; apart from having darker hair and eyes than the average Swiss, he was unremarkable in every way.

"Herr Asllani?" she asked, and he nodded, keeping his greeting-a-customer smile on his face.

"I'm Giuliana Linder from the homicide division of the cantonal police. I'd like to talk to you about a case I'm working on. Let me assure you that I'm not wearing a wire."

"Frau Linder," he said in acknowledgment of the introduction, not offering his hand, for which she was grateful, given her abhorrence for the way he earned his living. They stood about six feet apart, and then Asllani moved behind her to the shop's front door, hung a "Closed" sign on it, and locked it with a deadbolt, not a key. Good. She wasn't trapped.

"Come in," he said. The office was almost as large as the shop and contained a sofa, armchairs, and a coffee table as well as a desk and chair. "Have a seat." As he gestured her toward one of the armchairs, he reached into a desk drawer and brought out a sound masking machine, which he placed in the center of the coffee table and plugged into the wall. A whoosh of noise filled the room.

Finally, he came over and sat in the armchair next to her.

"Now," he said quietly, "tell me what this visit is about, Frau Linder."

She was surprised by how calm she felt. She'd spoken to many killers in her years as a cop, usually during an interrogation or after an arrest. Or she'd met them in the course of a case, without knowing yet what they'd done. But this man sold a drug that was responsible for the destruction of so many lives, both in an instant and over decades. She ought to be trembling with rage. But what would that accomplish? She took out the small notebook and pen that she'd kept in her jacket pocket, set them on the table in front of her, and said, "Twelve days ago, on the eighth of June, a young man named Simon Etter walked into this shop. I believe he came to ask you to invest money in a large indoor marijuana plantation, perhaps here in Bern, perhaps in the Seeland. On June 16 he was killed, and I'm trying to understand why. What can you tell me about him?"

Asllani leaned back and pressed his thumbs and fingertips together at his waist. *Just like Angela Merkel,* she thought.

"Are you here to offer me something in return for my talking to you?"

"No. I'll be very grateful for your cooperation, and the gratitude of the police can be useful. But I have no deal to offer." And how could she, when according to Jürg they had nothing on this man, even after months of observation?

"There's one thing I can promise you," she added. "If you talk to me about Etter here, in your shop, then you won't be required to come to the police station and talk about him to a group of people there. That may be worth something to you."

Asllani took several deep breaths. Giuliana waited.

"Herr Etter walked in here that Friday exactly as you said and spoke with me. He brought with him a surprisingly professional business plan for the facility he wanted me to invest in and balance sheets detailing his financial success, first as a salesman and then as an entrepreneur. And he had indeed been successful. He had eighty thousand francs of his own for the project, and he wanted me to add another one hundred sixty thousand. I'd get two-thirds of the profits, based on the size of my investment, and he'd have the option to buy up at least half of my shares after four years. Here, I'll show you."

Moving to his desk, he unlocked it with a key from his pocket, and pulled out a plastic folder of papers, came back to his seat, and handed it to her.

"You've probably already found it all in his computer, but here's his presentation. You can keep it."

Giuliana did not tell him they hadn't a clue where Etter's computer was. "Thanks," she said as she took the folder. "Was Herr Etter asking for *your* money, do you think, or that of . . . the people you represent?"

A shark's smile crossed Asllani's face, and his unremarkableness disappeared. "I don't think the kid knew the answer to that question himself, and I'm not sure he wanted to. For him, I'd say, money was money."

"And what did you say?"

Asllani's fingers were once again splayed, his fingertips pressed together. "I told him no. He asked me to think about it, and I still told him no. We aren't interested in his product. In addition . . ." He paused and, once again, Giuliana waited, not fidgeting, her hands on her knees.

Then he shrugged. "Never mind."

"If you know something about Herr Etter that might help us find his killer, I'd like to hear it. Please."

"No, no. It's nothing like that. It's just . . . well, a youngster like him, middle class, expecting the world to do him a good turn. A Swiss." He said the last word as though it contained a set of meanings only he understood. "He doesn't belong in our organization. Thinking he could buy us out in a few years. Ha! He'd be eaten up by then."

"So you're saying you turned him down in part to keep him safe," Giuliana said, striving for a neutral tone.

"Of course not," Asllani snapped, the first loss of control he'd shown. "We don't work with"—he searched for a word, perhaps one that wasn't obscene—"*Büebeli* like that. Weaklings."

"So you sent Etter away with no expectation that he'd get money from you—that you'd even consider giving him money." A whole set of assumptions was slipping through her fingers, and she felt almost sick with disappointment, but she had to know.

"That's right."

"Did you recommend anyone else for him to try his offer on?"

"No."

"Can you think of any reason he was killed?"

"Yes—because he was a cocky young fool playing out of his league."

"Any ideas about who might have killed him?"

"I'd know if it was anyone in our organization—and it wasn't. As for anyone else he may have talked to, I can't say. But, believe me, he wasn't a danger to . . . the trade as a whole. There are more than enough customers to go around. Now, if he was stupid enough to try to threaten someone with some information he'd picked up . . ."

Blackmail. The thought lit a path through Giuliana's dismay, and she missed the Albanian's next words as she focused on it. She and Jürg hadn't considered that Simu might have tried to use his bit of knowledge about hard-core dealing to get funds for his plantation. Good call, Asllani.

He'd finished speaking, and both of them were quiet for a moment. Then Giuliana stood up and Asllani did as well.

"Thank you for answering my questions," she said, and took one of her cards from her handbag. "If you hear anything about Etter's death, please call me."

He took the card with a nod of acknowledgment, opened the door for her, and, as she left, gave her another nod, this one akin to a tiny bow. "Good-bye," he said, as he turned his sign around to read "Open."

Out on the street, walking to her car, relief loosened every joint in her body, and she stumbled. What was the phrase? The banality of evil: that was it. But Asllani hadn't been banal. He'd been courteous, intelligent, articulate, and even, just possibly, kind—although he'd denied it—in his attempt to prevent Simu getting sucked into the world of organized crime. And yet he was a mass murderer, of sorts. How did he think about his career? Perhaps he saw no difference between himself and a tobacconist, except that heroin was illegal.

She felt as if the entire morning had passed, but it was only ten after ten. And what had the interview brought her? There was absolutely no reason for Asllani to have told her the truth about anything, but she believed he had. He had turned Simu down. So—where to go from here? There were other groups of organized criminals the police might have knowledge of but, honestly, what was the point? The photo of Simu entering his shop had given her leverage over Asllani. There was no reason anyone else in Jürg's dealer files would do more than laugh in her face. And that was assuming he had addresses for any other drug fronts.

She got into the car, rested her forehead against the steering wheel, and allowed herself to wallow in disappointment for a moment. Then she straightened up. Time to get back to the station, tell Jürg all about Asllani, and consider a new angle. Could Etter really have been so foolhardy as to try to blackmail someone in organized crime?

She started her car and, all the way back to the station, thought about this new idea.

25

Wabern and Haldiz,
Thursday morning, June 20

Every morning at five thirty, before Renzo left for the gym, he kissed his sleeping children good-bye. This morning as usual he stood between Antonietta's and Angelo's beds, drinking in their fine, tousled hair, small forms, and delicate faces. His beautiful babies. The extravagance of his feelings for his children continually surprised him. The compulsion to shield them from every sort of harm was overwhelming—he felt it in the morning when he kissed them good-bye and at night when he helped them wriggle into their pajamas and sang *Fa la ninna* to put them to sleep. Most fathers probably felt like this. Look at Ueli Brand. Renzo could easily imagine running blindly out of the house to find his daughter the way Ueli'd done with Isabelle. Passion did that to a person.

Passion was still on his mind as he drove in steady rain toward Haldiz, a route he was beginning to follow on autopilot. He relived kissing Giuliana the day before and all the joy he'd felt. Finally, finally, finally, he'd kept thinking, scarcely able to believe what was happening—and then she'd given her little speech about her marriage. He'd driven home far over the speed limit—thank God he hadn't been stopped—and all the while he'd felt . . . well, desperate didn't begin to cover it.

So once he was home, what had he done but have sex with Fränzi? He'd grabbed her the minute the kids were asleep, and they'd gone at it again later, too. Fränzi never turned him down; if anything, she was more eager than he was. But that was all she was interested in. At least, that was how she made him feel.

They'd chattered all the time when they'd first gotten together, hadn't they? But what had they talked about? Bands they'd heard, movies they'd seen, football matches they'd cheered at. He couldn't remember their talking about anything serious. She'd never been interested in his job, even though she used to think it was cool. Now that she knew how much of his time and energy it devoured, she didn't want to hear about it. In fact, since the kids had come she'd always seemed too tired or annoyed to listen to him talk about anything serious. Maybe sex had always been their main way of communicating. For a long time, it had been more than enough. But not anymore.

Why couldn't he be content with having great sex with his wife and great conversations with Giuliana? Why did he need to have it all with one woman—and that one not his wife?

Giuliana had said she couldn't risk her marriage. When he was in control of his anger, he could understand that, even if he didn't feel the same way about what he and Fränzi had. There was some relief in having everything out in the open, too. At least she hadn't totally turned him down, and she hadn't made him feel like a fool, either. He thought about the way she kissed him and knew she did care about him. She'd confided in him about Ueli—that meant a lot. So he'd just have to wait and try not to push her, even if it hurt like hell. Especially when he remembered how she'd responded to him.

He was on the outskirts of Haldiz. Time to think about work.

Bern had been merely cloudy, the drive rainy. Now, in the village, Renzo was immersed in fog. The Seeland was famous for it. Bern could be ablaze with sunshine and, twenty miles away, the region between the three lakes would be a sea of grey. He slowed to a crawl as he hunted for the parish center where the Lakers' meeting was taking place. Wisps of mist shifted suddenly past unseen obstacles and seeped around the corners of buildings, and the sound of traffic drifted to him from far away. He prayed a huge tractor wouldn't lumber out of a side street, because he'd never see or hear it in time. It was a relief to find the parking lot. The white steeple of the church appeared to hang in the air over his head; the low building next to it, where village events were held, was barely visible.

He'd arrived half an hour early. Instead of groping his way along the sidewalk to the Star for an espresso and a chance to pump Nadine Löffel for gossip, he was hoping to speak with Hirschi before the meeting began. Inside the parish center, he heard the farmer's voice echoing down the hall. The conversation sounded heated. Renzo slipped into a small office next door to the room where several men were arguing.

"*You* sell your tomatoes to Fraîche if you want to, but we are going to stick with Coop and Migros. They pay more. It's that simple."

Renzo didn't know who was speaking, but the next words were unmistakably Hirschi's.

"The Lakers' purpose is solidarity. We pool our produce and sell it together, and you've chosen me to find us good buyers. I think Fraîche is the best option for us."

"But why, Chrigu?" This was a new voice, older and more affectionate, addressing Hirschi by a nickname. "No one understands why you are so enthusiastic about Fraîche. It's fine if you and a couple of the other, bigger growers want to spread your risk around and use another grocery chain for some of your stuff. But why should the rest of us give up the advantages of working with huge, established buyers like Migros?"

Renzo crept back down the hallway. This argument had to do with the price of vegetables, not with Frank's death. Nor with marijuana. Still, he couldn't help asking himself the same question: why was Hirschi encouraging his colleagues to act against their better interests?

"At least hear Pfeiffer out," he heard Hirschi say. "Maybe he'll convince you." He sounded defeated rather than angry. When Renzo reached the far end of the hall, he called out, "Hello?" and walked noisily toward the small auditorium. Hirschi hurried out and greeted him with an enthusiasm that suggested he was glad to escape his questioners.

At seven thirty Hirschi stood up in front of a gathering of about thirty-five men and women.

"I've made a quick count, and it looks like almost two-thirds of the Laker farms are represented this morning. Thank you all for coming on such short notice. I've got two people who want to talk to you."

First he introduced Renzo, who came forward to explain about the two homicides and why the police believed the deaths were connected. He revealed some of what was known about Etter's marijuana business and his need for a new partner. The Lakers sat in rapt silence, following every word.

"I need your help," Renzo concluded. "It's possible that one of you—or someone you know—spoke with Simu in his search for a new partner. There is no reason to think Simu's partner murdered him or Herr Schwab; there's not even any reason to think that he or she is a dope-grower—yet. Until hemp plants with an average THC content of over one percent are discovered on someone's property, that person has not committed a crime. Besides, I'm not interested in drugs. I'm interested in catching whoever killed the two men. I need to know anything you can tell me about Frank Schwab and Simon Etter and what they were up to during the past few weeks or even months."

He pulled a stack of his cards out of a pocket and began walking among the farmers to distribute them.

"If you have information that might help the police figure out who killed Frank or Simu, call me. Don't worry about wasting my time. Sometimes details that seem unimportant end up being key to an investigation."

He examined each face. Everyone appeared to be more curious than hostile. Ruch and Niklaus smiled and shook hands with him as he passed. A few more of the attendees looked familiar from his walks and drives around Haldiz. One he could identify was Adrian Pfeiffer, who was going to speak to the group after he finished. The purchaser was waiting for him when he reached the back of the room.

"When you asked me about Frank the other day at Hirschi's, I had no idea he was a drug dealer. Now he has paid for that with his life. Such a tragic waste," he said. His mouth was pursed. Renzo decided that he was trying to look sad but only managing to look disapproving.

Although Renzo also didn't approve of Frank letting Simu use his field for dope, Pfeiffer's smugness galled him. "We have no evidence that Frank was selling marijuana," he said, and returned quickly to the front of the room. As he turned to face the group again, a man of about thirty-five stood up. His long hair was held back in a ponytail.

"I don't have to phone you. I can tell you right now that Simu came up to me in the Star and asked if I had a spare building he could rent from me. When I asked him why, he didn't beat around the bush. He said it would be for growing weed. Talked about getting money from friends to set the whole thing up with lights and all. I said I didn't want anything to do with it; too risky. I guess he was fooled by this." The man wagged his ponytail up and down.

As soon as he sat down, two others shot up simultaneously. One had elaborate tattoos on both arms. They looked across the room at each other in surprise and then chuckled. Someone else in the room, a bald man with a greying fringe, called out, "I told you not to get those tattoos, Benno. I said they make you look like a fool. Turns out they make you look like a drug dealer, too." The whole room laughed.

"He approached the two of you, too, I suppose," Renzo said. Benno nodded, while the other one spoke up.

"My story is more or less like Oli's"—he pointed at the man with the ponytail—"except that Simu tracked me down in one of my potato fields. I told him I wasn't interested. And to get off my land."

"I ran into him at the Landi," the tattooed Benno added. "He told me he was growing on Frank's land and wanted to move indoors, but Frank didn't have space for him. I don't have the space either. Nor much interest. Like Oli said, it's not worth the risk. But I wish you guys would hurry up and legalize. Then I'd switch fast enough." He grinned at Renzo.

Renzo smiled back; he had nothing against the idea. If three farmers could be approached about growing dope and take it so lightly, it really was time to make the stuff legal. "Hey, don't look at me. Tell the politicians. I enforce *their* laws."

There was a hum of talk that gradually died down. Renzo waited to see if anyone else would be inspired to speak, but the rest of the Lakers remained seated. Then Hirschi spoke.

"I didn't just call this meeting for Herr Donatelli, but also to bring in Adrian Pfeiffer, who is responsible for buying organic and conventional fruits and vegetables for Fraîche. You all know I sell some of my produce to him, and so do three other members of our group. He'd like to take on the bulk of our crops, and I've asked him to come and talk to you about his offer. Herr Donatelli, if you don't want to add anything, I'll introduce Herr Pfeiffer."

Pfeiffer started to rise, but Renzo held up a hand.

"You three men who've spoken up—just by confirming that Etter was asking around for growing space, you've helped the investigation. I appreciate your being so open. I need to take down your names and contact information and find out when these conversations took place. Don't leave here until you've spoken to me, please. If anyone else wants to talk, I'll stick around for a while after the meeting. And thanks to all of you for coming." He'd been about to add, "so early in the morning," but realized in time that most farmers had been up for hours by seven thirty, especially if they had cows to milk.

Trying to look as unthreatening as possible, he took a seat on the far side of the room. As Pfeiffer talked, Renzo watched the gathered Lakers' faces, hands, and bodies, searching for sidelong glances, twisting hands, rigid postures, or anything else that hinted at a secret someone hadn't shared. He saw nothing to indicate anxiety. In fact, he got two or three friendly smiles and, from one woman, such a blatant come-on that he himself turned away, swallowing a laugh. Only Jean-

Pierre Niklaus refused to meet his eyes, reminding him that they needed to talk.

Only half of Renzo's attention was on Pfeiffer's presentation, but he thought it made a good impression. The man's PowerPoint slides were uncluttered, his charts and figures were clear, and he explained all the advantages that Fraîche could offer the growers in a positive but not overly enthusiastic manner. When asked, he acknowledged that the firm couldn't pay as much per pound for the farmers' produce as its two more established competitors. It was a relatively new Swiss chain that was building up an organic foods department. But there were other advantages he could offer besides money, such as greater responsiveness.

Renzo studied what he could see of Christian Hirschi's face. The man struck him as a good leader: competent, well organized, and not given to bad-mouthing other farmers. But this enthusiasm for Fraîche seemed off-key. Pfeiffer hadn't said anything yet that would have convinced Renzo to make a switch, had he been a Laker.

The farmers offered polite applause at the end of Pfeiffer's presentation and asked no questions. Everyone seemed eager to get back to their fields. Renzo took down the information he needed from the men Simu had approached and walked over to Hirschi, who was speaking to the Fraîche buyer in an angry undertone. He broke off when he saw Renzo. Pfeiffer's lips were pinched, and he was breathing hard. Hirschi's fists were clenched at his sides, his body rigid. Renzo noted all this with interest. What were the two men angry about? Perhaps one of the farmers who'd been chiding Hirschi before the meeting about favoring Fraîche had made some insulting remark before he left.

"Herr Pfeiffer," said Renzo. "That was interesting. I'm going to keep an eye on how Fraîche develops in Bern—I know you already have a big store near the train station. Let me ask you a quick question. You must see a lot of farms in this region. Do *you* know anyone around Haldiz who might easily be tempted into growing marijuana?"

"This region isn't my only geographical focus. Still, what you said made me consider several local farmers in a new light."

Renzo opened the 'Notes' on his phone, but Pfeiffer shook his head.

"I'm not ready to commit myself yet. I have your card, so I can let you know."

This sudden reluctance made Renzo wonder if the purchaser really had a tip, or if he was just trying to make himself important.

"Call me, then," he said. "I need to speak with Herr Hirschi. Alone. Excuse us."

Pfeiffer seemed reluctant to let Hirschi out of his sight, but the young farmer moved off without a backward glance.

"What about you?" Renzo asked. "I imagine you couldn't speak up in front of the group, but do you have any suspicions?"

Hirschi spread his hands wide in a gesture of doubt that was more southern than Swiss, reminding Renzo that the man had lived several years in Spain. "Nothing," he said. "I can't imagine . . ."

"Fine. I'm about to check on Yves Lüthi. Can you tell me anything about him?"

"Yves Lüthi, huh? That's interesting. Lüthi is . . . well, he's had big problems, and he hasn't handled them well. He used to be a Laker, but twice we heard from Coop that they weren't happy with his produce. The first time we warned him, and the second time we dropped him. We have our reputation to protect. He's inspected by Bio Test Agro." Hirschi threw a questioning look at Renzo, who nodded to show he'd heard of BTA. "I think one of their inspectors worked with him, but I also called Bio Suisse to see if they could send someone to get him back on track. I said the Lakers would pay for a couple of hours of business consulting for him. But I heard Lüthi threw the adviser off his property about ten minutes into the first session."

"At least you tried."

"Yeah, well." Hirschi shrugged. "I haven't had any contact with him for over six months. I don't think going into business with him would be a good idea, but I'm not Simu."

"Thanks for your help," Renzo said. He turned to leave, but stopped. "Has anyone called you about your alibi? We're checking at least a hundred of them, so don't take it personally."

"My alibi for when Frank died? No one's asked me yet, but let me see. Last Friday, right? When?"

"Let's say, two to six p.m."

Hirschi got out his phone to check. "I had a long business call at two thirty, and then I supervised several trucks loading up produce. I wasn't there every minute, but you could check with the drivers."

"Good," said Renzo, taking notes. "And Saturday night?"

"What?"

"Simu's murder."

"Of course. Um, let's see. Saturday night I was out drinking until pretty late. I'm not sure what time I got home, but I think around one. Maybe a bit later."

"Who were you with?"

"Luis Díaz, a cousin of my wife's from Spain. He's a trucker. When he's passing nearby, he often stops to visit Asunción."

"Would your wife remember when you got home?"

"No. She's a heavy sleeper, and I didn't wake her." Hirschi frowned. "I'll give you Luis's number, but please don't bother my wife with this unless you have to."

He sounded like a husband who'd misbehaved. Had he picked up a girl in a bar? With a wife who looked like Asunción? In the company of her cousin? No way. Maybe it was just the late-night drinking Hirschi didn't want his wife to know about.

"Can't see right now why she'd have to hear," Renzo said. He took down the Spaniard's phone number. Hirschi didn't know the names of all the drivers from Friday, but Renzo figured he could get them through the grocery chains they worked for. "Thanks again for setting up this meeting."

Jean-Pierre had left. Why hadn't he grabbed him before talking to Hirschi? Should he go after him? He decided to see Lüthi first. On the way to his car, he glanced at his phone and saw it was a little after nine.

Giuliana had said she'd visit the drug boss first thing this morning. Was she with him now? Surely the man would want to avoid trouble with the cops, but still Renzo was afraid for her. He wished he'd gone over her head and insisted to Rolf that he be there, too. It was ridiculous that while Giuliana was in danger, he was away in the sticks, facing a chat with a failing farmer.

So get on with it, then. He stepped out of the building and found that the fog had lifted enough that he could see his car in the parking lot, although greyness still squatted over the village. He sighed. The sooner he saw Lüthi and Jean-Pierre, the sooner he could be back in Bern to check on Giuliana.

26

The Seeland,
Thursday morning, June 20

Renzo had considered Matthias Ruch's farm to be run-down, especially in comparison to Hirschi's immaculate place. But when he pulled into Yves Lüthi's driveway, he saw how wrong he'd been. *This* was what a run-down farm looked like. Peeling paint, skewed shutters, and a drooping crop of weeds in the former flowerbeds spoke of months of neglect. Cherries had fallen unheeded onto the courtyard from a gnarled tree and now lay rotting in the sun. The smell of decay added to the picture of desolation.

Renzo knocked on the farmhouse door. No answer. He decided to prowl around. The house and barn were under one enormous, deeply eaved roof. He wandered along the side of the building toward the wide-open barn door and peered inside. In one corner was equipment meant to be attached to a tractor—that was the best identification he could manage, although words like *winnow* and *harrow* came to mind. Most of the vast space was empty.

"Who the fuck are you?"

Renzo whirled around and found a large, gaunt man standing twenty feet from him.

"Herr Lüthi?"

"What the fuck are you doing here?"

Renzo reached for the police ID in his back pocket and held it out. "Renzo Donatelli from the *Kantonspolizei*. I'd like to talk to you about a murder I'm investigating."

"Fuck off!" Despite his words, the man crossed over to where Renzo was standing and peered at the badge with Renzo's name and photo on it. He smelled almost as bad as the cherries in his yard, and a wave of alcohol-tainted breath wafted toward Renzo as the man repeated, "Just fuck off!"

No use being subtle with this sot.

"Do you know a twenty-four-year-old from Bern called Simu Etter?"

Renzo had been expecting a blank look, but the man's eyes narrowed. Renzo could see him calculating.

"I know a lot of Etters."

Renzo got out the photograph, but Lüthi didn't even glance at it.

"Don't bother," Lüthi said. "I don't want you here. Just get in your car and leave."

"This Simu, he spent a lot of time in Haldiz," Renzo continued, ignoring the man's anger. "He was growing marijuana on Frank Schwab's land. Now he's dead."

"Simu's dead. So what?"

"You knew him."

"He drank at the Star; I drank at the Star. Back when I could afford it. Lots of people knew him. Now get off my land. Fucking *Tschugger*."

Jesus! Plucking information out of this boozer was like jiggling nails out of a plank. But Lüthi acted like he might know something worth the extraction.

"Over the past couple of months, Simu has been trying to rent buildings or land from farmers around here. Did he approach you?"

"No."

"I just want to know if he asked about using your space. That's no crime."

"Asking may not be a crime, but trespassing is. I'm not going to say it again. Get off my farm." Lüthi was snarling now; his fists were raised.

Renzo remembered Hirschi saying that this man had thrown a Bio Suisse adviser off his property. Rage seemed to be his natural state. He'd leave him to his misery—he had enough now for a search warrant.

Renzo turned to leave, but not fast enough to suit Lüthi.

The farmer shoved his shoulder into Renzo's chest. As Renzo recovered from his loss of balance, Lüthi gave him a powerful punch in the gut with his right hand. Breathing through the pain, Renzo grabbed Lüthi's right wrist and swung his own arm up to bash his left elbow into the hinge of the Lüthi's jaw. The farmer, who was already yelling at the top of his lungs, screamed and slumped forward. Thinking he was giving up the fight, Renzo moved in to hold the man upright, and Lüthi reared his body back, twisted sideways, and butted Renzo just over the temple with his forehead, following that with a knee in Renzo's crotch. Now it was Renzo's turn to scream, although he bit down on the sound as soon as he realized he'd made it. Forcing himself to stay upright, Renzo moved away from Lüthi, took a few seconds to master the agony in his groin, and then spun around and kicked the man on the side of the head. The fight was over. As Lüthi lay curled on the dirty stone paving, Renzo made sure he was breathing normally, took restraints out of his pocket, and fastened Lüthi's hands behind his back.

With the farmer immobilized on his stomach, Renzo leaned against his car and let the pain wash over him. Just trying to stand upright was excruciating. In between small panting groans, he muttered a string of Italian obscenities aimed as much at himself, for his careless inattention, as at the farmer.

"*Verfiggte Tschingg*," Lüthi mumbled into the ground. Apparently, he could recognize Italian when he heard it.

Renzo couldn't help it. He rasped out a laugh even though it made his gut hurt even more. Lüthi had called him a fucking cop and a fucking wop in just a matter of minutes, the latter while he was face down, hands cuffed. Lüthi was not easily cowed; you had to say that for him. Renzo limped over, hauled the farmer to his feet, and half-dragged, half-carried him to where he could sit on the ground with his back against a wall. Lüthi proceeded to try to wriggle away.

"Keep still, you maniac," Renzo shouted at him. He realized there was no way he could risk putting this man into the backseat of his car. Renzo wasn't sure he'd be able to respond fast enough if the fucker somehow managed to throw himself into the front seat or started banging his head against a window. The risk that Lüthi would hurt himself was too great. He might also crash the car. Renzo would have to call for backup. Shit. All he wanted to do was find some ice for his poor balls, and now he was going to have to sit around waiting with Lüthi. At least it gave him more time to try to get the man to talk. After he'd called Central and asked them to send the nearest police patrol, he propped the farmer back up against the wall he'd rolled away from and, trying not to clutch at his crotch, perched gingerly on the same wall.

"While we're waiting for the cops to get here, want to change your mind and tell me what you know about Simon Etter?"

"I don't know anything."

"The police are going to have you in a room asking you the same thing. Over and over. With no alcohol. Think of that. Why not save yourself some pain and talk to me?"

"Fuck you."

"Yeah, I think I got that message. But the one who's currently fucked is you, Lüthi. Even more fucked than you already were—if that's possible." Renzo glanced around the decrepit farm and bit off a nasty comment about the place. The man's wife and kids had left him. His entire life was a wreck. Now, bound with plastic ties, he sat in the mud and sagged against the crumbling wall at one end of his courtyard. All around him, every building seemed to sag with him.

"I want a drink!" he yelled.

"Shut up," Renzo growled, his burst of sympathy vanishing. He wandered out of earshot, keeping Lüthi well within sight, and started to phone Giuliana, before realizing that she might still be with the

Albanian. So he called Noah and told him what had happened. Thank God it wasn't Erwin he had to tell about this fuck-up. Noah's sympathy was bad enough.

"Get the patrol to bring Lüthi to us; we'll stick him in a cell and sic Erwin on him," said Noah. "That'll serve him right. You say you're pretty sure Etter approached him."

"He says not, but I don't believe him."

"Okay. In the meantime, get yourself to a doctor and make sure you're okay to drive.

"I just need ice and painkillers."

"You know the rules as well as I do. See a doctor."

"Yeah, I will. I'll do it. In the meantime, let me tell you about the Lakers meeting."

Fifteen minutes later, with Lüthi curled up against the wall snoring, Renzo was relieved to hear a siren in the distance. Now all he'd have to do was find the nearest emergency clinic.

It was after one by the time the doctor finished examining Renzo and diagnosed a mild concussion; the rest was bruising—serious but not dangerous. The doctor thought he should be monitored for a day or two, to make sure his head was all right, but Renzo refused to be shunted into the hospital, so he was commanded to go home and rest and given a packet of strong painkillers to ease the waiting time. With the first dose already dulling an infinity of aches, he hobbled into Giuliana's case-room. She glanced at his face and posture, did a double take, leaped out of her chair, and hurried over to him. She touched his arm tentatively, as if he were an unexploded bomb.

"Renzo, what is it? Sit down." She pointed to Sabine's padded desk chair. He approached it slowly and lowered himself onto it an inch at a time.

"What happened? Did you have a close encounter with a Seeland tractor?"

"Not a tractor—a man. I spend at least an hour at the gym every morning, take one combat class after another, and still manage to get myself beat up by a broken-down drunk at least ten years older than me. I've got a massive headache, a black-and-blue belly, and testicles that feel like beach balls. Good thing Fränzi and I aren't planning any more kids."

"Oh my God."

Giuliana's eyes were wide. It was nice to get the sympathy, but Renzo didn't want to scare her. "I'm completely fine, actually, and full of oxycodone. Don't worry about me—it will all heal."

"The farmer that the inspector woman said was going to pieces. Did he attack you?"

"Yeah. Yves Lüthi."

"Guess he hadn't quite fallen apart." He had to smile at that. "I'm so sorry you got hurt. Did he give you any information . . ." She stopped, looking stricken.

"Before he pulverized me? No, he wouldn't talk. But he's here in a cell. Erwin will get something out of him. At least he admitted he knew Simu."

"How was the rest of your morning in Haldiz?"

"I'm not sure it got us much further, except we know for sure now that Simu was searching for another partner. Or maybe even several at once."

He told her about the young farmers standing up at the meeting, and Giuliana listened, occasionally writing something in her notebook.

"Did you get a revelation from that?" Renzo asked.

"The three men who said Simu approached them," she began. "Perhaps one of them figured it would be better to *appear* virtuous, in case he and Simu had been seen together. Maybe he *did* make a deal with Simu."

"Could be. Noah said he'll send Pauline to get more detail out of them. But I think they're telling the truth; I don't think there *is* much more to their stories. Simu approached them, and they turned him down." Renzo tried not to wince as he moved in his seat.

Giuliana was gnawing on her pen. "Let me get you some coffee. Don't move."

"Wait. I came in here to ask you to give me something to do."

"Go home. I'm absolutely sure that's what the doctor prescribed when he gave you the painkiller."

"There's no way in hell I'm taking a break from the investigation at this point."

"For God's sake. Go lie down and let your pills do their work."

He didn't move. Damn it, he felt bad enough about letting himself get beat up without getting thrown off the case. Giuliana must have read the anger in his face because she said, "Okay, okay. If you're determined to stay, then you can have a look at these photographs. They're all from the night of the Dance-In."

On her desk, she had fanned out blowups of the best likenesses of Etter that she'd gotten from his family. She moved her chair aside, and Renzo drew closer, shuffling. "Here's Simu. Now, scroll through the photos on my tablet. I think I've found him in the first four. Do you agree?"

He moved slowly through the four photos, zooming in and out of each one. "Yes," he agreed, pointing at one figure in each picture. "That's him." Next, she showed him six "maybes," and he went through them with the same care.

"These three you can move to your 'definite' file. Check out the shoes. Those are Simu's."

"His shoes? Doesn't everyone wear high-top sneakers?"

"Yes, but look at his shoelaces. If you zoom in on this color photo and look closely, you'll see they are bright orange and exceptionally broad. They're distinctive enough that you can identify them even in the black-and-white pictures."

"How could I have missed that? Now I have to go back through all the preliminary identifications and look at shoelaces."

"I'll do it," Renzo offered.

"Before you start, have a look at this file. There are at least thirty men here Jonas thinks could be Simu's companion. A couple of the pictures are repeats of the same person, but mostly they're quite different-looking men with just a few things in common—short blond or light-brown hair and medium height and weight. No extreme facial features. All under fifty."

"If Jonas is making someone up, that's exactly who he'd choose—Fritz Average," Renzo said.

"Yeah. Like the sketch Bruno did for him: a youngish, unexceptional white male."

"Have any of the photos of Simu included someone matching that description?" asked Renzo. "Actually, that's a stupid question, isn't it? Half the men at the Dance-In fit."

"Still, I know what you mean. I've cross-checked the photos once without getting any definite results, but I'd be glad if you'd try." Giuliana gestured to Sabine's computer. "Sit there, and I'll get your tablet so you can access everything from the central database. Is it on your desk?" He protested her waiting on him, but she rolled her eyes and hurried to the office he shared with a group of other *Fahnder*.

For the next two hours, Renzo watched video clips and examined photographs until his headache became unbearable. He found only two tentative matches, which he didn't bother to show Giuliana. Instead, he started going through the photos Giuliana had rejected to see if the broad orange shoelaces made an appearance. Thousands of men in shorts and women in halter tops or tiny T-shirts flashed by, most of them with their mouths open, first singing and then, once the riots started, screaming.

He took a break to go to the toilet, drink water, and take another painkiller. Then he returned to the photos. Face after face. Until he recognized one.

"*Madonna*," he whispered. Giuliana turned to him.

"It's Christian Hirschi on Bollwerk." The time stamp on the picture was 1:50 a.m.

"Is he with anyone?" Giuliana asked.

"Can't tell. According to him, he went drinking that night with his wife's cousin from Spain. He told me he got home around one, but here he is walking down the street in Bern just before two. Why would he come to Bern when he could drink somewhere closer, like Kerzers?"

"Kerzers! It may be his nearest town, but it doesn't even have five thousand people. If I wanted to show a foreign visitor a good time, I'd take him somewhere more exciting. With the Dance-In going on, Bern was roaring last Saturday night."

"That's true. Hirschi could have driven forty minutes to treat his wife's cousin to a beer in Bern. But we're convinced there's a connection between Simu's and Frank's deaths, and now we have proof that an organic farmer from Haldiz, a Laker like Frank, was in Bern shortly before Simu was killed, walking around a few blocks away from the place where the homicide happened."

"Still doesn't seem so unlikely to me. Tell me more about him," Giuliana said.

"He's thirty-three years old, married, no kids, took his place over from his father, and made it organic. A very successful farmer who seems tremendously respected in the community. Already the head of the Lakers. People demand a lot of him, and he takes his responsibilities seriously. Ruch thinks he's on his way to a national career at Bio Suisse. Imagine what someone like that would have to lose by killing Frank or Simu."

Renzo went on to tell her everything he could remember about his encounters with Hirschi, first at the gleaming farmhouse and then at that morning's meeting.

"So something felt a bit off between him and his wife," Giuliana summarized, "and several Lakers objected to his recommending Fraîche as a buyer. Plus, you observed him arguing with Pfeiffer."

"I could be wrong about the marriage problems. He seemed crazy about his wife, but she was, I don't know . . . unresponsive? Not just to him, to everything. He also asked me to make sure she didn't find out he was drinking late on Saturday night."

Giuliana looked over Renzo's shoulder at the color photo. Someone else was the intended target of the shot. But the man off to one side, whom Renzo had identified as Hirschi, was in sharp focus as well.

"You realize Hirschi is blond, medium height, and has a pleasant-but-vanilla face," she said. "He fits Jonas's type. Is he Simu's companion in any of the photos that have been singled out?"

Together they combed the photo files, looking for shots of Hirschi and Simu together. They found three vague possibilities. Renzo spent long minutes examining a man who was behind Simu in one photo, his head turned partially away from the camera. Every time Renzo zoomed in on the figure, it went out of focus.

Giuliana leaned back in her chair in frustration. "Let's not waste any more time. We'll send the best of these to the lab. They can probably give us better-focused close-ups of some of the background figures."

Thank God for opiates, Renzo was thinking. He could feel all the pain in his body slowly receding. Unfortunately, his concentration seemed to be receding as well. He focused on what Giuliana was telling him, but her voice sounded odd to him. He murmured words of agreement anyway.

"We'll run the riot footage through the photo-recognition program again," she said, "this time looking for Hirschi. We'll need to give IT a good likeness of him for comparison. Once we have that, we'll also send someone to Bollwerk and try the photo in all the cafés and bars. Someone might remember Hirschi. And who he was with."

Renzo struggled back into focus. "I know where we can get his picture," he told her. "Hirschi and his wife were in a Migros TV commercial. If the lawyers can get Migros's PR department to let us have it, the lab can generate some good shots of him. Hell, it might even be on YouTube. There's only one problem with all of it," he added. "Why would Christian Hirschi hang out with Simu Etter? Based on everything I've learned about the two men, they don't have much in common. Hirschi didn't quite say so, but it's clear he wasn't a Simu fan."

"First let's find out if Hirschi was in Bern with his cousin-in-law or Simu. Or both. If it really turns out the two men were together, we'll focus on the reason."

"Okay," Renzo said. "Once you get the photo-recognition work lined up, I'll send IT a link to the commercial. And I'll look into Hirschi's farm. It's got to be inspected by someone."

"Find the ad, talk to the inspector if you must, and then go home and cover yourself with ice packs," said Giuliana. She was already on the phone and not paying attention to him when he shook his head at her and left, inching his way down the hall.

27

Nordring police station,
Thursday afternoon, June 20

Renzo poked his head into an office where two men in their thirties and a middle-aged woman sat at computers. "Hello. Did one of you check out Christian Hirschi's alibi for Frank's death?" he asked. "That was me," the woman said. She got up and followed him out into the corridor, where he introduced himself and asked for details.

"Hirschi checks out," she said. "The drivers who were at his farm until after six on Friday say his car was boxed in by one of their trucks. Plus, he was dashing around checking their loads and talking to his workers. They don't all agree on what he was doing for four solid hours, but he was definitely under observation for most of the time from two to six."

"Most of it?" Renzo asked.

"Yeah. See, Noah fixed us up with a map of all the houses and farms in Haldiz labeled with their owners' names. Hirschi's farmhouse is near the train station, a little over a mile from Schwab's place. Hirschi might have been able to sneak into the fields, walk to Schwab's, kill him, and return without tipping anyone off. But I calculated the whole process would have taken him about forty-five minutes, especially if he was trying not to be seen, and not that much time passed without one of those drivers spotting him. So I think you can assume Hirschi's alibi for Friday is solid."

"Well, so much for that, then," said Renzo, although he still thought that Hirschi could have made the round trip and committed the murder in less than forty-five minutes. "What about his alibi for Saturday night?"

"That depends on the wife's cousin, the Spanish truck driver, right? Chuy López speaks Spanish, so he's going to call him in Spain. But Chuy won't be here until five. Which means Hirschi's alibi for the time of Etter's death isn't confirmed yet."

Renzo returned to his desk and eased himself into his chair. While he searched for Bio Inspecta's phone number, he thought about Hirschi's alibi getting him off the hook for Frank's death. Had he and Simu plotted together to kill Frank, and then, after Simu committed the murder, had Hirschi gotten rid of his accomplice? But why go after Frank in the first place? Renzo knew greed was a powerful motive, but for someone as successful as Hirschi to be interested in the marijuana field on Frank's property—or in anything to do with dope—made no sense.

Reaching Bio Inspecta, Renzo asked for the director, Mario Valente. "Can you let me know in confidence if your firm inspects Christian Hirschi's farm in Haldiz?" he asked Valente after identifying himself.

"Hirschi! Yes, he is one of our clients."

"I'm investigating two homicides that we believe are connected, and I need to speak with you urgently, so I'd be grateful if you could clear the decks for me," Renzo said. "I'm also going to need your assurance that you won't talk to anyone about our conversation."

Valente was silent, but only for a moment, before saying, "I'd be glad to help. Give me twenty minutes. That way, I can take care of a few urgent things and cancel an appointment. I'll call you back."

"I understand. Let me give you the main police number in Bern—ask for Donatelli." That way, Valente couldn't claim afterwards he hadn't known Renzo was a cop.

As he waited for the call, Renzo scrolled through the Bio Inspecta website. The organization had ninety employees in Switzerland who inspected, certified, or advised five thousand organic farms and eighteen hundred food-processing establishments, large and small. He clicked around the professional-looking site. "Bio Inspecta assists farm holdings in sustainable development," he read under one heading and, on a page about inspection, "Most of our inspectors are practicing organic farmers who work in a responsive manner." It went along with what Pia Tanner had said about being more interested in helping farmers than punishing them. Not that he imagined they'd let sympathy get in the way of enforcing their regulations.

Renzo's phone rang.

"I assume this is about Frank Schwab," said Valente right away. "I don't think there's anyone here who doesn't know him or know of him. He's a legend to us—even if he didn't have Bio Suisse certification. Which, when you think about it, is funny. But nothing about his being killed is funny, so I hope I can help you."

"I hope so, too. You see, Frank's death may be related to a second killing, which occurred about thirty-six hours later. It's in connection with both these homicides that I want to talk to you about Christian Hirschi."

"I have to confess that that's . . . awkward. He's . . . um . . . in trouble with us."

An "Aha" filled Renzo's head. So Hirschi's perfect farm *was* too good to be true. More marijuana, huh? He knew it was great news for his case—but for a moment all he could feel was disappointment. He liked Hirschi, damn it. The man had let him down. So much for thinking he was good at reading people.

"Let's start with you explaining why Hirschi's in trouble," Renzo said.

"We've recently realized that his farm hasn't been properly inspected for years."

"How could that happen?"

"Let me give you some background," said Valente. "Hirschi

started talking to Bio Suisse about making the family farm organic when he was a seventeen-year-old apprentice. Eventually, his father agreed, and the two of them made the switch. One of our most knowledgeable inspectors guided them through the process of conversion and continued to advise them afterward. This man has been battling cancer, and three years ago he lightened his workload, but he kept a few inspection jobs."

"And one of them was Hirschi's."

"Right. The inspector took early retirement in January, and one of our new young inspectors was assigned many of his clients, including Hirschi. He eventually pulled Hirschi's files and started going over the forms. He discovered a mess. No, that's not true. The files are exceptionally neat. Hirschi has dotted every *i*. Only, some things don't fit. We checked the former inspector's records to see how he explained the discrepancies, and we found barely any notes. It appears that he hadn't walked that farm in years when he retired. He knew the Hirschis, father and son, and he always took them at their word."

"I gather that you haven't come to any official conclusions, but can you tell me how much marijuana you think is involved?"

"Marijuana?" Valente sounded bewildered. "We don't have any reason to think he's growing marijuana."

"What?" It had never occurred to Renzo that Valente's problems with Christian Hirschi weren't somehow related to marijuana. Everything else in this case seemed to be. He bowed his head over his desk in disappointment. Shit—this call had started so well, and now it was turning irrelevant.

"What worries us," Valente was saying, "is his balance. We're studying his production figures, and they don't add up. We haven't figured out what's going on yet. But we will."

Renzo wanted to get up and pace around the room, but he couldn't even get out of his chair. Stifling a groan, he sank back. "Hirschi's balance," he echoed. "Right. Someone at Bio Test Agro said you inspectors can predict how much a farmer should produce of each crop, once you know how much land he's using plus seed and manure and . . . whatever else is involved. If a farmer has too much of a crop, he's probably using more fertilizer than he's allowed to. Or breaking the *bio* rules some other way."

"That's it, more or less. Hirschi has a big farm, and he produces at least a dozen different vegetables and a variety of salad greens. He sells most of them to Migros and some to Fraîche. But something's wrong."

"Does he know you're looking into his farm?"

"The new inspector had a first chat with him two days ago, on Tuesday. The official inspection wouldn't normally be until November, but the new man wants to set up a preliminary visit as soon as possible, to get a handle on what's going on. Hirschi came up with lots of excuses for them not to meet—his wife's health, the stress of the harvest, an upcoming trip to Spain. All reasonable. But it fed our suspicions that he's hiding something."

"What's wrong with his wife?" Renzo asked.

"Umm." Valente's discomfort could be felt even through the phone. "That's gossip."

"Tell me," Renzo insisted.

"She grew up on a Spanish mega-farm in the south, surrounded by a big family, friends nearby. She and Hirschi have been married three or four years now, and she's very lonely. On top of that, she found out recently that she can't have children. She's being treated for depression. I imagine Hirschi's very worried about her. Not that he said so to the inspector, but I know all of this through a Spanish coworker of ours."

Renzo remembered the listlessness he'd noticed in Asunción. No babies. How terrible for them. Could she also be depressed because she knew her husband was doing something illegal? Or cheating on her? Could his lies about what he was doing on Saturday night really be something as simple as a girlfriend in Bern?

"What are your next steps?" he asked Valente.

"If he won't agree to an inspection, we'll pay a surprise visit to his farm. Probably in the next couple of weeks. But we're hoping to do it with his cooperation. He's well respected—and until recently nothing seems to have been irregular."

Renzo rolled his eyes at such vagueness.

"You are going to have to be clearer with me, Herr Valente. What exactly do you suspect him of doing? And are you sure it doesn't have anything to do with marijuana?"

Valente blew out a long, noisy breath. "I don't want to be obstructive but . . . well, these things are very bad publicity for us: customers being sold nonorganic food that carries the Bio Suisse bud. We think Hirschi has been doing that for two or three years now. As for growing dope, I don't see how he could do it, at least not on any grand scale. He's not selling too few vegetables for the size of his farm; he's selling too many."

Finally, something concrete. "So you think he's using banned fertilizer?" Renzo asked.

"Something like that," said Valente, taking refuge in obscurity again. "Look, do you really think this could have something to do with Frank's death? Or with the second death you're investigating? I'm positive Frank knew nothing about Hirschi's . . . irregularities, because if he had, he would have called Bio Suisse immediately. He was a strikingly straightforward man. Someone palming off vegetables that weren't really organic would have infuriated him."

From what *he* knew about Frank, Renzo thought the old farmer might have confronted Hirschi personally before doing anything else, and Hirschi could have killed him to keep him quiet. Friday afternoon's alibi sounded unbreakable. Still, the knowledge that Hirschi was running some kind of secret scam twisted both homicide cases into a whole new shape.

Renzo didn't give a damn about Bio Suisse's fear of bad publicity, but he decided to stop pushing Valente while he considered the implications of what he'd just learned. "The police need to know exactly what Hirschi's up to, so I hope you can figure this business out soon. And when you do, call me before you act on it. If it's fraud, the police are going to be involved anyway, and the sooner you get it out into the open, the better you are going to look for not covering it up. Whatever the hell 'it' is."

"I hear you," Valente said. "But we don't have all the facts yet, and we're not going to make anything public until we understand it ourselves."

"I am not the public," growled Renzo. "I need to know what you know, and I need to know it as soon as possible." Following this loss of temper, he took a deep breath, thanked Valente, and hung up.

Renzo thought about Hirschi's alibis for the two crucial periods of time: Friday afternoon, when so many people had seen him on his farm, and Sunday morning at almost two, when photos put him in Bern even though he'd claimed to be home by then already. If he was lying about what he and Díaz had been up to, chances were that his wife's cousin would back him up. Was there a way to double-check where the Spaniard had been that night?

Ignoring the throbbing in his head and stabs in his gut and groin, he reflected for a while and then looked up the number of the Star. The voice that answered the phone was hoarse from many cigarettes but still flirtatious—Nadine Löffel. He'd have to take a very low-key approach to this conversation. None of it could get back to Hirschi.

"Frau Löffel, this is Renzo Donatelli, the cop from Bern."

"Oh, I remember you."

"I hope you have time for a quick question. I'm doing some routine checking of all the Lakers' alibis, and at the moment I'm working on Christian Hirschi's. Has he ever come into the Star with a relative of his wife's?"

"You mean Luis? Sure. Nice guy. You don't think Luis had something to do with Frank's death?"

"No, no. I'm interested in him as a witness. Do you know if he was visiting the Hirschis last Saturday evening?"

"Last Saturday evening. Hmm. I worked until two in the morning, and I served a lot of people." Renzo waited while she thought back. "I don't recall seeing either of them. Luis tips well and he's cute, so I'm pretty sure I'd have noticed him. I don't remember his truck, but that doesn't mean it wasn't there."

"That's right. He's a trucker, isn't he?"

"Yeah, that's why he can visit so often. He drives a huge refrigerated truck full of Asunción's father's vegetables. He travels all over Europe. He says ordering a drink in German is nothing—he can order beer in everything from Estonian to Greek. Whenever he's got a delivery that brings him through Switzerland, he stops here. I don't think he and Asunción are real first cousins—more like second cousins twice removed or something. But he and Christian get along great."

"He must have fun trying to park that truck in the Star's parking lot," Renzo said, keeping his tone casual to disguise his excitement. "You've only got—what?—four spaces."

She giggled. "He always parks in one of Christian's fallow fields."

"His fallow fields," Renzo repeated. His words formed a statement, but she heard their question anyway.

"That's right, I forgot. You're a city boy. Fallow means empty. Unplanted. This year Christian has a fallow field along my route to work, so I usually notice if Luis's truck is parked there."

"And was it parked there last Saturday night?"

"I'm sorry. I don't remember." To someone else she called out, "Just a minute." Frightened of losing her, Renzo poured charm into his voice. "I'm so grateful to you for taking the time to help me. I can imagine how busy you are. If you could just give me two more minutes, I'll be done. I hope I can buy you a drink the next time I'm in Haldiz, too."

"I think I can find two minutes for you," she purred.

"Thanks. Think back to Saturday night. How late did the crowd stay?"

"It was almost one before I got rid of the last of 'em."

"Then you had to clean up. How did you get home?"

"I have a Vespa, but when I work especially late, my ex-father-in-law picks me up. He's a night owl anyway—but it's a kindness."

"So think about driving home with him last Saturday. Was there moonlight?"

"It was raining, actually—I remember that now, because I was watching the wipers go back and forth and trying not to let them put me to sleep before I got home. Hang on," she added. "I really have to take these orders. I'll be back."

Shit. She could never have seen a truck parked in a dark field through a rain-covered windshield. Renzo waited anyway.

"No truck Saturday night," she chirped when she picked up the phone again.

"You suddenly remembered?"

"Nope. But one of the guys who just walked in lives across the street from where Luis usually parks. The truck is so big that when it pulls in and out he worries about damage to his hedge. So he keeps an eye on it, and he says the last time he saw the truck in that field was ten days ago. He sounds sure."

"That's terrific. Does he know it's the police asking?"

"Of course not. They'd never tell me anything if they knew it was for the *Tschuggerei.* But I know *you're* okay. Just don't go getting Luis into trouble."

"Of course I won't," Renzo lied cheerfully. "We need him as a witness, that's all."

"You want me to let you know the next time his truck is here?"

"No, no. As I said, it's no big deal. Just routine checking. But I really appreciate your help." He repeated his promise about the drink and hung up. Then he wrote an urgent email to his Spanish-speaking colleague, Chuy López. Even if Hirschi had told Luis to back up his drinking story, they might not have thought of the truck. If Chuy asked Luis about his parking place in a casual enough way, he might answer without thinking and put the truck where Renzo now knew it hadn't been. That would provide honest-to-God proof that Hirschi was lying about Saturday night. Renzo added some questions Chuy could ask to keep Luis from seeing the trap. Then he phoned Chuy's cell. No answer, so he left a message telling him to read the email before he called the Spaniard; he'd call Chuy again just before five to make sure he was on board with the plan.

Now if only the photo lab would find evidence of a meeting between Hirschi and Simu in Bern during the Dance-In . . . But even if it all clicked—a clear photo of the two men together, a confirmation from Jonas that Hirschi had been Etter's companion—the question still remained. Why? Why would Hirschi want Simu dead? And what about Frank? Could Hirschi have killed him after all? Despite the investigator's conviction that there wasn't enough time, Renzo decided to run the path between Hirschi's and Frank's farms himself and see how fast he could do it. Then he slammed his fist on the desk as he remembered: in this state, he'd be lucky if he could crawl.

Renzo knew his painkiller was wearing off. His head hammered, and even the smallest movement hurt his gut, as if Lüthi's fist had been the size of a skillet. He forced himself to stop thinking about how much he ached. Giuliana needed to know what he'd learned about Hirschi's mysterious fraud and Luis's truck. Besides, maybe she'd heard something useful from the photo lab.

He tried to get up, and the pain grew worse. He pressed his lips together to keep from groaning, reached into his shirt pocket for the foil pack of oxy, and took half a pill. With both hands on the desk, Renzo lifted himself out of the chair. By the time he struggled to the door, the idea of roaming around in search of Giuliana seemed ludicrous. He propped himself up against the doorframe and fumbled for his cell. Fuck! It wasn't in his pants pocket, and he couldn't think where it was. Had he lost it at Lüthi's farm? He groaned, remembering how he'd longed to protect Giuliana from the drug boss and then been unable to protect himself from a drunk. *Testa di cazzo!* He was an utter fuck-up.

It was only four thirty, but a glass of white wine or—better yet—a frosted pint-mug of beer called to him. Several lines of the small print that came with his medicine warned him strongly against mixing it with alcohol, yet he couldn't imagine anything that would make him feel better—or at least less pissed off with himself. Some cold beer followed by unconsciousness, hopefully in bed at home and not over his drink.

He limped back to his desk and called Giuliana from the office phone.

"It turns out Hirschi may be a criminal," he told her, "but it has nothing to do with dope. If you want to hear more, you're going to have to come have a drink with me."

"You need a drink like I need a chat with the commandant," Giuliana said. "Your voice is slurred from the painkillers. You shouldn't be here; you know that."

Renzo tried very hard to speak clearly. "Seriously. I've found out from Bio Suisse that Hirschi is running a scam. Some of the veggies he sells aren't really organic. And . . ." He knew he needed to tell her about the truck, too, and the little trap he'd set for Asunción's cousin. But she interrupted before he'd gathered all the words he needed to explain anything so complicated.

"I can't come for a drink right now. That wasn't a joke about the commandant. Jürg and I are meeting with him in five minutes. He doesn't think we're making enough progress."

"Tell him about Hirschi's scam."

"Believe me, he isn't interested in vegetables. Only hard drugs. Specifically, in my proving that Etter had something to do with them, and they had something to do with his death. Ideally, the Reitschule should come into it somewhere, too."

Renzo heard the bitterness in her voice, but he couldn't come up with anything comforting to say except, "I'm sorry."

"Yeah, me, too. Listen, I *am* interested in what you've learned. Explain it to me in a message on my cell, and I'll listen to it as soon as this meeting is over. Okay?"

"Sure. Good luck."

After the call ended, Renzo sat unmoving. No Giuliana. So, if she wouldn't come for a beer with him, he'd go by himself. And then home. Otherwise he was going to collapse and embarrass himself even more than he already had. He'd walk to the train station, have a beer, and catch the no. 9 tram home. Surely he could manage that. Hmm. Maybe not the walk over the bridge to the station. He'd take the bus.

He was still gathering the energy to leave when his desk phone rang. It was Louise.

"Frau Fehr," he enunciated, conscious now of how he was beginning to slur. "I'm glad you called. Do you have information for us?"

"I phoned to ask if you had information for *me,*" she answered. "I can't stop wondering why . . . Frank and Simu. It makes no sense. I know it's only been two days since we talked, but I hoped you'd have something by now."

"I'm so sorry I can't talk to you about the case. But I believe we're getting there."

After a moment of silence, she said, "I hope so," and hung up on a sigh.

Renzo sighed, too. Now he wanted a beer even more than before.

28

Nordring police station and Wabern, Thursday evening, June 20

"... a clear connection between the dead man and the Albanian," the commandant said. "Etter was linked to hard drugs, as we suspected."

Giuliana was back at the round table, staring at the hanging pot of fuchsias in the boss's window again, this time with Jürg instead of Noah in the chair next to her. She kept her face blank to hide her exasperation with the commandant's words. *No, not "as we suspected,"* she told him silently. I *am convinced after talking to Asllani that Etter was only interested in getting money for his marijuana plantation.* You *are the one who wants Etter's death to follow the pattern you laid out for the press and the public.*

Both she and Jürg hoped to forget about Asllani for the present, although for different reasons. Giuliana was inclined to believe the man's story and thought they should look elsewhere for Etter's backer. Jürg was worried that if the police kept hassling Asllani, the boss in Albania might shut him down and replace him, and the narcs would have to figure out all over again who was handling heroin distribution in Bern. Giuliana and Jürg had spent time discussing who, if anyone, in the cocaine trade might be worth approaching. The South

Americans weren't as organized as the Albanians, so the target in Bern wasn't clear.

"I hear why you want to keep Asllani out of an interrogation room, Jürg," said the commandant, "but he has confessed to speaking with Etter. We need to bring him in."

Giuliana found herself protesting. "Tomorrow's Friday. Let's wait, say, five more days to pick him up. Until Tuesday. By then I may have other leads."

The commandant shook his head. "Etter was killed on Sunday, and we don't have a single real suspect. Asllani's arrest would . . ."

"I expect to have someone brought in for questioning tomorrow," Giuliana said.

Both men looked at her in surprise.

"Oh yes?" said the commandant.

"One of our investigators, Renzo Donatelli, has discovered a farmer in Haldiz who is involved in criminal activities." *Jesus, I sound like a rookie's report*, she thought, and carried on anyway. "The man knew both Simon Etter and François Schwab, and we believe he was with Etter just before his death. We should have enough evidence to bring him in . . . soon."

And I haven't even listened to Renzo's phone message, she thought, as she rolled out this tissue-thin tale for the commandant's inspection.

"Something to do with drugs, I assume?" he said.

"Mm . . . I need to get the details from Donatelli. I'll know more by Monday, though. Or earlier," she added, catching the commandant's scowl.

"Bring this farmer in now," he said.

"I'll do my best," said Giuliana, and to her relief, she and Jürg were released.

"Thanks for saving my ass in there—and Asllani's," said Jürg with a grin, "but I hope you didn't make up that 'criminal' farmer for my sake."

"Not quite," she told him, "but I'd better go do something about it."

She hurried back to the case-room to listen to Renzo's message.

It wasn't reassuring—Hirschi's problems clearly had nothing to do with drugs, which was not what the commandant wanted to hear, and Renzo's idea of catching the Spanish truck driver in a trap sounded too complicated to work. But he was right—this *was* something to follow up on. Giuliana was glad Sabine was out of the office; she needed to be alone to think.

Twenty minutes later her mobile rang, an unknown number.

"Linder."

"Giule. 'S me." She didn't recognize the voice. "'M using a man's phone. In the bar. C'n you have a drink now?"

Jesus, it was Renzo. He was a mess. Maybe that bang in the head had addled his brains. Probably just the oxy, though.

"Where are you, Renzo?"

"Train station. Meant to take the nine home, but . . . thought I'd better call you."

"I'll be there in fifteen minutes." *And thank God I don't have to find a legal parking place at the station.* "Renzo, don't order anything more to drink without me."

"Course not. Bye."

"Wait, wait. Which bar in the train station?"

"Dunno. 'S across from . . . Credit Suisse." He had some trouble with the *s* sounds.

"Okay. I know where it is. I'll be there. Wait for me."

"Always," he mumbled.

Oh no, not that again. "Just sit still."

Fifteen minutes later, she'd loaded a sheepish-looking and clearly hurting Renzo into her car, which she'd parked with supreme illegality right in front of the outdoor escalator closest to the lowlife bar where she'd found Renzo. She refrained from asking him why he'd chosen to drink in a place that he'd normally never be caught dead in. She wished there was a way to help him pull himself together before he got home to Fränzi. Maybe some fresh air. A couple of blocks from his apartment, she drove off the main street onto a small service road where she knew there was a bench overlooking the Aare.

"Can you talk?" she asked him, as he lowered himself to the bench where she was already sitting. What she really meant was, can you think?

"Yeah. Sorry. I didn't mean to do this." His voice was better now. "I only had two beers, but with the opiate . . ."

"I realize that. No problem. But I want to ask you something. Suppose Frank found out about Hirschi selling nonorganic produce. That's what Valente finally coughed up, right?"

"Yes. Bio Inspecta thinks Hirschi is ripping off organic-food customers. Valente is convinced Frank couldn't have known, because, if he had, he'd have called Bio Suisse. But I think he'd have gone to Hirschi first, to make sure it was true."

"And Hirschi has a reputation to lose," Giuliana said. "You've told me these Laker farmers look up to him."

"Not just a reputation. A livelihood. The big grocery chains only buy products that have been certified by Bio Suisse. If Bio Suisse kicks Hirschi out, he'll lose his market."

Renzo was hunched over, his arms wrapped around his belly. She'd been the one telling him to go to bed, and now she was keeping him talking. But if she was going to bring Hirschi into the station the next day, she had to have a good reason.

"Okay," she said. "So Hirschi couldn't let anyone know what he was doing. Suppose Frank confronted him with what he'd heard, and Hirschi suggested they talk about it last Friday afternoon. Then he came to Frank's place, killed him, and sprayed him with pesticide. Like, I piss on your organic principles, old man. Can you see that happening?"

Renzo nodded, just fractionally, and then his hand went up to his head and he closed his eyes. Opening them, he said, "Yes, it makes a kind of sense. But we have a practical problem. Hirschi's alibi. A lot of people at his farm were keeping a corner of their attention on him all through Friday afternoon. And you are suggesting that he grabbed a canister of pesticide and a spray wand, which were hidden somewhere on his *bio* property, ran like hell to Frank's, killed him, sprayed poison all over him and his shed, raced back, hid the pesticide, washed the stink off, and was calmly walking around his farm giving instructions before anyone could miss him. I suppose it's possible. But it wouldn't have been easy. We'll have to get someone to do a trial run between the two farms. I was planning to do it, but it'll be days before I'm fit enough to make good time."

"I'll set something up," she said, and stood. "Time to take you home. Um . . . does Fränzi know what state you're in?"

Renzo ignored this. "The other big problem besides Hirschi's alibi is: How did Frank find out about Hirschi's scam?"

She nodded. "The neatest solution would be that Etter uncovered it somehow. He told Frank, Frank told Hirschi, and Hirschi killed both of them so they wouldn't give him away."

"Hmm." Renzo didn't look happy.

"It doesn't work for you, does it?" said Giuliana. "Why?"

"I like Hirschi," he said. "Maybe he isn't Mr. Clean when it comes to farming, but I can't see him killing two people he knew, one after the other, just like that. Blim, blam."

"Okay," Giuliana said. "I hear you. But I think we have enough to bring Hirschi in tomorrow. The photo of him so close to the time and place of Simu's death is enough. Especially if the cousin lies about where his truck was parked. Plus, if Jonas identifies Hirschi from the photo lineup as Etter's companion, that will clinch it. Now, let's go."

Back in the car, Renzo closed his eyes. The pain was clearly worse. "When is Sabine showing Jonas the photo lineup?" he asked.

"The lab said the pictures would be ready by six," she told him. "Sabine promised to phone me as soon as she has Jonas's answer. Guess it's all running late."

"Call me when you hear," Renzo said, his voice slurring again.

She was not going to call him tonight, no matter what she learned—that was for sure. "You gon' talk t' Erwin 'n Noah 'bout this?" he went on.

"Hey, don't pass out. We'll be there in a minute, and I won't be able to carry you. Even Fränzi and I together can't manage it. Stay awake until you get home. To answer your question, yes. I'll phone Noah to let him know what's going on. And Rolf, of course. I'm also going to call Oliver about a search warrant for Hirschi's place."

"I'll go out to Haldiz first thing in the morning," he mumbled, but even as he said it his eyes fluttered closed. "I'll talk to Niklaus about his daughter's alibi and—well, I can at least walk the route from Hirschi's place to Frank's. I meant to do that today, until that fucker Lüthi hit me. But I'll finish up tomorrow."

Like hell you will. A minute later, she was unloading him at his door. While Renzo tried to wrestle his keys out of his pocket, she pressed the buzzer.

"Renzo?" a woman answered.

"Hi, Fränzi," she said. "Renzo's fine, but could you help me get him upstairs? I'm with the police, too," she added. "Giuliana Linder."

Fränzi burst out of the apartment building and gave a cry at the sight of Renzo being held up by the doorframe and Giuliana. Giuliana remembered her from their wedding six years earlier. It wasn't just her looks that made her so sexy, but something seething under the surface, an unquenchable energy. Which at the moment seemed mostly negative.

"What happened to him?"

Giuliana explained about Yves Lüthi, the doctor, the oxycodone, and the beer.

"He's not in any danger," she said, "unless he takes more pain-killers or drinks more alcohol. He just needs to sleep."

Fränzi shook her head. "Why do you *do* these things?" she asked. It was clear that, by "you," she meant the police.

Before Giuliana could figure out how to respond, Fränzi took a steadying breath and said, "Let's get him into the elevator." Together they maneuvered Renzo inside and stepped in with him. "'M okay," he said to his wife as they rode up. He rested his hand on her hip. "Got hurt. Stupid. Sorry."

"How badly is he hurt?" Fränzi asked.

Giuliana realized that she only knew what Renzo had told her;

she had to hope it was the truth. "Nothing that a couple of days of rest won't cure," she said.

"Well, that's a relief," Fränzi said, smiling at Giuliana for the first time.

Two small children stood in front of an open door, peering down the hall; the girl clutched her brother's T-shirt with both hands, and he had an arm around her. "Wait here for a minute," Fränzi said to Giuliana. "I need to get the kids back inside."

As soon as Fränzi disappeared into the apartment with the children, Giuliana turned and shook Renzo, before slapping him hard on the cheek. His eyes opened.

"Pull yourself together, or you'll scare your kids, and I know you don't want to do that. You're stoned out of your mind, but you need to walk from here into your bedroom like a normal person. Then you can collapse. I'll be beside you to prop you up."

"Got it," he said with unexpected distinctness. With his hand on the wall for support, he walked down the hall and into the apartment, where he called out to his kids in Italian, saying something about Papà being sleepy. Giuliana shepherded him into the bedroom, where she turned him over to Fränzi.

"I'll call tomorrow to tell you what the doctor says Renzo should do," Giuliana promised from the doorway.

Renzo was still managing to sit upright on the bed. Fränzi turned from where she was crouched, taking off his right shoe. Her face was tight with worry and anger.

"Yes, but tell me how I'm going to get him to do it," she said.

Giuliana gave her a crooked smile. "Good luck."

She knew she ought to feel sorry for Fränzi having to put up with all the "cop-crap," as Ueli sometimes called it. But her heart was with Renzo.

Back in the car, she noticed the time. Maybe Sabine had met with Jonas by now. She grappled her phone out of her purse, and, sure enough, her colleague had left a message.

"Hi, Giuliana. Bad news. I couldn't get Jonas to choose one of the faces. He kept saying he only saw the man in the dark, very quickly, and he couldn't really remember what he looked like. Call me if you want to talk. Otherwise, see you tomorrow."

Shit! She'd committed herself to bring Hirschi in for questioning. But no matter what she'd said to the commandant under pressure, there wasn't enough evidence. A photo of Hirschi and Simu together: that was what needed to turn up, and soon.

She crossed the Aare and took the narrow uphill curves between the Dalmazi Bridge and Helvetiaplatz. Fränzi's "Why do you *do* these things?" ran through her mind, and she realized she had been wrong to keep Ueli from saying all he'd wanted to say the evening before. Tonight, she'd listen without getting defensive and tell him that Isabelle could have been in danger from the police. Not at the detention center, whatever Ueli believed. But during the riots, a cop *could* have hurt her. Ueli was right about that, and she'd say so.

She thought about what she wouldn't tell Ueli, which was that she'd spent an hour that morning alone with a very dangerous man. Thank God procedure forbad her to talk about it. There were lots of other things she'd never told him during her many years of assignments. Which was just fine.

Her good resolutions came to nothing, however. Ueli was caught up in a last-minute assignment to write about the Swiss Farmers Union's angry rejection of a new federal trade agreement with Argentina, Uruguay, Paraguay, and Brazil. He was on the phone interviewing a member of the Mercosur trade delegation when she walked in, and only took time, once he'd hung up, to give her a quick kiss and an apology about dinner before focusing on his computer screen.

Giuliana sautéed onions, added cubes of frozen spinach to the pan, beat eggs, grated cheese, sliced bread, and soon had four omelets ready. She and the kids ate in the kitchen; Ueli at his desk. Lukas was full of talk about his class play, which was being performed in eight days, shortly before the end of the school year. The teacher had come up with a series of scenes about the Celtic hero Vercingetorix, who led the Swiss tribes of Helvetians against Julius Caesar. The play focused on Vercingetorix's short-lived victory, not his subsequent defeat and death. They'd had to draw lots to pick Romans, Lukas told them, because everyone wanted to be a Celt. *He* was a Celt.

"Can you listen to me say my lines, Mam?" he asked through a mouthful of omelet.

"What's your name again?" asked Isabelle. "Pain-in-the-butt-ix?"

Lukas was too pleased with himself to let his sister annoy him. "I'm called Crogix. That means brave. Sort of. I'm going to wear leggings with leather straps wound around them and a kind of poncho thing, only square. And I get to carry a spear."

Thank God no one expected her to sew costumes, thought Giuliana. All she and Ueli had to do was deliver a cake on the night of the play for the post-performance party. She could manage to produce a cake—if worse came to worst, she'd buy one.

"You put the dishes in the dishwasher as soon as supper's done, and then we'll go over your lines. Isabelle, wash the frying pan and wipe the counter when he's done, okay?"

Isabelle nodded, stuck her plate and glass in the sink, and ambled back to her room. Once Lukas was busy with the dishes, Giuliana knocked on her door.

"All we heard about at supper was the play. I want to know how you are," she said, kissing the top of her daughter's head. She perched on the arm of the overstuffed chair that Isabelle lay sprawled in, her school papers stuffed down the sides of the chair, her laptop resting on her stomach.

"I had lunch with Quentin again today," said Isabelle, the words coming out so fast Giuliana almost didn't understand them.

"Tell me about him." She prayed Isabelle wouldn't shrink from the question.

"Both his parents used to work for the UN. They lived for five years in Nairobi, and he went to an international school there. So his English is really good. And he's traveled a lot." Isabelle's eyes shone as she talked, and she looked right at Giuliana, not trying to hide her enthusiasm. "His focus is biology and chemistry, because he's interested in the environment. And . . . um. He's tall—with his hair in a bun. And he . . . he isn't someone who tries to be cool and ends up being obnoxious. He just *is* cool. He's nice, too. Not just to me, I mean—to most people at school. Kids *and* teachers."

Giuliana was relieved to hear Quentin was kind—even to teachers!

"He sounds like an interesting person." She knew better than to add, I hope we get to meet him someday. "I'll go listen to Lukas's lines. Are you thinking of coming to his play?"

"Sure, I'll come," Isabelle said. "Luna will be there. Her sister is in the band. Lukas's class and some of the younger ones are going to sing—did you know that?"

"They're singing?" She gave Isabelle a look of dread, and they both giggled.

"Yeah, the Romans are going to sing in Latin and the Helvetians in Gaelic—that was the closest the teacher could come to whatever they really spoke. Just two lines, Luna says, over and over—something about peace and brotherhood between different nations."

Isabelle was rolling her eyes as she described the treat in store for them.

"Oh, I see," said Giuliana. "These are politically correct, lefty Romans who aren't interested in conquering anyone. I can't wait to tell your father."

"He can write an article about it," Isabelle snorted. Giuliana stroked her hair and went off to listen to Lukas alias Crogix the Celt say his lines. Once Lukas was in bed with the lights off, she found Ueli at his computer, typing and stopping, typing and stopping, with a deep frown of concentration on his face. But when he heard her step, he looked up and chanted a few words of Latin. She laughed.

"I see you know all about the jolly Helvetians and the peace-loving centurions."

He stood up, stretched his back, took her in his arms, and kissed her. It was more friendly than passionate, but it made Giuliana smile.

"It won't do those bloodthirsty ten-year-olds any harm to get a dose of alternative history. Reality will descend once they start watching the news regularly."

"Want coffee?" Giuliana asked. "Tea?"

He shook his head.

"Everything going okay with your article?"

"I'm getting there. What about your murders?"

"We might, just might, have a breakthrough. Not a drug dealer, though. Which will give the commandant and the press a fit."

"Once you make an arrest," said Ueli, "no one's going to care what the commandant said about drugs and the Reitschule crowd. That's a constellation of troubles that's been around for decades. You know that better than I do. The media responds like Pavlov's dogs to each new rant against the Riding School, but it all fades pretty fast."

"I doubt we're talking about an arrest yet. Just more information."

"Well, I hope it goes well." He kissed her again and sat back down at his laptop.

"And I hope the editor likes your article."

He didn't respond; he'd retreated into the world of his writing. Smiling at his concentration, she wandered back to the kitchen to make her own tea. Then she opened her laptop at the kitchen table. She sent Sabine a quick email about their new interest in Hirschi but decided there was no point in disturbing her evening with a phone call; she also updated Oliver, who excused himself from the following morning's meeting but promised to be ready with the legal support for bringing Hirschi in and searching his place. Noah was next.

Before she could tell him anything, he said, "I was about to call you—I have good news. Or at least I think so—you'll have to explain it to me. One of the investigators, a guy named López, sent Renzo an email with a copy to me. I'll forward it to you. It says, "Luis Díaz confirmed that he and Hirschi barhopped until late on Saturday night, June 15. In Biel, not Bern. He claimed that he 'parked his truck in the usual place' and then drove to Biel with Hirschi in his car. I said, 'You mean that unplanted field off the Seestrasse?' as we agreed. He didn't answer for about ten seconds, then said yes. I didn't take it any further, so I don't think he got suspicious."

"That's great news, Noah. Now let me tell you what it's all about."

She explained about Renzo noticing the photo of Hirschi in Bern and about the trap set for Luis, and then summarized the call to Bio Inspecta and her idea that Frank might have confronted Hirschi with something he'd done that was against the rules of organic farming.

"You're saying Hirschi used the wrong spray on his lettuces or something. But he'd never kill Schwab over something like that," Noah protested. "I mean, it's nothing."

"It would destroy his reputation—Renzo says he's very well respected—and no one would buy his produce anymore. At least for a while. He could go broke before he got himself re-established as a conventional farmer."

"I stand corrected. Where do you think Etter comes into it?"

"Maybe Etter stopped by Frank's that afternoon and saw the murder—or figured it out. So Hirschi had to get rid of him, too."

"What does Rolf say?"

"I'm practicing on you," Giuliana said. "Now I'm going to talk Rolf through it."

"Well, I think you've got more than enough to question Hirschi."

Twenty minutes later Rolf had agreed that Giuliana and Renzo had enough evidence to act on, so she organized the pickup. The next morning at eight thirty the Erlacher police would ask Hirschi to accompany them to the Nordring station in Bern. She and Sabine should be interrogating him by nine fifteen.

29

Wabern,
Friday morning, June 21

Renzo woke up desperately needing to piss. Then he realized he couldn't move a muscle. Somehow, he got out of bed anyway. Trembling with pain, not standing, not quite crawling, he managed to reach the toilet. After that, he crouched for twenty minutes in the shower until he could stand upright. Slowly, slowly, he washed, shaved, dressed, took an oxycodone, and dragged himself into the kitchen. There on the table he found a note from Fränzi reminding him she was at work until one, and the kids were at his mother's all day. He filled the old Bialetti espresso pot with water and coffee and put it on the stove to boil, cut three slices of bread from the loaf, piled them with butter and apricot jam, and sat down at the table.

What had Giuliana and the others decided to do about Hirschi? Renzo had promised the Bio Inspecta guy that he'd call if they brought Hirschi in for questioning. That was something he could do from home, once he knew what was going on. But first, breakfast. The late morning sun shone through the window over the sink and made patterns on the table; the coffee, which was just bubbling up into the top of the pot, smelled like a blessing. Everything was quiet. He reflected on the luxury of being alone in his home. It almost never happened anymore, not since the kids were born.

The scalding espresso in his cup made him think of Matthias Ruch and his instant-with-goat's-milk. That was another comfortable kitchen. And a nice man. Every once in a while, he met someone through work that he really liked—and never saw again. He took a big bite of bread and smiled as he imagined driving over to Haldiz on a Saturday evening and asking Ruch to have a beer with him at the Star. That was never going to happen. Which was too bad, because he'd enjoy it.

His mind drifted from Ruch to Frank and then to Frank's last days. On Wednesday afternoon, a little over a week ago, Ruch had dropped by Frank's after lunch to have a chat. On Wednesday night, Jean-Pierre had forced himself to tell Frank about Simon Etter and the fungicide. Thursday evening had been the confrontation between Simu, Frank, and Louise. But what about Thursday during the day?

Renzo stuck his plate into the dishwasher and poured more espresso. Then he went into the small study he shared with Fränzi, sat down at their home computer, logged into the police central database for his case, and pulled up Frank's phone records, both landline and mobile. Other investigators had been through these, identifying all the numbers, but Renzo hadn't re-examined them.

Thursday morning Louise had called Frank's cell, probably about her plans to visit him that evening. Frank made no mobile calls out, but the landline records showed that he'd called the 062 area code. Whoever had been through the list of numbers had labeled that one FiBL, the Research Institute for Organic Agriculture. No details. Renzo felt for his own cell and with horror remembered thinking the afternoon before that he'd lost it at Lüthi's farm. He put his head in his hands, but, before he could start berating himself, he got a clear mental picture of it charging in his car. Thank God for that—but his car was still at the police station. God, he had been wasted yesterday. How was he going to function without his mobile?

Painfully, he fetched the family phone and dialed the 062 number.

"Hecht," a woman's voice said.

"Renzo Donatelli, Frau Hecht. I'm with the Bernese police, investigating François Schwab's death. I see he called you last Thursday morning. Could you tell me what that was about?"

"Oh, my God, yes. I heard about Frank. There was even a message from the boss here to call the police if we knew anything. But I . . ."

Renzo interrupted. "That's fine. What can you tell me about Frank's call?"

"He told me part of his land—he wasn't sure how much—had been contaminated with fungicide. I study the breakdown of chemicals in soil, so he asked me if I could check some samples for him. He also wanted his groundwater tested; I told him to send me that sample, too, and I'd get it to an analyst for him. Eventually we were going to work out a cleanup program together—but first we had to know how bad the damage was. He was coming by—this coming Monday. I've still got his name on my calendar. Oh, it's terrible to think that . . ."

The lamentations sounded genuine, but Renzo interrupted again, thanked the woman, and hung up. Okay. So Thursday morning Frank started planning the process of decontaminating Simu Etter's marijuana field, which meant he *was* going to destroy the unripe marijuana plants. It was helpful to have his intentions confirmed.

He continued to scroll down the phone records. There were three calls from Frank's landline to Simu's cell phone, the one his parents and friends used. These were short calls, probably messages. Presumably those messages were why Simu had turned up at Frank's that night and shoved him to the ground. On Friday, there was an early-morning landline call labeled "Fraîche." He remembered meeting Adrian Pfeiffer at Hirschi's, when Pfeiffer had mentioned a phone call from Frank to ask him about Fraîche's prices. This must be it. He sorted through the rest of the phone numbers, all identified: a place that delivered organic seedlings, then calls to several of Frank's health-food-store customers. No calls had been made from either phone after 1:45 p.m. Some time that afternoon, he had been killed.

Renzo thought with sadness about the man who had written that will. Perhaps he had sometimes been preachy, but that was no reason for him to be dead. Renzo's sorrow slid into a rage that had no outlet.

He called Erwin, whose ever-impatient "Sägesser" boomed in his ear.

"It's Renzo."

Erwin grunted. "Heard you took a headbutt and a knee to the nuts. You okay?"

"I'll live. I deserve worse for letting my guard down. But thanks for asking."

"Happens to all of us now and then. Just take it easy for a while."

"Hmm. Did you bring Hirschi in?"

"Yep. Giuliana and Sabine have been with him for a while now."

"Okay. Listen, I had to leave my car at the station yesterday, and my phone's in it. Can you tell Giule to call me at home when she can and fill me in on what Hirschi's saying?"

"Sure."

"Any calls you want me to make? My mouth still works, even if my ass is dragging."

"No jobs for you. Just two pieces of news. I'm about to break into Giuliana's interview and give her a photo. The photographers sharpened one of the pics you found and ran more facial comparisons. We've definitely got Etter and Hirschi side by side in Bern."

The photograph was a tremendous boost; Renzo felt like crowing and pumping his fist. Instead he mumbled, "Good to hear." Playing it cool with Erwin.

"Other piece of news is your man Lüthi. The fearless fighter. What an asshole! Says Etter did talk to him, and he—Lüthi, I mean—loved the idea of turning his barn into a dope plantation. But it never happened. Etter must have figured out what a loser the guy was and dropped him, because Lüthi never heard from him again. That's all I've gotten out of him. We'll hold him a while longer, and I'll squeeze him some more. But I think that's it."

"Thanks for dealing with him."

"You can owe me. Now be sure to nurse those nuts of yours." He gave a loud guffaw and hung up.

Renzo sat back in his chair with a great sigh of satisfaction. It was all coming together: Lüthi was out of the picture, and Hirschi had been in Bern with Simu. He just wished he knew what Giuliana was finding out from her interrogation of Hirschi.

30

Nordring police station,
Friday morning, June 21

By the time Giuliana and Sabine sat down with Hirschi, it was nine thirty in the morning. The interrogation room had a table with three chairs at it; there was a fourth chair in a corner behind Hirschi, where a uniformed man was taking notes, and an observation mirror in one wall. No windows. Some well-meaning soul had decided to paint the room baby blue, perhaps to create a calming effect. The light-colored walls were full of scrapes and scuff marks.

Sabine explained Hirschi's rights and asked if he wanted a lawyer.

"Not yet," he said. His skin was grey with fatigue, his eyes sunken, his expression dull. Giuliana had never seen Hirschi before, but she couldn't imagine a firm featuring him in an ad for healthy food. He looked like a zombie.

She'd decided to begin with the farming fraud. Her case for Hirschi as Frank's and Etter's killer depended on the threat of exposure. First, she'd have to make sure he'd actually done something he needed to hide.

"Herr Hirschi," she said, "we've learned that you are suspected of committing fraud, selling produce under an organic label for organic prices that isn't grown according to organic specifications. The inspection arm of Bio Suisse is about to confront you with its findings."

Hirschi closed his eyes. When he opened them, there was something new in his face. The exhaustion was still there, but dullness had been replaced by resolve.

"I've known this was coming since the new inspector called me," he said, "but I didn't know how long I had. It's a relief to know the wait is over."

Giuliana hadn't expected this. What wait? Did he mean he was relieved Bio Suisse had finally dropped the other shoe? Or was he implying he was tired of carrying Simu's murder on his back? She filed the comment away for further consideration and said, "It would be a big help if you'd tell us the whole story."

"It would help me, too . . . figuring it out. Explaining how . . . how it happened."

Whatever "it" is, Giuliana thought. "Please begin whenever you're ready."

Hirschi sat biting his thumbnail and staring over Sabine's and Giuliana's heads. "It all begins with my wife, Asunción," he said. "She's from the south of Spain."

"How long have you been married?" asked Sabine.

"Almost four years. She moved with me to Haldiz right after our honeymoon."

"How did you meet?"

Giuliana stayed quiet, glad to have Sabine leading at this point; she watched Hirschi grow calmer as he spoke about normal things.

"I wanted to get out of Switzerland before I settled down on our family farm, so I went to Spain for a year to experience something really different—working on one of those huge places that grow more vegetables than a Seeland farmer can imagine. Asunción's family farm was next door to where I was working. Her father offered me a more interesting job, so I switched. The land down there is very dry, but during the past thirty years they've learned to manage water better. My father-in-law, Don Beltrán, made the shift; he got very rich in only two decades. Anyway, Asunción and I fell in love. It took another four years of visits and phone calls and emails, but finally we got married, and she moved here."

"I imagine it's very different from what she's used to," Giuliana commented, with true sympathy. The Seeland fog could linger for weeks without a break; even locals complained about it. For someone from Spain, the chill, monotone grey sky, like a shallow soup bowl upended over the land, had to be hellish.

"Yes," he said. "The truth is, she's miserable." Giuliana made a sympathetic clucking noise as he continued. "I can't blame her. She's used to a lot of family, sisters and brothers and cousins; a big house; constant noise; and people singing and yelling. The sun shining all the time. She's also used to money. Servants. Shopping trips."

"The Seeland must seem quiet to her," Giuliana suggested. Sabine nodded her support.

"Exactly," Hirschi agreed. "I grew up in Haldiz, and even I wanted to get out. But I wanted to come back, too. Through her eyes, it's a dump: boring people, boring shops, boring landscape, boring cities nearby. Everyone has dinner at six o'clock and goes to bed by ten, when her family is just sitting down to eat. Everyone gets up at the crack of dawn and works all day. She expects me to sit around being a *patrón* like her father. He spends his time making deals, enjoying his wealth, and letting his employees do the work. But she forgets that he worked like a slave to get to where he is today. I can't afford to hire armies of workers the way Don Beltrán does. His Moroccans live in shacks with no running water."

"I hope your neighbors helped your wife to integrate." Giuliana's comments were meant to sound sympathetic but make Hirschi feel more desperate. It was cruel but effective.

"I think they tried at first—although she says they didn't. But she was so critical of everything, it put them off. They can't understand why she sleeps late or gets all dressed up just to go to the local store. You know how people in a small village can act toward someone who's different. And then there's her German."

"My colleague said she spoke to him clearly." Another twist of the knife that said: even with decent German your wife hasn't been able to fit in.

"But she isn't comfortable with it. If I lived fifteen minutes west of Haldiz, the farm would be in the Romandie. Then she could learn French, which would be much easier. She has taken classes in German, but she can't understand the Seeland dialect, and she gets angry when people speak it around her. I've tried to explain that they aren't doing it to be rude. I mean, not everyone in Spain speaks *castellano*: classic Castilian Spanish, that is. There's a dialect in her region, too. But she feels rejected."

"What about having a family?" Sabine asked. "Small kids can be a great way of fitting into a community."

"We want a family, very much. But . . ." He started to bite one of his nails again, before lowering his hand to the table to tap on his empty water glass. He looked up at last. "But it looks like we're going to have to adopt our kids. Because of infertility."

"I'm so sorry. That must be a blow for you both," said Sabine.

"Asunción's been diagnosed with depression," Hirschi burst out. "For the past year she's gone to see her family for longer and longer visits, and I'm afraid she'll decide to stay with them. So far, she has always come back, because we love each other. But now . . ." He stopped on a harsh sob and scrubbed tears from his eyes with balled fists.

Don't get angry, Giuliana begged him silently. *Don't lose your temper and clam up.*

"You said the fraud began with your wife," she said. Hirschi poured some water, drank it, and resumed tapping the glass. "Tell us what happened."

"God, where to start?" Ignoring his glass, Hirschi drank the rest of his water in a few gulps from the bottle. His eyes darted around the room; he wriggled in his chair. At last he seemed to reach a point of resolution. His hands clasped around the glass, as if for support, he said, "It started four years ago. On March first, the day organic farmers begin heating their greenhouses, I planted tomatoes for

Migros. They were contracted for a May delivery. No big deal. I had contracts for all my produce. Then came the most terrible spring I've ever had."

Sabine did her sympathetic face. "How was it terrible?"

"All the Seeland farmers, organic and regular, were facing blights and wilts that spring; every sprig of green was either sick or covered with mites. I was fighting with all the chemical products Bio Suisse would allow, along with my sweat and tears. I lost a lot of stuff but, in the end, everything I had under contract made it to the stores, except for the tomatoes. The tomatoes were—well, they just kept on dying. I did everything I could think of and called Bio Suisse for help, but I couldn't save them."

Giuliana had never grown more than a few flowers in pots, but it didn't take a green thumb to imagine what kind of a desperate fight a young farmer at the start of his marriage and career would put up to save his crops and his reputation. And how agonizing his losses would be. At that moment, her heart really did go out to him.

Hirschi needed no prompting to continue. "I had to tell Migros early on I wouldn't be able to deliver enough tomatoes, so the store made other arrangements. Come May, when my first pathetic crop came in, Fraîche agreed to take it and whatever other tomatoes I could give them until the end of the season. It's a relatively new Swiss-only grocery chain, and the organic produce line had started only the year before. I thought I'd be okay. But the fucking tomato plants didn't recover properly, and, by mid-June, I was afraid I'd lose even Fraîche. That's when I stopped pretending to Asunción that everything was going great and told her how scared I was. Today I know we were actually okay—we could have made it financially even if we'd lost the whole tomato crop, given all our other vegetables. But I was inexperienced, and I guess I just . . . lost my perspective or something."

There was a pause; Giuliana and Sabine looked at each other. It was time to speed this up. They had two murders to ask Hirschi about. Giuliana decided to ease up on the sympathy.

"Herr Hirschi, we've heard about your wife's depression, your difficult spring four years ago, and your terrible tomatoes. But none of this . . ."

Hirschi interrupted. "It was the tomatoes. That's what I'm telling you. I switched them. I gave Fraîche all the tomatoes they could use. But they were Spanish tomatoes from my father-in-law, not organic ones. Now do you see? I told Asunción and she told her father and he . . . well, it's no fair blaming him. He set the whole thing up that first time, but I went along with it. And then . . . then I just kept it going."

So that's why he said the fraud had to do with his wife, Giuliana thought. Without a Spanish father-in-law, he might never have become a criminal. Which, if she had things figured out correctly, would have meant no blackmail and no murders. At least he didn't seem to blame Asunción: nothing about the woman tempting him to sin. Perhaps he was smart enough to realize that two policewomen wouldn't be very sympathetic to that line of argument.

Giuliana looked over at Sabine, to see if she had any questions so far. Seeing only interest in her eyes, she nodded at Hirschi. "Thank you. Now tell us . . ."

"I'd like a toilet break, please," interrupted Hirschi.

31

Wabern,
Friday morning, June 21

Renzo decided to call Bio Inspecta and tell Valente the police had Hirschi, even without any information about Giuliana's interrogation.

"We haven't arrested him," Renzo explained. "But it's not looking good for him."

"It's not looking good for him here, either," said Valente. "Talking to you yesterday lit a fire under me, and we've decided to turn our data over to the police for further investigation. On Monday your Fraud colleagues can take what we've got so far and run with it. We don't want anyone accusing us of keeping this hidden to save our own skins."

"*Now* can you tell me what he's been up to?"

"Yes. It's a scam with tomatoes. The balance on the other crops looks perfect."

"So he's been delivering conventional tomatoes and calling them organic."

"Right. To Fraîche."

"Why tomatoes, do you think?" asked Renzo.

"Tomatoes are a great choice. The *bio* price is much higher than the regular one, and there isn't much difference in appearance. You couldn't use peppers, for example—the organic ones are smaller, differently shaped. With other vegetables, like cucumbers, the price differential is too small to make fraud worth the risk. Tomatoes are ideal."

Renzo found himself wondering how anyone could come up with a crime involving something as easily squashed as a tomato. And as cheap. "How many are we talking about, do you think?"

"An extra two or three million pounds per year. Added to his own three million organic ones."

Renzo's brain froze; he couldn't process what he was hearing. He forced himself to do a bit of arithmetic. "You're telling me that Hirschi's been selling three thousand *tons* of tomatoes per summer."

"That's not so many for a Seeland farmer. What gives him away is that it doesn't fit with the acreage he says he has planted."

"Yeah, right. The balance. Thanks for telling me what's been going on."

Renzo hung up and limped back to the kitchen to make more espresso, thinking about Fraîche buying millions of tomatoes. He stepped onto his kitchen balcony, dodged the recycling containers, and looked absentmindedly at the forested ridge surrounding his neighborhood. So here were Fraîche and Adrian Pfeiffer, back again. While Renzo waited for his second pot of coffee to boil, he considered Pfeiffer. The man was still trying to build Fraîche's organic line, and he was about to get hit with the news that a supplier had been conning him. Renzo hadn't warmed to Pfeiffer at all, but it was hard not to feel sorry for the fussy little pen pusher. He was perched on a hand-grenade and didn't even know it.

Renzo went back to the stove and poured another cup of espresso. Thank God the morning's oxycodone had kicked in. The pain was still bad, but now it felt manageable. He needed to do something more useful than just make phone calls. And he certainly didn't want to be home when Fränzi walked in from work at one and started giving him hell about getting injured. He owed her an apology for coming home so whacked the night before, but *not* for doing his job. He'd told Giuliana he wanted to talk to Jean-Pierre today, so that was what he'd do. And what about Asunción Rivera? Maybe it would be helpful if he visited her. In any case, he was going to Haldiz. At least he could clear up the business of Jean-Pierre's daughter.

The home phone rang as he was leaving to catch a tram to the train station. He was relieved to see the call was from Erwin, not Fränzi.

"A word from Giuliana," said his colleague. "She told me to tell you 'non-*bio* tomatoes from his father-in-law.' That was it. She had to get back to Hirschi. They were on a roll."

"Thanks." So Hirschi had confessed to the scam. Good for Giule. The extra tomatoes had been from Spain, which made sense. "You know," he told Erwin, "I feel pretty good, so I've decided to go back to Haldiz. Couple of things I want to check on. You got a problem with that?"

"Sounds fine if you're up to it."

"Think I should talk to Hirschi's wife before the two have time to compare stories?"

"Not till we know more about what he's given up in the interview. No clue how much longer they'll be in there. You haven't got your phone, right? Giule can't call you, so why don't you call her in a couple of hours? Maybe she'll have a job for you then."

"Will do."

Renzo hung up and wrote Fränzi a note. "Very sorry about last night. Thanks for coping. Home for dinner by seven." Even as he wrote it, he registered that he was being a coward, but his mind slid away from that thought as fast as it could and focused gratefully on Jean-Pierre and Jeanne Niklaus. He needed to think about the possibility that one or both of them had had something to do with Frank's death. Just because something was unlikely didn't mean it was impossible, he reminded himself, as he hobbled down the street to the tram stop.

32

Nordring police station,
Friday morning, June 21

"I never meant to keep selling my father-in-law's tomatoes after that one summer," Christian Hirschi told them.

They'd taken a break. While Hirschi was escorted to the toilet, Sabine fetched three coffees, and Giuliana phoned Renzo's cell. He didn't answer. Then she called Erwin, who told her about the photo of Hirschi and Etter together. A true confirmation of her and Renzo's theories. She hurried upstairs to get the picture from Erwin and leave a message with him about the tomatoes for Renzo, to show him they'd been on track.

After some fresh air and coffee, Hirschi seemed calmer.

"But I let myself get trapped," he added.

"The process can't have been easy to set up," said Giuliana. "Taking one Spanish delivery after another in secret."

"It helped that the guy who drives the produce truck really is a relative of my wife's, so his stopovers made sense. I switched to planting the same type of tomato my father-in-law was sending me, and I knew what crates to use for my own tomatoes that would match the crates coming from Spain. I built a remote warehouse to store the organic tomatoes in and took the Spanish deliveries at night. Anyway, never mind all the details—I made it work. But any normal inspector would have figured it out."

Hirschi was leaning forward, drinking his coffee and explaining his decisions as if he'd forgotten why they were there. It wasn't as though he were bragging about his cleverness. Perhaps he was just glad to get it off his chest.

"Inspector?" Giuliana echoed. "You mean the person who comes to your farm to renew its Bio Suisse certification?"

"Exactly. The new inspector, the one who called me this past Tuesday—he has already realized from my paperwork that I'm selling far too many tomatoes, without setting foot on the farm. But for years my farm was inspected by a friend of my father's, and he trusted me. He's retired now. God, when he hears about this, he's going to feel betrayed. I used him. If only I'd stopped after the first summer. I tricked him during his inspection that fall, but that would have been only once. An emergency situation, because so many of my own tomatoes had died. If only I'd never gone on with it."

Whatever short relief Hirschi had felt during his calm recital of details had vanished. With his elbows on the table, palms over his eyes, he looked ready to give up. Giuliana didn't want that. She nodded to Sabine.

"But you had to take the Spanish tomatoes because you needed the money," Sabine said. Her voice was kind and supportive: surely anyone would make that same choice.

"Yes," Hirschi agreed. He lifted his face from his hands but didn't meet their eyes. "Asunción liked showing her family how successful we were. When she met her sisters in Geneva, they stayed in five-star hotels and ate in fancy restaurants—and she treated them! She wanted them to be impressed with her new life, her new husband. I kept telling her that I'd never be as rich as Don Beltrán. She'd cut back for a while—and then I'd look at the credit card bill and see the presents she'd sent everyone. Crazy presents."

"No, no, not crazy," he said, glancing at them quickly. He looked frightened. "I don't mean that. She's never done anything crazy. And she rarely buys anything expensive for herself. Just for her family. Who don't need a thing. That's the cra—that's what I can't understand. They already have so much money. It has something to do with pride, I know that. And now she's going to be so ashamed of me."

Face hidden in his hands again, Hirschi sobbed. The harsh sound filled the room.

Sabine pushed a box of tissues closer to Hirschi, and Giuliana looked at her watch before stating, for the benefit of the transcriber, "It's eleven twelve. I am stopping this interrogation until Herr Hirschi is more composed."

33

Haldiz,
Friday afternoon, June 21

Renzo walked down Haldiz's main street toward the turnoff that led to Jean-Pierre Niklaus's farm. A large Migros truck was backed up to one of the outbuildings. Renzo could see pallets full of something green being loaded into it. The farmhouse itself was quiet. He rang the bell, waited, and rang again. After five minutes, he limped over to the truck, which was rapidly filling with zucchini, crates and crates of it.

"I'm trying to find Herr Niklaus," he said impartially to the four men clustered around the back of the truck.

A guy in rubber boots and blue coveralls who was crouched over so he could scan the barcode on one of the zucchini boxes said, "He's in the fennel."

"Where's that?"

The man stood, walked out from behind the truck, and said, "Go around the house, stand with your back to it, and look toward your ten o'clock. You'll probably see some people about . . . hmm, a quarter mile away. He's one of them."

Renzo did as he was told. On the other side of the old farmhouse he found a paved side-terrace and a patch of lawn. He crossed this to reach the edge of a field full of beans. Hundreds of tall vines planted in raised rows climbed perfectly spaced wires connected to central poles, with thousands of tiny string beans hanging in clusters on their green stems. It was an impressive sight. He looked beyond the expanse of vines, wires, and poles to where fine stalks and waving fronds formed a faraway mass of lacy green. Fennel, he supposed, since the distance was about right. Concentrating, he could see three people crouched in the rows around some plants. Should he walk out to them? The narrow valleys between the bean poles were very muddy.

He stood there a full five minutes, considering what to do, and, as he waited, the smell of sprayed manure that hung over most Swiss farming villages in summer grew stronger, and the pain in his groin and belly got steadily worse. Reaching into his shirt pocket, he fished out another pill and swallowed it. Just as he was planning to go back to the man in blue coveralls and ask him to phone Jean-Pierre, he saw one of the small figures in the fennel wave and start to walk toward him.

There were a garden table and six chairs on the terrace; Renzo sank down in one and waited. Over him was an apricot tree; the fruit would be ripe soon. His mind drifted until Jean-Pierre stood beside him. Renzo struggled to his feet and held out his hand, but Jean-Pierre only smiled and showed him his dirt-crusted fingers and palms.

"I'd like to talk to you again," Renzo said. "Do you have a few minutes?"

"I'll go wash." The old man stumped off toward the farmhouse.

Renzo leaned his head back and closed his eyes, listening to the chirps, whirrs, rattles, and hums of the countryside. He sat up when he heard footsteps. Jean-Pierre was coming back now, walking across the terrace with a large pitcher of water in one hand and an old-fashioned glass bottle with a rubber-and-glass stopper in the other. The liquid in the bottle was a magnificent reddish-purple color. Perched upside down over the neck of the bottle were two tall glasses. Jean-Pierre set everything onto the table, which was covered with twigs, bits of leaf, and dead wasps from the apricot tree. He swept the place in front of Renzo clean with his sleeve, set a glass in front of his guest, cleared another place for himself, put the pitcher and bottle between them, and settled into his chair with a sigh.

"Picked cherries all this week, and the wife made cherry syrup." He poured an inch of the garnet liquid into Renzo's glass, added water from the pitcher, and then did the same for himself, drinking half the glass in a gulp.

"Ah. That's just the way it should taste. Drink up, man!"

The color of the liquid had lightened, but it was still jewel-like. Renzo took a gulp. Sweet but not cloying, the flavor of perfect summer cherries filled his mouth.

"That's delicious. Fantastic! Thank you."

"Good cherries this year," Jean-Pierre said and was silent. Renzo realized he was waiting. He turned toward the old farmer and looked straight into his eyes.

"Did Frank tell your daughter Jeanne he was leaving you his land?" he asked.

Jean-Pierre didn't look away from Renzo, but he let his hands drop into his lap from where they were resting on the table.

"I'm a shitty liar, huh?"

Renzo nodded, unable to suppress a small smile. "It was when you were telling me about your alibi. All of a sudden, you thought of something, and it turned you into jelly. You must have remembered that Jeanne and her boyfriend were in Haldiz that afternoon. And you decided: If this half-witted cop got hold of all the facts about Jeanne and what she knows, he might suspect her or her boyfriend of killing Frank to inherit his land sooner rather than later. As soon as possible, even, in case Frank and I have another fight, and he disinherits her."

"Maybe you're not so half-witted after all. So, do you suspect the youngsters?" Renzo heard fear in Jean-Pierre's voice, even though he was trying to sound calm.

"Not the boyfriend, I'd say, assuming he and Jeanne are still together." It was cruel to tease the old man, Renzo thought, but he deserved it for all the information he'd withheld.

"What the hell does that mean?" Jean-Pierre growled, but Renzo just smiled.

"Are they still together?" he asked again.

"Yes." He was holding himself rigid as he answered.

"You'd never let your daughter stay with the man who killed Frank."

Jean-Pierre gave a choked laugh.

"Well, that's true enough. So does that mean you suspect Jeanne?"

"You're the one who lies so incompetently, so I'll ask: Do you?"

The farmer gaped at him. "Of course not. Jeanne's still a student. She doesn't need Frank's land right now. When he told her that he'd left it to me, she came to me terrified about how she'd manage a huge organic farm. She'd planned to convert our place here to *bio* field by field, learning as she went, not to take over a going concern and have to hit the ground running. I told her Frank was a tough old bird and wouldn't die for twenty years—by then she'd be an organic expert. Dear God. Who knew he'd be gone three months later?"

Renzo sat back and took another drink of cherry juice.

"The information you gave me about Simu spraying fungicide was important; you should have told the police right away instead of keeping it to yourself for days. That Jeanne and her boyfriend were in Haldiz the afternoon Frank died was also important, because they might have seen something that could help us solve the murder. Luckily, your wife told me about it. But in both cases, keeping quiet was . . ."

Jean-Pierre broke in. "Half-witted. Is that the word you're looking for?"

Now it was Renzo's turn to bark out a laugh. "You said it; I didn't."

Jean-Pierre shrugged. "I don't like talking to the police. Keeping quiet about whatever I know seems normal when cops are around."

"Yeah. It takes lots of people that way. Just give me Jeanne's phone number, so I can call her today. I should have gotten it from your wife, but I didn't."

He copied the number from Jean-Pierre's phone to his, drained his glass, and stood.

"Tell Frau Niklaus I think her cherry syrup is great. And show me how someone who wanted to go fast and not be seen would walk between Frank's farm and Christian Hirschi's."

"Why would you want to know that?" Jean-Pierre stared at Renzo and then said, "You're getting half-witted ideas again. Chrigu didn't kill Frank. No way."

"If that's true, the sooner you show me the shortcut, the sooner I can eliminate him."

Jean-Pierre brought up a map of Haldiz on his phone and traced out a path that either skirted or crossed a series of fields between the two farms. Then he glanced down at Renzo's pale grey running shoes and pristine black jeans and shook his head.

"I've got a pile of rubber boots; you'd better see if you can find a pair that fits you."

"Thanks! And—can I use your phone to call my colleague?"

But Giuliana still didn't answer her cell, so he left a message telling her how much he wanted to know what she'd wormed out of Hirschi. Another call to Erwin confirmed that the interview was ongoing. Five minutes later, wearing mud-encrusted boots and with his shoes draped around his neck, he set out to walk next door to Frank's and then, with his stopwatch running, to jog as briskly as he could to Hirschi's place on the other side of the village.

34

Nordring police station,
Friday morning, June 21

While Hirschi was calming down under guard, Sabine and Giuliana headed for the toilets and then into a corner of the parking lot for some fresh air. Sabine looked around first to make sure they were alone and then asked, "Is it time to push him toward Simon Etter? So far we haven't gotten a word out of him that points to either of the two murders."

Giuliana knew Sabine was right, and it was starting to worry her. Still, she shook her head. "I'd like to pursue the fraud a bit longer. Quite apart from the fact that it will destroy his career as an organic farmer, it's clear that he's ashamed of it. Which gives more credibility to the idea that he'd lash out at first Frank and then Etter if they confronted him."

"And in the end it will all be exposed anyway, since Bio Suisse figured it out," said Sabine. "Talk about two completely pointless deaths." She shifted as if to start back into the building and then stopped, adding, "I said push him toward Simu, but you're right—Frank died first. If Simu told Frank about the tomato scam on Thursday evening when they had their fight, then Frank must have decided to confirm what he'd heard with Hirschi either that night or Friday morning, because by midafternoon he was dead. So maybe we start with Frank."

"We'll play it by ear," Giuliana said, and they went back to the baby-blue room, where a red-eyed but subdued Hirschi was waiting, along with their patient transcriber.

"So this summer marks the fourth year of your selling the Spanish tomatoes to Fraîche along with your own organic ones—is that correct, Herr Hirschi?" asked Giuliana.

"Yes," he said. His leg was jiggling under the table.

"And until a few weeks ago, everything was going well, because no one except your wife and your in-laws knew about it," she went on.

"Christ! Is that what you think?" Hirschi threw back his head and laughed, before jumping up from his chair. Alarmed, the two women across the table leaped up, too, right hands automatically reaching for the pepper spray in their pockets; the man taking notes stood up, too. Hirschi was too agitated to notice their reaction; he was pacing the small space behind the table and muttering, "Jesus. If only. What a fucking joke!"

Still standing but more relaxed, Giuliana and Sabine watched him prowl around the room. What joke? Giuliana's mind was flashing through possible explanations, but she kept her face blank. "Please sit down again, Herr Hirschi," she said, and he looked at her in surprise, as if he scarcely knew what he'd been doing. Dutifully he returned to the table and sat. His leg resumed its frantic up-and-down motion.

"Why is what I said a joke?" asked Giuliana.

"Pfeiffer has known for over two years," he said. "That bastard. I can't stand to look at him, much less speak to him. I could kill him; I could pound him into pulp." He smashed his fist on the table as he said this, unaware that he'd just threatened a man with death in front of cops investigating two murders.

With Hirschi distracted by his rage, Sabine and Giuliana had a chance to exchange a look of pure astonishment. Nothing was more unnerving than having something totally unexpected turn up in an interrogation. For a horrible moment, Giuliana wasn't sure she knew who Pfeiffer was. Then it came back to her, and things started to get a little clearer. But only a little. She still felt blindsided, which made her angry with herself. What had she missed?

"Is Pfeiffer the buyer from the Fraîche grocery chain? The man Renzo Donatelli met at your house Monday afternoon?"

"Monday? Yeah, that's right. That's him, the slimy swine."

"Why are you so angry with him?" asked Giuliana, although she suddenly thought she could guess.

"He's a fucking blackmailer, that's why," Hirschi yelled. "I've been paying him for almost two years now, and he wants more and more. I've told him if he doesn't stop, he'll bring the whole scheme down, but he doesn't give a shit. But now he'll be truly fucked. I'm going to tell Bio Suisse everything, and I'll tell the police, too. Oh, yeah, that's right." He giggled in a way that made the two women give each other warning looks. "I *am* telling the police."

"And we're listening," said Sabine in her most soothing voice. Giuliana was impressed by how calmly Sabine was taking the new information; she only hoped she was managing to keep her face as serene. There was no time to go off in a corner and digest this new information, or, better yet, discuss it with Renzo. She was going to have to think on her feet—or on her bottom, in this case.

She shifted in her interrogator's chair and echoed Sabine. "Yes, please go on, Herr Hirschi."

35

Haldiz,
Friday afternoon, June 21

Even as he started across the fields from Frank's place to Hirschi's, Renzo knew he was wasting time. Hirschi had grown up in Haldiz and run around it since childhood. Renzo, by contrast, was hampered by his ignorance of the route, his injuries, and the damned boots, which were too big. But he trotted through the mud as fast as he could anyway, following the route Jean-Pierre had shown him. At least Hirschi's farm was close to the railway station, so once he finished this charade, he'd find a phone at the station and try again to reach Giuliana. Maybe she'd have something intelligent for him to do in Haldiz, like interview Asunción, as opposed to this idiotic dash through the dirt. If she didn't, he'd catch the train back to Bern and go straight to the office. That way, he could finally find out what was going on with the interrogation. Plus pick up his car and phone.

By the time he reached Hirschi's first outbuilding, he was breathless, aching, and lugging what felt like twenty pounds of soggy earth on each boot. Nine minutes it had taken him, for what it was worth. He sat down on a low wall out of sight of the house, since he didn't want to deal with Asunción. Gingerly he removed the dirt-caked boots, put on his shoes, and noticed that he had mud on his jeans. He shook his head. He really was a half-wit. He should have stayed in bed like everyone wanted him to. What good was he doing out here? The truth was, he'd run away from his wife and her reproaches. Ouch, it hurt his gut to laugh.

He realized that it wasn't just laughing that was making him hurt. He was a wreck again. But he'd taken a painkiller at Jean-Pierre's; he couldn't take another so soon. He slipped down until he was sitting in the dirt—mercifully dry—and leaning his back against Hirschi's wall. He looked at all the acres of vegetables he'd just run through and thought idly about how little he appreciated the work that went into growing them. He just put a few onions or potatoes into a plastic bag, weighed them, labeled them, and plonked them down in front of the cashier. He wondered if Fränzi ever shopped at Fraîche. He didn't. Not that he did the shopping very often, but when he did he always went to Migros, probably because that was where his mother . . .

Renzo sat forward suddenly and forgot his aching body. The question that had just shot into his mind required all his concentration. Frank had never sold to any of the grocery chains, so why had he called Fraîche? On Friday morning, the day of his death, Frank had phoned Adrian Pfeiffer, the man who bought organic vegetables for Fraîche. Renzo knew that was true, because he'd seen the call listed in black-and-white. On Monday, when Pfeiffer told him he'd had a call from Frank to ask about vegetable prices, Renzo hadn't known enough about Frank's principles to realize how unlikely this was. But now he was sure it was a lie. Pfeiffer had known the police would uncover Frank's call, and so he brought it up himself and offered an apparently good reason for it. Smart. But not smart enough. Because Frank didn't give a fuck about Fraîche, and Renzo knew it. So why had Frank called Pfeiffer?

If what he and Giuliana had speculated about the afternoon before was true, Simu had told Frank that Hirschi was involved in a scam. They'd assumed Frank would confront Hirschi with his new knowledge and theorized that Hirschi might have killed Frank so as to avoid word of the fraud getting out. But maybe Frank also decided to warn Hirschi's buyer. It would be just like Frank to want to protect all those Fraîche customers who were paying *bio* prices for *bio* vegetables and getting Spanish stuff instead.

The more Renzo considered it, the more it made sense. On Friday morning, Frank had called Pfeiffer not to talk about his own vegetables but to talk about Hirschi's. Specifically, about his tomatoes. Was that before or after he'd talked to Hirschi? Hard to know. Renzo imagined he'd been very cautious, not wanting to cause a scandal or get the young farmer in trouble if the whole story was just a rumor or another piece of evil mischief by Simu. But he must have decided he couldn't let it go unchecked, for the sake of Fraîche's customers. As if it mattered what kind of tomatoes people ate, thought Renzo, who had never knowingly eaten an organic tomato in his life. But it mattered to Frank. So he'd suggested to Pfeiffer that he have the tomatoes checked and make sure they were okay. And he hadn't called Bio Suisse to report a possible fraud, because he was waiting to hear back from Pfeiffer about the results of the analysis.

Of course Pfeiffer hadn't told Renzo the truth about Frank's call, because by now he knew that most of the tomatoes weren't *bio*, and he wouldn't want that getting out. Even to the police. Or perhaps especially to the police, since he'd been unknowingly involved in fraud. Renzo could see why Pfeiffer had lied to him, to protect himself and his employer, but it still pissed him off. He hated being lied to. It made him like Pfeiffer even less than he already did. He remembered the angry conversation he'd half-overheard between Pfeiffer and Hirschi the morning before, after the buyer had talked at the Lakers' meeting. Had they been discussing the scam? Had Pfeiffer gotten the results of the tomato analysis back by then?

He heard a creaking noise behind him and turned slowly, willing his body to move. Someone had walked through a pair of double doors into a large windowless building about thirty feet away. Good. He could ask to make a call on their phone. He got up with the help of the wall and limped toward the building, looking around as he went. During his shortcut across the fields he'd noticed scattered groups of pickers, human and mechanical, but here, near Hirschi's place, he didn't see anyone.

The person in the warehouse had pulled the doors shut. Renzo gave one of them a polite knock as he opened it and walked into the building. It was cool—somewhere a refrigeration unit must be running. No outdoor light got in, except through the gap of the partially opened door, but an overhead bulb burned, revealing a vast space half-filled with stacked crates of tomatoes. Hundreds of crates. Thousands? Renzo's first reaction was awe at seeing so many vegetables in one place. Then came recognition. These must be the infamous tomatoes, waiting to be picked up by a Fraîche truck. But where was the person he'd seen? He glanced around and called out, "Hello. Who's here? I came in to ask . . ."

"Herr Donatelli."

A man stepped out from behind a pillar of crates. Renzo recognized first the voice and then the figure, even though the light was bad.

Think of the devil and up he pops. Now Renzo could get the truth about Frank's phone call.

"Hello, Herr Pfeiffer," he said. "I'm glad to run into you."

36

Nordring police station,
Friday afternoon, June 21

"Pfeiffer didn't join Fraîche until about two years after I started mixing my organic tomatoes with the Spanish ones," Hirschi told Sabine and Giuliana. "I could tell from the start he was more uptight about details than the guy before him, but everything went on as usual for a couple of months. Then—it was in September almost two years ago, toward the end of the tomato season—he asked if he could drop by the farm for a chat. It didn't even occur to me to be worried." He gave what was clearly supposed to be a laugh.

The windowless room had grown stuffy; Giuliana felt groggy, and she was starting to get hungry. She was sure Sabine was tired, too. But this was no time to stop Hirschi, whose hatred of Pfeiffer seemed to spur him to talk louder and faster than before.

"That was . . . a terrible day," he said, "and the beginning of a terrible time. I was already worried about money and about Asunción's loneliness, and we'd started having fertility tests. Pfeiffer told me he knew all about my Spanish tomatoes and that his analyses had shown they were not only *not* organic but also contained higher quantities of some chemicals than were permitted in conventional Swiss produce. I figured he'd blow the whistle, but instead he asked me for a quarter of my profit. Otherwise he'd turn me in as a criminal and wreck my life. I didn't even take time to think about it; I said yes. Later I realized he'd never allow me to stop. I'd be stuck in the scam forever, paying and paying for Pfeiffer's silence."

"How did he figure out what you were doing?" Sabine asked.

"I'd worked out with Don Beltrán that he'd put my tomatoes in plain wooden crates, exactly like the ones I used here, and then I'd slap the same labels on all of them before they were picked up. But once in a while someone would screw up and use a crate with Spanish writing on it. Usually I noticed and transferred the produce to my own boxes, but now and then I missed it. Still, it never mattered; no one processing vegetables in the Fraîche warehouses is paid enough to think. But Pfeiffer was a control freak; he prowled and poked around. He saw the Spanish crates, found out they were from my farm, and got suspicious."

Hirschi looked calm, but his leg was jiggling madly.

"And since then he has asked for even more money?" continued Giuliana.

"He's out of his mind." Hirschi shook his head. "A year ago he asked for a third of my profits, and six months ago for half. Now he's talking about making me sell all my produce—my own stuff, all *bio*—through Fraîche instead of the other chains that pay more. Clearly, he wants to start skimming there, too. His latest thing is telling me to make the other Lakers go through him. How can I do that? I can't force them to change their contracts."

"Does your wife know about the blackmail?" Giuliana asked gently.

Hirschi lifted his head and shook it emphatically. "I couldn't tell her. I knew she'd pass the information to her family. Plus, she's never accepted that the substitution is a serious crime. She might have decided to tell Pfeiffer I wasn't going to pay anymore, because she wouldn't understand the terrible consequences. I've simply told her I don't like or trust Pfeiffer, and she shouldn't either. But she's incapable of being rude to anyone. The last time he came to the farm to harass me, she baked a cake! Homemade cake for that fucker. I should have put poison into it."

Giuliana decided it was time to shift the conversation from someone Hirschi wanted to kill to someone she was sure he had killed.

"You said your wife doesn't know about the tomatoes. But Simon Etter found out, didn't he?"

Hirschi cupped his hands over his mouth before standing up to pace back and forth behind his chair again, like a tiger at the zoo, while Giuliana and Sabine watched him. They looked at each other, and Giuliana laid a finger on her lips. Sabine nodded. They waited, silent and unmoving. Finally, Hirschi sat down again.

"Yes. Simu found out. He was prowling around my land at night, trespassing, and saw me unloading tomatoes with Luis. I guided him away toward the house, distracting him, trying not to show that he'd scared the hell out of me. But he understood what he'd seen. He phoned me—"

"When was this?" interrupted Sabine.

"God, I don't know. Today is . . . today is Friday. He called on Thursday. Two weeks ago." A week before Frank died, Giuliana calculated.

"June sixth," Sabine said for the record. "Simon Etter called you on Thursday, June sixth."

"And when did Frank Schwab get in touch with you?" asked Giuliana.

"Frank?" Hirschi stared at her with startled eyes. His leg stopped jumping. "What does Frank have to do with it? I don't know if . . . I guess he might have phoned me in the last two weeks about Laker business, but I don't think so. I can't remember the last time I talked to him."

Giuliana's chest grew tight, although she was sure she kept her face impassive. Shit! Hirschi's puzzlement at the intrusion of Frank's name into his story had a decisive ring of innocence to it. Perhaps Frank had not contacted Hirschi on the morning of his death, accused him of fraud, and died for it. Better to forget Frank for the moment, then—even if she wasn't ready to let Hirschi off the hook for his death so easily—and get back to Simu.

Sabine was already on top of it.

"Etter called you that Thursday," she repeated, as if Giuliana had never mentioned Frank. "What did he want?"

"That little shit wanted me to grow dope for him, of course," said Hirschi.

"Tell us about that," said Sabine.

"He catches me unloading tomatoes on a Wednesday night, and the very next morning he calls me to say that he's looking forward to our setting up a big indoor plantation together. I knew what was going on, but I played innocent. I told him I had more than enough work with my vegetables and absolutely no interest in weed. And he babbled right on as if I hadn't spoken, explaining what size building he'd need, how much he expected me to pay for the lights and other equipment. He talked about it as if we were going into business together. He told me we'd need to negotiate my percentage of the profits, draw up a contract. I was . . . speechless."

"No mention of blackmail." Giuliana made it a statement.

"I don't think he ever used the word. Certainly not in that phone call. When I said, 'Look, Simu, I'm not going to do this,' he said, 'Yes, you are. What else can you do?' But he said it in the friendliest way and kept assuring me that I'd make plenty of money. He wanted to meet right away, but I put him off. I needed a plan for pulling myself out of the pit he'd pushed me into. Day and night I couldn't concentrate on anything else, looking for a way out. By then I knew there'd eventually be a new Bio Suisse inspector who'd uncover whatever we set up on my property. But if I told Simu about that, he'd just suggest we do the growing somewhere else. It wasn't just my land he wanted—it was my money and knowledge."

Hirschi was sweating. He put his face in his hands again and slumped in his chair.

Giuliana knew they were coming to the night of the Dance-In, and at that point she wouldn't want to break into what she prayed would become a confession. It was after one; lunch had to be now or never. And they all three needed to get out of that windowless room.

"Let's break for lunch," she said. "Herr Hirschi, I'll have the guard take you to our cafeteria and then out of doors for a bit. We'll see you in about forty-five minutes."

She and Sabine went across the street to the bakery tearoom.

"So, looks like we're back to two murderers" was the first thing Sabine said as soon as they were alone. "Hirschi didn't kill Frank. You agree, right?"

"I'll push him some more," said Giuliana, "but I think he has no clue why we asked him about Frank. So now we've got Etter killing Frank to save his marijuana plants and Hirschi killing Etter over the blackmail. Noah is doing everything he can to find traces of Etter in Haldiz on Friday afternoon. Maybe Hirschi will have some idea about his movements."

They crossed the street dutifully at the light and entered the restaurant. There they were hit with the scent of puff pastries stuffed with chopped ham and onions that a teenaged apprentice had just taken out of the oven.

"We managed to overlook Pfeiffer, didn't we?" Sabine said, as they got in line to order some lunch. Giuliana had already decided on at least one of the fabulous-smelling pastries.

"Yes. That's Renzo's mistake, but I'm not sure how he could have known. At least he got us to look at Hirschi in the first place, so all this could come out."

"You don't have to defend him, believe me," Sabine said, and Giuliana cursed herself for being so transparent. "What a piece of work that man must be! Pfeiffer, I mean. Funny it isn't his death we're investigating," she added, "instead of Simu's."

"I guess being hit with a second blackmailer was finally more than Hirschi could bear," reasoned Giuliana, just as she reached the head of the line and had to decide what kind of salad she wanted with her ham-and-onion pastry. But Sabine was right. It was odd that the young farmer seemed to hate his buyer so much more than the man he'd actually killed.

37

Haldiz, Friday afternoon, June 21

"What are you doing here?" Pfeiffer's question came out on a rush of breath.

Renzo's mind worked fast, reviewing everything he knew and suspected about this man. He smiled and moved forward to shake Pfeiffer's hand, as if their encounter among the tomato crates was a normal social occasion.

"I've been speaking with Jean-Pierre Niklaus on his farm," said Renzo, "and he showed me a shortcut across the fields for getting back to the train station. When I realized I was on Herr Hirschi's land, I decided to stop and have another chat with him, too."

"Hirschi's not here. No one on the farm seems to know where he is. His wife took off in her car early this morning." Pfeiffer had a high-pitched voice in normal circumstances, but now he squeaked, as if he could barely draw air into his lungs. The man was afraid.

"That's a pity," said Renzo, making a sympathetic face. If he was right, Frank had told Pfeiffer about the scam the week before. Did he think Renzo was there to investigate the tomatoes, even though he was assigned to homicide? Was he that terrified of the fraud becoming public? Why? He'd been a victim of it himself.

"I'm here to make sure the tomatoes are ready for pickup this afternoon when the Fraîche truck comes by," Pfeiffer said. His breathing was steadying, and he was starting to lie again. Renzo was fed up with this son-of-a-bitch making a fool of him.

"The reason I'm so glad to see you," he told Pfeiffer, making himself more comfortable by leaning on a large forklift in one corner of the shed, "is because I want to ask you about that phone call Frank Schwab made to you on the morning of his death. You said it was because he was thinking about selling you his produce. But I don't believe that. I think he called to ask you to investigate these tomatoes." Renzo waved his hand at the thousands of crates on their pallets. "And when you did, you found out most of them were from Spain. I'll bet you were shocked out of your mind."

"I have no idea what you are talking about. These are Christian Hirschi's organic tomatoes that I've been selling for several years now. He's Bio Suisse's blue-eyed boy. Do you think they don't know whether his crops are organic or not?"

In the dim light, Renzo could see that Pfeiffer wore a bland social smile, which was odd. Whether he knew about the Spanish tomatoes or not, Renzo's accusation was nothing for him to smile about. Where was the fear he'd been showing only a minute before?

Something didn't compute. Wouldn't it make more sense for Pfeiffer to throw himself on Renzo's mercy, to say, "Yes, Frank called and told me, but I lied to you because my bosses made me. They don't want news of this fraud to get out. Imagine how bad that would be for Fraîche's image! We're going to stop doing business with Hirschi right away."

But the smug prick wasn't saying any of that. He'd stopped being scared and was gazing at Renzo in an oddly calculating way. What did he know that Renzo didn't?

Renzo hadn't realized how convinced he was that Simu Etter had killed Frank until he felt his brain tilt. Oh my God. Pfeiffer! He was in on the scam, and he'd killed Frank and Simu to protect his share of the profits. Because they'd found out about the tomatoes.

Renzo knew he had to get out of this building and find somewhere safe where he could call for backup. He pulled himself up from his slouch against the forklift and, trying not to show any pain or weakness, began to make his way toward the half-open shed door.

But he saw that Pfeiffer was moving out of the shadows toward him with something raised high over his head. Renzo wasted a precious fraction of a second reaching for a gun he wasn't carrying and then pivoted into a combat stance. Or tried to. Instead, his battered torso muscles seized up and froze him into an ineffective crouch. He felt his usual confidence vanish as he realized that he was literally paralyzed in the face of an attack.

38

Nordring police station,
Friday afternoon, June 21

When Sabine and Giuliana got back from lunch, Hirschi was waiting for them in the interview room with the door wide open. He was drinking coffee and had another bottle of water to hand.

"Any trouble?" Giuliana asked the man who'd supervised him.

"Not a bit," he answered. "We talked football." He shrugged and looked sheepish, as if discussing sports with a suspect was unprofessional.

"Why not?" Giuliana smiled at him. "You need to get your own lunch now. When does someone come to take your place?"

"She'll be here any minute," he said. "I'm fine."

"Good. Thanks." She could hear Sabine asking Hirschi how well he spoke Spanish. Simple, calming talk. She walked into the room and took her place. Hirschi finished his sentence and turned from Sabine to her, meeting her eyes. He looked a little less grey, a little more determined. She wasn't sure that was good.

"Herr Hirschi," she began. "The police know that you did not have a drink with Luis Díaz Saturday night, as you claimed. You were with Simon Etter at that time; we have a photograph from a closed-circuit camera showing the two of you together in Bern. Was this meeting with Herr Etter to celebrate signing your contract?" She calculated that the word *celebrate* would provoke him.

"Well, we both got totally smashed, but only Simu was celebrating." He hadn't looked away, continuing to hold her eyes. "A picture of us, huh? Shit. Not much point in lying, then, is there?"

Giuliana shook her head without breaking eye contact. She waited.

"I don't want to talk about that night," Hirschi said. He was looking down at his hands now, clasped tightly in front of him on the table. "I don't remember it very well. I haven't been so drunk since my years in Spain."

"What do you remember, then?" Giuliana knew this was a dangerous moment for the interrogation. "I suppose you remember the Dance-In."

"God, yes," he said, relaxing slightly. "I had no idea that was going on. I drove into town and half the streets were blocked. I finally found a place to park near the Monbijou Bridge and walked to Bollwerk. Some bar Simu suggested. I'd never been there. Shoving my way through the dancers was wild; I almost gave up and went home."

He stopped. *Got to get him talking again.* But before Giuliana could open her mouth, Sabine said, "Simu ended up celebrating, as you said, so I guess he forced you into this crazy partnership."

Well done, Sabine—let him think he's already told us so much he might as well keep talking.

"What else could I do? Simu told me what he wanted, and I agreed to everything. He got out his laptop, wrote up a contract, had me read it, and emailed it to me for my signature."

The missing laptop.

"He acted like we were business partners, friends even. And I was at the end of... at the end of everything. I was in the middle of getting the summer vegetables in, which is a ball-busting amount of work, and on top of that my wife never stopped crying, and Pfeiffer was pushing for more money. After that first call from Bio Inspecta, I was sure more pressure was coming from them, too. On top of all that, there sat Etter smirking and chattering and turning me into a dope dealer. All I could do was drink. Simu bought me beer after beer and jabbered about all the money we'd both be earning as soon as we got the indoor plantation going. At one point, I repeated that I didn't want to grow marijuana, that he was forcing me to do it. Suppose I walk out now, I said. I haven't signed anything yet. He just laughed and slapped my shoulder, as if I were joking."

Giuliana noticed that Hirschi's leg wasn't jiggling. He was approaching the moment in his story where he'd killed a man, but something inside him had relaxed. Or reached a point of resolution, perhaps.

"We kept drinking," Hirschi went on. "I thought about my wife and me not being able to have kids, and I think I was crying. Then I did walk out, just like I'd said I would, but Simu came after me; he wanted to take me for a tour of the Riding School. God knows why. After that, we were going to Frank's. Anyway, we ended up in the Schützenmatte. First a bunch of looters ran by and then the police, and after that one guy all alone. The cop Simu tripped. Thank God he was wearing a helmet, because he could have died, flying headfirst into a car like that. As it was, I was surprised he didn't break his neck. I was so shocked I couldn't move, and Simu stood there giggling. It was a hard fall, but the cop got up amazingly fast. Jesus, I was scared."

Hirschi stopped. His leg was jumping again after all, and he was gnawing on a thumbnail. Giuliana and Sabine waited for him to continue, but instead he pushed his chair back and stood up. This time, Giuliana and Sabine stayed seated, although the man in the corner stood again, a hand on the Taser in his belt. Giuliana watched Hirschi as he paced. Should she let him go on stewing in anxiety like this? Order him back to the table? Suggest a break? Change the subject to lull him into a calmer mood? She made up her mind.

"What happened next?" she asked softly.

Hirschi took a deep breath and walked back to the table, although he didn't sit down.

"I'd like to call my lawyer now," he said.

It was all Giuliana could do not to bang her fists on the table and yell curses. She'd lost him. Sabine wouldn't blame her, she knew that, but still she felt too ashamed to meet her eyes. She stared at her colleague's hands, breathing deeply.

39

Renzo was frozen. His body had shut down on him. Pushing with all his will through the pain, he somehow broke through it and forced himself forward. But clumsily. There was no time for finesse. He hurled himself at the man who was attacking him. As his feet left the ground, he felt a weight come down on the back of his head. Then agony.

Time passed, and now everything was strange. He knew he was face down on the ground, and hands were rolling him onto his back and fumbling with his belt. Christ! He heard himself start to pant, as adrenaline flooded his body. What was this person going to do to him? He knew he should know who it was, but he had no face in mind, no name. He strained to respond, but this time he truly couldn't move. His brain was no longer connected with any part of him; instead, it sloshed around in a sea of pain. Still, he could feel the way his body jerked as the hands ripped off his belt, and—despite knowing he was going to die—he felt relief when the nameless fingers groped at his feet, not his crotch. His belt was being used to bind his ankles. And his hands? Where were they? They hurt, he knew that; his arms, too. Not like his head hurt, but . . . Then the man with no name began to drag his body by the feet, and the biting pain in his hands told him they were scraping across the rough floor under his body. Tied behind his back, he told himself, and tried to free his feet from the panting man by swinging his legs and bucking. Maybe a kick in the head would . . . but no. His body stayed as limp as a wet towel, a heavy useless thing.

His eyes felt strange. Was he crying? Jesus Christ. His brain wouldn't shift an inch of his body, but it could still make tears pour down his cheeks. Or was it pesticide making him cry? As soon as he thought of pesticide, he remembered Frank's body, and then the name that went with the fumbling hands. Pfeiffer. The fucker had hit him on the back of the head with something and was dragging him through the tomato warehouse. Pfeiffer! The shame of being made helpless by that puny clerk spurred him to try again and again to lash out with his bound feet. He had nothing to lose, he knew that—he'd already lost everything. So he concentrated as hard as he could, kicking and kicking. But only in his mind. His feet never moved.

The dragging stopped, and he lay on the floor. His sight seemed to be coming back, and he could tell there was something looming over his face. A motor roared suddenly. Was he going to be run over? Then he felt the warm exhaust on his face and caught its reek. His body tried to cough, but his stomach muscles wouldn't respond. Automatically he held his breath for as long as he could. Which wasn't very long.

As he lay there, breathing in exhaust from—he concentrated and came up with an image—the forklift, the dim overhead light went out. Then there was a bang loud enough to be heard over the motor's racket. The doors. Pfeiffer hadn't even stopped to gloat. He was gone, and Renzo was alone in the cold, dark warehouse.

Renzo channeled all his strength into trying to roll away from the forklift. He didn't even twitch. So he relaxed. The faces of Antonietta and Angelo filled his mind's eye, smiling at him. Listening to their voices, he fell asleep.

40

Nordring police station,
Friday afternoon, June 21

Shit, shit, shit. After Hirschi requested a lawyer, Giuliana remained calmly seated, but inside she was beating herself up. She'd botched the interview, and nothing could be done about it.

"That is your right, Herr Hirschi," she said formally. Sabine had already stood up; they'd have to get Hirschi a phone so he could make his call, which would be monitored.

Giuliana had an idea.

"Before you call your lawyer, I wonder if you'd be willing to answer a question I have about something you said earlier. It's not about . . . the Schützenmatte."

Hirschi smiled. It was after three in the afternoon, and she couldn't remember him smiling once since they'd started talking. But now there was a real smile on his face.

"Ask the question, and I'll see if I think I can answer it," he said. The note-taker in the corner behind him sat back down.

"You told us that Simon Etter wanted you to go with him to Frank's farm. In the middle of the night. Why was that?"

Hirschi kept smiling. "Okay, I can talk about that—at least as far as I can remember. Don't forget how drunk I was." After a pause, he said, "At some point after we finished with the contract, Simu started to rant about Frank not letting him harvest his marijuana plants. So he wanted to . . . move them. That was it. He said he and I—I was his best buddy at that point—had to go to Frank's place that night, while Frank was asleep, and rescue the plants. Um. Wait, now I remember. He wanted to go very, very quietly with my smallest tractor—as if any tractor is quiet!—dig up each plant, pile them in a wagon hitched to the tractor, drive them back to my place, and replant them in one of my fields until the indoor growing facility was ready. According to him, we had to act right away. That very night. Before Frank could destroy them. He was very worried about that. 'He's going to burn them,' he kept saying. 'He told me so, and he means it.' Still, a few minutes later, he got excited about taking me on a tour of the Riding School, as if he'd forgotten about his plants. Or were we going to get them afterward? I'm confused about that part."

"So you're saying Etter believed Frank was alive," Giuliana said.

Hirschi shrugged. "He was so worried about digging up the plants quietly and in secret that I can't believe he knew Frank was dead. No one knew, did they? Not until Matthias found his body Sunday evening."

"The person who killed Frank on Friday afternoon knew he was dead," Sabine said grimly. "So if Etter was talking on Saturday night about not waking him up . . . well . . ." Her eyes, as they met Giuliana's, said, "There goes another suspect."

Giuliana cursed silently again. First Hirschi, then Etter—two perfectly good Frank-killers flown right out the window. She made a last-ditch effort. "Do you think Etter was only pretending to be drunk?" she asked Hirschi. Perhaps, she speculated, Etter had planned to use Hirschi to establish his innocence, by acting as if he believed Frank was alive.

But Hirschi was shaking his head. "No way. Simu smelled like dope when he came into the bar, and then I watched beer after beer go down his throat. He added a couple of shots of schnapps to the mix, too. I know how hammered I was, and I didn't have any dope or schnapps. He's got to have been way farther gone."

"Thanks for answering the question," Giuliana said. "Now I'd like to try one more that's urgent for us. It involves Adrian Pfeiffer. We need to know more about him in order to arrest him for fraud."

"I'm happy to talk about him." Hirschi's smile was wolfish now, and his eyes were bleak.

"A few days ago," began Giuliana, "since the deaths of Frank Schwab and Simon Etter, you got a second call from Bio Inspecta."

"That's right," Hirschi said. "That's when I knew it was all over with the Spanish tomatoes. I decided not to try any desperate tricks with my paperwork before the new inspector came. I was ready for it all to be over."

"So what did you tell Herr Pfeiffer?"

"You mean, did I tell him about the new inspector. Of course not. I..."

Giuliana couldn't help it—she interrupted her witness.

"And when Simon Etter called you on—when was it? June sixth—and made it clear he knew about the scam, did you tell Pfeiffer?"

Hirschi seemed to swell at her question. There was no smile of any kind on his reddening face. "I don't tell that fucker anything. He tells me. He orders me around like a beaten dog, and it's all I can do not to . . . I wouldn't tell him if his head was on fire!" He paused to take a deep breath and lowered his voice to a growl. "Everything in my life has turned to shit, but I can still do one thing. I can take Pfeiffer down with me, that filthy prick! *Dä huere Souhung! Dä dräckig Siech!*"

Sabine and Giuliana exchanged a long look, while Hirschi called Pfeiffer one obscenity after another. Then Giuliana broke in.

"I need to be sure I understand you. So please stop that and pay attention now." She hadn't meant to sound like a first-grade teacher, but it worked. Hirschi stopped swearing and tried to calm his breathing, though his eyes were wild, and his fists clenched.

"Are you telling us that while all this has been going on—Etter blackmailing you and Bio Suisse cracking down on you—Pfeiffer continues to believe that the goose is still busy laying its golden eggs? That all is well with your tomato business?"

"Well, this goose," Hirschi slapped his chest, "is about to run out of fucking eggs, but . . . yes. As far as I know, Adrian thinks his only problem is keeping me in line."

"I see. Thank you," said Giuliana. "That is extremely helpful. Now we need to let you make your phone call."

Five minutes later, Hirschi was alone in the interrogation room, talking to his lawyer on a police phone, a guard waiting just inside his door.

Giuliana and Sabine had only gone as far as the cafeteria, where they sat alone, drinking more coffee.

"What do you think?" Giuliana asked Sabine.

"I think it's clearer than ever that Hirschi killed Simu. He was working up to telling us, then got cold feet and decided to lawyer up. But Frank's death is a mystery. Both those youngsters believed Frank was alive on Saturday night, so neither one killed him."

"I agree," Giuliana said. "But let me tell you what's on my mind—I need to know if this makes any sense. When Frank and Simu had their fight about the fungicide Simu had sprayed on the weed, Simu was already blackmailing Hirschi, right? He knew all about the scam."

"Yes," said Sabine, nodding.

"Suppose, when Frank threatens to burn the plants, Simu yells something like, 'You and your organic horseshit. If you knew what your precious Laker boss was up to with his tomatoes, you wouldn't waste time freaking out about me and my tiny patch of weed.'"

Friday afternoon coffee break: the room was noisier than usual. One man at a nearby table was telling a long joke; people were laughing uproariously even before the punch line. Sabine paid no attention. "I can imagine that," she said.

"Simu clams up, because he realizes how stupid it is to give his secret away, but it's too late. Frank's caught on. Who knows? Maybe he'd already noticed the Spanish truck once too often. But let's assume Frank gets suspicious and decides Hirschi's tomatoes should be checked. If he'd called Bio Suisse and told them to check it out, all would have been well, at least for him if not for Hirschi. But instead he calls Fraîche and asks to speak with the person who handles Hirschi's tomatoes. That would be Pfeiffer, and Pfeiffer is part of the scheme. Which Frank doesn't know."

Sabine saw it now; her eyes were shining. "Yes. Frank says something like, 'I'm suspicious about some Seeland organic tomatoes you're selling. I think you should have them tested.' And Pfeiffer asks him if he's told anyone else about his suspicions and he says no, because he doesn't want to cause trouble if the rumor isn't true."

"Right." Giuliana took up the story again. "So Pfeiffer says, 'I'm going to be in Haldiz this afternoon, and I'd like to come by your place and talk to you about this. Maybe I'll have some results on the tomatoes by then.' So he drives to Frank's farm and kills him, because he thinks Frank is the only one who knows about the scam, and he knows Frank is the kind of man who can't be bribed or blackmailed into silence about it."

"Could Pfeiffer have killed Simu, too?" asked Sabine. "Instead of Hirschi killing him. We've always liked the idea of only one killer. Did Pfeiffer eliminate first one and then the other of the two men who knew about the tomatoes?"

Giuliana shook her head, even as she said, "Well, maybe, if Frank told Pfeiffer that the rumor about the tomatoes came from Simu—but why would he do that? And how could Pfeiffer have been in the Schützenmatte to pick up Jonas Pauli's baton? Unless he was trailing Hirschi, which is . . . no, no, it's too far-fetched. Hirschi killed Simu. But what do you think of the possibility that Pfeiffer killed Frank? Now that we feel sure Simu and Hirschi didn't do it."

"It makes a lot of sense. What shall we do about it?" asked Sabine.

Good old Sabine. She was always practical. "We bring Pfeiffer in—immediately. Now that Hirschi has requested counsel, we have to put the rest of our talk with him on hold, anyway. Let's stick him in custody and agree to continue questioning him with his lawyer tomorrow morning. That work for you?"

Sabine nodded.

"Great," said Giuliana. "Why don't you and I run upstairs and explain all this as fast as we can to Rolf, Erwin, and Noah. All at the same time if possible. Frank is Noah's homicide—he may not like our ideas."

"I know. But I think he'll go along."

I wish Renzo was in on all this, she thought as they hurried to the homicide office. *He's going to be so disappointed. Bad enough to miss the interview with Hirschi, but now he's home in bed during this excitement with Pfeiffer. Of course, if it all blows up in my face, he won't have to take any blame either.*

For a moment she considered calling him, just to run her theory by him, but she knew it was a bad idea. He'd only insist on coming into the office when he ought to be recovering.

Erwin wasn't answering his mobile, but Rolf and Noah were at their desks. She told them as briefly as she could why she and Sabine wanted Pfeiffer.

"No point in waiting," Rolf agreed. "Fraud's going to want Pfeiffer soon enough. Whether he's a murderer or not, let's get him in here before he hears that Hirschi's been busted and starts wiping his computer and shredding paper. What is your next step?"

Sabine had already walked over to the keyboard on her desk, phone at her ear.

"Sabine's calling Fraîche in Lausanne to find out if he's there," said Giuliana. "Noah, do you want to go after this guy? Just for the satisfaction of finishing your case? That's assuming I'm not making a hash of it."

"No, you two bring him in," Noah said. "Besides, you've got to find him first. I'll help with that."

Adrian Pfeiffer wasn't in Lausanne. He was "out in the field," Sabine was told. Even after the inquiries escalated to a higher level, no one seemed to know which farms he was visiting that day. Information about the make and plate number of his van led to a four-canton-wide be-on-the-lookout command. With his mobile number, they hit the jackpot. "Pfeiffer's been calling the same cellphone every half hour since nine this morning," the federal specialist told Noah, who had her on loudspeaker. "Hirschi, Christian. Pfeiffer varies the pattern by calling Hirschi's landline, too. Kind of obsessed, huh? Leave this with me. I'll pinpoint him as best I can by the nearest tower and call you back."

"I think he's in Haldiz, staking out Hirschi's farm," Giuliana said. "He must suspect something has gone wrong, or he wouldn't keep calling."

"I hope he's leaving lots of revealing messages," said Noah. "Let's check Hirschi's mobile."

But Pfeiffer was too smart for that. After his first "Call me back right away," followed half an hour later by, "Where are you, for fuck's sake? Call me now," there were no messages on Hirschi's phone. The four detectives stared at each other for a moment before Giuliana said, "I'm worried about Hirschi's wife. Maybe Pfeiffer found out that we brought Hirschi in for interrogation, and he's sealed up in the farmhouse trying to squeeze information out of Asunción. Or even holding her hostage."

"After what he did to Frank's body with the pesticide, I'm not convinced the guy is firing on all four cylinders," said Sabine. "Maybe he's decided to destroy the tomatoes. Or something even screwier that we can't imagine."

Giuliana spoke up. "I recommend that Sabine and I and two uniformed officers drive to Hirschi's farm right now and check it out. No SWAT stuff or anything dramatic like that—not until we know what we're facing. If it turns out there's any kind of hostage situation, we'll back off and wait for a negotiator. That goes without saying."

Just as Rolf finished setting up a car with a driver and an additional officer, the telephone specialist called Noah back. Sure enough, the last place that Pfeiffer had called from was within a half-mile radius of Hirschi's farm in Haldiz.

"Okay," said Rolf. "Giule and Sabine, you get going as fast as you can. Meanwhile, Noah, you go talk to Hirschi. Tell him Pfeiffer might be on his farm. See if he can reach his wife and make sure she's okay. Ask if he has a clue what Pfeiffer's up to. Find out if Pfeiffer has keys to any of the farm buildings, if he has a favorite place to hang out there or in Haldiz, anything."

"Wait," Giuliana said as Noah started out the door. "Before you talk to him about all that, get his keys and meet me at the parking-lot door with them. Have him mark the house key. It will save time if we don't have to break in. Oh, and tell him to postpone his lawyer until tomorrow morning."

It was great to be doing something active at last instead of endlessly asking questions and analyzing answers. She felt full of energy, like she could sprint a mile. But it was Noah who left the office at a run. Sabine had already fetched Giuliana's and her own SIG Sauer P228s from their lockers, with holsters and ammunition. Shrugging on bulletproof vests, they were driving to Haldiz three minutes later, siren screaming and blue light flashing. In the backseat next to Sabine, Giuliana put on her hip holster and settled her pistol into it, turned her cell phone to vibrate, checked one pocket for wrist and ankle ties and the other for pepper spray, and hung her flashlight on her belt. She wiggled the house key off Hirschi's key ring—Noah had passed it to her as planned—and handed it to Sabine, putting the rest of the bunch in the pepper-spray pocket.

"I may have been in charge of the Etter investigation, but this arrest is a joint operation," she told Sabine. "Assuming you're okay with that." Sabine nodded, so she went on. "I think you and the two guys"—she pointed to the men in the front—"should tackle the house. That's why I've given you the key. In the meantime, I'd like to check and clear the outbuildings. I don't like the idea of this nutjob creeping up on us from some shed."

"If you're sure you're all right alone, that makes sense," said Sabine. "Just don't forget he could have a hostage out there instead of in the house."

"You're right," she said, and then leaned forward to tell the driver, "I'd like you to cut the siren in a few minutes, as we near Haldiz. I'll give you the word."

"Got it," he answered. They'd left the highway and were on a two-lane country road. Her phone vibrated, and she put Noah on speaker for Sabine and the men in front.

"Hirschi says his wife isn't answering the house phone or her mobile, which means we can't eliminate a danger to her," he said. "And the only building Pfeiffer has a key for is the storage shed with the tomatoes, which is about fifteen hundred feet southwest of the house—behind it and to the right, a big grey concrete building. But there's no Fraîche pickup today, so Hirschi can't think of any reason Pfeiffer would be there. And he doesn't believe he'd set fire to the tomatoes, for what that's worth. Too greedy, he says."

"Thanks for checking," said Giuliana. "Siren off now," she added to the driver. The car drove on in silence.

Noah continued. "We've alerted the regional operations center that we may be needing cops from the field to converge on Haldiz, so they'll be ready to respond if we call. And finally some good news: Pfeiffer has no firearms license. I'm sending a photo of him to your and Sabine's phones. Coat-and-tie shot from the Fraîche website."

"Thanks, Noah. We're in Haldiz now. Phones silenced. Text us if you get any update on Pfeiffer's location. We'll keep you informed."

"Right. Good luck."

As the car sped toward Hirschi's farm, Giuliana's mind was on Asunción. Until she knew the woman was safe, she couldn't relax.

41

Haldiz,
Friday afternoon, June 21

Giuliana jumped out of the car as soon as it stopped and set off at a run along the side of the farmhouse. She'd start at the tomato shed on the farm's border and work her way back toward the house on its western side, clearing outbuildings as she went. If Sabine didn't need her at the house, she'd follow up by checking the buildings on the eastern side of the property. She smiled as she reviewed her "plan." The truth was she'd play it by ear. But a bit of strategy never hurt.

She was running through a field now—or, rather, jogging in the mud between rows of what she thought were potato plants. She'd assumed she'd pass people picking produce or loading trucks or something, but she didn't see a soul. On a hot, muggy midsummer Friday afternoon with the boss missing, maybe that wasn't so surprising. But she hadn't expected to feel so isolated. There was something almost eerie about the emptiness of the land.

There weren't as many sheds and outbuildings as she'd anticipated: perhaps ten in all, many made of wood. The grey cement warehouse she was heading for was much larger, separate from the others, and obviously newer. Approaching it from the direction of the farmhouse as she was, she could see no doors, so she assumed they faced away, out into the fields. Hirschi had obviously done everything he could to keep curious eyes away from this building and its contents.

With the additional weight of her vest and gun, not to mention the mud, she was starting to tire. She slowed to a walk and suddenly felt like a target. She'd talked to Sabine about Pfeiffer creeping up on them, and now, in her hurry, she was failing to cover her back. The nearest building, apart from the windowless warehouse, was only about three hundred feet behind her, an easy rifle shot away. Maybe the man had no gun license, but that didn't guarantee he didn't have a gun. She drew her SIG and, keeping it at her side, turned slowly 360 degrees. Still no figures in sight, no glints of metal. But she couldn't shake her feeling of exposure and, forcing herself into an awkward sprint that almost brought her to her knees, she reached the doubtful cover of the grey warehouse and stopped to catch her breath and listen. The buzz of crickets, an airplane far overhead, whooshing traffic on the distant *Autobahn*, a child's cheerful shriek, and a motorized hum. A loud hum. Someone was running an engine, but there was no vehicle in sight. As she began to trot along the side of the building, it became clear that the noise was coming from inside the shed. Someone must be in there.

She half-ran, half-scurried to the end of the wall and peered around the corner, weapon ready. Finally, she'd found the entrance. She scanned the surrounding fields and faraway farms and then, with her back to the wall, moved crabwise until she reached the double doors. They were locked. Had someone locked them from the inside? Could Pfeiffer be inside with Hirschi's wife or some other hostage? Or was Asunción alone? The woman was depressed, and the noise from behind the doors sounded like the muted rumble of a motor. It could just be a loud refrigeration unit. But she had to check, and she had to check fast.

She holstered her gun and drew the bunch of at least twelve keys from her pocket. Not a single one was labeled, which made her want to throw them against the door. Instead, she spread them out on her palm, praying for a clue. Many of the keys were small, as if they opened padlocks. They also looked old—so did several of the larger keys. Only two normal-sized keys looked new; both were printed with the letters SEA. She tried the first with a shaking hand. No luck. Taking a deep breath, she tried the second. It worked.

She pulled one of the big doors open wide, all the way to the wall, and then flattened her back against it, in case someone was waiting for her inside. Fast as she'd moved, a cloud of exhaust still enveloped her. Coughing, she turned on her flashlight and peered carefully in the dark space, her SIG at the ready again. She could see nothing, but the sound of the engine was a rumble now. She took a deep breath and held it as she looked for a switch first right and then left of the entrance. There it was. She clicked on the dim overhead light. A sweep of the room showed her mountains of produce boxes; not until she looked away into one corner did she see the forklift whose roar she'd been tracking. She was backing up to gulp fresh air when she realized her eyes had taken in something half hidden behind the vehicle.

She replaced her gun, rehooked the flashlight on her belt, and ran straight for the shape. It couldn't be . . . could it? But it *was* a person. Only after she'd crouched over and grabbed the ankles did she realize they were belted together. No help for it—she had to breathe. As she took a shallow gasp of the stinking air, she started to drag the body toward the door. Coughing and shuffling backward, she almost dropped the feet in horror when she moved into a circle of light from the bulb and saw Renzo's face. No, no, please no. The words repeated themselves in her mind even as she forced herself to try to understand that Renzo was here in Haldiz instead of at home in bed.

As soon as they were in fresh air, she cut through the strip of cloth that held Renzo's wrists together and freed his ankles. Then she slipped her arms under his shoulders, lifted his upper body, and lugged him to a low wall at least twenty feet from the door. As she knelt at his side and tried to feel for a pulse, a fit of choking and retching seized her. With it, she felt terror rise. If Renzo was alive—and he had to be alive; she wouldn't accept anything else—then every second counted, and all she could do was cough.

Stop, she raged. *You aren't allowed to panic.* She forced herself to take calm, deep breaths of fresh air. Then she tried his pulse again. His flesh was very cold, which terrified her until she remembered the temperature in the shed. Of course, it was refrigerated. That was why it was so well sealed. Was his heartbeat fluttering under her fingers, or was it her own trembling? As for his breathing, she couldn't feel anything against her cheek. His face was sooty, and she wiped it with the tail of her shirt. Still no sign of life.

Joining her hands, she pumped his chest, counting to thirty. She pressed his forehead back, pinched his nose, and gave him two breaths. After two more cycles, she pressed her fingers to his carotid artery again. Now she felt something. She was sure of it. But still no breath. More blowing into his mouth. She was starting to tire: she had to call Sabine for help. But she was afraid to stop CPR. Then she heard a noise behind her and leaped up. Without any time for thought, her SIG was in her hands, her body in a shooting stance.

A man had come around the side of the building and was running at her, one arm raised over his head, something white in his hand. "Stop. Police," she tried to yell—it was more of a squawk. "Stop or I'll shoot you," she said again, clearly this time but no longer yelling. No need to. The man was less than ten feet away and moving fast. The weapon in his right hand was swinging in a wide downward arc toward her head.

She shot him.

The bullet lodged in the hollow of his right shoulder, and he crumpled to the ground. His weapon shot forward as his limp hand released it, but it sailed harmlessly over her head to hit the dirt with a thunk. She jogged to him. Just as she'd intended, she'd missed the shoulder joint, and he was breathing normally—she hadn't hit the lung. Nor, from the way he was bleeding, a major vessel. She fumbled in her pocket one-handed for restraints, never taking her eyes off the man. He was moaning, but she didn't think he was unconscious. She ripped off his jacket, which caused him to scream, and then zip-tied his wrists behind his back. She rolled the jacket to make a rough bandage, tied the sleeves around him like a sash to secure it, and zipped a restraint onto his ankles. It all took less than a minute. Only then did she focus on his face and recognize Adrian Pfeiffer from the picture on her mobile. Well, at least she'd shot the right person. She giggled from sheer relief as she leaped up, ran back to Renzo, flung herself on her knees again, and did two more sessions of breathing. No change. Christ, she mustn't cry; she couldn't do CPR if she cried. She took a second to steady herself, gave him another set of breaths, and then called Sabine. Talking was hard—she was wheezing and croaking.

"Giuliana. I was just about to call you. There's no one in the . . ."

"I shot him. Pfeiffer. Think he's killed Renzo. Get ambulances."

"Oh God. Where are you?"

"Big cement building beyond a field. Grey. Can't talk. CPR."

She laid the still-connected phone down beside her on the grass and put her mouth over Renzo's, stopping periodically to get her own breath back and rest a hand on his chest, feeling desperately for a rise and fall. Then her hand detected a slight movement. Yes, yes. She did another round of breathing. He convulsed and rolled onto his side, choking and gasping. She gripped his shoulder to steady him, and all the silly, soothing, loving words she'd ever murmured to her children flowed out in a whisper.

"That's right, that's right. Everything's going to be fine, little bean. Come on, just breathe in and out. You're doing a great job, mousey." She stroked his matted hair back from his forehead.

It took a while for Sabine to find them, but eventually she burst around the building. Giuliana gazed up at her from the ground, where she sat with Renzo half-lying in her lap. His head was propped on her shoulder, so she could support him as his body spasmed with coughs.

"Glad to see you," Giuliana wheezed.

Sabine was so out of breath she couldn't speak, but she sat down in the dirt next to Giuliana and draped an arm around her while she panted, her eyes on the trussed-up Pfeiffer.

"Renzo okay?" she asked finally.

"He's alive, but . . ."

"What happened?"

"Poisoning from exhaust."

Sabine recoiled. "Any idea how long?"

Giuliana shrugged. The question shook her; she couldn't even bear to contemplate it.

"Shit," said Sabine. She touched Renzo's cheek and then met Giuliana's eyes. "The ambulances are coming. And you're okay, thank God. So I'll keep looking for Asunción, just in case she's in one of these other buildings."

"Yeah." Giuliana closed her eyes. Renzo's weight on her was growing uncomfortable, but she didn't move. He seemed to be quieting a little, but his color was bad. Suppose his brain was damaged from the lack of oxygen. He'd hate her for saving him. If he had any brain left to hate her with.

Then she heard the thread of a whisper. She put her ear to his mouth.

"Giule."

She was afraid to believe that she'd heard him speak.

"Mousey?" he whispered. "Li'l bean?"

She laughed and then cried, kissing the top of his head as she held and rocked him.

"How do you feel?" she asked softly.

"Head . . . terrible." His voice trailed off. Then, in a voice almost too hoarse to understand, he added, "Pfeiffer got me."

"Yeah, he stuck you in the refrigerated tomato shed with the forklift's motor running and left you under the exhaust pipe. Thank God it's such a big building."

She should get up and check on Pfeiffer. She should look for his weapon. What the hell had he hurled at her anyway? She should at least go turn off the forklift—although sooner or later it would run out of fuel. And she should tell Rolf what was going on.

But she didn't move. All the frantic urgency she'd felt since the word *hostage* had come up was gone. Renzo was speaking sensibly, and Sabine was looking after things. She lay still, arms around Renzo's chest, drifting on the edge of sleep until the whine of distant sirens shook her into alertness. She slipped out from under his body, laid him gently on the ground with his head on a raised patch of dirt and grass, and got to her feet as an ambulance came into sight, still quite far away on a service road through the fields. The white object Pfeiffer had tried to hit her with lay on the grass a few yards away. She shook her head as she recognized what it was: a sock. She poked it with her toe. No, a cosh, she corrected herself.

She turned toward Pfeiffer himself, where he lay bound on the ground. Sabine had tightened his makeshift bandage and left him alone. Now he met Giuliana's eyes, and she stared right back at him in complete silence. Later, she'd approach him like a professional. Right now, she hoped he could feel her hate like a needle under his thumbnail. "You are going to jail, you evil bastard," she said to him—under her breath. That he'd killed Frank was as obvious to her now as if she'd been a witness. But she had to know about Simu. She moved until she was standing only a few feet from him and squatted down.

"You killed François Schwab," she said matter-of-factly.

He smiled and said nothing. *Try and prove it.* She heard his unspoken words clearly in her head.

"And Simon Etter."

His smile slid into a frown, and then his expression became blank. He was probably trying to work out what her words meant for him, trying to decide if this development was good or bad and how he could use it. But in the second between the frown and the blankness, she'd seen his eyes fill with bewilderment.

The idea of him turning up in the Schützenmatte to wield the fallen police baton had been far-fetched in any case. It would have been nice to tie up the cases with only one killer, but she'd never really thought Pfeiffer had killed Simu. Christian Hirschi had done that.

42

Nordring police station,
Friday night–Saturday morning, June 21–22

Giuliana rode back to Bern with Sabine and one police driver; the other sat in Pfeiffer's ambulance on the way to the hospital. Pfeiffer would be guarded around the clock now. Giuliana wondered how long it would be before he recovered enough to be questioned.

"We found stuff in Pfeiffer's van," Sabine said.

"The pesticide?" asked Giuliana. It was hard to stay alert. Her head was pounding, and her throat was sore; she didn't know if it was the exhaust, too much CPR, or just a post-stress reaction. But this was no time for a trip to the doctor.

"Yep. A canister with a wand. I don't know if the lab will be able to match it with what was sprayed at Frank's. Then there was a brand-new shower cap, still in its packaging, and a box of thin plastic gloves, with several pairs missing. They were hidden in the tire well."

"Which is part of how he managed not to leave DNA in Frank's greenhouse."

"I wonder why he wasn't wearing the cap and gloves when you shot him," Sabine murmured. "Maybe he thought leaving traces on Hirschi's farm wouldn't matter. That was a place everyone would expect him to be."

"Let's hope he left traces on Renzo. You didn't forget about his clothes?"

"I didn't forget," Sabine answered, unruffled. "The guard will tell whoever undresses him to stick everything in a laundry bag for us."

"Sorry. I should know better than to . . ."

"If my forgetting something will screw up a whole case, you sure as hell should remind me. I'd have reminded you."

Giuliana's eyes were closed, her head back, but she patted Sabine's arm affectionately. "Mind if I rest till Bern?" she asked. "Need to get a grip on myself."

"Have a nap," Sabine said. Giuliana sank into sleep..

When they reached the station, there were only a few reporters and cameras, nothing they couldn't get through. Word had spread about a "shoot-out" in the Seeland, and most of the press had converged in Haldiz. One bullet fired into one shoulder by one cop, and it was news. Giuliana was deeply grateful that she wouldn't have to talk to a journalist.

She took some time in the bathroom to clean herself up and take aspirin. Then the debriefing began. Rolf, Noah, and Erwin all questioned her; so did the two prosecutors. The commandant sat to one side and listened. Despite her exhaustion, she was glad for the speed of the reaction—she wanted to tell the story while all the details were fresh in her mind. She talked about Pfeiffer's blackmailing activities and gave Renzo credit for pursuing the organic-farming angle of the two murders from the very beginning. *While the rest of us were running around distracted by drug dealing at the Reitschule*, she wanted to add. But she didn't.

Rosmarie Bolliger, the prosecutor assigned to Frank's death, had been asking her about the links between Pfeiffer and Frank. Now she said, "Are we assuming Pfeiffer killed Simon Etter, too?"

"I don't think so," Giuliana said. "My money is still on Christian Hirschi."

"We'll continue his interrogation tomorrow morning," added Sabine before turning to Giuliana to say, "His wife is fine—staying with a woman friend in Fribourg. She has given us assurances that she'll remain in Switzerland."

Giuliana nodded and broke into a fit of coughing. Rolf looked at her sharply and said, "Thank you for cooperating with the debriefing. A driver will take you to the hospital now. You're spending the night there."

"What?!" She started to argue further with Rolf and then remembered the commandant was in the room. *Never give your boss a hard time in front of his boss.*

"If you think a trip to the hospital's necessary, then I'll go," she said, hoping she didn't sound as sulky as she felt. *But I'll be back here early tomorrow morning to talk to Hirschi*, she added to herself.

It turned out she had to be cleared by a medical professor who only made rounds in the morning, which meant it was ten on Saturday before she was able leave the Insel Hospital. She asked the nurse about visiting Renzo first, but when she heard Fränzi was with him, she decided against it.

It was after eleven by the time she sat down—this time in the largest of the interrogation rooms—with Sabine on her right and a fresh note-taker in the corner. Hirschi and his lawyer sat across the table from them. A stack of papers lay next to the lawyer. Hirschi wore a fresh shirt; it was still creased from its packaging. Although the police cells had no showers, he'd managed to wash and shave as well as change his shirt. Still, he looked like a man who hadn't slept.

His lawyer was a dapper man of about fifty named Binggeli. Thanks to her father's fifty years in defense, she knew most of Bern's criminal lawyers by name and reputation and was acquainted with many of them. Herr Florian Binggeli was new to her, which meant he probably handled Hirschi's contracts and business affairs. As a policewoman, she hoped he'd be a pushover; as a lawyer's daughter and general believer in justice, she hoped he'd give Hirschi good advice. She wondered if he'd ever sat next to a client in a police interrogation before. She gave him a friendly smile. His expression grew rigid. *Okay, then*. She'd tried.

Hirschi, despite his exhaustion, seemed eager to speak. As soon as Sabine had announced the time, date, and participants for the transcript, he burst out with, "Is it true you got Pfeiffer?"

His lawyer must have shown him a morning paper; if a guard had given him one, there'd be trouble. "Herr Pfeiffer is in the hospital, and he'll be charged with a variety of crimes once he has recovered sufficiently to be accused."

"Yes," said Hirschi, pumping his fist. "Thank God. I'll do anything I can to help you keep that bastard locked up for as long as possible. I promise."

"Thank you," said Giuliana, noticing that Herr Binggeli was goggling at Hirschi. *You mean he's just going to talk, and I have to cope with it?* he seemed to be thinking.

"Now," she continued, "let's go back to you and Herr Etter standing in the Schützenmatte. He tripped a policeman, and the policeman jumped right up. That's what you've told us. What happened then?"

"I . . . I was drunk, so it's hard to say exactly. I know I yelled, 'We're sorry, we're sorry' over and over. I was afraid."

"Why?"

"The cop was running toward us with his club raised, and he hit Simu. Simu screamed and clutched his head, and later he fell over and there was blood all over his neck and shirt. He kept moaning and making these weird noises in his throat, and I . . ."

"Stop," said the lawyer. Giuliana had been just about to stop Hirschi herself. Clearly, he was lying. There had been two blows, and she knew the first blow had not been heavy. If Simu fell over, it was because he was drunk. And he didn't bleed—she knew that—because Jonas's blow hadn't even broken the skin. Only Hirschi's own blow had done that.

Herr Binggeli was talking quietly, reminding Hirschi that he didn't have to answer. When he paused for breath, Giuliana spoke, her voice steel.

"The policeman ran toward you, hit Simu, dropped his club, and ran away. And then you hit Simu. That's why he was lying on the ground bleeding and moaning. Not because of the policeman. Because of you."

She couldn't see Hirschi's face—he was turned toward the lawyer.

"Look at me," she said harshly, and he stared at her, his eyes wide.

"I didn't hit Simu. The cop did. He was furious. At first. Then I think he was scared. That's why he ran away."

"I know he ran away. That's when you picked up the club and said to yourself, this is how I get rid of at least one of my blackmailers, and . . ."

"No," Hirschi yelled. "No," he repeated more quietly. He didn't look shocked anymore; he looked terrified. "Listen to me. I assumed you knew what happened. I never . . . it never occurred to me that you thought I'd hit Simu. That's not why I had to get a lawyer. It's because . . ."

Binggeli opened his mouth to speak, but Giuliana plowed over his voice.

"So tell us again. The cop ran up and hit Jonas once—where did he hit him?"

"The first time was on the top of the head, and the second time was on the side, near his ear. That's why his shoulder and that side of his shirt were all bloody. The first time the cop hit him, it didn't bleed at all. Simu didn't fall over. He just clapped his hands to his head and yelled. But the second time was worse. A lot worse."

"The second time was you!" Giuliana said, her voice so loud that she felt Sabine put a hand on her leg under the table.

"Frau Linder," said Binggeli, "stop yelling at my client. Listen to him."

She was so dismayed she couldn't find words anyway, appalled not just at her loss of control but at what was staring her in the face: the idea that she was wrong.

Sabine took over smoothly. "Let's go over what you think you saw in detail again, Herr Hirschi. Please. Slowly and carefully. Tell us exactly what the policeman did, and what you did, as best you can."

Hirschi closed his eyes and bent his head. "The first time the man hit Simu, the baton came down on the . . . the crown of his head." Hirschi touched the top of his own head. "Simu didn't fall, but he yelled and put his . . . his right hand over where he'd been hit. The cop was cursing him, and I was yelling, 'Stop it' and 'He's drunk' and maybe still saying that we were sorry; I'm not sure. There was a kind of pause, not long, but long enough that I thought maybe it was over and we were okay."

"How long a pause, would you say?" said Sabine.

"Ten, fifteen seconds?" Hirschi said. "That sounds like no time, but when you're scared, it's long."

"And then?"

"Then the cop lifted the hand with the baton up over his shoulder, with his body twisted, and whipped the knob on the end into the side of Simu's head."

"Can you be more specific about where he was hit?"

Hirschi reached up and felt around his own head, his eyes still closed. He covered the crown of his head with his right hand as he did this.

"Left," he said, putting his left hand over his left ear. "He hit Simu above his left ear. The right ear was already half-covered by Simu's arm. Besides, the club was in the cop's right hand."

That was the blow that Simu had eventually died of, lying on the parking-lot blacktop bleeding inside his brain for an hour or more. It had been on his left temple. Giuliana felt sick. She'd watched Hirschi the whole time he'd been talking—could he really have so perfectly acted out the scene if he himself had been the one to hit Simu with the extended baton? Was he that cold-blooded? But surely the killer couldn't have been Jonas all along. And yet . . .

"What did the policeman do then?" Sabine asked.

Hirsch's voice was low. "He stood there looking awful."

"Awful how? Threatening?"

"No, not like that. Like . . . like he was terrified. I know, because I was terrified. I was sure he was going to hit me, as well. He stood there looking at me, and I looked at him. Then he dropped his baton, just dropped it by his side; ran over to get his shield—it was lying by the car where he'd fallen—and raced away, toward the Riding School."

"And Herr Etter?"

"He . . . he . . . he," Hirschi stuttered. He was almost whispering now. "He was on his knees, bent over, both arms crossed over his head, making hurt noises. Awful ones. His hair and one side of his face were full of blood; it was running onto his left shoulder, soaking into his shirt. I could see the cloth getting darker and darker. Then he fell over onto his side and vomited. I took his shoulders, pulled him clear of the vomit, and turned him onto his back. His eyes were open, but he didn't say anything."

"Could you hear him breathing?" Giuliana asked, taking over from Sabine at last. Her rage with Hirschi was dissolving; she was ashamed of it. She'd almost wrecked an interrogation just so she didn't have to hear a truth she didn't want to believe.

"I knelt beside him. He was breathing but in a strange way, loud and slow and deep in his throat. And he kept staring at me without seeing me. I said, 'Simu,' several times, but he didn't answer."

"Did you call an ambulance?" It was suddenly clear to her, the reason for the lawyer.

Hirschi said nothing. Herr Binggeli's moment had come. He sat up straight, and both hands held his sheaf of paper to his chest, like a shield. He didn't look at the contents.

"I've consulted the law about failure to render first aid. Article 128 of the Swiss penal code talks about an immediately life-threatening situation. In this case . . ."

Hirschi had turned away from his lawyer. He looked into Giuliana's eyes, and she looked back. She saw the moment when something in him reached out to something in her for . . . what? Pity? Understanding? Whatever it was, he must have found it, because he interrupted his lawyer, who turned a stricken face to him.

"Chrigu, no. Let me talk to them," he pleaded, using a nickname for Christian, which showed he must have known his client a long time. Whatever the limits of his talents as a defense lawyer, he clearly cared about the person he was here to help.

"I have to, Flöru; I have to," said Hirschi. "I'm sorry to bring you here and then . . ."

He glanced over at Sabine, then refocused on Giuliana's face, and spoke again.

"I knelt by Simu and thought about what would happen if he died. I would be free of the nightmare I'd been in since he'd seen me unloading tomatoes. That's what I thought at the time. The truth was, I wouldn't have been free at all: Simu was just the newest of my problems. But I'm telling you what I was feeling that night, kneeling there with the blood and vomit and trying to decide. I knew he was very badly hurt—I could see that. All I had to do was call an ambulance, and he might die anyway. Or, if I walked away, someone might find him two minutes later and save him. But if I was going to do anything, I had to act fast."

He took a deep, shuddering breath and went on. Giuliana didn't move. She just nodded and held his gaze.

"First I had to get everything off him that might identify me. So I took his stuff: his laptop, which was in a shoulder bag he was still wearing when he fell over; both his phones—it turned out he had two. His wallet, with his IDs and credit cards. He had one hundred and fifty francs and some change in his trouser pocket—I left that. But I took anything that might have identified him or me. Even the plastic sack he'd been selling weed out of.

"I loaded up his big shoulder bag with all that stuff, and then I had to decide what to do. My last chance to call for help. His breathing was very loud by then. He still didn't speak or follow me with his eyes. If he had . . . I don't know. I left. I walked fast, and the weird thing was that I ended up walking right through the Bahnhofplatz and past the burned-out trash cans and smashed ticket machines and shops with all their broken windows. Broken glass and garbage and loot from the stores were all over the ground. There were at least a hundred policemen around me, ambulances, fire trucks, journalists with microphones, camera men from TV—a crowd of people—and no one said a word to me. I had Simu's blood on my hands and my shirt, and it was as if I was invisible. I didn't even think about the crowd; I was in a faraway place."

He looked like he'd gone back to that place again—his gaze was distant now, and his expression blank. His leg went up and down like a piston.

"I walked to the Bundesgasse and turned right, then left onto Monbijoustrasse. That's where I'd parked, near the Monbijou Bridge. But I didn't stop at my car. I knew there was a staircase from one end of the bridge down to the Aare. So I walked down the stairs and past the traffic circle to the bank of the river. The first thing I did was wash my hands. Then I put rocks into the bag with the laptop and phones and ID cards and threw it as far as I could into the fastest part of the river. I took off my shirt and waded into the Aare to wash it. But I knew I'd never wear it again, so I tied it around a rock and threw it into the river, too."

He stopped. Now he was panting as if he'd been running. Herr Binggeli's face was drawn with worry—he appeared to have aged a decade in an hour. Giuliana turned to Sabine, but Sabine was looking at Hirschi. Her face was full of compassion.

"You must have been cold," Giuliana said, trying to catch Hirschi's gaze again.

"I was," said Hirschi. He sounded surprised, as if he'd forgotten that part of the story. "I was freezing. It must have been three in the morning by then, and I was drenched. After that blazing hot evening, the Aare felt icy cold."

"You walked back upstairs to your car?"

"Yes. Shirtless and with the legs of my jeans soaked and my shoes and socks dripping. I drove home and collapsed into bed. Asunción never woke up. I slept a few hours and then got back to work. It was Sunday; that morning we were picking cucumbers, romaine, and a couple of other kinds of lettuce, and that afternoon we had the Lakers meeting, the one where Frank turned up missing. Life . . . kept on going. For me. Not Simu."

Hirschi stopped. He was finished. Giuliana was finished, too. She wondered where she'd find the energy to walk out of the room. Christian, Simon, and Jonas, three young men with ruined lives, one now dead. What a fucking mess they'd created among them—and what a tragedy!

They needed to talk about bail for Hirschi; someone had to decide if he was a flight risk. Someone, but not she.

"Let's take lunch," she said, standing up. "Herr Hirschi, thank you for everything you've told us. I know this was very hard for you. Herr Binggeli, we'll continue at two."

She had to push on the table a little to get herself to her feet. She shook hands with both men and walked out, not forgetting to ask the guard in the hall to keep an eye on the prisoner and his lawyer while they were at lunch. For the first time in years, she approached the elevator and pushed the button instead of walking upstairs to homicide on the third floor. Sabine came up behind her.

"Are you all right?" she asked.

"I . . . will be. I need a few minutes. Somewhere. Not here."

The elevator arrived; they got in and, before Giuliana could push "3," Sabina pressed the Open Doors button.

"Go outside, get something at the bakery, and sit in the park to eat it. I'll tell Rolf where we've got to in the interview. I don't think Erwin and Noah are in but, if they are, I'll brief them, too."

"We have to get Jonas Pauli."

"I know. But that doesn't mean you can't take a lunch break." Sabine smiled at her. "I can't imagine why you're feeling so burned out," she said in a girlishly emphatic tone quite different from her own voice. "Yesterday you were attacked by a murderer and watched someone you care about almost die, then you were in the hospital being messed with by docs and nurses all night; this morning you listened to a terrible confession, and this afternoon you get to arrest a colleague. Gee, I wonder what your problem is."

Giuliana managed a smile. "And don't forget—I shot someone, too," she said, trying to match Sabine's facetious tone.

"And thank God for that," Sabine said in her normal voice and gave her a hug. "Go on—I can hold the fort alone for a while. Are you sure you don't want us to handle Jonas without you?"

"I may want you to, but I'm not going to let you. I'll see this to the end."

"Hirschi could be lying, you know. He may still have done it himself," Sabine said.

Giuliana stepped out of the elevator; Sabine stayed in. Two uniformed men were at the doors; they couldn't keep the elevator there any longer.

"Maybe. But I don't think so," Giuliana said to Sabine as the doors began to close.

"No. I don't either." She heard Sabine's voice as the elevator rose, and then realized she could at least have ridden up to the main floor. She turned to climb the stairs, thinking about what Sabine had said. Yes, someone she cared about had almost died. A man she loved. It was important to say it and know that it was true, no matter how conflicted it made her feel.

Ten minutes later she sat on a bench under a tall linden on the edge of Breitenrain Park, spooning a mixture of oats, yogurt, grated apple, honey, and chopped fruit and nuts out of a large plastic container: the bakery's homemade *Birchermüesli*, which came with a whole-wheat roll. Comfort food. She'd had the foresight to bring extra napkins for wiping the bench dry of rain. A few drops still fell on her from the tree overhead, but she ignored them.

Jonas Pauli had hit Simu Etter. Not once, rising from the ground full of rage and fear and adrenaline after his spectacular fall, running toward the man laughing at his pain, and giving him a clip on the head before getting a grip on himself. No, not once, but twice—the second strike aimed at Simu's temple, the skull's most vulnerable place. A killing blow, delivered to an unarmed man who was under the influence of drugs and alcohol and doing nothing except laughing.

She finally believed Jonas had done this terrible thing. And then he'd lied about it. He'd let a police investigation rise up around him to solve a homicide he'd committed himself. Ueli was right. He'd been right all along about what the police—her police—were capable of. And she would tell him so.

It was starting to rain again. She got up, threw her empty *Birchermüesli* container into the bin by the bench, and hurried back to the police building. She had to get Jonas Pauli into custody.

43

Nordring police station and the Old City, Saturday afternoon, June 22

From her desk, she dialed Werner Rindlisbacher, Jonas's lawyer, on his cell.

"Werner," she said. "It's Giuliana Linder."

"Is it Jonas Pauli?" he asked at once. "Tell me."

"We have new evidence, and I need to see him. Now. I'm sorry it's Saturday, but you'll need to be here. Shall I have him picked up or . . . ?"

Werner interrupted. "No. Let me call him. I'll get back to you in the next ten minutes and tell you how soon I can have him there."

Fifteen minutes later, she and Sabine were set to meet with Jonas and his lawyer in a small conference room at one thirty, and the transcriber from Hirschi's earlier interrogation had been asked to take notes. Now she checked the day's roster of uniformed people in-house and asked Stephan, a large, calm man in his midforties, to come to her office at 1:20. She hoped things with Jonas wouldn't turn ugly, but they'd need a guard, and Stephan would do well.

While she waited the half hour until the meeting, she phoned the hospital and asked about Adrian Pfeiffer and Renzo. Pfeiffer's wound was clean, she was told, he was receiving antibiotics, and no one saw any reason to remove the bullet unless there were complications. As for Renzo, according to a nurse on his ward, he was being kept until Tuesday at the earliest for observation and tests but seemed to be recovering well—in fact, his wife had spent the night at the hospital, and other members of his family had been showing up since eight in the morning.

She swiped at tears of relief and hoped he was getting enough rest with so many visitors. Then she told herself not to be stupid. Renzo was not her responsibility.

Walking with Stephan to the conference room where they were meeting Jonas, she briefly filled him in on what was coming. The policeman listened without interrupting. When she finished, he said, "The kid should've called an ambulance and come clean. Now it's bad. Really bad."

By the following day, all the cops in the canton—no, in the whole of Switzerland—would be talking about Jonas's arrest. Stephan's take on it was only the first of thousands, but it comforted her. And it was true. What Jonas had done was awful. What he'd failed to do afterward was worse.

Sabine was already there, and Giuliana took a seat next to her at the round white table in the featureless room, whose only decorations were two bedraggled philodendrons, one at each end of a low shelf under the window. Stephan took a parade-rest stance in the corner and, a few minutes later, Jonas walked in with his lawyer. Did he know that Giuliana had interviewed Hirschi that morning and the day before? Probably; the police grapevine worked as well as any office's did, and he must have friends at the station who were convinced of his innocence and keeping him posted. She supposed that, for the past two days at least, he'd been waiting desperately for something to happen.

The strain of that wait showed in the jerky way he entered the room. He met her eyes at once, and she kept her face stony, watching his feeble beginnings of a smile vanish. Werner sat down at the table, but Jonas just stood there behind a chair, his body stiff. He reached shaking hands to grip the chair's back. Behind him, Stephan stood in front of the closed door.

"Sit down, please, Jonas," said Werner Rindlisbacher.

Jonas didn't move, and Rindlisbacher nodded, acknowledging his choice to stand. Sabine leaned over her notebook, and Giuliana said, "I've spoken at length to Christian Hirschi, the man who was standing with Simon Etter when you hit him. He told me that you hit Etter twice before throwing down your club. The second blow was fatal. I am therefore putting you in custody, so that this case can be taken over by an outside police force."

Silence.

"Jonas, do you understand that this case can no longer be investigated by a member of the canton of Bern force?"

He stood there, his whole body trembling. "I don't understand why you believe this man Hirschi and not me. You know me; we're colleagues. Etter's friend is a crook, isn't he? That's what I've been hearing. So why am I the liar?"

"I don't know for sure that you *are* lying. But the story I heard from the man who witnessed what happened that night makes sense. It is my responsibility to take it seriously. That's why we're here."

I know you're just a kid and you made a terrible mistake, she wanted to tell Jonas. *I'm sorry for you. But I'm much, much sorrier for Etter's family*. She didn't open her mouth, but she didn't look away from him either. He deserved her full attention.

The hands that gripped the chair back were white; so was Jonas's face.

"Do you have any questions about what I've said?" she asked him.

He went on as if he hadn't heard her. In fact, she didn't think he had. "You were attacked in the Seeland yesterday, and you defended yourself by shooting your attacker. But you're lucky: you didn't kill him. Now you're a heroine who saved the life of another cop. I was attacked on the night of the riots, and I defended myself with my baton, but I wasn't lucky like you. What's the difference? What's the difference, for Christ's sake? My bad luck?" His voice rose. "Don't you know what it's like to be scared?"

"Yes, I do," Giuliana said, her eyes never leaving his face. "I know what it's like to feel terrified and helpless and to shake with rage, and I know what it's like to want to punish someone for making me feel that way. Every member of the police does," she said. But she didn't go on. There was no point in adding the obvious message about self-control. Jonas knew exactly what he'd done wrong, which was why he'd thrown his baton on the ground. She remembered Hirschi saying he'd seen terror in the young cop's eyes. Terror for himself, yes. But was that all he'd felt?

Jonas was still on his feet, but he'd bowed his head over the table. Then he straightened slowly, like an old man, and turned to Stephan. "Okay, Steph," he said, "I'll come with you now." The big man took him by the arm gently and said, "I won't cuff you if you don't make me."

Jonas nodded. "Thanks," he whispered, and Stephan led him out the door.

Giuliana stood up as soon as they were gone. "Thanks for coming, Werner," she said. They shook hands. "I'll go get myself a cup of coffee while he's processed," the lawyer said. "Then I'll talk to him. Which department will be taking this over?"

Sabine spoke at last. "Probably Zürich, but we don't know yet. It's all happened fast—and on the weekend."

"Yeah," said Werner. He reached out a hand to Sabine, too. "See you . . . next time," he finished lamely, addressing both of them, and then he, too, was gone. Left alone with only the skimpy philodendrons, the two homicide detectives looked at each other, and Sabine put a hand on Giuliana's shoulder. "You're going home, right?" She looked at her watch. "Almost two, but everything will be fine with Hirschi. We're more or less done with him anyway."

Giuliana nodded. There'd be charges—not only would Fraud be all over him for the tomato scam, but he'd be charged with failing to give help to someone seriously injured. But homicide was almost through with him. "Thanks, Sabine. I really appreciate it."

Sabine went on. "I'm going to push everyone to let him go back to the farm for now, at least long enough to find someone else to supervise his harvesting. His livelihood will be hurt badly enough by the fraud without us making him miss getting his crops in."

"Brilliant!" said Giuliana and meant it. She should have thought of it herself—but for now she was too tired to reproach herself.

"I'll keep you posted," Sabine said, moving toward the door. She was almost through the doorway when Giuliana called out, "Jonas . . ." Sabine turned. "You heard everything Jonas said to me. Did he express any remorse for killing Simon Etter?"

Sabine stood still in the doorway, biting her lip. "Not a word," she said.

"Yeah," agreed Giuliana. "I didn't hear it either."

Upstairs, the homicide room was empty except for Rolf, who looked like he was packing up to go home. Whoever was on call that weekend was probably busy somewhere else in the building or out in the field, and she knew Noah and his wife were running a half-marathon somewhere in French-speaking Switzerland.

"Ciao, Rolf," she said. She hoped she'd given her voice the energy she wasn't feeling.

"Jonas in custody?"

"On his way. Where's Erwin?"

Rolf made the creaky noise that was his way of laughing. "He's so eager to start on Pfeiffer that he drove to the hospital to talk a doctor into pronouncing him fit for interrogation."

"That's got to be a waste of time."

Rolf shrugged, still grinning. "Erwin can be very persuasive, in his own way."

"Does the commandant know about Jonas yet?" Giuliana asked, moving to the window.

"I've briefed him. He'll let Lilo talk to the press this time. Luckily we have your rescue of Renzo to counteract the bad news about Jonas." She closed her eyes, shaking her head. "I know," he said. "But still, well done!"

Giuliana perched on the desk across from his, facing him, and said, "That's not the way my encounter with Pfeiffer will be presented by the press. Think of the talk shows: 'Not even a week has gone by since a cop beat an unarmed bystander to death during the riots, and now another one of these butchers has shot a suspect armed with a sock.' That'll be the show hostess. Then the guest psychologists will start up. There's the outside investigation of the shooting, too. God, Rolf."

"You'll get through it," he said. The words were callous, but his voice was kind. "And the investigation will clear you—I know that. The public may not take a cosh seriously, but, believe me, other police will."

"I don't have to meet any press, do I?"

"You have an email from Lilo in your mailbox at this moment telling you under no circumstances to talk to journalists. I got a copy of it. I can't talk to them either. The way she writes, you'd think she was forbidding us a treat, instead of saving us from agony. I guess, for her, dealing with the press *is* a treat, or she couldn't do her job. Thank God I don't do it."

Still sorting what he wanted to take home into his briefcase, Rolf examined his watch, before meeting her eyes with a stern look. "You know as well as I do that we're going to have months of work preparing these cases for trial. But for now, we're done. You did an excellent job, Giuliana." As he said this, he walked toward her with his hand outstretched, and she took it. "Now go home. I don't want to see you until Monday."

"I'll go, I'll go. But there's something I'd like to do first. Assuming she's at home, I want to tell Frank's partner, Louise, what's been going on."

"She probably read the stories about the 'Seeland shoot-out' in this morning's papers, don't you think?"

"All the more reason to explain what really happened."

He pressed his lips together as he reflected and then said, "Go ahead. But not a word to Etter's family. When they find out Jonas killed their son . . ." He trailed off.

"Oh, God. Everything about Jonas's situation is going to be hell to deal with." *Including telling Ueli about it*, she thought. He'd come by the hospital the night before to bring her a change of clothes and some toiletries, but to protect her voice the doctor had forbidden her to talk—to her relief. Was she stopping by Louise's in order to avoid Ueli for another hour?

Giuliana drove to her own street, parked two blocks from her house, and snuck off before anyone in her family saw her. Louise, who was expecting her, lived a ten-minute walk away: down a long hill, past the bear park, and into the medieval part of town. The hill she walked down sloped steeply to the Aare, its green flanks temporarily home to a dozen sheep. She looked across the wide river and saw the bulk of the *Münster* with its delicate spire and, on either side of it, a row of centuries-old buildings with gables and red-tiled roofs. Louise lived in one of those buildings. It was odd to think they'd never met; Renzo's conversations and written reports had given her a vivid sense of the woman's personality.

Giuliana turned left at the bottom of the hill and crossed the Aare on the Nydegg Bridge. Under blue skies the river could be a rich moss green, but now, under dirty-white cloud cover, the water flowed grey. All her life, no matter where she'd moved, Giuliana had lived within five miles of the Aare. She'd hiked its banks, picnicked by it, paddled in its shallows, thrown stones into it, swum in it, rafted on it, and crossed it on all of Bern's bridges more times than she could count. But she never took it for granted. It was the aorta of the city.

Louise let her in, and she climbed the stairs to the second-floor flat. It was full of antique woodwork, as she'd imagined, but all of it was painted white—beams, doors, wainscoting, and window frames. The walls and ceilings, with their elegant stucco decorations, were also white. In the living room, where Louise brought her, all the rugs and upholstery were in shades of blue. Louise gestured her to a royal-blue armchair and said, "Tell me."

For twenty minutes, Giuliana talked and Louise listened. Several times the older woman hid her mouth behind her fingertips or wrung her hands, and once she got up and walked around the room, but she didn't interrupt. The story emerged: Hirschi's tomatoes and Pfeiffer's financial interest in the scam, Etter's drug-dealing ambitions and subsequent blackmail, and Frank's decision to report Hirschi to Fraîche. She followed that with an abbreviated version of Renzo's pursuit of the case and an even more truncated version of her own involvement. When she stopped talking, the room was silent, except for the rush of the Aare coming through the open windows.

"I convinced my boss to let me tell you all this because I was sure you'd never talk to a journalist about it. These deaths have generated three trials: Pfeiffer's, Hirschi's, and that of the young policeman we've arrested for killing Simu. Preparations for the trials will start Monday, although it will be months before we're ready to go to court. Anything you say in public risks messing up the trials. Still, I felt you had a right to know."

"Thank you," said Louise. "And you're right—I would never want to jeopardize the trials. I don't think I should discuss this with anyone, not even my daughter, because although I won't talk to the press, someone else might. So, I'll give you a promise: not a word."

"Good. And now I have a question for you. If we hadn't made these arrests, I'd try to force you to answer me; now you don't have to. But I'll ask anyway. Why did you take a much later train to Zürich on Friday afternoon? My colleague Renzo told me that you answered every question as straight as string until he asked you for an alibi for Friday afternoon, and then you lied. I don't need your alibi anymore, obviously. But . . ."

Louise was sitting on a paisley-patterned sofa across from Giuliana; she leaned forward and touched a small white bowl on the low table between them.

"I'm going to make a pot of black tea," she said without looking up. "Will you have some?"

"Tea would be nice." Giuliana stayed in the living room, giving Louise time alone in the kitchen to think. She walked to one of the large windows with its dark-blue wooden shutters folded back against the outer wall and watched the Aare boil far below.

Only when both women held cups of strong, milky tea did Louise finally speak.

"I'm sorry I lied. It must be such a problem for the police. Here you are, trying to figure out something vitally important, and everyone lies to you, not because their activities have anything to do with what you're investigating, but for their own ridiculous reasons. Perhaps only one person out of all the ones you talk to lies because of the crime. But how do you know which one that is? It must drive you crazy."

Giuliana smiled. Louise had summed up exactly the way she felt when she questioned people. "You're right. It's maddening. And such a waste of time. In your case I don't think we ever considered you a suspect. Still, we were troubled."

"You've just told me something I promised not to tell," said Louise. "Now I'll tell you something that I also consider . . . well, if not secret then very private. I drove back to this apartment from Frank's last Friday morning, and while I was here getting the last of my things together, my ex-husband called. David. He and I have talked and texted several times since the twins' birth, but we haven't seen each other for weeks, and he was calling to ask me to lunch. He lives in the Marzili, and he suggested I meet him at the Marzilibrücke restaurant to celebrate the birth of our grandchildren. I told him I was just about to catch a train to Zürich, and he said of course he understood, not to feel bad, it was just a thought. But he sounded so disappointed. So I called our daughter, told her I was delayed, and met her father for lunch. We drank champagne. He lives two minutes from the restaurant, so I went back to his place, and we ended up in bed. I didn't catch the train until four."

By the time she finished speaking, Louise was staring into her cup as if she were reading her fortune in the tea leaves. Giuliana had guessed where the story was going as soon as she'd heard the word *celebrate* but enjoyed hearing it to its end.

"So you got out of bed with Frank in the morning, and by two in the afternoon you were in bed with David. Hell, if I was over seventy years old and having sex with two men in one day, I wouldn't be embarrassed about it. I'd be crowing."

Louise glanced up, saw Giuliana grinning at her, and breathed a tiny laugh. Then they were both laughing. Giuliana had to set her cup down so as not to spill her tea.

"I couldn't tell those two policemen," said Louise, sobering up at last. "Not when we were talking about Frank's death."

"I can see that," Giuliana said. "But I appreciate your telling me."

Louise's face turned serious. "Loving two men, even when you love them in very different ways—it's painful. And messy."

Yes, Giuliana said to herself, *it is*. She waited, hoping for advice, but none came. Louise finished her tea in silence, and Giuliana took her leave. As she climbed the hill to her street, she rejoiced that her own dilemma hadn't resolved itself with a death, as Louise's had. It had come close, though. Very close.

44

Kirchenfeld,
Saturday evening, June 22

Giuliana knew the moment she walked into the apartment that Lukas must be out, because the place was so quiet she could hear Ueli's keyboard clicking. She hoped he didn't have an important deadline; now that she'd made up her mind to talk to him about Jonas Pauli, she wanted to do it without delay. She took off her work shoes, set her bag down, saw that Isabelle's room was empty, and walked to where Ueli was writing. When he looked up, she kissed him.

"No kids?"

"Isabelle went to an early movie with Luna and afterward they'll hang out. She'll be back by midnight. Lukas is spending the night at Niko's. I checked—his parents are okay with it."

"Can you take a break?" she asked. "How about a walk to the rose garden?"

"That sounds good. I was going to suggest going out to dinner, if you feel up to it. I'll call and see if there's space in the restaurant there. Shall I try for a table on the terrace?"

"Sure. I'll go change."

It was a little after six. From the bedroom window she saw that the flat grey blanket of cloud Bern had endured since Thursday was thinning. Blue sky was showing; the summer was reasserting itself. She showered and put on a black-and-white patterned shirt, wide black pants, and black sandals and brushed out her hair, leaving it loose around her shoulders.

It was a fifteen-minute walk to the city's rose garden, which was above the Aare on a hill even higher than the one their apartment house perched on. But with a dinner reservation at seven, they took a roundabout route. Ueli slowed his pace to match hers, and they walked side by side, not holding hands but almost touching.

"Isabelle had her date with Quentin last night," Giuliana said, as they strolled past a nearby pond that was a haven for mallards and the occasional swan, "and I was in the hospital. Did she tell you anything about it?"

"Nothing, not even what music they listened to at the Reitschule. She said the evening was 'fine' and rolled her eyes at me when I tried to find out more. She did get home at one, though, right on time."

"Did you tell your parents what you did when you were out with girls?"

"Of course not." With deliberate exaggeration, Ueli rolled his own eyes, and they laughed.

"It's retribution, isn't it?" Ueli said.

"Definitely. Here's what I think, though. Sometime over the next few weeks, when we're least expecting it, she'll start talking about Quentin. That is, assuming she's in love with him. Remember how hard it is not to talk about the person you've fallen in love with? I bored my family silly talking about you. Paolo used to stick his fingers in his ears and go, 'La, la, la,' when I said the word *Ueli*, just to tease me."

"You never told me that."

They continued in silence. Then Giuliana could wait no longer. "You know it was the young policeman—Jonas—who killed the man in the Schützenmatte. Just as you thought all along. And I shot Renzo's attacker. He'll be all right. But I could have killed him."

"Were you trying to kill him?"

"No, I was trying not to. But a bullet is . . . A breath of wind can change everything."

"Giule," he said, but she interrupted, speaking fast. "You were right, Ueli. You've been right from the first. The police are dangerous. Over and over since Monday I've pictured Isabelle running at the cop in the passageway. I told you she wasn't at risk, because we're trained to use the amount of force appropriate to the situation. Well, that's not true, or Jonas and I wouldn't be facing inquiries. What Jonas did was wrong, and, in spite of everything, I think what I did was right. But we both acted on instinct. In that tiny moment of time, anything can happen, including terrible mistakes. The temptation to use all the violence you're capable of is . . . huge. I felt it."

Ueli put his arm around her shoulders. "I only know what I've read in the papers and seen on TV. Do you feel like telling me the whole story? You know I won't pass it on."

So once again, this time in detail, Giuliana went through what she knew or guessed about Frank, Simu, Hirschi, and Pfeiffer. She also told Ueli about the drug-selling angle that had distorted the cases. Explaining everything to him felt like exactly the right thing to do. By the time she finished, they were sitting on a bench at the edge of the rose garden's vast lawn.

"Do you think I did the wrong thing?" Giuliana asked, before Ueli could speak. "I want your true opinion."

"Absolutely not," said Ueli, reaching out to take the hand that lay in her lap. "If someone attacks you, you have to defend yourself, and you were defending Renzo, too. Suppose you'd hesitated and that bastard had cracked your skull open. My God. I'd have spent the rest of my life wondering if our argument had caused your death. And probably Renzo's, too."

"You say that because you love me. But if you were a stranger reading about the shooting in the newspaper, you'd feel differently. You'd ask yourself why the policewoman in the article, faced with a man holding a cosh, didn't drop her weapon and hit him. Wasn't she trained in unarmed combat? Did she really warn him before she pulled the trigger? Why didn't she withdraw to a safe place to phone her nearby colleague for backup? Or let the man run away, knowing he wouldn't get far, since there was an alert out on his van? I know you would ask those questions, because I keep asking them of myself. They're the kind of thing I'll be asked during the investigation into the shooting, you know."

"You did the right thing, sweetheart. Never hesitate to protect yourself. Please."

"Thank you," Giuliana said simply. She leaned over and kissed him. "I will try to protect myself. But now that I've shot someone, I don't want it to be a little bit easier for me to fire the next time, when it might be a kid in an alley, a kid that I only think is a threat."

"I know," Ueli said, wrapping his hand gently in her loose hair. "That's why I was so frightened for Isabelle. But you've been in the police for almost twenty years now. Follow your instincts. Otherwise, you won't be able to do your job."

"Do you trust my judgment?" she asked him.

"I do."

"I love you, Ueli."

"I love you, too." They held each other's eyes for a moment, and Giuliana slid her arms around her husband's waist. He drew her toward him. Side by side, flanked by rose bushes, they held each other for a long time, until Ueli said, "Hey, it's after seven. Come on—let's go eat before they give our table away."

They walked across the lawn to the restaurant, hand in hand. "The guy who died, Simu, and the cop who killed him were the same age, right?" asked Ueli.

"Twenty-three, twenty-four, something like that."

"I think I'll do a piece on both of them, figure out how they got to where they were, what led up to that scene on the Schützenmatte. There'll be info I won't be able to use pretrial, but I can work around that. What do you think?"

Giuliana considered the two families, Etter and Pauli, and how such an article could hurt them. But everyone would be writing about their sons, and Ueli would do it honestly and with sensitivity. She was a policewoman; he was a journalist. He, too, had to use his best judgment to do his job.

"I think it's a great idea," she said.

45

Bern's Insel Hospital,
Sunday afternoon, June 23

"Scoot up here so I can see you better."

Giuliana moved her chair to the head of Renzo's hospital bed. She placed a ribbon-tied cellophane bag on his night table, which already held an Italian paperback and a small bunch of wilted dandelions in a water glass.

"Did Antonietta bring you those?"

He turned his head slightly toward the yellow flowers and smiled. "Yeah. And Angelo brought me his favorite bulldozer. Luckily, it's small. Chocolate from Nobile?" he asked, eying her gift.

She nodded. "Milk with hazelnuts and dark with orange peel, which I think is your favorite."

She couldn't stop grinning at him. Just hearing his voice, hoarse as it was, was a gift. The oxygen tanks by the bed were disturbing, but she was determined not to show him how emotional his helplessness had made her feel—and still did.

"I almost came by yesterday morning before I was discharged, but you had your family with you," Giuliana said.

"They're coming again at five. Fränzi and the kids, my mother, my sisters, and my brother, all with spouses and kids. Plus, some of Fränzi's family. They'll eat most of the chocolate. But I'll keep some of the stuff with the orange peel for me. Mm. Thanks."

He settled himself against his pillows so he was facing her and said, "First question: what the fuck did Pfeiffer hit me with?"

"A homemade cosh. It was a thick white football sock filled with two-franc pieces. If he made it up new every time he needed it, he'd never be found with a weapon on him—just an odd sock on the floor of his car and a surprising amount of change in his pocket. He came at me with it, too."

"Ah," said Renzo. "Clever. No weapon in his possession. It was effective, too. The doctors say I have quite a concussion. First the head-butt from Lüthi and now this. Another hundred thousand brain cells up in smoke."

"You can spare them." She kept smiling but couldn't stop thinking of the amount of time he'd been without oxygen. "Are they positive you're going to be fine?"

"So far so good. But I feel like an idiot for not realizing that Pfeiffer was a threat."

"*You* feel like an idiot? What about us? We got obsessed with drugs when it was the vegetables that were important. Calling the Bio Suisse guy—that was brilliant of you."

He smiled and shrugged against his pillows.

"My main motivation was curiosity, you know. And now I've missed the end of the story. So what happened to Pfeiffer? No, wait. First tell me about Hirschi."

Giuliana took him through everything Christian Hirschi had told her on Friday afternoon and Saturday morning. As she spoke, Giuliana noticed Renzo's breath was still rattling in his throat. She was glad he listened quietly.

"I can't help feeling sorry for him," he said when she finished. "He waded into disaster one step at a time. When he figured out how deep into the shit he was, it was too late to get himself out."

"Lots of people much poorer than Hirschi suffer bad harvests and stay honest," said Giuliana. "He should have had the strength to stand up to his father-in-law about the Spanish tomatoes and told his wife to stop spending so much money."

"What do you think's going to happen to that marriage?" Renzo asked.

"I think she's going back to Spain."

"I think so, too. Poor Hirschi. He's so in love with her."

Giuliana snorted. "I hope you aren't going to tell me you feel sorry for Pfeiffer, too."

"Pfeiffer!" Renzo said his name with loathing and then settled back into his pillows like a child looking forward to a bedtime story. Mischief was back in his eyes, and his typical expressiveness, which had been so frighteningly absent on Friday, was returning to his face. She took his hand and squeezed it, not caring that her eyes were tearing up.

"What can I get you? Is this a pitcher of tea? Can I pour you some?"

He grimaced. "Tea, my ass! That pitcher gets refilled every few hours with a lukewarm brew that tastes like grass clippings, and they make me drink it. You tell me about Pfeiffer, and then I'll ask for some espresso. The nurses have a little coffee machine in their break room, and they sneak me cups when the other patients aren't looking."

Ha! If Renzo was well enough to flirt with his nurses, he was himself again. "Fine," she agreed, "Pfeiffer first and then coffee." She explained how she'd come to shoot the man. "Now he's here in the Insel, just like you. We still can't question him."

"He must have hit Frank with the sock before he suffocated him. But why the pesticide?"

"You know more about Frank than I do. What do you think?"

Renzo was silent, and Giuliana cursed herself. She shouldn't put him under strain when he was concussed, he might . . .

"Everyone in Haldiz knew about the bug-killer that blew from one farm onto the other," said Renzo. "I bet Pfeiffer heard a version of that drama from someone in the village and decided to frame Jean-Pierre for Frank's death."

"That makes sense."

"If Frank hadn't been so full of organic principles," Renzo went on, "he wouldn't have called Fraîche and gotten himself killed—just when Bio Inspecta was about to reveal everything anyway. His death was so . . . senseless."

"Senseless and very sad," Giuliana agreed. "Which reminds me—I met Louise."

"You liked her, didn't you? I knew you would." Renzo's face was starting to look drawn. "Okay, time for coffee," he said.

"I hope you don't mind, but I think I'll skip coffee. With all your relatives coming later, you should rest, and I'm going to go home to be with Ueli and the kids. Starting tomorrow morning, we'll go into high gear doing trial prep. Can you believe we still haven't found the place Simu stored the rest of his dope?"

"Giuliana." Renzo sat up and turned toward her, all mischief wiped from his face.

"What's wrong?"

He leaned forward and drew her into a fierce hug. His lips met hers, hard. Then, as quickly as he'd crushed her to him, he let her go. Leaning back against his pillows, his eyes held hers. She fought to keep her breath steady and looked right back at him, not caring what he read in her face.

"Thank you for my life," he said. "It's good to be here."

"I'm glad you didn't die." She took his hand in hers and didn't let it go.

They smiled at each other. Then, dropping his hand, she stood. "See you at work."

"See you," he answered, and his eyes closed. By the time she'd set her chair back in place and picked up her purse, his breathing told her he was asleep.

Acknowledgments

Christian Sohm is one of many people who have worked for years to make organic farming in Switzerland a success. When I started doing research for this book, he was a buyer of fruit, vegetables, flowers, and plants—both standard and organic—for Coop, one of Switzerland's biggest grocery chains. I told him I wanted to shape my book's plot around some kind of scam where standard produce was sold as organic, and no one noticed the switch. He was immediately inspired. "Well, you couldn't use cucumbers," he told me, "because the price difference isn't big enough to make it worth it. Apples or peppers would pay off, but the organic ones look too distinctive. Now tomatoes—hmm. They all look more or less the same, and you can charge enough more for the organics to make money. Why not write about tomatoes?" So I did.

Previously, in a magazine article, I'd written about the speed with which farms were going out of business in Switzerland. Farming itself, however, is unfamiliar to me. I know all my father's stories about his summers as a boy in northern Louisiana, working on his Aunt Ella's and Uncle Elijah's small farm. But I have never even planted a row of beans. Many organic farmers and farm inspectors, agricultural researchers, and journalists generously spent their time educating me about much of what appears in the previous pages. Thank you, Andreas and Kathrin Schneider, Manfred and Andrea Wolf, and Regina Fuhrer; thanks, also, to Katrin Portmann, Ueli Steiner, Beate Huber, Lukas Inderfurth, Sabine Lubow and Paul van der Berge. Organic farming produces a few villains in this book, but in real life the men and women who practice a form of agriculture that is safer for the planet do heroic work. I also want to acknowledge the help of Chantal Guggenbühl, who supplied me with exactly the farming statistics I needed.

I found the courage to write a police procedural set in Bern in large part thanks to Gabriele Berger, a high-ranking policewoman in the cantonal police—and my neighbor. After getting her boys into bed, she'd leave her husband in charge and join me for a glass of wine. She patiently answered all my questions about solving murders in the canton of Bern, filling me in at the same time on how the police interact with each other and with cantonal prosecutors. For example, you may have wondered why none of the detectives or investigators in my book have titles like Chief Inspector or *Kommissar.* That is because, in Bern, police are simply called *Herr* or *Frau* by the public; among each other, they use first names. Gaby read this manuscript and corrected some absurdities that had crept in despite her advice. Any mistakes that remain, however, are certainly my fault, not hers.

Other advisers about questions of police procedure and the law were Ursula Hirschi, then head of the homicide department in the canton of Bern; public prosecutors Philip Karnusian and Peter Müller; and lay magistrate Katrin Grüter. Clerk of the court René Graf made it possible for me to attend two trials, for murder and attempted murder, at the Bernese courthouse. Thank you!

Pesticide went through version after version over a period of years. Those drafts benefitted from the feedback of many friends and relatives, some writers themselves. I'm very grateful to: Giuliana Berset-Brignoli (who also lent her first name to my heroine), Malcolm Boother, Betsy Draine, Dominique Düby, Esti Dunow, Patsy

Encinosa, Yolanda Gama Terrazas, Tara Giroud, Donna Goepfert, Alex Griswold, Melina Hiralal, Regula Jalali-Strahm, Ellen Klyce, Kimball Kramer, Min Ku, Matthias Lerf, Joan Porter MacIver, Pia Malmquist, Thomas Malmquist, Robin McElheny, Melanie Mettler, Igor Metz, Lisa Müller, Clare O'Dea, Susanne Oesch, Rosalind Philips, Barbara Porter, Catherine Puglisi, Dan Reid, Julia Reid, Isabel Roditi, Susan Rose, Karl Spälti, Nina Spälti, Susan Spälti, Lyn Spillman, Michelle Stucker, Peter Stucker, Thomas Stucker, Deborah Valenze, Bettina Vollenweider, and Paula Wagner. If I forgot any of my readers, please forgive me; it's not a lack of gratitude, just poor recordkeeping.

My cousins Bob and Darlene Hays deserve special thanks for not only critiquing the manuscript themselves but sharing it with a group of their friends, who then provided many helpful comments and corrections. Until I can someday meet them and thank them personally, I have to content myself with listing the following readers: Nancy Archer, Dale Herron, Joanne Manthe, George Morrison and Peter Moser. Yay, Minneapolis critics!

Missing from this list of valuable readers only because she deserves special mention is my sister Natasha Hays, who critiqued and proofed *all* the drafts of the book and provided unsparing praise, support, and encouragement. For that reason, among many others, *Pesticide* is dedicated to her.

Many authors only find the time to write and rewrite their novels when they aren't busy bringing in money. My husband Peter Stucker earns my heartfelt thanks not only for encouraging me to become a full-time writer but for making it possible by supporting us.

Between first draft and printed book, I've been lucky to have input from several people in the book business. First of these to advise me about *Pesticide* was Gail Fortune of The Talbot Fortune Agency; another was editor Angela Polidoro. Agent April Eberhart steered me toward Seventh Street Books, for which I will always be grateful, and Dea Parkin of the Crime Writers Association was warmly supportive when I was short-listed for the 2020 Debut Dagger Award. When I needed advice on my publishing contract, I got it from Helen Corner-

Bryant of Cornerstones Literary Consultancy and Margery Flax of Mystery Writers of America. Thanks to Margery, I found Daniel Steven of Rockville, Maryland, one of whose areas of expertise is publishing law. He gave me clear explanations and detailed advice. In addition, Bryony Hall of the UK's Society of Authors and Michael Gross of the US's Authors Guild kindly commented on my contract clause by clause.

Kathryn Price is a professional editor for Cornerstones; she's also coauthor of *On Editing* (John Murray Learning, 2018) which I strongly recommend to anyone with a manuscript to revise. To me, she has been first an adviser and then a mentor and friend. Over the past several years, she has helped me see problems in my books, often requiring me to do major amounts of rethinking and rewriting, without once making me feel a loss of ownership over my work. She is a great editor and a lovely person, and her support has been precious to me.

And, speaking of unstinting support, *Pesticide* would never have become a book if Dan Mayer, editorial director of Seventh Street Books, had not rescued it from his slush pile. Heartfelt thanks for everything you've done for me along the way, Dan, and thanks, too, to Jennifer Do for a wonderful cover and to her and the rest of the Seventh Street Books experts for shepherding my book through the processes of production and promotion.

The music and lyrics of "Crossroads," the song quoted on page 42, were written by blues guitarist Robert Leroy Johnson (1911-1938). The song has since been covered by many singers and bands; Cream first recorded it in 1966.